Head over Heels

SUZANNE MOORE

VIKING

VIKING

Published by the Penguin Group
Penguin Books Ltd, 27 Wrights Lane, London w8 5tz, England
Penguin Books USA Inc., 375 Hudson Street, New York, New York 10014, USA
Penguin Books Australia Ltd, Ringwood, Victoria, Australia
Penguin Books Canada Ltd, 10 Alcorn Avenue, Toronto, Ontario, Canada m4v 3b2
Penguin Books (NZ) Ltd, 182–190 Wairau Road, Auckland 10, New Zealand

Penguin Books Ltd, Registered Offices: Harmondsworth, Middlesex, England

This collection first published in Great Britain by Viking 1996
10 9 8 7 6 5 4 3 2 1

These pieces were first published in the *Guardian*

Set in 11/13.5 pt Monotype Bembo
Typeset by RefineCatch Limited, Bungay, Suffolk
Printed in England by Clays Ltd, St Ives plc

A CIP catalogue record for this book is available from the British Library

isbn 0–670–87074–9

Contents

Contents

Acknowledgements

Thank you to all the usual suspects – you know who you are – and as ever to Lorraine Gamman and Thone Braekke.

Thanks to Georgina Capel and Margaret Bluman for getting the show on the road.

I am indebted to everyone at the *Guardian*, especially Pat Blackett, Sarah Marshall, and the editors that I have worked most closely with: Georgina Henry, Roger Alton and Deborah Orr. You have been and continue to be just fantastic.

I am also grateful to all the people who have written in response to my work, if only to tell me that I've got it all wrong.

Special thanks to my girls – Scarlet and Bliss – and my mother, Monica Costello, who died in 1995. This book is in her memory.

Introduction

I never asked to become a newspaper columnist. I never applied for
the job. There was no interview, no job description, no game plan.
It certainly wasn't part of the family business. After a few years of
freelancing I was just asked to be one. So I guess I got lucky because
I found myself with one of those rare jobs where you can make it
up as you go along. I wish I could say it was what I always wanted to
do because now I think it is. Having your own column is a freelance's dream – a steady gig with regular money means that you can
join in the phallic boast 'I have my own column. It appears regularly
and yes, it's quite big.'

A column of one's own means you get a little picture with your
by-line; it means that over time your readers get to know what you
think and you certainly get to know what they think. They love
you, they hate you, they are disappointed by you, you let them
down, you cheer them up, you say what they would have said if they
had had the chance, you make them see things in a different light,
you are the reason that they buy the paper, you are the reason they
will never buy the paper again, you are a vile lesbian, you are going
to be the mother of their children, you are exactly like them, you
understand nothing of what they are like, you are their representative, you are the enemy. In short, it's a relationship like all relationships with its ups and downs, its 'fear of commitment'. You offer
both the comfort of familiarity and the distress of sometimes not
being the person they thought you were. They take it personally
because you have the luxury of writing personally.

Indeed, newspapers are now filled with columnists, commentary and opinion. As more and more people get their news from other forms of media, the role of newspaper journalism has become more interpretative and subjective. In these times of media saturation and its subsequent neurosis – information anxiety – columnists in their idiosyncratic ways wade through the mire of information about the world we live in. One response to the changing role of print journalism has been the rise of the increasingly intimate columnist who writes only from their own experience, whether it is about their baby being sick on them or their dating crises. This is the columnist as a kind of virtual friend. You don't actually know him or her, but you know all about them, and they become part of an imaginary extended family which you can gossip about.

What I do is different. I do draw on personal experience if it is relevant or entertaining, but that is not the subject of my writing. Basically, I do not consider my own life interesting enough to sustain a weekly column. There are so many other things happening out there in the world that to ignore them in favour of my own particular catastrophes would be narcissistic beyond belief. My experience in newspapers is also that female journalists can too easily be pushed into this role, emoting about the mundanities, leaving the boys to analyse the big stuff about policy and politics. On a good day, I find myself attempting to tread the fine line between the personal and the political, between the 'real issues' of the day and the things that people actually talk to each other about in the pub. It's a balancing act between the agenda set by what is happening in the news and my own personal agenda.

I have been in the fortunate and increasingly rare position of writing for a newspaper that has given me the freedom to explore that agenda rather than set one for me. It is a liberal newspaper in the best sense of the word, in that it is not afraid to give voice to opinions that are not necessarily those of its readership. I am well aware of the stereotype of 'the *Guardian* reader' who knits their own muesli. In fact, I must confess that my job would be a lot easier if that stereotype was true, but I'm afraid it isn't. The responses I have received over the last three years have constantly surprised me. When I think I'm going to upset 'the readers', I have received only support. When I think I am saying what they want to hear, they are outraged. The largest mailbag I have received in my journalistic career was in response to a mocking aside I made about Morris dancers. It is my duty, therefore, to warn any prospective journalist out there that Morris dancers are a powerful pressure group whose wrath should not be lightly incurred.

I'd like to pretend that choosing the subjects I write about is a far more organized process than it actually is. Basically, my ground rule is to find something that interests me, that I feel strongly about. There is little point in writing an opinionated piece about a subject that you are indifferent to. You can't fake it, and if you try it shows in the writing. Surrounded by a glut of commentary I also have to feel that what I have to say is not simply the same as what everyone else is saying. I'm always looking for that journalistic cliché, an angle, and my angle should be at a tangent to the rest of the newspaper. Sometimes it will go against the grain, sometimes just be slightly slanted. Often there are worthwhile subjects that I am loath to comment on because I feel that they have been so well covered elsewhere and with great skill by other journalists.

Some weeks it is obvious what I should write about. It would have been strange not to comment on the James Bulger case or the Hugh Grant fiasco, because these are things that gripped the public imagination. At other times I am casting around for a subject, still having last-minute conversations with my editor on the day that I have to produce the article. The hard work, I always think, is getting the idea for the article rather than the actual writing of it.

That said, it would be ridiculous to suggest that I don't bring a whole set of concerns to bear on a given subject. Those who want to dismiss me would use the words 'feminist' and 'left-wing' to indicate their distaste. There are others who continually complain that I am neither feminist nor left-wing enough. The truth is that I find myself increasingly negotiating and re-evaluating my own relationships to these particular sets of politics. That I happen to be doing this at a time when many others are too, works, I hope, to my advantage. The old divides between left and right are no longer so easily classifiable and other far more interesting divisions are

emerging. The new questions are about the limits of the state, whoever runs that state. We often talk in terms of morality rather than
politics. Issues of social justice, fairness, public accountability and
the creation of sustainable communities are part of the contemporary political agenda.

One theme that I find myself returning to again and again is the
changing demarcation between what is private and what is public.
Are politicians to be held accountable for their private lives? Does it
matter how the future king of England has behaved in his marriage?
Are those who lead unconventional lifestyles, such as New Age
travellers, to be criminalized by the state? The cross-pollination
between mounting media invasion into what was once considered
beyond the bounds of legitimate public interest, and the growing
realization that the feminist mantra 'the personal is political' may
actually be relevant, have produced an entirely different news
agenda. To dismiss this as nothing more than the tabloidization of
serious matters is to underestimate its significance. The highest
authority in the land – the monarchy – is now under threat because
of the gossipy revelations about how its various members conduct
their private lives.

That which was once held up as a separate sphere from public life
– the sacred space of the family – is now also at the heart of these
debates. The punitive attitude towards single parents is something
that I have often been impassioned about. I have a stake in this
debate: I am a single parent myself. When the Tories first started
their onslaught, I remember saying to a friend: 'I feel personally
attacked by all this.' 'That's because you *are*,' he said. For some, the
nuclear family is under threat – torn apart by a horrid mixture of
those underclass bogeymen and women, loose lone parents and
feckless fathers. In reality, family life is in a state of transition. This
transition has been brought about by a number of things, not least
of all a changing economic climate which has altered employment
patterns and the rise of the new technologies. The increase in part-
time work for women, accompanied by a decline in full-time work
for men, is having a profound effect on the relationship between the
sexes, which is no longer founded on the economic dependence

of women. The repercussions on all our lives have been enormous and continue to resurface in all sorts of unexpected ways. The anxieties that the changing position of women produces are visible not only in government policy but in our most popular fictions, in the stories we tell ourselves about the world and the fantasies that they produce for us.

While some lament these changes, I welcome them, and while I stand accused of being too hard on men, I see my attitude as one of mere impatience. Many women of my generation and younger, whether or not self-identified feminists, have expectations that have been fuelled by feminism. What is ever more apparent is that feminism has leaked into the culture in such a way that, while heightening female demands, it has not managed to produce the men to meet these demands. I write less and less about feminism explicitly, but there is in many of the pieces here an implicit feminist agenda, in that I am always arguing for more choice and more opportunity for women, be they film stars, nurses or politicians. I am not against men so much as on the side of women and children – which should not be unusual, but still is. This strikes me as a question of balance.

Newspapers are dominated by men, men often being at worst gratuitously nasty or at best uncomprehending about women's lives. Inevitably and quite unconsciously, I often find myself putting across the other side of the story. It just so happens that these days I get far more response from men than women. There are many men out there grappling with the same problems, there are many women bringing up sons, there are many boys who feel lost, there are many fathers who are too busy working to read their kids a bedtime story. Not all of them are happy about this state of affairs.

At the forefront of any examination of contemporary sexual politics, though, is the debate about how we as a society treat homosexuality. In my opinion, a culture at ease with itself would have little problem with sexual difference; but we are far from that. Issues such as the age of consent for gay people or the ban on gays in the military or the phenomenon of outing are continuing to set the terms for any discussion of sexual politics. I find many of the ideas coming out of gay activism far more focused and exciting than much of what passes for feminist debate, which is either located in the purer reaches of academia or is still treading deeply worthy water.

Sometimes I find myself translating or interpreting these discussions, and so obviously my work is informed by debates in that loose and much-maligned area known as 'cultural studies'. Cultural politics was once defined as 'a struggle over meaning', and struggling over meaning is as good a description as any of what I am aiming for. One way of doing this is by questioning why things mean what they do or how they have got to be defined that way. Where, for example, did that all-purpose insult 'politically correct' come from? Does it mean what we think it means? Who has decided its meaning? To do this within the context of popular journalism means inevitably that I take popular culture seriously. It seems bizarre to me that, at this late stage of the game, one still has to argue that popular culture is worth taking seriously to begin with, but we do. To suggest that the best of popular culture is as beautiful and as complex as anything that sanctified high culture can offer us still remains a radical and controversial view. This is not, however, the same as saying that all products of the culture industry have equal value or that there isn't something outside of culture. In fact, I sense a sea change in these cultural and political currents. Many people in the eighties who were vaguely on the left moved into culture because they saw it as the only space where it was possible to make a difference – for us the realm of straight politics was a no-go area, a dead zone. Two things happened of significance that shook up all cultural refugees. The first was the big bang caused by the fatwa against Salman Rushdie, and the second was the resurrection of the very old arguments about cultural value. Those who had embraced postmodernism with all its reactionary content had come up against the limits of relativism. The word 'judgement' was once more in the air. If we could make aesthetic judgements, could we not make moral and political ones too? It seems that we not only could but that we had to.

My instinct is that this brought about a revived interest in more traditional politics and in power itself, power as a material rather than abstract presence in all our lives. This coincided with two interlocking forces – the rise of extraparliamentary politics and the formation of the Blairite project. Looking back, I see this move in my own writing. The personal may be political, but if we concentrate purely on the personal we lose sight of the wider political picture. We have reached a point, I feel, where we have to acknowledge that sometimes things are *only* personal. Knowing the difference is what makes the difference.

So, while challenging what so often presents itself as 'common sense', I have found myself up against other kinds of dogma that I dislike equally. To present one's own opinion as common sense, good sense rather than nonsense, is the columnist's trick. It requires that mystical attribute – a voice, a persona if not an actual personality. If you want to make sense to people, in my experience, being common also helps.

Above all, though, the joy of writing a weekly column is that it is a gift for those of us with short attention spans. The pieces in this book are arranged in the order in which I wrote them, from 20 March 1993 to 21 December 1995. The journalist's privilege, compared to the author of massive tomes, is one of uninhibited speculation. We are a feckless, promiscuous, faithless bunch. A newspaper article only has to be meaningful for a few days; if it lasts longer, this is a bonus rather than a precondition of writing it in the first place. There is a huge freedom in this and I still get an enormous kick out of it. There is a real buzz involved in writing about what is in the news, in reacting fast. There is another kind of pleasure in sometimes quietly observing, whether it be the machinations of a party political conference or a fashion show. So I can honestly say that I have had real fun writing the pieces in this book, whether my intention at the time was to be taken seriously or not. So enjoy yourselves and feel free to differ – that surely must be what it's all about.

ADVENTURE ON PLANET MODEL

'You can't sit there. That's for press,' snaps the blonde Sloane. 'I am press,' I say indignantly as I take my seat by the catwalk. I may be 'press' but I am sure she has spotted the fact that I am a stranger in Fashionland. Please be gentle with me, I want to say, I am a fashion virgin – this is my first time. She leaves me alone and I settle into my chair trying to pretend that I have seen it all before. But I have never seen anything like it at all; the bright white catwalk with the photographers all banked up at one end, the rows of ladies with Ray-Bans clamped down over their noses, the frantic kissing and waving going on all round me. This show is by Edina Ronay, a designer loved by the South Kensington crowd, the ladies who lunch, the ladies with money.

It is being held at Claridges. Outside, the chauffeured Daimlers are lined up. Inside the paparazzi cluster around any hapless celebrity they can find. Oh, look, it's Rula Lenska. And there is that man from *The Crystal Maze*, Richard O'Brien. Some woman in fake leopardskin demands to be seated. She is eased into a chair and the music starts to play. Fifty-year-old women start tapping their toes to rap. They have to – it's fashionable.

Then down the catwalk comes the first model, stalking, turning sulkily, bathed in flashbulb light. Then another and another. Out they come, these weird creatures. These aliens from the Planet Model. I am mesmerized. I can scarcely look at the clothes at all. Sure, I have seen models in pictures, on TV, even doing coke in nightclub toilets, but I have never seen them like this. Close-up and working. Walking this peculiar walk. Making the most artificial of movements look natural. That is the skill. That is why grumpy Naomi Campbell is considered good; she almost looks like she means it. Almost. But no one in real life walks like this. As the week goes on I will stop my naïve comparisons with real life. Almost. For in Fashionland real life is not a place where you live. It's just somewhere to get ideas from occasionally.

Ideas like let's revamp the seventies, let's make women look like little girls, let's do that grunge thing, let's go hippie. For, as a hippie friend of mine used to say when he was particularly stoned, 'If things don't change, they'll remain the same.' And in Fashionland things must never remain the same because the lifeblood of fashion is change, restlessness, dissatisfaction. So strong is this urge to constantly live in the present that if the fashion beast cannot find fresh blood, it will eat itself, consume its own previous creations so that it may throw you the future out of its own undigested past. Fashion, like all the arts (if it is an art) has replaced innovation with this endless regurgitation. And now there is a crisis. Because fashion differs from art in its function. We all have to get dressed. One way or another. And we like to think that one way is better than another. Me? I'm reviving the late eighties. I'm obviously ahead of my time. For currently the only decade which is not in some way trendy is the previous one. Having created the power-dressed eighties the fashion beast is in reaction. It has to do something new, something different.

So a series of oppositions is being duly manufactured. Out go the hard lines of the eighties. In come the soft, floaty silhouettes. Out go the Supermodels. In come the tiny Super Waifs such as Kate Moss – the one with the dodgy eyes. Out goes the glamour of conspicuous consumption. In comes the grunge of conspicuous recession. But the whole grunge 'aesthetic' is a difficult one even for the fashion beast to swallow. Its message is basically an anti-fashion one that says dress down, don't bother. It makes the fashion editors feel queasy. They know that large doses of the stuff would destroy their *raison d'être*. No wonder that the influential Suzy Menkes of the *International Herald Tribune*, is wearing a Grunge is Ghastly badge under her Lacroix jacket. There is thankfully no grunge at Bella Freud but there is a better class of celeb – mainly because her dad, Lucien, is there. There is no catwalk either and the models have to walk on carpet, which makes them look even more pissed off than usual. Carpet, I ask you – can you imagine how awful it must be for them?

It's awful for the fashion press, too, because the show starts late. Everything is late in Fashionland. The later you are, the more fantastically talented you must be. Journalists sit around trying to outdo each other with stories of incredible lateness. 'Oh, do you remember in Paris. We were there for Vivienne – doing our bit to support her and the lorries with the clothes hadn't even arrived. Two hours we sat there.'

Opposite sit the buyers, even though many of them will already have bought the clothes direct from the showroom. I am starting to realize that the purpose of a fashion show is not actually to sell clothes, but something much more elusive. It is to sell the idea of a designer as already successful. It is to generate excitement, buzz, hype, publicity, and this is exactly what the symbiotic relationship between the designer, the press and the buyers actually achieves.

At least at Bella Freud, I notice the clothes mainly because they are so unlike anything I could imagine anyone I know wearing. Very little girlie and English. Amanda de Cadenet comes out carrying a dog and wearing something see-through. A scary woman next to me starts screaming at her photographer, 'That's Amanda de Cadenet. Get it. Get it.'

Later on, at Red or Dead, I chat to an American fashion student and try to explain why I didn't like Bella Freud. 'Not modern enough for you?' he asks. 'Yes,' I say. It sounds more sophisticated than just saying that I think that sub-Westwood look is horrible. 'You'll like this better then,' he says. Red or Dead have a reputation for being 'street'. They are so groovy that the invite to their show is made of pasta. By the time I get back from Milan, it will already be covered in mould. The atmosphere is buzzy, the music is loud. 'That was what was wrong with Bella,' says the young American. 'Terrible music. You've got to have "up" music so that the models move well. You've got to keep them coming out – pack the catwalk. You put the worst clothes on the best girls.'

Here is a man who knows. He was downstairs with the models at Bella's. What are they like, these alien beings? 'Oh, they are on another planet definitely. They play snooker all the time, moan about having to go to Paris and have got trackmarks on their arms.' The idea that they are all junkies appeals to me. It explains their extreme thinness and the strange look on their faces, though when I ask other people in the business about it they tell me this is rubbish.

Red or Dead is more like it. Women with birdcages on their heads. Leather holsters with cider bottles in them. Not just grunge but crusty grunge. Do models ever say I am not going out there looking so ridiculous? 'Of course not,' explains my guide. 'The more stupid they look the more photographed they are and that is what they all want.' This is the first show, too, where I've seen male models. They apparently don't have to do the silly walk of their female counterparts. Instead they just affect a sullen saunter, a studied 'wish I wasn't here' look.

At Central St Martin's I see clothes that I actually want. Beautiful dresses tied together by Wai Tao, gorgeous red prints by Virginia Yuk Lin Lau. But at Ghost it's young girls and skinny boys with hunched shoulders. 'If they are the finest examples of British man-hood, well please . . .' Iain R. Webb of *The Times* exclaims later, sitting in the bar at Heathrow. Sarah Stockbridge, the blonde model that Westwood always uses, is at Ghost. She's the one who shows her knickers although she often doesn't wear them. Helen Storey has lots of see-through stuff. In Fashionland there are no such things as bras. Breasts must be bared at all times.

The circus moves on to Milan – the centre of the huge scandals rocking Italian public life. But, hey, why talk about bribery and corruption when we could be discussing hemlines? Instead, just be thankful for the little presents that fashion editors receive. Enjoy your press discount. Time was, apparently, when the clothes sizes of certain journalists would be faxed over before the show. When they opened their hotel wardrobe there would be waiting the jacket, the perfect suit . . . There are only empty hangers in my wardrobe. But Sandra Bernhard is staying in my hotel with a model 'friend' so why complain?

Dolce & Gabbana is the next big thing. The audience is full of more beautiful people than in London, or perhaps it is simply that there are more Italian people. The show is lovely. But the press release babbles on in the nonsense language that dominates Fashionland: 'A wind from Eastern Europe is howling which with an ordered confusion is charged with cashmere and leafless roses.' Or my favourite from Bella Freud: 'Handbags are glossy and great.' At Max Mara there are lots of coats. The country casual look loved by the wealthy who apparently see no irony in the fact that these endlessly tasteful coats are modelled to the strains of Alice in Chains and Guns 'N' Roses. At the end twenty or so models march out in long black dresses. They all look exactly the same. It's the image I will take home with me.

Moschino doesn't bother with a show. Instead you can go to the showroom, watch a video, and actually look at the clothes. It's much more relaxing and fashion's own court jester has rummaged through the seventies to conjure up a collection that looks like an expensive jumble sale. I like it but fail to understand how anyone could pay so much money for it. There are jackets made of sewn-together Smiley badges. All of this is socially significant. The collection, the publicity woman tells us, is 'multi-ethnic: Moschino would like people to go together just like his clothes go together'. In the corner two men are having a similarly *Absolutely Fabulous* conversation about this daft attempt at social comment. 'You see it's multi-ethnic,' intones one. 'How often do you shave your head?' asks the other. Five minutes later they're still talking haircuts.

The next day bunches of mimosa are on sale everywhere for Women's Day. A huge display of them is in the entrance to the Emporio Armani show. This is the most highly organized event so far. 'I've always thought Armani was ever so slightly fascist,' confides the stylist beside me. Two queens in the next row are bitching about 'label-girls' when Suzy Menkes makes her entrance, wearing the sort of velvet hat they sell in Camden Market plonked on her head. 'What does she look like?' 'Oh, I think it's called Widow Twankey – have you seen the back view?' The show itself is boring, or rather my interest in looking at clothes is flagging. At the end

Armani comes out wearing a Comic Relief-style red nose to indicate what a hip kind of guy he is. In Fashionland red noses or red ribbons for AIDS awareness are fairly interchangeable symbols.

Sandra Bernhard is at Callaghan, there to watch her friend who is modelling. It's a small show livened up by the presence of André Leon Talley, the big black creative director of US *Vogue*, who nips the models' bums as they go past. His revered colleague Grace Coddington is there too. André stage whispers: 'It's good. If Grace scrawls, it's fucking good and she hasn't looked up yet.'

A full moon hangs over the Duomo as we head off to Versace. I am looking forward to this one. He is the man who does the incredibly expensive high tack that would not look out of place on an East End sunbed girl. But when we arrive there is a crush to get in. I wait for a long time while hyperactive women screech and wave their tickets all around me. '*La Stampa*'. '*American Vogue*'. 'Emanuela. Let me in now.' They are desperate, I am shoved up against a barrier and choking in a cloud of a thousand perfumes. They won't even let Cindy Crawford through. These people are behaving like animals and I feel I can't really make the kind of effort required to scratch my way to the front. I wander off to get a drink. Desolate individuals are crying because they have not got in. An English girl comes up to me. 'You got a cigarette?' 'Didn't you get in?' I ask. 'No,' she says. 'I can't stand the indignity of it all. Sometimes you just have to think to yourself it's only a fucking fashion show. That's all it is. It's just clothes. That's all it is in the end.'

HOME ALONE HOME ALONE MUM

'You bitch' screamed the headline on Tuesday's *Daily Mirror*. It gave me a jolt, reminding me of the 'Kill the bitch' slogan audiences chanted at Glenn Close in *Fatal Attraction*. I saw it from a distance and thumbed mentally through all the women in public life who could have deserved such tabloid scorn. Even with today's disillusionment with the royals, surely not even the *Mirror* would describe our monarch or her daughter-in-law as a 'bitch'?

Of course not. This bitch was not a famous person, though she longed to be. She was Yasmin Gibson, the 'Home Alone Mum' accused of leaving her eleven-year-old daughter Gemma on her own while she went on holiday to the Costa del Sol. Luckily Gemma was found by the police, who called in social services a day after her mother went away. Gibson, who claims she'd made arrangements with a neighbour, was arrested 'after being flown back by the *Sun*'.

The whole sorry tale smacks of tabloid 'news management'. After the recent Home Alone episode in the US, in which a couple left their two children with a fridge full of sandwiches while they went on holiday to Mexico, they were rapidly elevated into America's 'most hated couple'. The details of the case continue to fascinate and appal: when arrested at the airport, they did not ask about the kids but if their luggage was OK.

How awful it all is but what a great story. And now we have our very own version, with Gibson in the kind of star role of which, as an out-of-work actress, she could only have dreamed. But was she sure what the part would entail when she talked to tabloid journalists in her 'Spanish hideaway'? Did she know the price of her fifteen minutes of fame when she gave that silly interview saying she hadn't done anything wrong and wasn't coming back? Could she have known that blurting out her ambivalent feelings about her own child – 'She hates me having any fun and is quite jealous and spoiled' – was simply winning the case for the prosecution? No. Because she didn't realize that, in this case, the prosecution was led by the very people who had promised to give her fame, attention, money and a safe ride home – the tabloid hacks themselves.

OK. So all of this is pretty dumb. As is having blonde hair and admitting to rich Arab boyfriends. It all adds up to the stereotypical picture of the amoral good-time girl, the selfish mother. But some of the condemnation heaped on Gibson this week has nothing to do with her. Her story – of the woman who deliberately left her child alone – has been cruelly juxtaposed with the appalling murder of James Bulger. In a week in which we have been made to feel we cannot take an eye off our children even for a second, what could be worse than a mother who does just that, who does it in public and who appears to know no shame?

Now we have our revenge. Gibson, distraught in the cells, protesting her innocence, her face streaked with tears of mascara and anger. No more 'saucy' poses, for she has shown us what we really wanted to see all along: the face of a fallen woman.

Undoubtedly she was wrong to leave her child alone. I am not saying otherwise. But witnessing the sheer hatred projected on to this sad and infantile personality makes me wonder how women can ever begin to express their difficulties with their children without for ever being labelled 'wicked' or 'bad mothers'. If Yasmin Gibson had been able to say that she could no longer cope with her daughter, maybe she wouldn't have had to take such drastic action. Yet while we live in a society in which the idea of motherhood is sanctified, the price of this involves a wilful denial of reality. So it's hard to say that children can be bloody awkward, demanding little beings and that everyone longs to get away at some point.

To say these things is not to say that children aren't wonderful, but if you actually think they are wonderful all the time, then I suspect you are not a parent. When I wrote a column about how it feels to be stuck at home with bored, ill children, the most hostile letters I received were from other women telling me how selfish I was, how sorry they felt for my kids, how I had sold out to male values by preferring to work than to be at home. One slightly more supportive letter came from a psychotherapist who advised me to get in touch with my own inner child and learn to scream. (I'm working on it.)

Gibson, on the other hand, strikes me as someone so in touch with her 'inner child' that she could forget the real-life one for whom she was responsible. This strikes me as sad rather than bad. She needs help, not hatred, now 'the bitch' is broken.

But while Gibson could not cope with her responsibility, I am left wondering why she should have had to. Two people presumably produced this child. Where is the father in all this? After all, he has abandoned his child for a lot longer than a day but there is no headline that says 'The bastard' because, let's face it, men leaving their kids is so routine that it is not even considered newsworthy. Can you imagine someone being dubbed a Home Alone Dad?

As long as women shoulder the responsibility for bringing up children, they also shoulder the blame when something goes wrong. With so many women now bringing up kids on their own, the surprise is not that such circumstances occasionally produce a conveniently archetypal 'bad mother' but that they actually produce so many good ones.

ONCE UPON A TIME IN THE
NUCLEAR FAMILY

Let me tell you a story. A long, long time ago, everybody in the land lived in little nuclear families. Everybody was happy. The Daddies went out to work to get the money; the Mummies didn't do much except look after the house and children. Oh and wear nice aprons. Sometimes Mummy went out to work too but only to get a few extras. It wasn't like Daddy's job. There were no muggings, drugs or Gameboys. Everyone knew their place and they could have lived happily ever after had it not been for the nasty feminist witches who came along and put a spell on the Mummies, making them think perhaps they weren't so happy after all.

After that, everything went wrong. The Mummies said crazy things, like they worked as hard as the Daddies. The Daddies couldn't find jobs anyway. The Mummies said they would be better off on their own and the sobbing children were left with nothing to do but sniff glue and shoplift.

This, after all, is the kind of fairy tale that has been regurgitated at various intervals over the past few weeks. Such a moral panic could sustain itself only by attaching to some suitable target the free-floating anxiety we all felt at the James Bulger murder. After years of being told no such thing as society existed, we are all now supposed to be concerned about its breakdown. And at the heart of this breakdown, of course, is the decline of the nuclear family.

Rather than trying to look at what is an *international* trend, the tendency has been to bathe the past in sickly nostalgia and blame everything that has gone wrong on the left, feminism and progressive education. Reality must not be allowed to intrude into this daydream because if it did, things would look very different. Far from the family being destroyed by outside forces, what has most undermined it has been the unbearable tensions within, tensions that were always already there. These may have been repressed for the myth to retain its power but they have not gone away. In fact, the very idea of the family under siege, the family as a safe haven from the brutal outside world, depends often on the deliberate repression of what we know goes on inside many families.

Feminism did not create the dissatisfaction that many women felt but it began to describe and name it. One of the reasons why feminists focused on the family was not because they thought it unnecessary and easily replaceable but quite the opposite. They saw the importance of the family in socializing children, in shaping our notions about work and leisure, the public and the private; they identified it as the fundamental unit of social cohesion. But what they did, that still remains so shocking, was to violate what was considered a personal, private space with an essentially political analysis. To say that what goes on in the home is also part of society, not separate from it, runs counter to the prevailing belief that, for men at least, home is somewhere you go to escape the outside world.

Yet behind closed doors, escape for women has not been so easy. The majority of violent crimes take place in the home. Family life may also include child abuse, marital rape or, more mundanely, the double shift of work and childcare that most women end up doing. For many women, families are something to be escaped from, not to, and those who want to turn back the clock should not forget the drudgery and misery that family life may entail. They should be forced to talk to some of our young homeless people, many of whom would rather sleep on the streets than return to their families.

Where feminism is responsible, if you like, is simply in raising women's expectations, but what has made the real difference is growing female financial independence. More women initiate divorce proceedings because they are no longer dependent on their husbands. Serial monogamy seems to be the trend and alongside that comes general restructuring of the family.

Of course, the family has had to change before – the Industrial Revolution demanded a different set of household arrangements from what had gone on previously – but because we insist on seeing it as a natural rather than a social unit, we forget this. Now, in this period of transition, perhaps we should look back to some of these older definitions of family. While we understand the word to be entirely based on kinship, it once indicated household or co-residence. Your family were simply the people you lived with.

When you listen to what people are actually asking for, or mourning the loss of, it is not the nuclear family but the extended family, a looser network altogether. Single parents (when we are not too busy producing delinquents, smoking crack and stealing giros) often need help with childcare. We might want someone to look after the baby while we nip out to the shops. This is a different demand from the one for institutionalized childcare and one that is equally unmet because of the decline of the extended family network.

In the inevitable process of restructuring that the family is now going through, women can no longer rely on the old obligations which, however oppressive, have not as yet been replaced by any new ones. Consequently, many men have simply opted out of family life altogether. This is far from ideal but surely the future depends on facing up to family life as it is lived now, with its advantages as well as disadvantages, rather than telling ourselves fairy stories about the past.

LET'S TALK (AND TALK AND TALK) ABOUT SEX

The female rappers Salt 'n' Pepa sang: 'Let's talk about sex, baby, let's talk about you and me . . .' and look how we have obliged them. These days we talk of little else, the overriding sexual imperative has become not the urge to do it but the urge to talk about it.

Are we doing it properly, often enough, adventurously enough? Are we concentrating as hard as we should be working it out, contacting our real desires, coming as many times as we really could? I tell you, this sex business is a real labour of love. Labour being the operative word.

You can now do your proficiency tests with an array of alarmingly uninhibited experts on videos, TV programmes and books. Only the other day I woke up next to one called *How to have an orgasm as often as you want.* How was it for me? I'm afraid I did what came naturally and turned over and went back to sleep. For the central message of all this hyperactive gush is that sex is somehow natural; when in fact the very opposite is borne out by the enormous production of material around the subject. What can be natural about an activity that is performed, packaged and policed in such intricate ways? How can one ever separate out the act from the attitudes that surround it?

One way of doing this is to ask 'How was it for you?' not of an individual but of a culture. This is what Paul Ferris does in his book *Sex and the British: A Twentieth Century History*, where he surveys British sexual attitudes of the past 100 years. To say that sex has a history is automatically to concede to its cultural construction, but it's an approach that tends to fit everything rather too neatly into a story of our progressive enlightenment on the matter.

At times Ferris is guilty of this, though he remains healthily grumpy about the efforts of the various sexual reformers throughout the century. Of Marie Stopes, he writes 'she was, perhaps, not quite sane', and then proceeds to give us the juicy details of the annulment of her marriage to Ruggles Gates. Asked in court about the rigidity of her husband's 'parts', Stopes replied 'I only remember three occasions on which it was partially rigid, and then it was never effectively rigid.' It had apparently taken this sexual pioneer a year or two before she realized that there was anything wrong with her marriage.

But Ferris's thrust, if that is the right word, is that the British have tended to suit themselves, not paying much heed to the reformers, the moralists, the educators. While some attitudes have clearly shifted, many remain ready to be recycled at any opportunity. Victorian imperialism stressed moral discipline as one of the ways that we were superior to loose-living foreigners. Then both the Germans and the French were seen as potentially contaminating influences. Now the pro–censorship lobby warns against the tide of filth that will flood in from Europe, citing *Red Hot Dutch* as a perfect example. In the real world, meanwhile, pirate decoders change hands for as little as forty quid.

The truth is that since sex became an object of scrutiny, we can scarcely take our eyes off it. Havelock Ellis, Stopes, Krafft-Ebing, Freud, even Baden-Powell (with his bizarre theories about the 'rutting' season of young men) have all contributed to the cataloguing and monitoring of sexual behaviour. That there were always those ready to do the dirty work of actually hounding couples engaged in the activity does strike one, however, as peculiarly British.

The National Vigilance Association in 1900 busied itself combing the streets for the 'workers of impurity'; the Suffragettes took in prostitutes; in the name of social hygiene, women's patrols during the First World War evicted couples from damp grass, boarding up seaside seats used by lovers. The Mass Observers of the 1930s ludicrously tiptoed about Blackpool beach after dark to find 120 couples embracing. 'What we found was petting and feeling' (though in 1937 four cases of actual copulation were duly recorded).

National traits also present themselves in an abiding interest in flagellation and punishment – subjects which preoccupied the otherwise respectable pages of *Picture Post* – and an obsession with the evils of masturbation. Stopes called it 'utterly loathsome', while D. H. Lawrence wrote that it was 'perhaps the deepest and most dangerous cancer of our civilisation'. What Lawrence was in favour of, you'll be glad to know, was 'warm-hearted fucking'. But what changed things for most ordinary people were the arguments of neither the moralists nor the radicals. Both wars brought with them freer attitudes because people felt they had to live for the moment, the cinema began to peddle its romantic fantasies, and above all, contraception became more effective and more widely available. Moral panics about abortion, prostitution and VD continued through to the 1960s, but it was the Pill (described by one of its defenders as 'a wafer of love') that was a hugely liberating force.

Was this new found freedom a sign of society's maturity, or one of anarchy? Ferris is good at highlighting the anti-sex strand of feminism which had, at various times, lined up with doctors and clergy to resist both contraception and the divorce law reforms – which were first dismissed as 'a Casanova's charter'. Now we take it for granted that they have helped women enormously. But he is less good at analysing what the recognition of female pleasure meant. 'The clitoris would soon be regarded as dispassionately as the thumb,' he writes somewhat astonishingly of the early women libbers. Perhaps, though, this is better than Prince Charles's comment at feminist protests: 'Basically, I think it is because they want to be men.'

From thereon in, the book takes up the familiar narrative of the *Oz* trial, *Oh Calcutta!*, rows over sex education, video nasties and the Operation Spanner case. His conclusion is basically that sex is not subject to immutable laws and that people in the end do what they want to do anyway. This is fine as far as it goes, and Ferris provides a fascinating summary of the last 100 years or so. Yet, as with so many books about sex, one can't help feeling that something essential is just beyond reach, that whatever its proclaimed subject, this isn't really a book about sex at all. For a chronological ordering of facts cannot explain why people feel sex to be such a powerful force in their lives; it cannot explain the transcendental space we accord it, or why, as Ferris hints in his introduction: 'Pleasure is too persuasive, it smells of anarchy.'

Sexual discourse may have taken over from sexual intercourse but this discourse depends on two parallel lines that must never meet – that of repression versus expression, both of which are over-rated by their champions. But each, of course, depends on the other. For Herbert Marcuse or Wilhelm Reich (or even Richard Neville) to think that sexual liberation could bring about a political revolution was precisely to accord sex a subversive, disruptive power that is derived from it being repressed in the first place. Sexual politics is the third term that can interrupt this hopeless duality because it doesn't treat sex as magically separate from the rest of our lives. It understands that sex is always social, that we may have animal urges but that we are also cultured beings.

Another approach is simply to forget all this culture and get back to nature, and this is what Helen Fisher does in her book *Anatomy of Love: A Natural History of Adultery, Monogamy and Divorce*. Now, I know that these sub-Desmond Morris DIY anthropology books are very popular, but I fail to see what light they throw on human sexual behaviour. It may help you to know that flirting occurs in all species, and that 'Codfish bulge their heads and thrust out their pelvic fins', but I'm afraid it doesn't do much for me. While Fisher accepts that culture sculpts diversity from common human genetic material, her real interest lies in the biological bases of our behaviour.

Yet this emphasis on unchanging biology, and the similarity of our mating rituals with those of other animals, ignores precisely what separates us from other animals. We have language, and with language comes immortality, through inter-generational know-ledge, abstract symbolic thought, not to mention morality. This is why I am not that much reassured by the cases of adultery she finds among baboons and Swedish blackbirds. An instinctual basis for adultery may be just what you have been looking for, but surely it means something different for us than for a red-winged blackbird? Her main finding is that a four-year rather than a seven-year itch is in evidence when one looks at divorce patterns around the world, and that serial monogamy, alongside adultery, can be found in many species and many cultures.

It is hard not to concur with W. S. Gilbert's rhyme: 'Darwinian Man, though well behaved, at best is only a monkey shaved.' If you are content to think of yourself as little more than a shaved monkey, then you will like this book. If you feel your sexuality to be some-what more complicated than that, you may be disappointed.

Sex as nature, sex as culture? Take your pick. Yet for all their overwhelming amounts of information, I wonder in the end if either of these books tells us any more about the whole mystifying business than Dorothy Parker when she wrote: 'By the time you swear you're his, Shivering and sighing, And he vows his passion is Infinite, undying – Lady, make a note of this: One of you is lying.'

NOT ANGELS, NOT DEVILS, JUST KIDS

Over the past couple of weeks, children have not just been in the news. They have been the news. Murdered children. Murdering children. Children who rape teachers. Children killed by terrorist bombs. Children lost at sea. Children who are out of control. To have read the popular press over the past week, one could have forgotten Bosnia, Yeltsin, the boring old economy and instead shared in the mourning for Johnathan Ball or the teenagers lost in the canoeing accident. The front page of Wednesday's *Daily Mail* had two sombre headlines: 'Johnathan, my beautiful angel. Father recalls bomb victim's last words' and 'Lost hours in the icy seas'.

It goes without saying that these are terrible tragedies, that the loss of a child is the hardest loss of all, that, yes, these deaths touch us in ways that much 'news' doesn't. But what is most peculiar about the macabre milking of these tragedies for every last tear is that accompanying them is another sort of story altogether. As the *Sun* discusses the 'sea-terror', looking for someone to blame under the dramatic banner 'Why did they let kids die?', its own front page screams, 'Boy, 13, rapes teacher in class'. 'We're growing used to the young monsters in our midst,' thunders its editorial.

Somewhere between the talk of angels and devils, innocent victims and evil kids, lies an anxiety, a disquiet about what we have actually reproduced in our society. Simplistic though this tabloid dichotomy might be, one can sense that it enables people to ask the big questions in a way that is comprehensible to them. A bomb, an accident, a hand held out in a shopping centre, the very arbitrariness of life itself – how do we explain these things in an age of little faith? How do we cope with the sheer injustice of a young life suddenly taken? How do we carry on? How do we look after our own children?

Clearly we are not even sure these days when children are no longer children any more. The line between childhood and adult-hood is becoming more blurred. Are signs of criminal activity now the only rites of passage available to our youth? How much can we hold children responsible for their wrong-doing?

More specifically, however, with all this resurrected talk of evil and innocence, we are asking again whether we are born or made, what part nature has compared with nurture. For the morality at the root of the moral panic about the 'monsters in our midst' is one that has had enough of all those theories about social construction. It is a morality based on retribution, condemnation, and it has little truck with explanations which it sees as excuses. It calls for the law to be changed so that ten year olds can be punished as if they were adults. But this morality depends for its existence on the belief that chil-dren are either absolutely pure or absolutely corrupt.

We project these fantasies on to kids, for they are fantasies until the monsters become like alien beings, not children at all, not our responsibility. If kids are mirrors of ourselves, in which we see our hopes and fears, we now have one group who embody our fears, who are hopelessly out of control. With the death of our 'angels', we are perhaps reminded not to hope too much.

Yet in all the public grief that has been poured out, there is some recognition that children are a collective responsibility. The privat-ization of family life has meant that while some kids are driven from ballet to violin lessons to pony-riding, many can't wait to leave their own burdensome childhoods behind and will do whatever it takes to be seen as adult. We can blame their parents as much as we like but it will change nothing. It's no use complaining that today's kids grow up 'too soon' when children themselves sense what is valued in our culture and what is not.

And children, precious angels that they may be, have only to look around them to see that ours is a culture that does not actually like children very much. Parents pay a fortune so that offspring may still be caned in private schools, restaurants and hotels claim the right to refuse those under a certain age, and a discussion about children's rights is still a long way off.

The big horror stories of the past few years – about child abuse, the scandals in children's homes, the lack of opportunities for many kids – are still swept under the carpet. While the faces of dead children haunt us, we continue to ignore the pleas of many of those still among us. A healthier attitude would be to allow children some autonomous existence. They are contradictory beings just like us, neither good nor bad. They are not metaphors for the *fin de siècle* breakdown of society but flesh-and-blood beings.

Yet to allow them some autonomy would remove the power of these fantasies. Our tabloid concern does nothing to change the real powerlessness of children in our culture. It is as if we are so keen to see ourselves in our children that we can no longer see them as they really are. While they remain reflections of our own confusion, they continue to be seen but, in proper English fashion, never actually heard.

LITTLE ME AND NOT SO SILLY JILLY

If I started off this column by telling you that I am a dizzy, daffy kind of girl with scarcely a thought in my head, would you carry on reading? If I described myself as an impossibly daft individual who, by a marvellous stroke of luck, gets to witter on every week in a national newspaper, would you be impressed? Perhaps not. But maybe I've been reading too many Jilly Cooper interviews in which the self-proclaimed doyenne of silliness has been demonstrating what I hope is a dying art – one perfected by so many women – that of appearing to be less intelligent than they really are.

Silly Jilly ('I know at heart I'm a flibbertigibbet') may be a hopeless gusher with low-brow aspirations ('I couldn't write a literary novel because I like happy endings') but the fact is that she is a highly successful author, her books topping both hardback and paperback lists. You don't have to be a fan to recognize some skill in her endless permutations of the riding and rogering scenario. So why the false modesty, the twittish persona ('Are we still in the eighties? I get so mixed up')?

I have a feeling that a woman with a first print run of over 100,000 knows damn well which decade she is in, but the point of all this conspicuous idiocy is surely strategic. And it's a strategy at which women excel. From the 'Here's one I prepared earlier' at a dinner party to the 'Oh, this old thing', women consistently downplay their achievements. The debates in the seventies about wages for housework were exactly about making visible what was largely invisible. This invisibility can be extended to the whole range of tasks that now go into the production of femininity. How many more articles can you read about how to put on make-up so that you look as if you haven't got any on? The natural look we are supposed to achieve in the end actually takes up an enormous amount of time and energy.

This consistent denial of the sheer labour that goes into being a woman with children, a job, a novel to write and a face to put on is so galling that when it is mentioned, it is rather embarrassing. I read with ambivalent feelings the interview in this paper with Candia McWilliam, in which she talked about how motherhood had made her less prolific as a novelist than her male counterparts. 'With the birth of each child, you lose two novels,' she said. By her reckoning, the world has been spared four of my epics but to admit this makes me edgy as it so easily plays into the familiar whine of 'Women can't be artists because they have children'. Biology becomes not just destiny but lack of literary recognition.

So what do we do? Deny that bringing up another human being might actually take a bit of time, might actually make us tired? Or do we carry on writing blockbusters with one hand, baking soufflés with the other, while breastfeeding the twins at the same time? Privately, we may dream of being Martin Amis with a flat of one's own; publicly, we pretend it's so easy that anyone could do it.

For Cooper (the woman has a surname, after all), a pathological desire to please has resulted in this strategy. Early on, she must have learnt what was thought pleasing in a woman. Intelligence, obviously, was not listed. So she did what a lot of women do and played dumb, denied the hard work she puts in and smiled a lot. Psychoanalytically, this is known as the masquerade. Joan Riviere, a contemporary of Freud, wrote about women who mask their cleverness under excessive femininity so as to reduce its threat to men.

It is one of the oldest tricks in the book but, thankfully, it now seems like an unfortunate throwback. Even Diana 'I'm as thick as a plank' Spencer has come to, and a new generation of women continually remind us how clever, how in control they are. Even women who are entirely famous for their looks, like models, don't want to be thought of as stupid. They are more than just pretty faces and they have financial advisers to prove it. Madonna, Sharon Stone, Demi Moore are as desperate to show us their business skills as their muscles. While time-warped Jilly Cooper may act like a complete bimbo, women like Amanda de Cadenet rush around as if they are world leaders.

Such women take themselves very seriously indeed, sometimes too seriously, but isn't this better than the simpering silliness of women who are afraid that to be taken seriously might mean they are not liked? Ultimately, to take ourselves seriously means we cannot pretend either that we are stupid or that everything in our lives is incredibly easy. It means giving up the patronage of men and the conspiracy of silence perpetuated by women. This may be hard. But not as hard as realizing that, when it comes to women faking stupidity – or orgasms, for that matter – most men can't tell the difference anyway.

WHO'S AFRAID OF ANITA HILL?

Who's afraid of Anita Hill? Quite a lot of America apparently. Eighteen months after she mesmerized the nation with her testimony to the Senate about the activities of her former boss, Clarence Thomas, the Anita Effect is still going strong. Thomas *was* confirmed to the Supreme Court, but with the highest number of negative votes ever for a successful nominee.

Hill, meanwhile, has been fêted by Hillary Clinton and Gloria Steinem. Last year, she was one of *Vanity Fair*'s Women of the Year. Emily's List was started. The record number of women elected to Congress was attributed in part to her. More women than ever applied to women-only colleges; the numbers complaining of sexual harassment rose by 45 per cent; the election of Clinton himself was described by sociologist Michael Kimmel as 'Anita Hill's revenge'. Most significantly, perhaps, opinion polls show that, while at the time of the Senate hearings the majority of Americans believed Thomas, a year later they favoured Hill.

It is not surprising, then, that some sort of backlash should occur. Anita Hill has become a symbol of a broader cultural conflict, a feminist martyr, a civil rights heroine. But by turning her into a myth, her own supporters have ignored the complexities of this case and conflated two very different issues: greater awareness about sexual harassment is not in itself proof that this particular case occurred. What exactly went on between Thomas and Hill we shall never know. There is no hard evidence and no witnesses. Just his word against hers.

This was precisely what was so compelling about the phenomenally high-rating televised hearings. Here was a story that had it all: race, sex, ambition, power. Yet ultimately it all hinged on a simple choice. Who do you believe, him or her? Was this the sort of man who talked about pubic hair in Coke cans? Was this a woman who would make up stories about a porn star called Long Dong Silver?

We could only speculate. And that is what a new book does. *The Real Anita Hill: The Untold Story* by David Brock isn't the first book on the subject. There was the collection of essays, edited by Toni Morrison, with the unwieldy title *Race-ing Justice, En-gendering Power*, which assumed, fairly uncritically, that Hill was telling the truth. Brock's book, on the other hand, is a cool character assassination of Hill. It was aided by a grant from the John M. Olin foundation, a champion of conservative causes, which prompted Anna Quindlen in the *New York Times* to comment: 'The book is not only steeped in ideology; it was financed by it'.

In the ideological chasm that separates Hill's supporters from her detractors, the word 'ideology' itself is thrown around like a hand grenade. For conservatives, Hill's supporters are ideological warriors, thought police who use the obscure machinations of political correctness to destroy the American way; for liberals, Hill's enemies are steeped in the ideology of patriarchal objectivity. They know not what they do. Which is why, as so many women said at the time, the men 'just didn't get it'.

Brock's book, however, is just one part of a concerted attack on Hill. The state legislator has demanded she be fired from a job in law school and there is strong opposition to the creation of an Anita Faye Hill Chair for the study of gender-based law issues at the University of Oklahoma Law Center, where she teaches; Republican Oklahoma City Senator Leonard Sullivan has said they might as well have a David Koresh Chair.

Hill herself has kept quiet, though there are rumours she will answer critics with her own book. While she makes $12,000 per lecture, her public statements often seem steeped in the worst non-communicative PC jargon. She is 'the Ross Perot of feminism'. Everyone knows who she is but no one really knows what she stands for. Indeed, Brock's book challenges the media representations of her. While they tended to treat the whole scandal as a kind of national referendum on sexual harassment, Brock uncovers a different story. Far from being the demure Baptist girl with Republican sympathies, he says the real Anita Hill was obsessed with gender and race issues. Worse, she appears to have been a sexual being. But while his overt sympathy is always with Thomas, he does uncover discrepancies in Hill's testimony.

What is revealed in detail are the politics of judicial nomination. The judiciary is seen by both sides as another branch of government, which forces Supreme Court nominees to behave like political candidates. Ever since right wing Robert Bork's nomination was defeated in 1987 by what Brock calls the 'shadow senate' after 'a caricature of his record', the word *bork* has meant this organized attempt to defeat a nomination by any means. When Clarence Thomas's nomination was announced, the Republicans desperately wanted a black conservative in the post – and Patricia Ireland, president of the National Organization of Women, declared, 'We're going to bork him.'

Thomas was repeatedly described as an Uncle Tom, a self-hating race traitor. This portrait arose from his opposition to racial quotas and affirmative action, the sacred cows of the liberal establishment. The irony of course, was that when Thomas himself complained during hearings that this was just the 'hi-tech lynching of an uppity nigger' everyone knew that he had never been at all uppity.

Hill, on the other hand was painted, in some quarters at least, as a courageous woman who had come forward only to tell the truth. Brock sees this as a last-ditch borking strategy and says that Hill, who for some time had insisted on anonymity, had been pushed to the forefront by 'fervently committed Senate staffers' out to beat the Thomas nomination.

That Hill wanted some control in the process, however, does not seem as damaging to her case as other facts Brock unearths. Why did she, after the harassment had occurred, change jobs so that she could still work with Thomas? Why did she keep in touch? Brock also claims that Thomas does not fit the part of the 'typical harasser'. He doesn't, for instance, believe he has ever used pornography and no other women have come forward since, which one would have expected. Actually, Angela Wright did but backed down at the last minute, perhaps put off by seeing what happened to Hill, who had to sit while a psychiatrist described her as having a delusional system fuelled by erotomania.

Brock's subtext is that Hill was a woman scorned, given jobs far beyond her capability because of the dreaded quota system. While he bends over backwards to believe Thomas, he conjectures wildly about Hill. Does anyone really believe, for instance, Thomas's declaration to the Senate that he had never discussed the *Roe* v. *Wade* decision on abortion, probably the most controversial judgment made by the Supreme Court in twenty-five years? He fails entirely to explain 'how Hill could have been so persuasive to millions of viewers'. In the end, he concludes that no sexual harassment took place.

In the end, though, it's just his word against hers. Again. In the end, one feels he just doesn't get it. For whatever did or did not happen struck a chord with so many women in particular that they felt what was being told was some emotional truth beyond the comprehension of the men in suits.

What is so extraordinary about this case is the way it has been perceived as such an enormous threat by the right. The discrediting of Anita Hill goes far beyond what happened in an office ten years ago. It is about discrediting a whole movement. Why is it so important for the right to secure a consensus against her? Why else does the *Sunday Times* publish extracts from the book? Why else do you still see 'Anita For President' T-shirts on the streets of America?

Barbara Amiel wrote recently in the *Sunday Times*: 'One doesn't want to make ludicrous comparisons' and went on to make one: 'It seems fair to say that America today, *vis-à-vis* feminist thought, is at the point Germany reached before the Nazis took over.' This echoes Leonard Sullivan's equally crazed statement: 'Not many people believe her, except her feminazi friends.'

Who's afraid of Anita Hill? These people certainly are because they know that more people believe her now than ever. Are all of them feminazis? I don't think so somehow. And while Thomas sits on the Supreme Court, he will still have to live with the fact that *Conquering Cock*, the Long Dong Silver movie to which he supposedly referred, has been re-released on video, bearing the legend, 'The Supreme Court's Highest Rating, The All-Time Favorite of Justice Clarence Thomas!'

RIP THE 'REAL' ROSEANNE

'The old Roseanne is dead. A new Roseanne is being born,' Roseanne Arnold announced, painfully, this week. Speaking with difficulty because of a recent facelift, she joked that one day her lips would move again. Loudmouth Roseanne has finally been silenced by that most banal of desires, the wish to be beautiful. And what is wrong with that? The woman who played the She-Devil in the film of Fay Weldon's book knows a thing or two about plastic surgery herself: she's already had a breast reduction and a tummy tuck. This is the new Roseanne. It must have been the old Roseanne who once said, 'I'm fat and proud of it. If somebody asks me how my diet is going, I say, "Fine. How was your lobotomy?"'

The new Roseanne, as fans of her show will know, grows more glamorous week by week. Gone is the lank, stringy hair and tracksuits; now her brunette mane is as shiny as the silk shirts she wears. She is remaking herself in public. And it hurts. She says the pain of these operations is worth every penny. But is this what we expect of a woman who has continually traded on her 'realness'?

Her TV show, consistently in the top five in the US, is considered revolutionary because it is about 'real people' with 'real problems'. Roseanne represents, according to US comic Alan King, 'the hopeless underclass of the female sex. Polyester-clad, overweight occupants of the slow track.' For her critics, she is precisely the reason we need fantasy. Or, as her husband Tom Arnold says of the Roseanne phenomenon: 'We're America's worst nightmare: white trash with money.' Money enough, it appears, not to have to look like white trash. Doesn't it all sound so neat and tidy? These nips and tucks, this relentless self-construction? Let's be honest: we never expected the Roseanne Arnold work-out video. As Marjorie Garber, author of *Vested Interests: Cross-dressing And Cultural Anxiety*, explains: 'We expect miracles, not self-discipline from our cultural heroes.'

What makes a miracle exactly is less appetizing. A tummy tuck sounds almost gentle until you think about what it is. Incisions are made in the lower abdomen and fat sucked away; the navel is 'freed' from the abdominal wall; skin and fat are removed and the wound sutured; the navel is 'relocated'. This is not embroidery we're talking about here.

Does having your navel relocated make you any less real than before, though? Does Roseanne have an obligation to look like a blue-collar slob to make the rest of us feel better about ourselves? Obviously not but this question of realness is a tough one for women. Mirror, mirror, on the wall, who is the most real of them all? Roseanne, Kate Moss, Joan Collins? Has anyone ever seen a 'real woman'? Could they tell the rest of us, so we have a point of reference?

Schooled from birth to be as unreal as possible, we spend large amounts of time making ourselves over. For a small fee, you too can be immortalized in gooey soft-focus as a magazine cover girl. You can say, I looked like that. Once. The possibility of transformation, even for a single day, is a compelling fantasy for many women. How else do you explain the success of a magazine devoted to bridalwear?

Many successful women appear to be successful because they have lost all faith in the idea of realness being any kind of advantage – they simply play the game. Edwina Currie's advice to ambitious women has nothing to do with policies or expertise. It is simply this: 'Lose two stone and buy a suit.' All around us we see the results of this wisdom, and some would say men are increasingly subject to the same kind of pressures.

This is not the case, however. While male politicians may have got themselves a decent suit, they are not required to make over their personalities as well. For as Roseanne has her spare parts physically removed, Hillary Clinton is having her personality cosmetically altered, to judge by the endless profiles in the American media. Hillary the cover girl, Hillary the saint, Hillary the loving wife and mother. Forget Hillary, one of the hottest lawyers around; see her in the kitchen scrambling eggs for sick little Chelsea. All this is about as convincing as Margaret Thatcher's 'I'd rather bake cakes than drive a tank' act.

Paradoxically, though, all this mannered domesticity is an attempt to show us the 'real' Hillary. This tinkering with her image, this toning down and dressing up, is no doubt the result of long-thought-out strategies. A photogenic First Lady is still more important than a clever one.

It is the malleability of female identity that is on show, however, with both Hillary and Roseanne. While men just are, women are continually becoming. To admit to cosmetic surgery or to being aware of one's image is always, for men, a feminizing move. Surgery may transform Roseanne's body, soft-focus may make Hillary's smile look less gritted, but these sisters are still doing it for themselves, aren't they? These days there is little comfort to be found in the idea of the natural. Indeed, successful women parade their transformations in public as if they were the most natural thing in the world. No one is born a 'real' woman but, hey, we get the picture. With the right light, enough liposuction and a feigned interest in the right way to scramble an egg, any of us can do a damn good impersonation of one.

BRIGHT WOOLLIES CAN'T WARM SO COLD A WORLD

When is an advert not an advert? When it is banned? When it is art? When it tells the truth? The latest Benetton ad was, apparently, devised after the organizers of the Venice Biennàle invited the company's creative director, Oliverio Toscani, to show his work in the avant-garde section of the festival. It features fifty-six sets of genitalia, belonging to men, women and children.

The picture recently appeared as a double-page ad in *Libération*, alongside the familiar United Colours of Benetton slogan. In Britain, however, the Obscene Publications Squad has sought to bar distribution of the French newspaper on the grounds that it risks infringing indecency legislation, mainly because there are children shown in the ad.

Toscani claims this is not exploitation as the children featured are his own – a questionable defence. Benetton's London headquarters are quoted as saying: 'It was not a new campaign, it was not really an advert at all – you shouldn't know about it anyway, it's been banned here.'

But we do know about it here, just as we knew about the campaign featuring a newborn baby which was eventually banned, and the ad showing a man dying of AIDS, which some magazines refused to run. Benetton's potent images have been disturbing us for some time now. Yet what is disturbing is mostly that these pictures of birth and death, of terrorism and racial harmony, hang in our consciousness, disconnected and dislocated from any context in which we might make sense of them.

These images are unanchored except by the meaningless legend

'United Colours of Benetton'. Toscani may talk a lot of guff about their universality, that they are there to remind us that we are all the same, that we are all equal. But their real intention, lest we forget, is to inspire brand recognition and loyalty. They are there to sell us jumpers. Not to change the world, merely to clothe an affluent part of it. This, more than any one particular image, is the real obscenity. In all their postmodern detachment, these campaigns manage to exploit all of us.

At least it's a reminder, if we ever needed one, of what advertising is really there for, however much contemporary advertising denies this, pretending some dubious higher purpose. Advertisers' highest purpose has never been to teach the world to sing, only to buy CocaCola.

The veneer of glamour attached to the ad industry conceals the lowest common denominator of the deal closed, the quick sale, the sparking of free-floating consumer desire. You don't know what you want? I'll show you things that you never even knew you needed. I'll make you want ... Benetton at the Biennàle?

The thin line between culture and commerce that Andy Warhol needed, if only to disregard it, has faded into memory. Does it matter? Not if you think that art-directed means the same thing as art itself. Then it doesn't matter at all. All categories are blurred. Gee isn't that the fun of living *right now*. Benetton's supposed attempt to show us things that matter flips into its exact opposite. Nothing really matters except brightly coloured casual wear. That is, after all, the meaning of life.

Irony, that sad excuse for not caring any more, is now the dominant aesthetic. Advertisers are so hip that they claim that their ads are not sexist, but a comment on sexism. The Vauxhall Corsa ad wasn't the old girls-lying-on-cars number. No, it was a very highly paid girls-lying-on-cars number. We were all in on the joke – including, of course, 'the girls' themselves. Another very funny ad, hysterical if you like that sort of thing, is the new Do It All one, showing all kinds of locks and bolts under the caption 'Lock up your daughters'.

Or what about the advert for Linn Hi-Fi, carried by this paper, which shows a picture of an attractive woman with the words: 'She's terrific in bed. She's witty, intelligent and makes her own pasta. She doesn't have a Linn Hi-Fi but her sister does, and she's the one I married.' Please don't get offended or take it seriously – it's obviously just a laugh. I mean it's all so knowing. These days everyone knows there is more to women than what they do in bed and in the kitchen, don't they? While the impotent Advertising Standards Authority received several complaints about this one, the good old-fashioned sexism that has crept back into ads in the name of ultra-modern in-jokiness is often far more insidious. Female bodies are still used as blank screens on to which every available fantasy can be generated. I find this much more offensive than pornography. Porn may sell the idea that all women are sexually available, but at least you know what you are buying.

Advertising also sells this idea but in the guise of trying to sell us something else instead. The ad for the Metro Rio doesn't show a woman lying on a car, instead it shows a woman with a tattoo of the car, its name and price on her shoulder. Who owns what, you might ask.

Men's bodies are no longer immune from this kind of treatment. Hunky torsos are now used to persuade us to buy Ajax: 'New Ajax Liquid. Because you don't want him to spend all his time cleaning.' (Why not?) Indeed some advertisers claim that they are trying to counter the innate sexism of the industry by showing men in domestic roles. Cow and Gate showed a dad feeding his baby; the Oxo dad now has to cook the occasional meal; Persil put a man at the kitchen sink a couple of years ago. But simply reversing the old formula is not enough to counter the way women are consistently portrayed.

The new Nike adverts incorporate this knowledge. One of their ads shows women of all different shapes who are naked, save for loin cloths. 'It's not the shape you are it's the shape you're in that matters' it says. Another of its ads shows a picture of a baby girl and asks, 'When was the last time you felt really comfortable with your body?' The copy reads: 'So who defined your template of beauty?

Who said you weren't OK?' To which one is tempted to answer, 'Well, actually the advertising industry hasn't exactly helped.'

For all this instant feminist empathy, don't forget this ad is still trying to get us to buy one kind of training shoes and not another. A right-on message with your running shoes, two for the price of one. What more could a nineties woman want?

Quite a lot actually. In the eighties, the advertising men might have convinced themselves and some of us too that they were agents of social change, capable of flogging governments as well as washing powder. But we won't get fooled again. Now we all know so much better, don't we? Maybe only someone without a sense of humour would think that any of this superficial world meant anything at all. Oh and Luciano Benetton, who knows how profitable such a loss of meaning can really be.

NOT A SINGLE ISSUE

I wonder, can you help me? I'm looking for a Sugar Daddy. I want someone in my life who will always be there, be faithful, and provide the basics, if you know what I mean. I don't want much. Just a run-down council flat and £60 a week will do. In return, I'll bear a few children, each with a talent for stealing cars or dealing crack, and I promise, for better or worse, to remain a member of the underclass all my life. I wouldn't be asking but the thing is, you see, I've tried a few real men and though they provide the children, they never provide the cash. They're just not reliable.

OK, so I'm joking. But not much. As a single parent myself, I have a vested interest in our image, which has taken a down-turn of late. We are part of an 'epidemic', a new kind of social disease, both symptom and cause of society's decline. Some say we are a result of the permissiveness of the sixties; others blame individual-istic Tory policies.

Under the headline 'Do They Want To Marry A Man Or The State?', a thoroughly offensive cartoon appeared in the *Sunday Times* of a feckless pregnant bride marrying a male figure called Social Security, while pig-like children crawled among her skirts and a tattooed man stood in the background pouring lager down his throat. Behind them, of course, the obligatory tower blocks, the other symbol of urban decay. The overclass's view of the underclass is not a pretty sight.

Yet, despite the pontifications of Peter Lilley and John Red-wood, who cannot be totally ignorant of the Government's plan to cut welfare spending, many of John Major's players are struck surprisingly dumb when it comes to the crux of the matter. For if this issue is not about gender politics, then I don't know what is. It is still far easier to blame women than to hold men accountable for this problem. Either the single mothers themselves are scapegoated or a shadowy group called 'the feminists' are vilified as the root of all evil. Traditional party politics has little to offer us because it prefers to maintain its inarticulacy about gender; on the left, to talk about such things is often regarded as divisive.

Surely, though, the rise of the one-parent family indicates the limitations of a politics based on old left/right allegiances. Though some Tories talk of morality, it is obvious that it is not morality at stake but the ultimate in privatization. The fact is, under this Government you can have any morality you like, as long as you can pay for it. Morality becomes the prerogative of the state only when the state is expected to hand over benefits which it then believes it can use like a stick or a carrot.

How quickly it then returns to those detestable Victorian values about the poor, dividing them up into the undeserving and deserving. Make no mistake about it, the current debate is a concerted effort to shunt single mothers from one group into the other. Though the majority are divorced or widowed (so have tried and failed for whatever reason to attain the ideal of the nuclear family), the caricature of the lazy breeder who allows herself to be impregnated in order to jump the housing queue is the one routinely resurrected.

It's their own fault, is the message. Can you imagine a similar attack on pensioners as parasites who, selfishly, expect the state to provide pensions because they don't have private ones? Yet how much does the Government really want single mothers to be independent when it will not provide childcare or tax relief to make work worth their while?

Meanwhile, the invisible fathers of all these children remain out of sight and out of mind. Though there is a growing consensus that men should be financially responsible for their children, no one

37

knows how to make them responsible emotionally. Instead, generations of men are considered, often by the women with whom they have children, to be redundant: they cannot or will not provide cash, cannot or will not provide any sort of care. They are infantilized to such a point that they feel little sense of responsibility. No amount of Tory rhetoric will turn them into suitable husband material. While everyone talks vaguely about the need to support family life, what we actually need is to extend the definition of family life itself so that so many of us do not feel members of families that have in some way failed.

Nor is it any use to see only single-parent families as having problems; the family *per se* is shifting. It is undeniable that feminism has played a part in this, by heightening women's expectations. More and more women now initiate divorces because they are simply not prepared to carry on. Fifty years ago, for instance, would Princess Di have gone ahead and separated from Charles, or would she just have laid back and thought of England? And would such self-sacrifice have made her morally superior? Are we to condemn as perverse a desire for an intimate and equal relationship with a man?

The question remains: why is public debate so keen to stigmatize single mothers while turning a blind eye to or washing its hands of the men involved? Could this be because the kind of irresponsible behaviour we are talking about here cannot just be confined to a bunch of jobless teenagers, but is only one end of the continuum of acceptable masculine behaviour? It is not only unemployed men from inner-city dumps who feel it is perfectly OK to procreate and move on. All kinds of men think children basically belong to women, that their part in the process ends as soon as they put their trousers back on.

Tracking absent fathers and getting them to contribute financially is probably the limit of what we can expect the state to do. We are all keen that it should not interfere in our private lives but if we are to have a public debate about all of this, then the cultural as well as political aspects have to be addressed. However much all the male pundits involved might want to tell us what the real issues are, please let's stop pretending that we can even have a debate if no one is going to ask the most obvious and fundamental question: how do you get men to change?

OUT OF ACTION

Popular culture depends for its livelihood on magical incarnations of sex and violence. The public wants them, and the public gets them. Art favours relationships and death, which we kid ourselves are more morally uplifting. But it is those who show a special aptitude for entertaining us with sex or with violence that we truly reward. For it is they who speak the universal language of drives and of instincts, and it is they who are lifted into the pantheon. They are the ones that we make into icons.

Take a look at Arnold Schwarzenegger – the man whose most famous line is 'Fuck you, arsehole', whose major talent is for playing a cyborg, whose film *The Running Man* contained 146 atrocities an hour – now to be seen toning down his movie violence, re-inventing himself for the nineties as a caring, sharing kind of guy.

Arnie danced with Madonna at Cannes once and everyone said how small he looked compared with her. Sex and violence dancing together, so much in common. Both Arnie and Madonna have made careers out of personal discipline and public excess. They fastidiously re-created themselves, pumped iron and pumped egos until the surface became the reality. They got what they always wanted. They thrilled us in the eighties: she played femininity as a charade; he always managed some kind of distance from his macho image. They reminded us continually that everything was a game, that ambition was more important than talent, that the desire to be rich and famous was the most fabulous desire of all. They were postmodernism on legs. Forget the theory, feel the irony. Just float, face down, in the endless sea of signifiers. You can do it. Just stop taking everything so seriously. Whaddya mean, you think Schwarzenegger's not a good role model? Get a grip, it's only the movies.

But that was then. This is now. And something has shifted. The excesses of the last decade now feel ever so slightly embarrassing. Maybe they were too much of a good thing, or maybe they were just too much. Anyway, worries about the violent imagery produced by Hollywood have finally been taken seriously. Although whipped up by the *Sunday Times* serialization of Michael Medved's inaccurate and patronizing book on the subject, the moral panic about screen violence is not, as some critics complain, a self-regarding media affair. Talk to anyone who actually works with kids and they will express a concern about what they see as the effects of the bombardment of violent imagery that today's youngsters are subject to.

Yet, what is really at the heart of all this is an almost atavistic fear of the screen itself. We are not just frightened by movies or by television programmes but also by computer games. All images that come from screens are now somehow suspect. We have reached a stage, the argument always goes, where we can no longer tell the difference between what happens on one side of the screen and what happens on the other. Kids playing Sonic; US generals playing even more expensive video games, and in press conferences describing dead civilians as 'collateral' – well, it's all the same, isn't it? Arnie making a wisecrack just before he power-drills someone to death; security cameras eerily and anonymously recording the abduction of a two-year-old in a shopping centre . . . But even in an image-saturated culture, which of us does not know which is the more chilling vision? No special effect in the world can scare us more than the cold reproduction of reality. And we shouldn't forget that.

However, even Hollywood moguls, with one eye on the growing distaste for gore and another on the huge grosses for family films like *Home Alone* – in its way an extremely violent film – are now talking about 'responsibility'. It's a nicer word than censorship certainly. But how, if you made a billion dollars in the eighties from playing killing machines, do you adapt to this new-found sense of responsibility? How do you stop yourself from turning into yester-day's hero?

It's hard to know what is real about the world's best-loved Austrian (Mozart comes second) any more. Arnold Schwarzenegger has almost no private identity, he is proud of his depthlessness, self-analysis is anathema to him. Publicity is all. So what will this man, whose true self is entirely dependent on his celebrity status, do about the latest round of publicity that has come his way, the pub-licity for his new film, of which he is executive producer, *Last Action Hero*?

Directed by John McTiernan who made *Die Hard* and *The Hunt For Red October*, it has already been declared a massive flop in the States. Pitted against Spielberg's monster *Jurassic Park*, *Last Action Hero* has definitely lost out. Maybe it's because, like Madonna, Arnie has simply been too successful for too long. Backlash is inevitable. McTiernan puts the spate of terrible reviews that have greeted the film in the US down to this: 'It's called the OMF theory. It's not enough for some people to succeed. Others Must Fail.'

Failure is too strong a word. After all, whatever happens Arnie still gets $10 million plus a percentage of the merchandising on *Last Action Hero*. But maybe we *have* had enough of Arnie. There is something so unremittingly smug about the film that one can see why, as one American critic said, 'It also feels like a farewell of sorts to Arnold. Or at least to the action hero Arnold.' It has variously been described as 'a joyless, soulless machine of a movie' and as making Madonna's *Truth Or Dare* look like an exercise in humility.

In the past, Schwarzenegger has defended the violence he por-trays. 'I don't think violence does damage. I myself have seen an endless amount of violent movies – the John Wayne movies, the Clint Eastwood movies, and it had no effect on me. As a matter of fact the effect it had on me was that it released a kind of desire for violence and I could let it go through fantasy by seeing it on screen.'

Now, though, Arnold Schwarzenegger wants it both ways and in

Last Action Hero is clearly attempting to distance himself from his violent image. It is difficult not to think that by insisting that the Arnie dolls merchandised with this film shouldn't have guns, Schwarzenegger is doing too little too late. For the new film ingeniously weaves the moral panic about screen violence into its plot. This could be interesting if the movie was brave enough to tell us anything about the relationship between the two things. Instead it opts for trying to parody what is often beyond parody. How do you satirize movie violence, while still dishing it up?

Last Action Hero's basic set-up is a sort of '*Cinema Paradiso* from Hell'. We start off with action hero Jack Slater (Schwarzenegger) striding into view. Slater can dodge bullets, take on an army of thugs single-handed. He is tough. He is the quintessential Schwarzenegger hero. He is also a fiction within a fiction, as we realize when the camera pulls back to twelve-year-old Danny, alone in a cinema, watching a Jack Slater movie.

Reality for Danny is not that great. His Dad is dead, leaving his Mom working all hours to support them both. They are poor and they live in a violent neighbourhood. Action films are Danny's escape. He daydreams about them all the time. In one ludicrous, hilarious, sequence, Schwarzenegger turns up as Hamlet in the Olivier film that is being shown in Danny's literature class. Arnie as the prince turns the plot around; Elsinore becomes just another backdrop to ultra-violence, blown up by a hero who doesn't have a procrastination problem. Then, by the entirely contrived device of being given 'Houdini's magic ticket' by the cinema's projectionist, Danny is actually able to get inside Jack Slater's latest movie. Here again, as in Woody Allen's *The Purple Rose Of Cairo*, is the idea of the screen as semi-permeable membrane, a surface which can be passed through.

Once inside the movie, Danny finds himself in an altogether more glamorous world than the one he is used to. The Los Angeles Police Department, the streets, the video store, all are peopled with women who look like models or actresses. 'That's because it's a movie,' Danny tells Slater. 'No, that's because this is California,' says Schwarzenegger. Danny, you see, is out to prove to Slater that they are both in a film. But Slater doesn't realize that he is a fictional character. He thinks the endless round of baddies, violence and winning through, is real life. He doesn't know he's really Arnold Schwarzenegger, actor and superstar.

This play on reality allows all sorts of in-jokes. Like in the video shop, where Danny takes Slater/Arnie to show him some of his other films and thus prove he's an actor. At first when he asks where the Schwarzenegger movies are, the assistant tells him that 'foreign movies are over there'. When Danny does find the action movies, we all see the famous cardboard cut-out advertising *The Terminator* standing there large as life in the store. But the camera pans up to reveal the face of Sylvester Stallone on Arnie's body. 'I love that guy. He's my hero,' says Slater/Arnie.

These jokes all pivot on the differences between real life and movie life, with Danny constantly in a position to advise Slater because he has watched enough movies to know the formula. At one point he holds up a handwritten note to Slater, asking him to read it. 'If you're not in a movie, read this word,' challenges Danny. Slater doesn't say the word aloud, proving Danny's point. 'See, you can't possibly say that word because this movie is PG 13.' Slick huh?

Eventually, in his pursuit of villains, Slater/Arnie also visits the other side of the screen. Reality is deeply disturbing to him: 'How would you feel if someone made you up?' Danny reassures him that he will survive this latest adventure: 'You can't die until the grosses go down.' On the other side of the screen Slater also meets the real Schwarzenegger, who is attending the première of the latest Jack Slater movie, and as usual is naffly plugging his restaurant with his wife Maria Shriver by his side. 'Don't do that, it's so-o-o embarrassing,' the real-life Shriver tells her real-life husband.

Confused? That's the whole point. The movie is so top-heavy with self-referentiality and parody it topples right over. There are constant visual references to all of Arnie's other films, continual pokes at the formulaic appeal of action movies, with real-life movie stars like Sharon Stone and Jean-Claude Van Damme making an appearance. There is even an animated cat from *Roger Rabbit* on the loose. At the centre of the film there is only the hollow laughter of Arnie playing with his sense of self yet again.

But this time it doesn't work. On one level, the film demands of its audience an almost Spielbergian sense of innocence and wonder. We are asked to believe in the magic ticket that enables all this through-screen traffic. On another level, we are supposed to be knowing and cynical enough about the tricks of cinema to laugh at the jokes. And because they are so knowing we cannot possibly care about any of the characters.

Though Arnie has repeatedly said that he is only giving the public what it wants, here he appears to be despising them for wanting it. Unlike *The Player*, which stripped Hollywood naked and asked it to laugh at itself, *Last Action Hero* does the same thing, only to laugh at its audience – a cynical and complacent move. Self-consciousness and parody can be great fun – look at *Wayne's World* – but here the parody is exclusive rather than inclusive of its audience. This is why it is all so heartless.

The irony is that the movie contains all the themes that have made Arnie's film career so fascinating. It's about the gulf between reality and fantasy, about control and authenticity, about identity itself. But for once Arnie has been defeated by his real limitations. When the fictional Schwarzenegger comes face to face with the real one, frankly, my dear, none of us could give a damn. Jack Slater realizes he is fictional. The tragedy is that the real Arnie never has.

But at least the real Arnold Schwarzenegger has proved himself to be good at adapting. Take his life story. Take your pick, because there are at least two versions. There is Arnie's version and the unauthorized biography. In the first, he grew up near Craz in Austria, started body-building at sixteen and transformed himself from a wimp to the youngest-ever Mr Universe in 1967. As a ten-year-old he already exhibited extraordinary business sense, carting ice-cream to the other side of the local lake to sell it. This enterprising spirit has not left him and indeed blossomed when he came to what he calls 'the promised land' – America. There he found 'no limit to one's vision', moving from body-building to real estate to movies. His trick, he says, is to 'stay hungry'. Arnie's story is one of cultural assimilation *par excellence*. He epitomizes the American Dream at a time when it is falling apart. He is still reticent about his political ambition for, unlike that other right-wing actor of questionable ability, he will never be president as he wasn't born in the USA. None the less there is talk of Conan the Republican becoming Conan the Senator.

Wendy Leigh, his unofficial biographer, tells a different tale. He grew up, she says, in East Germany, the son of a Nazi. She claims to have obtained Gustav Schwarzenegger's Nazi party membership number from the Berlin Document Centre Archives. His father was a disciplinarian who made young Arnold's life a misery. Arnold started taking steroids at the age of thirteen to build himself up. (Schwarzenegger has admitted to taking steroids but says that it wasn't for long.) Leigh documents the ''roid rages' of a man who, she says, is basically a bully. Leigh claims that he favours cruel practical jokes and, she alleges, organized a vendetta against her when he got wind of her book. Though Arnie cannot be held responsible for the politics of his father, what he describes as 'these Nazi smears' were not put to rest when he invited Kurt Waldheim to his wedding. He also invited the Pope. He didn't show up either.

Whether you believe any of Leigh's sensational, suggestive version of the Schwarzenegger story or not, it is undeniable that in re-creating his identity as carefully as he has built up his body, Arnie has managed to marginalize his past until all that really exists is his future. And the land of his future is always America. It is in this respect that Arnie is still the perfect role model. Change everything you can. What you can't change, turn into a registered trademark. His accent, still improbable after twenty years of elocution lessons, makes him sound like he just got off the boat – the sub-*'Allo 'Allo* German, the strange ungrammatical sentences he uses to make himself fresh and foreign.

Schwarzenegger's greatest strength has always been his ability to make the most of his limitations, to turn his defects into assets. People said he couldn't act, so he hasn't even tried to. He knows he's not Robert de Niro but he also knows that by playing himself every single time, he has built up a loyalty to the Arnie persona. What you get in a Schwarzenegger film is unadulterated Arnie.

But the cleverest move he ever made was to take the criticism that he acted like a machine on board. If he acted like a machine, he would act a machine. And that was what he did so well in *The Terminator*. This is the nearest Arnie has ever got to method-acting. 'You have to get into the character,' he said. 'If you have a walk like a terminator then you see yourself as being a machine. And machines walk different.' As Arnie instinctively knows, machines do indeed 'walk different'.

And it is this ability to be so utterly non-human that has lifted him above his rivals. While Stallone is all underdog sincerity, Arnie is *ubermensh* superiority. While Stallone is desperate to be an intellectual, intellectuals are desperate to be like Arnie. College lecturers are not interested in wordy wimps like Woody Allen, but they just adore this monosyllabic Germanic slab. Arnie provides instant access into the world of pop culture. At a time when the word 'unreal' is a compliment Arnie has unwittingly provided a hook on which to hang all sorts of ideas about simulation, authenticity, and the glorious parody of masculinity that can be found in his movies.

I first encountered this nearly ten years ago, when a sensitive kind of boy, a Godard fan no less, told me he was going home to watch *Commando* on video. 'But that's like *Rambo* or something, isn't it?' I asked. 'No, you don't understand. It's got this wonderful sub-text. It's all about masculinity, and the way his body is filmed. Completely fetishized.' From then on it was obvious that Schwarzenegger was going to get even bigger, though for a while he remained a culty kind of secret. We who were in the know could watch all this death and destruction because we knew there was a sub-text. What did this subversive little sub-text whisper to us? It said 'Don't worry, lads. [It always addressed us as lads because sub-texts understand that in the dark of the cinema we are all promiscuous in our gender identifications.] It's not because it is full of macho violence that you like this movie. You are better than that. You like it not because it *is* those things but because it is *about* those things.'

And with a nod and a wink Arnie could remain miraculously

detached from that which he represented. Poor old Sly Stallone, poor old Chuck Norris – sad irony-free zones, they were far too real for us. With Arnie it was different. We could have our violence, our car chases, our out-and-out sadism, and a laugh too. All the power, none of the responsibility. How cool could it get? Arnie always had the edge, verging on camp sometimes. And from the risible depths of *Commando* and *The Jayne Mansfield Story*, Arnie would skilfully pick scripts which reflected the concerns that made him the perfect postmodern hero: *The Terminator*, *The Running Man*, *Total Recall*. From now everything was on fast-forward. It was all one big video game, full of zapping from one parallel universe to the next.

From Arnold the goof-ball hunk with that crazed smile and oh-so-perfect gap between his front teeth, we began talking megabucks and Nietzsche in the same breath. Yet while in real life (remember that?) Arnie was cementing his identity effortlessly, marrying into the Kennedy clan, making speeches for George Bush, begetting cute little baby girls, opening restaurants, his movie personae were growing ever more confused. In *Total Recall* he finds his whole life has been a sham, a memory implanted into his mind. At one point he asks: 'If I'm not me, then who am I?' 'You're not you, you're me,' comes the reply.

Total Recall director, Paul Verhoeven, liked to talk about conspiracy theories and psychosis and defended this splatter-fest of a film with the excuse that he was in Holland during the German occupation. Arnie carried on raking it in, even branching out into comedy with Danny de Vito in *Twins*. Good old Nietzsche had now been taken on as a script consultant, his presence felt even in this light comedy – the scientist who has genetically engineered him tells Arnie that while he contained all that was 'purity and strength' his twin brother Danny de Vito was made up of all the crap. *Twins* made over $100 million.

So Arnie can do funny. But can he do sexy? *Last Action Hero* suggests that he can. When Slater gets into the real world, Danny's Mom falls for him: 'You're much more intelligent than you appear on screen, Arnold,' she simpers. When other stars at the Slater première are being interviewed about the real Arnie, one guy says, 'I don't like him, but my girlfriend really gets off on him. And I like to be around when that happens.' But whatever new personae *Last Action Hero* attempts to open up for Schwarzenegger, he's still not sexy. It is not a question of whether women find him attractive or not, or even whether size matters, because Arnie has a basic deficiency which no amount of direction can change: Arnie can't do sex because he can't do human being and so he certainly cannot do relationships and all that yukky stuff. Not in the movies anyway.

What we like best about Arnie has nothing to do with sex and everything to do with power. This raw power, unfettered by any memory of the past, is about purity of will. He is indestructible, invulnerable, impenetrable, all the things we know we are not. At first we read this from his body. This massive body that wears its muscles like a coat of armour. Like all the best starlets, as Schwarzenegger has made it up the ladder he reveals less and less of that body. Gone are the days of loin-cloths and weapons strapped on to naked flesh. Now we have to read everything from that impassive face. But we don't ever expect to read too much, for the former Mr Universe's world is still overwhelmingly physical, not mental.

His muscleman's body is a fantasy of the body as impossibly hard and self-contained, the shield of musculature hiding the messiness of the soft machine inside it. Such bodies reveal no weakness, no signs of age, no acceptance of the inevitability of time passing. If Arnie's body breaks down, as in *The Terminator*, it can be rewired, it is miraculously self-repairing. This futuristic vision of technology melded into flesh, the electro-cyberpunk riff sits uneasily with a reality where bodies naturally decay, where immune systems falter and there is not a damn thing we can do about it. Yet if Arnie's body can feel no pain it can certainly inflict it. Arnie is often pitted against scores of villains all of whom can be shown no mercy. The motives behind this are often not that clear, beyond those of winding Arnie up and then letting Arnie go. For in Arnie's world death is funny, an excuse for a one-liner.

This is why people say it's only cartoon violence. But though many of his films share a cartoon-like wish to destroy all in their path, cartoons have a different function. In *Tom and Jerry*, Tom, the powerful character, is routinely flattened but always reconstitutes himself. Both characters get to have their cake and eat it. In Arnie's films he is the only one that gets the cake – his victims are too dead to eat anything. But the comparison with cartoons is valid in the sense that there is something overwhelmingly infantile about Arnie's appeal. Many journalists have reported that when they meet him he is like 'a big baby'. Certainly his screen persona is one of pure id, he is without guile, simply a physical presence.

It is this combination of immense power and retarded emotional development that threatens his role-model status. For the cultural embodiment of the kind of masculinity that he represents has disastrous consequences for all of us. What if people don't get the subtext? In other words, what happens if we take him for real? Well, if we take him for real, he's the last action hero.

Last Action Hero is Schwarzenegger's attempt at having it both ways, just like he does in the movies – his attempt to be a Terminator and a moral guardian at the same time. But in real life it's impossible. Doesn't he remember that line in *Twins* when he says 'I hate violence' and Danny de Vito just looks up at him and replies, 'Yes, but you're so good at it'?

KISS AND DON'T TELL

Some of Bill Clinton's best friends are. Gay, that is, though I'm not sure you'd know it from the 'honourable compromise' he has offered homosexuals. The issue of gays in the military has been bugging Clinton for some time; it has become a test of how much he is prepared to keep his election promises and how far his liberalism goes. He has to be seen to be doing something, so what he has come up with is a set of guidelines that allows gays into the military but does not allow them to exhibit any overt homosexual behaviour, on or off duty. This is the so-called 'don't ask, don't tell' formula and it is more than a compromise, it is plain daft.

It is not a case of allowing gays into the military; they are already there. Rather it is a case of the extent to which they are supposed to hide their sexuality while in service. Now, being gay will no longer be a bar to military service, as long as you don't do anything about it while you are there or, in the Pentagon's jargon: 'The military will discharge members who engage in homosexual conduct, which is defined as a homosexual act.' What sort of double-think is this?

Well, it's the sort of double-think that's prevalent here too. We are tolerant of homosexuals as long as they don't 'flaunt it' or demand 'special treatment'. By flaunting it, we often mean nothing more than behaving in the way heterosexuals take for granted, such as holding hands in the street. By special treatment, we mean the same rights as everyone else.

Clearly, we are still very confused about what homosexuality actually means, as the debate over the 'gay gene' has shown. While Clinton's muddled guidelines accept the existence of a homosexual identity, it is somehow seen as possible to separate this out from homosexual acts or behaviour. In many of the articles that appeared around the gay gene issue, homosexuality was referred to some-times as an identity with its own corresponding lifestyle; at other times as a behaviour pattern. Yet all this scrap of genetic 'evidence' pointed to was a predisposition towards same-sex attraction. A pen-chant for Judy Garland is not, I'm afraid, encoded on one's DNA.

Gay activists also often embrace this notion of a fixed gay identity which is totally separate from a heterosexual one. The notion of outing depends entirely on revealing an essential truth about some-one. Peter Tatchell, writing in this paper, tells us that gay men are more sensitive, caring, creative, while lesbians are more independent and assertive than straight women. Is this wishful thinking or simply another kind of stereotype, albeit a more positive one than the idea of the homosexual as a dirty pervert bringing about the end of civilization as we know it?

The difficulty here is that the establishing of a gay identity was a strategy necessary for demanding civil rights. Historically, it's a rel-atively recent phenomenon but what it tends to do is to categorize us all rather too neatly as gay or straight, with a few waverers in the middle, whereas we know from other cultures and other historical periods that it is perfectly possible to engage in what we now define as homosexual acts without in any way defining oneself as homo-sexual.

Clinton wants the opposite of this: you get to define yourself as homosexual, you just mustn't do any of the business, or rather must not do it publicly. The only person made happy by such an ar-rangement would be Brett Anderson of Suede, who defines himself as bisexual, though says he has never slept with a man – and he hardly strikes me as someone desperate to be admitted into the armed forces. So, while the US military will now officially tolerate homosexuality on the condition that it remains a private activity, it fears its public face. Homosexuality as contagion is the model here, though the anxiety it causes the toughest of marines makes you realize just how fragile the institution of heterosexuality must be.

Indeed, in a brilliant article in the American magazine *Details*,

John Weir goes to Camp Lejeune, a military base near Jacksonville to discuss this issue. He writes: 'This is how to end up going home with a straight marine: stand in a gay bar near a military base and wait. For it is as easy to have sex with a marine as it is to get bashed by one for being a fag.'

Weir does go home with a marine, fantasizing that he's Whitney and the other guy is Kevin Costner. They have sex. For the straight marine it's an act; for Weir, a New York homosexual, it is part of an essential identity. Split the difference if you like but no amount of genetic research will explain exactly what has happened. Clinton might stop worrying about the cohesion of the military – bombing Iraqi civilians looks pretty cohesive to me – and start worrying about the cohesion of a society that inevitably is made up of people of varying sexual persuasions. Instead of fearing the moral backlash from the right-wing bible-bashers, he should realize that this is an issue on which he has to lead from the front. He relied on gay support during the election, but instead of returning this support, he has asked gay sexuality to remain in the closet, discreetly out of sight of those it might offend. Congress, he explained, would over-turn any unconditional ending of the ban, therefore he has had to step down. The question, he now informs us, is not one of 'group rights but individual rights'. No amount of semantic posturing, however, will convince me that there is much that is honourable or even workable about this ludicrous compromise.

ABORTION: I HAVE . . . HAVE YOU?

A third of British women will have one in their lifetime. Actresses Liza Goddard and Janet Suzman have had them. I've had one. Most women I know have. Most men I know have had girlfriends who have. I'm talking about abortion. As offensive as this subject may be to some people, it seems to me a fact of life rather than a dirty secret. Yet when the National Abortion Campaign wrote to hundreds of well-known women asking them to declare publicly that they have had abortions, in support of tomorrow's public meeting, 'Speaking Out For Choice', many refused. Though they supported the campaign in private, it was perceived as too potentially damaging to their careers to go public. Others said yes, then pulled out at the last minute on the grounds that there were still key family members who had never been told.

Such reasons are, of course, perfectly valid. There is no point in 'coming out' about something so personal if you still feel guilty and ashamed about it or so compromised that it jeopardizes the rest of your life. This is precisely why the strategy of 'outing', practised by certain gay activists, ultimately fails. Instead of the closet doors being joyously kicked down, there is only the pathetic spectacle of certain individuals clinging to the wreckage as they are dragged, kicking and screaming, out of it. Likewise, on this issue, one feels that being pro-choice must inevitably mean being pro-privacy.

There are times, however, when the retreat into privacy not only hides the widespread nature of the experience of abortion itself but also plays into the hands of the anti-abortionists who regularly claim that women are ashamed to admit that they have

54

had abortions. While the National Abortion Campaign emphasizes that abortion may often be a difficult choice, they say: 'It need not be a cause of shame.'

This need to speak out has also been precipitated by the announcement by the extremist US anti-abortion group Operation Rescue that it will be back in Britain this month. Its tactics include intimidation and assault of clients and staff in abortion clinics. So high do feelings run in the US, that last spring a doctor in Florida was killed; more recently, another was shot and wounded in Kansas.

Yet, if women are ashamed, what exactly are they ashamed of? What does having an abortion say about you? That you have had sex and are therefore a loose woman, an amoral being, a failure at all the wonderful methods of contraception we have available to us? That you are an unnatural woman, a child-hater? Does choosing not to become a mother when you are single, broke, miserable, already have enough children, or are just absolutely unprepared for it, make you a bad person?

If this is the case, then an awful lot of us are bad. Some of the men who played a small part in the conception of these unwanted babies may be worse, but abortion remains resolutely a women's issue. A thing that women have to hide away, like menstruation, menopause and all that other yukky stuff that women's bodies are wont to do.

Those who oppose abortion, often for religious and moral reasons, would rather talk about the theoretical sanctity of life than the lives of ordinary women. Yet we live in a world in which real-life babies are bought from impoverished South Americans and sold to doctors in the West who remove their internal organs for transplant and let them die. While sanctity of life for them looks like a sick joke, the 'rights' of the unborn cannot take priority over the rights of adult women.

If we are going to talk morality, then – to some of us – valuing a female life as less than an eight-week embryo is in itself immoral. Yet the battle between the pro-choice lobby and anti-abortionists is a thoroughly modern one between moral relativism and moral absolutism. While I do not wish to impose my beliefs on others – I would want no woman to have an abortion if she didn't want one – the anti-abortionists are perfectly willing to impose their beliefs on me. As their campaigns go far beyond the issue of abortion, also opposing contraceptive services and sex education for the young, so too has the pro-choice lobby had to take on the increasingly complex debates about reproductive rights.

The battles of the present, never mind the future, go far beyond the sloganeering of a woman's right to choose. To choose what? A baby guaranteed free of genetic predispositions to all sorts of hereditary disease? To choose to abort anything other than a perfect human being of the right sex? Or, more basically, how can we talk about choice when so many of the world's women live in economic slavery?

At the same time, however, it is important to remind ourselves of what has been achieved. Despite numerous attempts to overturn it, we have had twenty-five years of legal abortion in this country. In opinion polls, this is supported by both sexes. Though the situation is far from perfect, with only about half of the women seeking abortions on the National Health Service able to obtain them, it is far removed from the days of injecting soap solution into the womb or simply clipping the cervix so that women would later deliver stillborn foetuses in public toilets.

So things have improved: no one is gaily flushing foetuses away with merry abandon. Abortion remains, however, even for those of us who are prepared to go public, an individual experience. Some women need to grieve afterwards, others to get wildly drunk. Some feel incredibly relieved, others not much at all. Some may feel bloody awful, some are back at work the same day. Some benefit from counselling, others are simply irritated by it. None of us, however, needs to feel this burden of shame attached to always having to pretend that it hasn't happened to you.

Personally, I have an inbuilt aversion to the confessional mode that sometimes dominates feminist gatherings: you tell me yours and I'll tell you mine. I am about as interested in the details of other women's abortions as I am in their mortgages. What I am interested in, though, is the implicit McCarthyism that is in operation, so that when many women are asked in public: 'Have you or has anyone you know ever had an abortion?' they still have to lie through their teeth and say no.

A SLIVER OFF THE OLD BLOCK

What a responsibility it must be to be a modern sex symbol, like Sharon Stone. One minute you're just another Californian girl with a bad hairdo, playing disposable blondes in disposable movies. The next you are the new bad babe on the block, threatening to depose even the material girl herself.

Sharon Stone has been on every magazine cover in the past couple of months; the British press, meanwhile, has greeted Madonna's forthcoming tour with yet more tales of how she is finished. This latest backlash is founded on the notion that Madonna has done too much, we have seen too much, and we are all strangely unintrigued by the prospect of yet more Sex.

While it may be the case that Madonna Inc. has reached media saturation point, the idea that we can ever have too much sex from our sex symbols seems paradoxical. After all, what are these icons of sex for if not to reinvent the clichés, to give us new variations on the same old theme? We have certainly seen a lot of Sharon Stone: 'All the way to Nebraska' as she said of the infamous scene in *Basic Instinct*. The point is that we still want more.

In retrospect, however, whether we want more of Sharon Stone herself, or of her character in *Basic Instinct*, is the key question.

No one will claim *Basic Instinct* is a good movie, whether read as a tale of homophobia, male anxiety or a paean to the hopelessness of Michael Douglas's dress sense. But what caught the public imagination – and particularly the female imagination – was the Katherine Tramell character, a beautiful, sexy, clever woman who does what the hell she likes and gets away with it.

Stone was established, like Madonna, as a sex symbol for women as well as for men. And she has been trading on this particular sexual persona ever since. In interviews, she is sharp, sassy, full of bold one-liners such as: 'Since becoming famous, I get to torture a better class of man.' Meanwhile the tabloids have rushed to print stories about how hard and heartless she really is: she once hit a man at a party; her producer boyfriend left his wife, who not only miscarried but went public about the whole affair.

Stone was by now where we wanted her to be: firmly in control. When asked what she thought about Madonna, she replied: 'I try not to.'

Madonna, however, does seem to have thought about her, attempting to do a 'Sharon Stone' in the dismal *Body Of Evidence*. Stone, meanwhile, was busy revamping the predatory Katherine Tramell character for a Pirelli ad and choosing her next film role with care.

That is why *Sliver* is such a disappointment. Not only does it remind us that the roles for sharp, sexy, sassy women just aren't there, if this is the best offer Stone has been made, but its dot-to-dot 'erotica' just doesn't hit the mark. The scene in which Stone masturbates in the bath is remarkable simply for the fact that it has been cut in such a way that she appears not to be using her hands at all. I don't hold this against Stone; the ability to orgasm without manual stimulation is, as we know, an absolute prerequisite of all women in Hollywood movies.

Sliver, scripted by Joe Eszterhas (*Basic Instinct, Jagged Edge*), hinges on the plot device he has already milked to death, i.e. that you have the best sex with a psycho killer. Stone plays an upmarket book editor with all the accoutrements of cinema's version of the modern career woman: beige cashmere, loads of Evian and absolutely no friends to speak of. This is a movie in which a first date is a work-out, for God's sake. She is fragile and insecure, which in Hollywood terms means she is about to be 'sexually awakened'. This is the cinematic euphemism for the more familiar phrase 'All she needs is a good . . .'

Stone was drawn to the part, she says, because of its vulnerability.

Sure, it must be hard work being a full-time bitch-goddess. No wonder, then, having played a sexually *desiring* woman in *Basic Instinct,* she has made the basic mistake of retreating into the much more familiar role of object of others' desire. All Stone has to do is look good, which she does beautifully. She gets her knickers off in public again but only because she is told to by her boyfriend. This ain't what I call transgression but regression.

Whether all this is 'erotic' is a matter of taste. Although, if you are sitting there thinking, 'I wonder if this is erotic?' during the course of the movies, then it probably isn't. The way Grace Kelly kisses James Stewart in *Rear Window,* the way the male prisoners blow smoke to each other in Genet's *Un Chant d'Amour,* the way Kelly McGillis returns Harrison Ford's gaze when he watches her washing in *Witness* – these moments are all far sexier than the choreographed bonking that now passes for eroticism.

But then, what is a symbol of sex meant to be doing in the nineties, I wonder? Selling herself to Robert Redford for a million dollars? (As Jo Brand so aptly remarked: 'That's ludicrous – I'd shag him for a tenner.') Crawling around in head-to-toe rubber *à la* Pfeiffer or flogging herself to her richest client like Julia Roberts in *Pretty Woman*? In this context, it's no wonder Stone made it on the basis of just one movie. What she sold us was far sexier than mere sex. It was the ultimate aphrodisiac – a fantasy of power. If audiences understood this, how come Hollywood still can't?

LOOKING FOR THE REEL THING

Unrequited love may be the safest form of sex but traditional ideas of romance come a close second. In the magical world of candlelit dinners and sparkly rings proffered with the purest of intention, the red roses smooth over the nasty cracks on the path to true love. Such as sex. For genitals, the exchange of bodily fluids, even boredom do not feature in the romantic vocabulary which talks instead of those special moments, of just knowing when something feels right.

Sometimes, though, things don't feel right. There is such a thing as trying too hard. The film *Sleepless In Seattle*, which has already been elevated from the ranks of mere movies to the status of a 'phenomenon', tries very hard indeed to be a sloppy, weepy, cute, romantic movie for the nineties. It has been a huge hit in the States. It's about feelings, destiny, about following your heart instead of your head. It's escapist nonsense, just like movies ought to be, so how come I wasn't carried away? Is it because I am a cynical old witch?

No. Actually it's because *Sleepless In Seattle* is a cynical movie. It's a wised-up new film pretending to be an innocent oldie. This isn't a romantic film. It's a film about romance which isn't the same thing at all. But perhaps we can't tell the difference any more because, like everything else, you can buy your romance ready-made. Hey, these days we can say it with flowers, say it with balloons, we can flash it up in neon, we can send each other those awful gooey cards saying, 'I don't know how to say this but . . .' We may not know how to put our feelings into words but someone will, which is why newsagents are stocked full of rhyming declarations of love, lust and loneliness.

If you're not sure what love is, you can find out from the side of a mug. If you want people to know how you feel about each other, then propose on primetime, get married on *The Big Breakfast*, tattoo her name across your heart. It can always be cosmetically altered at a later date.

I guess Annie and Sam, the couple in *Sleepless In Seattle* – who don't even meet until the end of the movie – don't need these props. They are just meant to be together. She is a dizzy kind of chick, though naturally enough a career woman, a journalist, no less. He is a widower (clearly Hollywood is peopled with eligible widowers) with an adorable son, convinced he will never love again. She hears his voice on a radio phone-in, is in floods of tears and soon enough is on the plane to Seattle because, as the press pack helpfully reminds us, 'What if someone you never met, someone you never saw, someone you never knew, was the only someone for you?'

Annie has got a stable though allergy-prone boyfriend back home, but she gets on that plane anyway because she has wept over enough old Cary Grant movies to know that if two people are made for each other, they have to find each other.

Now, I can take the idea of falling in love on a phone-in. In fact, my friend's mother has a relationship with a guy she met in this way. What is more difficult to swallow is this business of destiny, this self-conscious idealization of movie-style love. It's probably true that we all have a special person on the other side of the world whom we will never meet, but the dull fact is that most people meet their partners at work or in the pub, not a million miles from where they already are.

Trying to superimpose such overblown notions of destiny on to the average relationship is pretty hard work. Which is where romance comes in.

Who actually does this work, though? Well, just like in this movie, it's usually the woman. All Sam has to do is sit there. Like much female labour, however, the work of romance remains invisible, involving, as it does, a kind of active passivity. One must simply wait to be wined and dined, sent flowers, swept off one's feet, though actually most women are continually prodding and poking at men to fulfil these statutory obligations.

In between these magic moments – from the first kiss to the white dress – that are freeze-framed in the female imagination, is something else altogether: it is the long-drawn-out waiting, the mundaneness of everyday life, the unfulfilled longing that wants it to be like it is in the movies. This has an infantilizing effect. It certainly does on Meg Ryan in *Sleepless In Seattle*, in which her kooky *When Harry Met Sally* persona becomes just irritatingly little girly.

Fans of *Sleepless* will no doubt claim it is a harmless fantasy, yet surely the reason for its massive success is that the fantasy it offers is even more out of reach than ever.

On the same day that I saw this film, I came home to watch a report on single mothers on *Panorama*. Here were girls who, at fifteen, had given up on the idea of 'proper' relationships with men. They had instead settled for their babies, their flats and in some way each other. Boyfriends were around but not in any central role, rather as something of a nuisance. Where was the romance in these girls' lives, I wondered? Did they really need another instruction, albeit fictional, to trust their hearts and not their brains? Should their quest be eternally to find 'the fireworks' in a relationship or to find a way of earning a living?

Of course, the idea of romance is one of the reasons that girls ever put up with boys in the first place. The skilled operator learns at an early age to translate the crude reality that what boys actually want is sex into some sort of hazy mysticism in order to find them acceptable at all.

It's still hard for young girls to say that they might want sex too. Indeed, it is clear in the movie that what Annie wants is not sex but, you know . . . magic. It is the very vagueness of the language of romance that creates so many misunderstandings. In the name of 'magic', women tolerate misery. They shut up about what they want and simply wait to be given it. They are often disappointed, except of course in the movies, which is why, though romance may appear to make sex seem safe and soft, it is a dangerous thing. It will truly break your heart.

HAVE HANDBAG, WILL HIT BACK

So she is back. Like Freddy Kreuger, like Banquo's ghost, like a mongoose hypnotizing a snake, the not-so-repressed Lady Thatcher returns. And the political commentators mix their metaphors because no one metaphor quite captures the power of the woman, the power of the myth.

She shall go to the ball, they say, but this is no Cinderella awaiting her prince. As Major well knows, her standing ovation will always be bigger than his, so she must not be allowed to stand alone on the party platform. The back-seat driver must never again be allowed to take the wheel. For, three years on, Thatcher has, according to Nigel Lawson, not come to terms with the manner of her leaving. She is hurt, betrayed, and although the Tory men only gesture towards it, we all know hell hath no fury like a woman scorned.

Three years on, though, I wonder if any of us is any closer to coming to terms with it. What role did we want her to assume? What role is there for an elder stateswoman? Did we really expect her to devote more time to her family? Or to become a cross between Ted Heath and the Queen Mother? She could have smiled beatifically and handed over the baton to a chosen one like a saintly grandma. But this does not suit her, for the doting elderly relative who sees no bad in her progeny is an entirely female part and one she has never wanted to play.

'We are a grandmother' she once said, that infamous 'we' somehow turning a personal event into a political institution. Thatcher was always able to invoke her own experience as a woman, a mother, in such a way that glossed over the reality of family life for most women. She could domesticize politics – it's all a matter of housekeeping – when her own life wasn't a bit domestic.

The fantasy of family life that has once more gripped the Tories is enormously strong. It can withstand an awful lot of pressure – and enormous contradictions. On one hand, John Patten can talk about the importance of parent power; on the other, we read that Carol Thatcher is thinking about emigrating because, largely as a result of her own parent's power and indeed policies, she cannot find work here. It is she who will take the place of the prodigal son, Mark, who has now returned from the desert and made good. It is the daughter who admits to not voting Tory in the last election, while the son ties up the big deals for Mummy's memoirs.

Of course, whatever Margaret Thatcher 'meant' or means now goes far beyond the realms of her position within her own family but because she so cleverly used the idea of family to prop up the Thatcher myth, it is interesting to see where that has led her. In traditional families, as women age they are allowed a degree of power; they can become grand matriarchs, presiding over their clans or, in this case, the Conservative Party.

Anyone who has watched will know, however, that Thatcher is ambivalent about such a role, as she has been about every traditional feminine role. She is, on the contrary, a patriarch. Her heroes are her father and Winston Churchill. Her great strength is in bringing together masculine and feminine. As Beatrix Campbell wrote in her fascinating book, *The Iron Ladies*: 'She has not feminized politics . . . but she has offered feminine endorsement to patriarchal power.'

Or, to put it crudely, as that other material girl Madonna did: 'Pussy rules the world, but I have a dick in my brain.' Thatcher is resentful of being tucked away, to be brought out like a mascot for the adoring masses, for 'the dick' demands a place in public life. Home is still not where her heart is. If she cannot be the giving matriarch, there is the terrifying possibility she will turn into the other archetype of the old spurned woman: the mother-in-law who knows the dirty secrets of her offspring, the witch who will destroy what she can no longer control.

For all the fuss about the damaging effects of her memoirs, the tedious in-fighting between newspapers, is anyone really surprised at what has been revealed so far? Did anyone think she would have thought any of her predecessors good enough? That she thought half her Cabinet intellectual drifters, even buffoons, is really no great shock. We all think that anyway.

The credence we give to her ability to destroy the entire government is a testament not to her actual political power but to the pull she still has over something that politics seeks so desperately to deny. The symbolic. The unconscious.

No better example is there than the continuous and barmy obsession with her handbag. Handbags are part of the great mystery of women. What on earth do they keep in there? What has she got in hers? Well, you never can tell. According to this paper, it is a cash register. The *Sun*, meanwhile, says: 'That shiny black handbag is as lethal as ever.' The *Mirror* captions her picture with: 'Lady Thatcher checks her handbag is loaded as she is driven through the rain to appear as a star guest.'

Now, you may not accept the Freudian interpretation that handbags and purses represent female genitals but you have to admit that we are pretty fixated on what she's got inside her bag. While senior Tories are clearly horrified at what might be unleashed, the party faithful are still aroused by her particular brand of passion.

Yet if Thatcherism were a coherent ideological project, a response to a particular historical situation, the question still remains: can it survive without her? Its supposed softening, its transmutation into 'Majorism', is entirely unconvincing because, for all its social concern, it still ruthlessly seeks to blame the victims of the past fourteen years for all that we can see has gone wrong. And that, surely, is more frightening than anything that might be revealed in Thatcher's book or even, God forbid, in the contents of her handbag.

THE HOME TRUTH ABOUT BRUTALITY

From the end of this month, at a cinema near you, is something that you really do not want to see – a real-life horror film. Sandwiched between the girl fellating her Flake in the bathtub and another wacky banking ad is a film that should make your blood run cold. *Don't Stand For It* is a ninety-second commercial about domestic violence and it will be showing nationally for three months from 29 October.

The film, made by Penny Gould, was not commissioned, no one was paid to work on it and the Home Office covered the £18,000 distribution costs. It is an incredibly powerful piece of work that uses horrific pictures of battered women alongside typical quotes from them, such as: 'I'll just give him one more chance.' To counter this, the facts also appear on the screen. Every year one hundred women in the UK are murdered by their partners. On average, a woman will have been assaulted thirty-five times before she goes to the police. Forty per cent of all murders occur in domestic situations. As image after image of bruised, burnt, cut bodies appear, Lyle Lovett sings 'Stand By Your Man'. The project was fully supported by Tammy Wynette, who wrote the song, although she no longer controls the rights.

The aim of the film is twofold: it offers a helpline number to women who are trapped in violent relationships but, just as importantly, seeks to give a very clear message to men and women that violence is unacceptable. Of course, not everyone will want to be reminded of what goes on behind closed doors. Domestic violence for a very long time has hardly been a sexy media issue.

Like rape and hysterectomies, it is somehow perceived as worthy and depressing, 'a women's issue', which translates as 'a women's problem'. Battered women are still interviewed with anthropological zeal, as though they were another species. Special psychological syndromes are invented to explain their passivity, and why, on average, women will put up with seven years of abuse before they go to an outside agency. The Stockholm Syndrome was originally identified in hostages who became emotionally entwined with their captors and is now thought to be applicable to some women in this situation.

In some ways, though, we are all responsible for neglecting this problem. Part of the progress that feminism has made over the last few years has been a move away from anything tinged with a boringly politically correct agenda. Now, as we are told repeatedly, girls just want to have fun. This is because many women, and I count myself among them, got tired of the continual representations of women as men's victims. It is all so much more exciting to think about the arousing power play of an S & M encounter than to think about the power play of a man pushing his wife's face into a boiling chip pan.

While we are busy celebrating images of powerful women, the stills in *Don't Stand For It* remind us all too graphically of what being powerless actually looks like. Whether that powerlessness is psychological or financial or both, it looks like a woman with her nose knocked across her face. It looks like hell on earth. It looks shameful.

So, if we are ashamed of – though I hate the phrase – 'battered women' because we perceive them to be the ultimate victims, it is really not surprising. Do you remember Erin Pizzey, who founded the first women's refuge in this country, coming up with the appalling theory that some women who grow up with violence just get addicted to it?

Yet, what I see in this film is at last a way of moving the issues back into the mainstream. Domestic violence has surfaced in soap operas like *Brookside* and *Roseanne*. The case of Sara Thornton and the release of Kiranjit Ahluwalia have provoked discussion about

whether long-term physical abuse can legally constitute provocation. This month, both *Elle* and *Vanity Fair* carry domestic
violence stories although, of course, *Vanity Fair* doesn't advertise its
story as such. You may remember the case of John Wayne Bobbit's
penis, hacked off by his wife and thrown out of a car window. This
case which, according to *Vanity Fair*, 'tapped into the core of the
female *zeitgeist*' now – surprise, surprise – reveals a long and familiar
story of abuse. Bobbit had repeatedly beaten and raped his wife.
Her vigilante justice may have turned her into a hero for some.
Camille Paglia's response was: 'It's a wake-up call. It has to send a
chill through every man in the world.'

However, let's be clear: these are not cries of revolution, but
desperation. These may be the cases making headlines but they are
not typical. They are the exception to the rule that it is men who
murder and mutilate the women they live with. In London alone,
the number of reported attacks has risen from 5,130 in 1990 to
9,800. Scotland Yard says this figure represents 'a tiny tip of the
iceberg'. Last year, over 100,000 women used a range of Women
Aid services. That's why I didn't laugh at comedian Jim Davidson's
explanation for his ex-wife's two black eyes: 'Pushing her away
from me, I caught her in the eye with my thumb, bruising her and
dislocating my thumb . . . A few days later she asked me to throw
her the keys . . . I flung them over and the bunch hit her in the
other eye.'

Domestic violence has too long been considered a private issue.
Now it is, necessarily, being made a public one. This is not a problem that was sorted out in the seventies, this is not some loony
feminist cause, this is not just part of what happens in relationships.
It is a crime.

While Neighbourhood Watch schemes have been concerned
with protecting the contents of homes rather than the people in
them, isn't it about time we started caring as much about the violation of women as the theft of a few videos.

MEETING WITH THE ENEMY

You may wonder what a nice girl like me is doing in a place like this. Let me introduce myself properly. I am 'the enemy'. I know this because a sweet guy I met recently said: 'I always read your column, Suzanne. I like to know what the enemy is thinking.' He was just being friendly, I guess. So I thought, 'Smile at me again and I'll do you for sexual harassment. Touch me just once, and I'll cry rape. If you dare to ruin my evening, watch out: just for the hell of it, I will ruin your life.'

That's the way 'the enemy' thinks, isn't it? That's what is expected of feminists, isn't it? I was just doing my job. Take this date-rape thing. Diggle and Donnellan, decent young men destroyed by 'the zealots of Political Correctness'. Donnellan has been cleared. Quite right too. Anyone who has been following the trial could see that his accuser was a confused and daft young woman. Daftness and confusion, however, are not crimes, though the way that some people have been baying for her blood, you'd think they were.

Clearly both she and Donnellan have in some way been casualties of the sexual confusion that we keep hearing about nowadays. Men are confused, we keep being told, because they have no way of interpreting the ambiguous signals women send out. Young men always want sex. Particularly, it would appear, with girls who are so drunk that they describe themselves as a 'semi-comatose vegetable'. Women are just confused. We are supposed to believe this is a new phenomenon; that, once upon a time, no one was confused, that sex and love and courtship conformed to easily understandable patterns. First base, second base . . . wham bam, thank you, ma'am. Everyone knew where they stood. Everyone was happy.

But the whole point is that everyone was not happy. Some women were not happy at all. So those nasty feminists put a spanner in the works by saying such crazy things as 'no means no' when everyone knows that girls always say no until you make them say yes. Then there was all that palaver about AIDS and, Jesus, you even had some women saying that penetration might not be the be-all and end-all of sex. It was obvious what they needed.

Somehow it all got so bitter and twisted that, while sodomizing a woman with a Coke bottle got to be referred to as 'date-rape', it was men who cast themselves as the new victims. An argument about whether we need different categories of rape turned into a scenario where now, apparently, it is men who are persecuted, who must live in terror of a false accusation.

And, as the *Daily Mail*, standing up valiantly for this new oppressed majority, told us this week: 'Men, too, deserve justice.' I can't say I'm surprised. In January, I wrote: 'A year or so after the importation of the term from America, I am wondering if the advancement of date-rape as a feminist cause has done much for women at all.' Witnessing the crowing accompanying the clearing of Donnellan, I am even more convinced that it hasn't.

Yet practically all female journalists writing about this case have been perfectly happy to admit that Donnellan should have been cleared, that his young woman accuser behaved stupidly and that women can behave as badly as men. Give them an inch, though, and they take away your rights. The anonymity given to women in rape cases has now also been called into question on the strength of this one, highly untypical case. As though one false accusation undoes statistic after statistic about the numbers of rapes reported. As though one silly girl whose main problem is that she is simply very young represented all the women who claim they have been raped.

Can we learn anything from all this? Apparently not, because we are far more interested in blame than in truth. A tiny minority of feminists still cling to the wreckage of old ideas – all men are rapists, no always means no, raped women are traumatized for ever. But they are the extremists that men fear, the ones that demand sex by contract. They are the enemy. But are they about to seize power? Of course not. They are more likely to be worshipping the goddess in a field in Wales than trying to get a leg up the judiciary.

But, by God, men need to see this enemy everywhere. While feminists are accused of tarring all men with the same brush, some men generalize wildly about any woman who doesn't consider herself a doormat. They need to in order to construe themselves as victims of the new war. 'Is not the pendulum in danger of swinging too far?' the *Daily Mail* asks.

Women's right to anonymity in rape cases is now referred to as a 'statutory privilege'. The balance of power has shifted ever so slightly and already the boys are feeling wobbly, being ever so slightly hysterical about the whole issue. They report the fact that students have sex as a major news story. A culture of drunken casual sex emerges, something far more recognizable and healthy to me than this strange world of dating that is talked about. A Doris Day world – where women are rented for an evening, where the perfect date is Rock Hudson – is not my idea of a good time.

You see, although apparently I am the enemy, I am pretty bad at it. I don't have the certainty of those who seem to believe that teenage girls are fully in possession of themselves sexually. I'd be deeply suspicious of anyone who said they always knew exactly what they wanted, when and how. You find out what you want sometimes by doing what you don't want.

And, generally, I'd go for a lover who preferred me conscious to unconscious, but there you go . . . perhaps I'm just being choosy. The thing is, you see, I've thought a lot about being responsible and irresponsible and I know I'm capable of both. Any good that can come out of this whole messy business is if men can do the same. I'd even be so extreme as to suggest that men might have better sex with women who actually wanted to have sex with them. But rather than examine their own sexuality, for many men it's easier to point the finger, to construct an enemy, a persecutor where often

73

there is none. So cast me as the enemy if you like, because it's been obvious for a long, long time that you need me far more than I ever needed you.

WORRIED ABOUT THE CHILDREN OR SCARED OF SEX?

Last night I sat down with my kids and enjoyed a good bit of sex and violence on the television. It was another nature programme.

In it we saw two giraffes about to copulate. 'What is *that*,' asked my daughter, having, I presume, never seen a giraffe's erect penis before. My answer was lost as they collapsed into giggles. 'That's sex, that is,' the older one said, an expert in such matters because she has seen the group, Take That.

Sex yes, but not as we know it. I realize that for kids, as ridiculous as the sight of giraffes bonking may be, it is really no more ridiculous than the idea of adults having sex. They are at a stage where they find sex alternately revolting, fascinating and hysterically funny. I can relate to that.

Is it any wonder kids have mixed-up views about sex? Look at us grown-ups. This week the Family Planning Association published a book for use in primary schools. It suggests that sexual education begins as young as four. A predictable outcry has risen from the family-values mob.

John Patten, the Education Secretary, viewed the book with 'considerable anxiety', saying: 'Education about sex should begin in the home as should all education.' Valerie Riches, of the Family Education Trust, bemoans classroom 'condom culture'. 'Most booklets and videos have no religious or moral basis. Look what happens – more abortions, illegitimate pregnancies and family breakdowns.'

Indeed, it is because the FPA has looked at what happens – that one in five people have sex before the age of sixteen, that seven out of a hundred adolescent girls become pregnant and that a third of those pregnancies are unplanned – that it has produced this material. Despite what Mr Patten may think, 96 per cent of parents look to schools to be the main providers of sexual education.

Those disturbed by the idea of four-year-olds being able to name nipples and testicles often use the argument put forward by the former Education Minister Sir Rhodes Boyson: that a degree of sexual knowledge destroys the innocence of childhood as if child-hood were some hermetically sealed state.

Anyone who has been around little children will know they are incredibly sexual, finding enormous pleasure in their own bodies, though to acknowledge that remains difficult in a culture that denies it.

The division of the world into a pastoral daydream of childish innocence and an adult world of deep, dark sex is no longer work-able, if it ever was. We live in a highly sexual culture. Four-year-olds will have sung 'I'm Too Sexy' because they will have heard it in the playground or on the radio. They will already have seen endless imagery of sexy people doing sexy things because, let's face it, that's what most of us surround ourselves with.

They may well be like my friend's little boy and be so appalled at the sight of snogging that they pretend to throw up, but they certainly will not be able to avoid it.

Calling a nipple a nipple is hardly going to corrupt a kid who has grown up singing Madonna's 'Like a Virgin' or seen her mother feeding her baby brother. Indeed, most toddlers I know lift up their shirts and try to breast-feed their dolls.

What we are all so afraid of is that any kind of sexual information will lead to imitation – that if we tell kids how sex is done they will automatically go and do it. It is a blinkered view, as if sex were an idea we put into their heads rather than one that is always already there.

I wonder who we are really afraid of: our kids or ourselves? I have a lot of sexual information that I choose not to act on. Are children persuaded to do things they have no desire for simply because they know how?

Surely the real problem here is that the mechanics of sex have little to do with our complicated feelings about it. Many adult sexual fantasies are a mystery to adults themselves and contain information that children are simply unable to process.

Sensitive sexual education is always bound to be difficult because it is often attempting to do the impossible, to make sex into something it is not: an always healthy, loving, comprehensible and rational act, a snigger-free activity.

That simply is not what most people's experience of sex is like. That is why Woody Allen's one-liner 'Sex isn't dirty but it is if you're doing it right' is funny. On one hand we are telling kids sex is not dirty, on the other we still feel it is. Such ambivalence can be deadly, which is why adult sexual education about HIV has proved so difficult.

Whether we are talking about masturbation or mathematics, it is widely accepted that to teach children well, information has to be given gradually. The danger is that if we give them more information than they can handle we end up confusing them. The greater danger, however, is that if we think the subject is best avoided kids will carry on having sex and getting pregnant.

The major difficulty with sex education will always be that kids are able to grasp the biological concepts before they have experienced the emotional context in which those concepts materialize. You cannot teach 'intimacy'. The best we can hope for is that good educational practices teach respect, sexual and social.

Let us do away with hypocrisy dressed up as concern for our children. What we are worried about is our own ambivalence and discomfort about sex. Like the Victorians, we can avert our eyes and in the name of children's innocence pretend that what we know goes on does not really.

Ignorance has never proved to be bliss and no morality can change that reality.

BEYOND GOOD AND EVIL

Blood stains. It's a job to get rid of them. This much we know. This much Child A, one of the murderers of James Bulger, knew. Before he became Robert Thompson, when all we saw of him was an artist's illustration of the back of his head, he told the police about the blood. 'Cos blood stains, doesn't it, and then me mother would have to pay more money and he was pouring with blood so I put him back down.'

I can't shift this remark, either; it's indelible. It stains us all because this is clearly a child talking, a child who feels responsibility to keep his clothes clean, a child who understands the price of things, a child who doesn't want to burden his mother with cleaning bills. Yet this is the child who killed another child.

Now the floodgates have opened. Child A and Child B have become children with names, faces, families and futures filled with the dull certainty of institutionalization. One is struck by the terrifying oscillation between intimacy and anonymity: a couple of days ago, we knew nothing of these boys; now we know the details of their family lives.

A week ago, the boys and their barristers were blaming each other. A and B, Tweedledee and Tweedledum, agreed to have a battle. We knew that Child B cried in court when he heard the other boy's QC saying: 'They will never have a normal childhood.' And we knew that he wanted to take the gerbils home at half-term. That's a normal thing to want to do.

Hanging out and getting into mischief in a shopping centre is not so strange really. After all, shopping centres are there to encourage you to want things. Want things that maybe you can never have. So, surrounded by the goodies on display, instead of the usual pens and sweets, they took some paint and they took something else, the most precious commodity of the lot. A two-year-old child. They took him for a walk and took his life.

This baby, whose image has haunted us, put his hand in the big boy's hand, a gesture we understand, yet viewed through the distance of the video camera, it became the ghostliest vision because we knew by then what had happened to James. The image lied to us because it made James present, it made us feel intervention was possible.

So we saw the image and could do nothing. Presumably the security men saw the image and did nothing. The thirty-eight witnesses who saw the abduction did nothing. The jurors wept when they saw the pictures of what had been done to James because by then it was too late to do anything.

The gap between seeing and doing grows ever wider. We were made to witness what had occurred. We watch but leave the real surveillance to someone else. We are safe in the knowledge that other people will be watching, so it's not our responsibility to intervene. Just hold your own child's hand tighter than ever and kid yourself as a parent that you know everything there is to know about your own child and your child would never . . .

Or imagine. For this is what all these images help us to do. Our tears fall so easily because we can begin to imagine what this little child went through, we can imagine some of what it must be like for his family. We can imagine a toddler running towards the same person who was throwing bricks at it. The gap between strangers and ourselves closes. The anonymous wreaths – 'RIP Little One' – show the kindness of strangers, some sort of attempt to bridge the gap.

Yet as these sobbing eleven-year-olds are taken to be locked up, there are those who don't want us to imagine what it is like for them or their families. For they are evil. The word 'evil' signals the end of a conversation before it has started. These are evil children who found each other. The police told us. The media is enthralled by this concept of evil. Never before have I heard it bandied around with so much glee. The vocabulary of the Old Testament has swamped us and we have scrabbled to make sense of it. Treatment or punishment? Repentance or forgiveness? Redemption through divine grace or through psychology?

What unites all of us – wishy-washy liberals or those with firm religious beliefs – is that there is a bottom line, that what these boys did is so terribly wrong. While we have heard endlessly about moral deterioration, what we have witnessed in the response to this murder is a nation that has not lost its moral certainty. Murder is not a relative act but an absolute one. Quite rightfully, no one has tried to slot this particular agony into the agony of other sufferings. We know enough to know grief cannot be quantified.

What is to be done with this grief is another matter. Sean Sexton, the Bulgers' solicitor, has said that it is dangerous to extrapolate lessons for society from this case, which is an aberration. Already, however, such extrapolations have been made. Broken homes, truancy, video violence have predictably been made to play their part. In all of these respects, the murderers' environment was not so different from that of thousands of other children.

Much has been made of the boys' mothers struggling to manage. *Newsnight* featured a report on the work of child guidance clinics in repairing mother/child relationships. Again, parenting has been equated with mothering. There has been little talk of fathering. It is easier to ask about the moral values of a pluralistic society than to raise questions concerning men, responsibility and parenting. Easier to talk of evil than empathy.

Thank goodness Professor Halsey, on yesterday's *Moral Maze*, made a distinction between evil acts and evil people. If we fail to do this, we may as well join the crowd outside Preston Crown Court and bay for more blood in the legalized murder of these boys. Such is the potency of this case that even those who believe in rehabilitation whisper that it will take a brave Home Secretary to release these children ever.

Like it or not, from now on these children will be analysed and examined through the eyes of experts who will use largely internal and psychological models to try to understand their behaviour. Some of this has already emerged in the trial. Thompson's protestations that if he had wanted to kill a baby, he would have killed his own brother reveal that this is what in a sense he did. But more generally – and we know this from adults who abuse children – the hatred of their own vulnerability, their own babyishness, becomes so strong that it is punished, killed off through the body of another.

Speaking personally, which is all any of us can do in this situation, the idea of the punishment of vulnerability has a lot more resonance than the time-warped ramblings of archbishops. It is the most vulnerable in society who have been punished in the past fifteen years, it is weakness that is thought of as the ultimate sin. Strength, willpower, inflexibility – these are to be encouraged. But James was vulnerable, as we all are. As, indeed, his killers now appear. So before we leap to unflinching moral absolutes, let us speak of this shared vulnerability so that it may be acknowledged and protected rather than despised.

MORAL SEX, THE TORY WAY

Recite after me the Back to Basics times table: Two parents are better than one. One man and one woman make a marriage. A family is indivisible. Divorce into marriage doesn't go. AIDS cannot be multiplied by anyone, except homosexuals. Two people of the same sex never add up. You can never subtract from the age of consent. To solve any equation use the formula known as compulsory heterosexuality. Call line one reality, draw a parallel to it and call it government policy, and the two lines will never meet.

The sum total of all this may be ignorance, poverty, misery and disease, but learn it off by heart, my friends, because these are, according to John Patten in his new draft circular on sex education in schools, the values 'that should be common to all of us'. The fact that they are patently not, represents not only a gross miscalculation, but a refusal to acknowledge the figures that even Mr Patten must be aware of, on everything from the changing face of family life to the statistics on teenage pregnancies.

It is not that most of us are unconcerned with the moral education of our children. What I find so shocking is the presumption that this kind of morality, which has been tried and tested for a good while now, is the only morality acceptable to the state. I say this not because I am immoral or because I am a *Guardian* writer/reader cocooned in some dangerous time warp, but simply because I cannot close my eyes to what I see going on around me.

The books I read, the television I watch and, yes, even the people that I meet, do not seem to me bereft of moral values, though they often seem weary of having to pick a path between human weakness and a sense of how things could or should be. Most contemporary soap operas from *EastEnders* to *Neighbours* to *Brookside*, which – if you bother to ask them – is where most young people say they get their sex education from, are stuffed to the gills with moral dilemmas. Should Mark in *EastEnders* have told Shelly right from the start that he was HIV positive? How will she cope? Should Pauline take Arthur back, even though he has committed adultery and so on?

This is sex education, not as the mechanics of reproduction but as the stuff of life itself. This is sex, not as an irresponsible pastime but as an act imbued with all sorts of complex emotions and consequences. It seems to me a far richer world than Mr Patten's, where values such as fidelity and responsibility can be inculcated alongside algebra and the periodic table. Of course, it's more difficult to communicate this to teenagers than showing them films of wiggling spermatozoa. It is really no wonder that most parents would rather leave sex education to schools than do it themselves.

The problem facing many teachers, and the rest of us who are prepared to take it on, is that because we live in a highly sexualized society, most kids will already have an enormous amount of information about sex before they even get to see a diagram of the reproductive system of a rabbit. Sometimes, that information will be plain wrong, sometimes misunderstood, sometimes it will be understood intellectually before it can be understood emotionally, and sometimes that information will have already been so morally loaded that young people will just not know how to deal with it.

My own sex education, for instance, consisted largely of horrible films about venereal diseases with graphic close-ups of babies born with syphilis. This was only after a girl in my year complained of period pains on a school trip to Belgium and went upstairs and gave birth. By then it was decided that something must be done and the result would doubtless have met with Mr Patten's approval. Our deputy headmistress strode into a biology lesson demanding to know what the purpose of sex was. My friend Anita's hand shot up. 'Pleasure, Miss,' she said, and was promptly told to 'Get out of this classroom'. We were then informed that sex was purely for procreation and that the best method of contraception was a brick wall. This to the girls who spent lunchtimes huddled around desks discussing Linda Lovelace and who had done it with who.

Did the attitude of my teachers produce a generation with happy marriages filled with gloriously satisfying sex? Did it eliminate the sins of homosexuality and adultery? Of course not, which is why, like so many people, I am prepared to try something different. I'm with Anita on this one. I think pleasure might be a good place to start. Indeed, educating boys about female sexual response would do more to encourage marriage than all Patten's sanctimonious waffle. It's not that better sex education leads automatically to sex being any easier, any more than it leads children to have unlimited sex, but it can help. If it is to start before kids start putting into practice what they know in theory, then it has to start in primary school. The moral worries here are those of context. In what kind of relationship is it acceptable to have sex?

If children are to be taught that the only acceptable context is within marriage, what on earth are they to make of what they see around them, including their own families? I guess they can always condemn a little more, understand a little less, the society they live in, and do John Major proud. They will also perhaps feel slightly lost as the sex education videos tell them not to have underage sex and then how to have it. The ever-vigilant Mr Patten has also warned teachers that advising individual girls under sixteen about contraception is a criminal offence. What kind of morality is this, I wonder?

To me, it is a criminal offence not to give a girl, who is clearly going to have sex, information about contraception. It is an offence that Mr Patten and his cronies will be condemning this same girl when she becomes a teenage mother nine months later. Call this Tory policy if you like, call it the flounderings of a party who can only look back, but calling these guidelines 'moral' is an affront to those of us who, though we do not share Patten's claim to the moral high ground, have a pretty good sense of right and wrong.

DIANA – HER TRUE COLOURS

With familiar blushes and winces of nervousness, a speech is blurted out at a charity lunch. And a soul is available for diagnosis by everyone from Marje Proops to Nigel Dempster. The fracturing of a fairy tale is a strange sight to behold. For as dreams sour it is difficult to remember the story we told ourselves in the first place. If there ever was a story at all.

Even those glued to their sets on the day of the Royal Wedding knew that life – anyone's life – wasn't like the spectacle on their screens. All the same, the nation seemed happy to drown itself in icing sugar, heedless of cynics among us who saw Diana as a sacrificial lamb on the altar of a monarchy in decline. But, as the years passed, the drama became more watchable, because a twist appeared in the plot. Diana started to come out of the coma she had been brought up to function in. And, by then, if anyone needed a fairy tale it was her – not us.

As Diana, the fairy-tale princess, gets tired, emotional, litigious even, her myth has given way to something much more mundane. She wants 'time and space', and though she never stooped quite so low as to say the words, we all know that this means time and space 'to find herself'.

So what is there for her to find – inside or outside the role that she has played for twelve years – that can be disentangled from the fairy tale? Somewhere between colonic irrigation, *Vogue* covers and holding hands with lepers there is, we are led to believe, a personality, a thirty-two-year-old with, as James Whitaker so quaintly reminds us, 'all the desires and urges of a young woman'.

Which means that the first part of the fairy tale has been shot to pieces already. Fairy-tale princesses don't have urges. They leave that job to their princes. Unfortunately, while Charles's urges extend to Camilla Parker-Bowles and ecologically sound farming methods, for some time now they clearly haven't extended to his wife. One could sense the fading of the urge as far back as the time when a mortified Charles looked on as Diana chose to dance to 'Uptown Girl' with Wayne Sleep. This certainly wasn't part of the Prince's fairy tale. Where it fitted in to Diana's, I don't know. But then this fairy tale has always been rather vague.

If anything, Diana's story (though not the one she told Andrew Morton) seems to resemble a mutated version of 'The Sleeping Beauty'. Instead of a long sleep, ending with a prince's kiss and the inevitable happy-ever-after marriage, Diana appears to have been put to sleep by a prince's kiss, to have gone sleep-walking through a marriage and to have woken up only a year ago. Then we learned that Diana could not only walk but that she could talk as well. And talk she did, about eating disorders, hugging children, depression and her desire to 'disappear like a Dispirin'.

This Sloaney woman, who once described herself as 'thick as a plank', may still have blushed scarlet as she spoke, but she did have opinions. She had become conscious. While Charles continued to ramble on against modernism, and for recycling, Diana continued to jig up and down at pop concerts and hold the hands of the sick and the needy.

During the marriage such instinctive populism did not sit well either with her husband or with some others at the Palace. But it always sat well with the public. A year after the separation Charles is still floundering around looking for a role. Who could read Douglas Hurd's remark, 'He would be a star even if he were not Prince of Wales', with anything but incredulity? Charles's tragedy is surely that he is not a star even though he *is* the Prince of Wales.

While Hurd seems unqualified to determine star quality in anyone, it is undeniable that Diana is still regarded as a star. Yet she does not glow as brightly as she once did. While she may sell any magazine that she is pictured on the cover of, there has been less public interest of late and this has possibly contributed to her decision to take a break. At an official engagement she attended in September, although the police had erected barriers because of the expected crowd, only two women turned out.

But then who would want to catch a glimpse of the Princess, fully dressed, in the flesh when any of us can see pictures of her frolicking on a beach, working out in a gym, or crying, on the news? Her great ability has always been to be intimate in public, to emote under the flash bulbs, to *feel* in front of a camera. No wonder she feels so empty the rest of the time. What is the point of feeling if there is no one there to document it?

From the very beginning, we all knew about her prized virginity, the thing that made her suitable bride material for Charles. That most private part of her life was already public property. Not quite bought and sold but, how shall we say . . . arranged. While Charles was brought up knowing that whatever the basis of his marriage, it would not be love, Diana's mistake was her belief in the fairy tale. Though the aristocracy have always favoured arranged marriages in order to protect their estates and their gene pools, Diana was dumb enough to fall for it all, even to fall in love with Charles.

Maybe she needed the fairy tale more than the rest of us, because the reality was really quite horrible. Even for a young woman of limited intelligence, to be used as little more than a brood mare is unpleasant. And who can say it wasn't like that? Virginity and then fertility was her value. What's love got to do with it? Frankly, my dear, very little.

And Diana did both virginity and fertility so very well. Wham bam, thank you ma'am and two heirs to the throne in quick succession. Diana did her duty all right. No wedding dress, no matter how many pearls are sewn on to it, could disguise what had happened to her. Her *haut bourgeois* values of true romance had no place in the cynical game plan of a monarchy under attack. As Barbara Cartland, who told the biggest fairy stories of them all, said: 'The only books she ever read were mine and they weren't awfully good for her.'

'Trapped in a loveless marriage' and continually on display, she opted for desperate self-improvement, every part of her body and behaviour under the scrutiny of an expert. When that didn't work she wailed at Charles, chucked up in the loo and even made some spectacularly daft attempts at suicide. In public, however, she continued to glitter, to look up from under her eyelashes like a five-year-old and play dumb.

Her silence was a marvellous asset because, as with all great stars, blankness is mistaken for charisma. Diana became a blank screen available for all kinds of projections. She was supermother, saint and sex symbol. For Camille Paglia she was nothing less than a goddess. For tabloid editors the world over she was simply a gift horse who never opened her mouth.

We – that is you and me – were insatiable, we just couldn't get enough of her. That's what we were continually told anyway. There could never be too many images of her. We wanted to see her on duty and off, and we did. Pregnant in a bikini, taking her children to school. There was no such thing as off duty.

Her announcement last week has been referred to as an exile, even as an abdication, but it is really nothing more than a break from public engagements. Yet the reaction to it has signalled that her life is one permanent public engagement in that, without the oxygen of publicity, we can barely imagine her life at all. She will, says Cartland, be 'bored stiff'.

There is, of course, a huge amount of hypocrisy in all this. While Diana lives for her children, apparently, they live thirty weeks of the year away from her at boarding school. While she is credited with giving them a much more affectionate upbringing than the traditional royal one, she has not broken with the aristocratic habit of getting rid of your children for as much of the time as possible. Call me old-fashioned but no amount of rides at Thorpe Park can make up for that. But, and she well knows it, it is her children that ensure she cannot be excluded from royal circles. Even after the rumoured divorce she is, all said and done, the mother of the future king and she will, as she promised, somehow without irony, endeavour to give her sons 'an appreciation of the tradition into which they were born'. One can't help wondering if this means she will explain to them the difference between love and marriage, between duty and destiny.

While the tabloids talk of Charles and Diana as though they were at war, this latest decision to retreat from public life has been seen as a surrender. Charles ultimately has all the power of the Firm behind him and she doesn't. She cannot be, as Philip said, both inside and outside the family. She cannot operate an alternative court. This downgrading has been seen in the way that her chauffeur, her bodyguard and dresser have all been recently removed. She is reported to be very distressed at this – one has to ask what kind of life it is when the people closest to you are, in fact, your servants.

Others, however, see her temporary retirement not so much as surrender but as a time to regroup. They expect Diana to come back with more energy than before, ready to take on the world. They see a manipulative woman who has learnt to use the media as much as it has used her. Her media virginity went a long, long time ago: she knows how to plant a story. Her engineering of public opinion at the time of the separation would have done any political spin doctor proud.

The emotive farewell, for instance, could have been less public, if less public she had wanted to be. The murmurings of senior royal aides, 'without elaborating, there is more to her decision than meets the eye', ring true in light of how she has handled her affairs in the past. Her expertise in making calculation look spontaneous should come as no surprise and, of course, if she ever needed to remind herself of what she has to lose there is always the forlorn Fergie to look at.

Nor can she ignore the fact that, photogenic as she may be, she is vulnerable in a way that Charles will never be. After twelve years in this family she ought to know how it works by now. She has seen, close up, naked hereditary privilege protecting itself; she has seen patriarchy unconstrained by any notion of decency. She has been surrounded by those who must believe in the notion of natural superiority if they are to snip another ribbon, shake another hand, take another posy of flowers from a child or another few thousand pounds from the Civil List.

She has also seen a royal family struggling to maintain its position in the modern world. The enormous public sympathy that Diana has attracted reflects how the world has changed. Her refusal to be satisfied with public duty and personal misery strikes a chord in millions of women. Her expectation of a happy marriage, while totally unrealistic in the circumstances, is one we feel she is still entitled to. Charles's perceived lack of involvement in his children is no longer tolerable in the way it would have been fifty years ago.

And while Charles has sought to change the world in large-scale public ways, Diana has actually changed attitudes with small personal gestures. Holding the hand of a person with AIDS probably did far more good than all of Charles's pompous pontifications about rain-forests. Against Charles's cold rationality, Diana appears to be so in touch with humanity that she is continually brimming over with emotion.

Yet, without an audience to second all this emotion via the endless snapshots of her, what will she do? She can certainly choose to be less royal than she is but she cannot choose to be less of a celebrity. Having achieved celebrity through marriage and motherhood, she must now find a celebrity that is hers alone. She needs to matter. Just as she was getting nearer to her goal, the strain began to show. Charles was said to be jealous of her public profile, and rumours of friendships with men were once more mentioned. She was often reminded that this fairy-tale princess never could be crowned queen. So, instead of the happy ending, we have two lonely people who, despite their vast wealth, don't seem to have a clue what to do with themselves. (Just proves that all that money doesn't make you happy, doesn't it? Which keeps the rest of us in our place.)

But Diana's journey is not over yet, and she knows it. To present herself as hounded out of public life by the media, when so long ago she made a pact with them, is disingenuous beyond belief. She could, of course, have her privacy but that would mean giving up the privileges that go with the title. She doesn't want to make such a choice and who can blame her? So I wouldn't cry too hard for her now that she has woken up to find herself 'a prisoner in a gilded cage'. At least her cage is gilded, unlike most. And though not quite the fairy-tale ending some of us might have hoped for, 'the gilded cage' would make a great title for Barbara Cartland's next novel. That is, if she hasn't already used it.

FOR FEAR OF THE QUEER

Let's all breathe a sigh of relief. Back to Basics is not about personal morality, it's not about public morality either. Now that's been made as clear as a muddy windscreen by the Tory automatons anxious to get themselves out of another fine mess that they have got themselves into, we can rest assured that the state does not want to interfere with our private lives. Tolerance and decency, that's what concerns Mr Major. And I'm glad to hear it.

I am also glad to hear that this commitment to tolerance will be tested in next week's free vote in the House of Commons on lowering the age of consent for homosexual men. Currently set at twenty-one, it is higher than that of any other European country. In Italy, Belgium, the Netherlands and Portugal, it's sixteen. In Denmark and France it's fifteen. In Spain it's twelve and even in Ireland, hardly known for its liberal legislation, it's seventeen.

What looks likely is that MPs will reach for the compromise option of eighteen. This, of course, means that there will still be inequality between the age of consent for homosexuals and heterosexuals. Some Conservatives, running scared after the events of the last week, will not want to be seen as pushing through the 'radical change' which will lead to equality under the law for gay men.

It has been left to Edwina Currie, an unlikely champion of gay rights, to table the amendment to the Criminal Justice Bill to make the case for lowering the age of consent to sixteen. The sight of Currie quoting Oscar Wilde in the house – 'You cannot make men moral by law' – may have been a drag queen's delight but in the current climate it struck me not only as courageous but as the kind of moral leadership that the Cabinet may talk about but rarely demonstrates.

For Currie understands that what matters is not what people say but what they do, an insight clearly lost on senior politicians. She understands that just as old ministers will have affairs, young men will continue to have sex with one another if that is what they desire. That the latter should live in fear of prosecution because of a consensual act that harms no one is nonsensical.

The law does not initiate changes in society but drags several years behind them. The great liberalizing reforms of the late sixties on divorce, homosexuality and abortion reflected the coming of age of British society, a society with a sense of the future as well as the past. The war was finally over. This freeing up of a culture brought with it enormous complexities and problems, but for people such as myself it is impossible to imagine a time when women were trapped into marriage and childbirth because they had no choice. Or one when men lived miserable secret lives because they had no choice.

A nation which feels itself to be modern is not afraid of choice, indeed it encourages it. Nor is it afraid of its own citizens. Some of its citizens will be gay and some straight; but most of them will feel their sexuality is in some way innate, rather than a matter of choice. We can argue all day that sexuality is actually a lovely, gooey, fluid thing but the fact is that most of us have defined ourselves at an early age as being either homosexual or heterosexual.

Those unsure must be left to their dabblings, though most would not be dumb enough to claim that sharing a bed with someone of the same sex is nothing more than an effort to save on expenses.

Those who feel threatened by homosexuals simply insist that they have made the wrong choice, that they can be brought back into the wonderful world of sugar and spice and all things nice. For them homosexuality features largely as a form of contamination. The great concern that is voiced about lowering the age of consent to sixteen is that young boys will be preyed upon by older men, as though a sixteen-year-old lad might not have some inkling himself of what he wants to do. Now many of my best friends are heterosexuals, and I can assure you that they have been preyed upon by older men. Some of us have even liked it. If we are going to start legislating against predatory male sexuality, gay or straight, I'm afraid the consent threshold will have to be set at pensionable age.

What remains fascinating is this great bogeyman of seduction. There is already a law to protect children from men and women who sexually exploit them. Such exploitation constitutes abuse; it is not acceptable. No one disputes this. But the great myth of the male homosexual remains that of the great seducer forever on the look out for his innocent heterosexual prey. The most repulsive of straight men always imagine themselves to be some sort of catch for a gay man. They are deluding themselves entirely. The kind of seduction that they are so wary of happens largely in their dreams.

To seduce you have to find someone willing to be seduced. And it doesn't matter if you are male or female, gay or straight, sixteen or sixty. Though as Simon Fanshawe says: 'I've never seduced anyone. I just beg.' But in trying to protect the youth from the gay man, the gay youth – and believe me he exists – is denied the information about safe sex that he desperately needs, because to give him that information would be seen as condoning an illegal act. Exactly who are we protecting here?

Neither Mrs Currie, nor Marje Proops, who is a convert to the cause since having a chat with that nice Ian McKellen, is up there with the activists calling for A Queer Nation, but all of this makes me think we are a very queer nation indeed. Not least the fact that female homosexuality remains as invisible as ever.

The most perverse thing about all of this is not what gay men do in private. Rather, it is the weird way that those against lowering the age of consent to sixteen while desperate to reinforce heterosexuality as the true and rightful path, end up presenting it as such a precarious institution that equality before the law might make it topple over at any minute.

YOUR PENIS OR YOUR LIFE

In this world what is most valuable – a life or a penis? This is one of the questions the jury has to consider in the Lorena Bobbit trial. She is the woman who cut off her husband's penis with a kitchen knife. According to an American friend, people are phoning in sick because they can't tear themselves away from television coverage of the case. 'You hear the word penis every thirty seconds – it's amazing.' The word 'Bobbit' has transmuted itself into a verb.

Lorena Bobbit's defence is that she was temporarily insane when she did the deed, which was brought about by years of physical and sexual abuse. Her lawyer Lisa Kemler claims 'it was his penis from which she could not escape. It had caused her the most pain and the most fear. You will come to one conclusion; a life is more valuable than a penis.'

Howard Stern, the radio host and supporter of John Wayne Bobbit, summed up the opposing view when he said 'a guy's whole life is his penis'. Well, Bobbit's penis, now happily re-attached, has taken on a life all of its own. The three players in the case appear to be John Wayne, Lorena and the piece of severed flesh.

If Lorena had cut off his ear, for instance, would the case have attracted anywhere near the same sort of publicity? Of course not. But Lorena Bobbit cut to the heart of the matter – male power. I don't happen to think that male power, or pleasure come to that, resides solely between men's legs. Men have a lot more going for them than their pricks. But there you are, I'm obviously a pussycat at heart.

Lorena Bobbit is not my heroine – what she did was an act of desperation, not revolution. But that doesn't mean that I can't make jokes about it, or help noticing the smiles on women's faces whenever this case is mentioned. Or, underneath the smiles, pick up an enormous amount of female anger.

Does that mean that under every giggle is a castrating feminist just dying to get out? No. It just means that a lot of women from all walks of life are extremely pissed off. Lorena Bobbit was a manicurist, not a man-hater. Her husband said in court that he had not been raised to hit a woman but admitted he never indulged in foreplay. Just how brutish he was is up to the courts to decide.

All of this is unfortunately real life. Which is why trying to slot the characters into cyphers for various positions doesn't really work. Unless you accept that the dirty deed turned Lorena overnight from the classic victim into feminist vigilante.

Victimhood is out anyway. The new power feminism as advanced by Woolf, Roiphe and their kin has given an acceptable gloss to the half-crazed rantings of Camille Paglia. Understanding, rightly, that not all women want to be patronized by being talked about as victims, they are also bending over backwards to tell us how much they lurve men. No wonder they are having a hard time with this case. Although not all women are victims, sometimes I'm afraid some are.

They are beaten up and raped daily and it's not because they feel bad about themselves or have been got at by some zealous politically correct propaganda. The bottom line is that life for many women is made miserable by the men who are supposed to love them because we live in a culture that tolerates an awful amount of male violence.

The Zero Tolerance Campaign launched by the Association of London Authorities to raise awareness about domestic violence (you may have seen the posters that say 'Behind every successful man is a woman they put into casualty') is sending out a message about women's growing lack of tolerance to such violence. This violence is not located in men's dicks but in their hearts and minds. I just hope that all those men who feel tender hearing details of the

Bobbit case feel as vulnerable as I do every time they read about another woman being mutilated in equally horrible ways.

I do not know of a single case where a self-proclaimed feminist has physically castrated a man. I do know that as long as men see female equality as essentially emasculating that we have a job to do. Part of this may entail liberating men from their genitals. I'm talking symbolically here. It might be saying not that the penis is a weapon and we will disarm you but that there might be more to being a man than having one. The Bobbit case cannot be reduced to little Lorena versus his big thing.

John Wayne appears to be the same ape with his penis either severed or re-attached. The enormous symbolic power attributed to the Bobbit appendage doesn't quite square up to the pathetic piece of flesh found by policemen and deposited in a plastic bag. But then phallic symbols are always much more awe-inspiring than their real-life counterparts.

All women know this. Most men do too, which is why they have such a huge investment in them in the first place. If Lorena mistook the symbol for the reality and reduced the problems that she had with her husband to the existence of his penis, she was in a de-mented way reinforcing the dominant view of male sexuality that the penis has a life of its own, that men just can't help but being led around by their dicks.

If I was a man I would resent being categorized by this 'wicked willy' view. Yet this idea of the uncontrollability of the male sex urge is one that we hear time and time again. Men just can't help acting on impulse. This time around nor could Mrs Bobbit. And though we have heard a lot lately about how women must take responsibility for their own desires, which of course we must, we have heard far less about how men must do the same thing.

I don't want to reduce men in all their glory to little more than attachments to their penises. I want them to have as much pleasure as possible. But if that pleasure is at the expense of women then it's not their attachment to their actual penises that I want to see removed but their attachment to the power that having a penis may give them. To sever this connection is more complicated than

97

getting out the kitchen knife. So if any of this makes men feel slightly anxious, let me reassure you that it's not your willies we are after. It's your symbolic bollocks that you really need to worry about.

HACKNEYED WORDS FROM PC BASHERS

Can it really be true that the fabric of our nation is being undone not by poverty, unemployment and deprivation but by a mere idea, a half-baked one at that? Apparently yes. The virus of political correctness is out to get all of us. And if it can't get to us, well, then it will get to our children. They will, after endless multicultural school assemblies, no longer be the right-thinking British children we want them to be; they will become mini-ideologues obsessed with chairpersons and the vertically challenged.

Deprived of decent nativity plays and the odd ballet, they could grow up thinking that differences of race or sexuality should not automatically mean disadvantage. My God, what is the world coming to? Let's deprive our children of books, of school buildings, let's put them in overcrowded classrooms, let's give teachers less teaching time and more forms to fill in, let's refuse to teach them modern history, but whatever happens we must never ever deprive them of an outing to see a ballet of *Romeo and Juliet*. Of all the things that the children of Hackney need, suddenly this is what they need most.

The furore surrounding headmistress Jane Brown's decision not to go to the ball has been quite incredible. The remarks she made about *Romeo and Juliet* were stupid, and she has since apologized. This decision, however, like most decisions in education, was not simply based on ideals but on resources. That this story – not in any way a new one – broke in a week when, if anyone noticed, John Patten had to stand down on just about every recommendation he has made, was no coincidence.

Brown has, according to the *Daily Mail*, 'sensationally held on to her job', the sensation being presumably that she had the support of the majority of the governors and parents. Parent-power, which we have been so generously granted by this Government, may now indeed have to be overruled by the Department for Education.

There is some strange double-think going on here. The problem of political correctness, we are always being told, is that it rewrites the rules to suit its own particular ideological agenda, which it then imposes on everyone else. This is largely the work of middle-class public sector professionals. 'Ordinary people', whoever they are, have no interest in such discussions, they just want their kids to learn to read and write. Yet here is a situation where, in the name of opposing the madness of political correctness, not only are the rules being rewritten to suit a particular ideology, but the procedures drawn up by the Government itself are now being thrown into question.

Ordinary people, i.e. the parents of the children in the school concerned, are interested in the discussion, so much so that they sign petitions and turn up in support of Brown and, surprise, surprise, their support turns out to be premised on the fact that, 'in spite' of Brown's championing of equal opportunity practices, she is a good teacher who has turned round an inner-city school.

What a useful thing the bogeyman of political correctness turns out to be. We used to have to make do with loony lefties – long before the reds under the beds. Now we have a case that manages to encapsulate every kind of threat that decent folk live in fear of. But what does it actually mean? And – more to the point – what is its opposite?

It seems to me that 'political correctness' is yet another meaning-less American phrase imported with little regard for the different context in which it finds itself. The context in the US was origin-ally the restructuring of the humanities syllabus at some American universities to include more female and black writers. The intro-duction of Alice Walker alongside Dickens on reading lists hardly represents the end of life as we know it. Yet the idea that the curriculum is not neutral, that it has not just fallen out of the sky, but is the result of a mishmash of largely political and historical decisions, is not to everyone's liking.

Since then, the secret agents of political correctness have been given much more credibility than they could ever have dreamed of. From being a debate about literature or language, PC is now referred to as a movement, presumably with its leaders firmly underground, as we are never given any names. I have heard this movement referred to by people from the left and right alike as a form of Nazism. This is cheap beyond belief. We have real Nazis in our midst; it devalues the power of the word to use it to describe anything we don't like.

You see, I think language matters. I think there is a difference between using the word 'black' and the word 'nigger'. Was it a dose of premature political correctness that people demanded to define themselves with their own words, whether those words were 'black' or 'gay'? Had they all been got at by some sinister bureaucrat with a sneaky political agenda up one sleeve and a mission to deaden our vocabulary up the other? Or did they just feel it was time for a change?

Change, after all, must be what it's all about. And that's why I ask what the opposite of political correctness is. It appears that those so vehemently opposed to the very concept are doing very nicely, thank you; the world may be full of kikes and dykes and whingers of all descriptions who want a piece of the action, but that's tough. The fact, though, that some of them may even be getting it means something has to be done.

As Robert Hughes points out in his book *The Culture of Complaint*, the cultural power of what was once 'the left' is out of all proportion to any real political power. This is why the stakes are so high, why a private comment by a teacher can become headline news.

But don't be fooled again – the opposite of political correctness is not tolerance. Instead, PC is being used to lunge at the heart of anyone who suggests there is something wrong with the status quo. There are many things wrong with the notion of political correctness, chief of which is that it mirrors so precisely the faults of its opposition. Both understand that language is a vehicle for ideology. Both camps seem to believe that language, literature, indeed culture, is a fixed rather than fluid entity, that the substitution of one word, one text, one sentiment for another somehow changes everything. Both are appallingly literal, concentrating on text at the expense of context. Why else, for instance, have we had to endure another spirited defence of Shakespeare, one of the 'dead white males' least in need of resuscitation.

Both camps want to change things from the top down, whether it be the National Curriculum or the terms we use to refer to each other. Both deal in ideals and not practicalities. The rest of us are in the middle and know that our world is not so simple. We know that no one text, whether it be *Romeo and Juliet* or *Neighbours*, is the be all and end all. It's not a question of Alfred the Great versus Martin Luther King (both, incidentally, subjects of my daughter's recent homework – given to her by a Hackney primary school teacher).

I am glad she is learning about both figures. But what I hope she also has available to her is a language that is able to talk about social change. For I fear that none will be left. Liberal, leftie, commie, these words are now insults, or at best anachronisms. We are being made so afraid of being tarred with the all-purpose insult of political correctness that we hardly dare talk about injustice.

This is as insidious as the censorship done in the name of PC. Indeed, it struck me reading J. K. Galbraith's lecture about what a decent society should aim towards, published in the *Guardian* this week, that this was the most politically correct piece of writing I have read for a long time in that it talked about what should be and how it might be achieved.

And if we can no longer talk about how things should be, then the opponents of PC, those very people who purport to represent common sense in the face of lunacy, will have won the day and not only our language but our lives will be truly poorer.

THE PLEASURE IN GORGEOUSNESS

'I don't make political art,' says Barbara Kruger. This may come as a surprise to those familiar with her work. Even those who don't know Kruger's name will probably have seen something she has done. Her trademark style of blown-up, close-cropped photographs emblazoned with bold slogans – 'I shop therefore I am', 'We won't play nature to your culture', 'We don't need any more heroes' – has appeared in galleries, magazines, newspapers and on billboards and book covers. Her art, if you like, is in your face.

If ubiquity is a sure sign of success – and how can it not be – Kruger is extremely successful. Her work is as instantly recognizable as an advert by the Benetton crew, who also know a thing or two about the manipulation of images and words. Manipulation is, of course, a loaded word, implying as it does that there are visual and verbal signs that come to us in a virgin state, untampered in any way. And no one believes that any more. Unless of course they are forced to.

It goes without saying that Barbara Kruger obviously doesn't believe in the transparency of language, the possibility of direct communication and all those other dangerously dated concepts. Well, of course, none of us does. But it makes doing an interview with her rather difficult.

It is not that she is difficult; she is charming enough. But a conversation with her is a slippery encounter, as she consistently refuses any category, term or definition that might be applied to her work. What she forces is not so much a disagreement but a constant shifting of the terms of debate. So, for instance, she doesn't make political art, rather she makes art 'about power, the exercise of power, about how pictures and words construct us'.

She doesn't do agit-prop because 'that term doesn't mean anything anymore; is the evening news agit-prop?' When I ask how she has fun, she immediately counters with: 'I would rather use the word pleasure. I like walking down the street. I like the sun on my face. I live in the present as much as possible. I am not nostalgic about the past.'

When the journal *Flash Art* asked her for a statement about her work and a photograph, she responded by talking about the picture she sent in: 'Although this picture isn't verbal in the literal sense, it speaks none the less. It joins with other received information about "Barbara Kruger" and works to biographize my body, siphoning out the palpability of incremental moments, laughs and touches, leaving an outline, a figure which has a life of its own.' Unsurprisingly, she doesn't want her photograph taken by our photographer.

He may just be trying to do his job but that doesn't appear to fit in with the sophisticated game of peek-a-boo that she is playing. Don't get me wrong. I like some of Barbara Kruger's work. Even 'Barbara Kruger's' work come to that. I like some of her writing reprinted in her new book, *Remote Control: Power, Cultures, and the World of Appearances*, very much indeed. What I can't stomach, I guess, is the geekiness of so much art-world language which vomits out half-chewed-up bits of theory, blissfully unaware of the context of that theory.

Yet the source of Kruger's strength and popularity, the very thing that made her rich and famous, is the immediacy with which she handles both her medium and her message. Having worked for eleven years at Condé Nast on magazines such as *Vogue* and *House and Garden*, she learnt how to grab attention as a picture editor and designer. This understanding of what makes images 'work', what makes them shout, garnered from the commercial world is exactly what she has used in the 'cottage industry' of the art market.

Culling images from all over the place, she blows them up, tinkers with them and covers them with her Krugerisms, an often eerie mix of the banal and the profound, but always in the same typography. So, instead of explaining the images in any way, she either subverts or makes ironic their content, rejecting the terms 'appropriation artist', 'guerrilla semiologist', or 'image-scavenger' that have been applied to her by critics; none the less Kruger, along with artists such as Jenny Holzer, made it big in the eighties.

Though she admonishes me for thinking in decades, her bank statement would surely tell her that her raiding of the image-bank went down rather well at the time. For the last four years she has been making installations. Indeed, that is what she is in London to do. She has been given a room at the Serpentine and has covered the wall and floors with vast slogans: 'Talk like us', 'Look like us', 'Think like us', and 'Do like us'.

Installations may have been given a bad name lately, mostly by Brian Sewell, but I have to say I can't really see what she is doing with installations. They may be an extension of her work in terms of the physical space she is covering, but in many ways they are simply a repetition of what she has been doing for a long time, but on a grander scale.

For her great ability is that, unlike many contemporary artists, her work actually has far more impact in a public space – as a poster or book-jacket – than in a gallery. She is without doubt a commercial artist in the best sense of the word, happily dissolving the dumb distinctions between commercial and fine art.

Indeed, some of her best-known projects over the last few years have been designing posters for the 1989 Pro-choice March in Washington – 'Your Body is a battleground'; a 1992 AIDS poster – 'Girl, don't die for love'; and a billboard in San Francisco aimed at fighting violence against women. This featured a picture of a woman's face up against a wire fence. Against a red background are the words 'Get out'; at the top it says, 'If you are beaten, If you are hurt, If you are scared, If you need help'. At the bottom of the poster is a phone number. Here she uses her visual technique to reinforce the message, the close-cropping of the photograph giving the whole poster a terrifying sense of urgency.

Even if she refuses to say that she makes political art, she will accept that: 'Working on specific projects, on a single issue. Yes, it is different.' Critics may see her techniques as coming from a long line of 'political artists' working with photography and montage such as John Heartfield, but she sees what she does as 'a mutation of my job as a designer. When people start talking about my similarities with Heartfield, I say, excuse me, but I didn't know that he did any work on gender. The similarity is just that we both worked in magazines.'

In an image-saturated culture, Kruger may just be attempting to turn the spectacle back on itself, to give voice to that which is often silenced, but those who don't like her work often complain about the harshness of her aesthetic. There is something fascistic, menacing even, about her style, with its repeated use of personal pronouns: 'You invest in the divinity of the masterpiece', 'Your gaze hits the side of my face', 'Your comfort is my silence', 'I can't look at you and breathe at the same time'. The work is directed at a vague but omnipresent authority – men? patriarchy? art dealers? Yet it speaks itself with the voice of authority. It uses the same techniques of persuasion.

As Kruger writes: 'We loiter outside of trade and speech and are obliged to steal language.' And stolen it she has. But for whom? In one of her clearest statements she has said: 'I see my work as an attempt to ruin certain representations and welcome a female spectator into the audience of men.'

'The thing about personal pronouns,' she offers, 'is that they are free-floating. They cut through the grease, they have a certain velocity.'

Yet while conjuring the great absence at the heart of authority, of control itself, women, whether those who respond to her form of address or indeed those pictured in her work, still often appear to be silenced, passive, threatened. 'You molest from afar', for instance, features a shadowy image of a man. But is it a case of mistaken identity to read her work as little more than social commentary? She may be telling us one thing but what she is actually showing us is another.

She is staging for us the techniques, the poses, the stereotypes that produce our own subjection. As she has written about Andy

Warhol: 'He understood the cool hum of power that resides not in the hot expulsions of verbiage, but in the elegantly mute thrall of sign language.'

Her expertise in sign language though, she insists, has nothing to do with the books she has read. 'I don't read a lot of theory.' This is disingenuous coming from someone who wants to replace 'fun' with 'pleasure'. But like it or not she writes in the kind of whacked, stunned but sassy way that characterizes those who have taken Baudrillard and his gang at face value.

So her project, as much as it surfaces in her writings, is to do away with the 'tired militarism' of binary opposition – public versus private, political versus non-political, commerce versus culture, art versus pop culture, woman artist versus what? – the genius magically free of gender that is our definition of the male artist.

Writing extremely well about taste, she throws up for question words like moral, value, community, standards, at a terrific rate. But I wonder what happens when all those words come down again, as they inevitably do. I wonder for myself as much as her, how all this slithery postmodern refusal to commitment actually pans out for a woman who, it seems, is still committed, who still adheres to some fairly old definitions of what politics is about, such as gender, race, class. And money.

But there are a lot of things that Kruger does not want to get into publicly. Except her work. Political correctness is not something she will talk about. Certainly I think she is at her best when she moves away from the old certainties, the us versus them, of so much of her work – and gets less sure, when the ambiguity is less clever, less knowable. The essay that she wrote on Howard Stern for *Esquire*, 'Prick up your ears', is wonderful because she likes the racist, misogynistic Stern, who repulses her politically and makes her laugh out loud.

Having divided the world up into two types of people, creeps and assholes, she compliments Stern by designating him 'vintage gaping asshole'. She recognizes in Stern the barrenness of the categories that may be tossed off theoretically, but in the flesh turn out to be something else altogether. She likes it when things get complicated, when the rules of the game no longer apply. What she wants is 'More art, more art, more books, more movies, more television, more diplomacy that sparkles with clarity and generosity and intellectual rigour. And gorgeousness.'

Thankfully she didn't explain to me the cultural construction of gorgeousness. And maybe for the first time in the conversation I knew exactly what she meant.

NO LONGER A MAN'S MAN'S MAN'S WORLD

A man's gotta do what a man's gotta do. And what is it that men do exactly? I'm not being facetious, because for a long time we knew exactly what men did. They went to work. They had jobs. They provided for themselves and their families. The majority of men defined themselves and were defined by what they did. But clearly those days have gone. Once again the latest unemployment figures reveal not just that the recovery is 'faltering' but that the structure of work itself is changing.

Unemployment among men is said to be 13.4 per cent, well over double the 5.3 per cent rate for women. There are problems with these figures in that if women are living with men and are on income support they will not show up as officially unemployed. None the less, everyone agrees that there is a decline in the number of full-time jobs for men and an increase in the number of part-time jobs for women. Most new jobs are going to women.

Such shifts are about more than just figures; they have repercussions for how society at large organizes itself. But so far it seems we are loath to talk about what these changes might mean. The discussion is polarized between those on the left who invoke the mantra of 'full employment' as the only goal worth pursuing, and managers who talk about the need for the work-force to be increasingly flexible in order to be competitive.

Flexibility in human terms means more part-time workers with fewer rights, more short-term contracts with no long-term security, more people having to leave their families to work away, more retraining, more people willing to see themselves as having three or four careers rather than a job for life.

Indeed, the idea of a job for life now seems as quaintly historical as the picture that appeared this week of the Durham Miners' Gala whose very future is in question. This once huge pageant of working-class solidarity which, in its hey-day, used to attract up to a quarter of a million people, is having its funding withdrawn by the National Union of Mineworkers. There are no working mines in the region anymore. How can there be a miners' gala when there are no jobs in the mines?

And with the closure of the mines, the heroic images that the pageant produced – the magnificent banners, the colliery bands, the lined faces of solid, hard-working men, the very feel of marching with tens of thousands of people who share a way of life, will be consigned to the history books. To say that these images were essentially images of a particular kind of masculinity is not in any way to denounce them, but it does make me think there is a need for new kinds of images of work that tell it how it is now rather than how it used to be.

For every time we speak about work we do so in the language of gender, albeit in a coded way. A post-Fordist economy automatically means a shift from the old manufacturing industries which we define as hard and male to the newer, softer and more feminine service industries. Employers themselves speak this language, too. As Paul Convery of the Unemployment Unit says: 'There is a growing perception among employers that women find it easier to adjust to new methods, that they are happier with multi-skilling and with an undemarcated structure. Maybe they are more culturally accustomed to juggling tasks.' Men coming from the heavy industries are more used to doing one task at a time within a much more demarcated structure.

If you pick up any of the books by the business gurus they also talk about the 'feminization' of management skills. Gone are the strict hierarchies and specialisms. Now the code word is organic. Networks and webs are where it's at. Lateral rather than vertical organization is the key to efficiency. It is peculiar how much psychobabble has crossed over into the world of work. The other day on the train I heard two people having a conversation that could have been had by two women in a consciousness-raising group in the seventies. 'Success is not a destination, it's a journey,' said one to the other in all seriousness. They happened to be two young guys, sales reps talking business – but talking business through a language of emotion rather than of targets and goals. I'm sure they will go far.

Perhaps we should question why certain approaches are defined as masculine and others as feminine. Neither of them are really suitable to describe what is actually happening, but at a more basic level the loss of identity experienced by unemployed men alerts us to just how tied to these definitions we remain. What we see of the effects of unemployment for men – particularly no hope of long-term employment for young men – surely signals the need to create masculine identities not totally based on the workplace. We have yet to see such identities created. Instead, we are still numbed by the anaesthesia of nostalgia every time we see a picture of a grimy miner from 'the reservoir of men's men'. In his fascinating book *Male Impersonators*, Mark Simpson writes of 1992's pit closures: 'Unasked, the miners have been assigned the burden of representing authenticity in an inauthentic Britain . . . Their labour – hard, masculine and productive – is an antidote to failed, frivolous and "feminine" service industries.' As the title of his book might suggest, Simpson doesn't see masculinity as innate but rather as something that men perform. This way of thinking is surely more productive given the current situation. As long as authentic masculinity depends on labour then we will carry on condemning 10 per cent of our young men to feeling not quite real. Yet it appears that many men will continue to feel uncomfortable because the old model of work depended on a kind of gender complementarity – men do one thing, women do another; men get their power at work, women within the family. So what is to happen when women do a bit of everything? What place does that leave for men?

No wonder this is causing resentment – dressed up in the new victim culture that some men have embraced. Given the poor conditions and low pay that most female part-time workers have, it is a sign of the times that they are still envied, while men feel themselves to be 'the disposable sex'. This is taken to the limit in Warren Farrell's book *The Myth of Male Power*, where he describes the emergence of 'the multi-option woman and no-option man'. By this he means that women have a choice of work, whether they combine it with mothering or not, whereas men are obliged to make money, so have no options. There may be some truth in this although the myth is actually that women choose to work to amuse themselves. They do so largely because a family cannot be raised on a single income or they are the sole breadwinner.

None the less, if the labour market is readjusting itself so that women are perceived as both being a better bet and as having more choice, then the discussion will have to be not just one of rights and conditions but of rehabilitating all these lost boys. It doesn't help that at the top of the tree we see Diana, who like many women continues to make herself busy, while Charles just doesn't know what to do with himself. At least he doesn't have to sign on.

SLOTH ABOUT THE HOUSE

I am intrigued by the prospect of a 'Newish Man'. It is not a phrase I had heard until last week. I know full well that New Man is old hat and long ago disappeared into the mists of media myth from whence he came. I know too that New Lad was but a trendspotters' flash in the pan. But Newish Man? The term has been invented by experts at Mintel 'to capture the one-fifth minority of Britain's male population who are only just beginning to see the sexual egalitarian light'. This turns out to be a guy who doesn't share equally the household tasks but takes responsibility for just one job around the house.

Well, big deal. Newish man, puny offspring of the peculiar liaison between fantasy New Man and clapped-out Oldish Man – is this vague entity really what we have to settle for? Apparently, yes. Unless of course we divorce him. Mintel researcher Angela Hughes is quoted as saying: 'This total selfishness is often what prompts women to divorce.' Half of married men were happy to admit they are 'sloths' who have far more leisure time on their hands than their wives.

Given the choice between a Newish Man, a sloth and a selfish pig, it's really no wonder that home is where the heartache is. Or that one of the biggest factors in women saying no to sex with their partners is their tiredness. It takes a lot of energy to work part-time and go home and service a sloth, yet increasingly this is how women are expected to live.

If I sound impatient, it's because I am. It's one thing to read that attitudes 'to the roles of the sexes are too deeply ingrained to be rewritten in a single generation'. It's another to watch sensible women vacuuming under their boyfriends' feet as they sit pretending not to notice what is going on.

If work patterns, as I wrote last week, are changing to demand a more flexible approach to work, then clearly this flexibility also has to be transferred to the home. Reports this week have been full of how men are facing an age of insecurity, how uncertain and vulnerable they are. A quarter of them are living on their own, due mainly to marriage breakdown. The word 'bachelor' has bounded back into our vocabulary – though I have never heard anyone use the word except as code for being gay.

'This Newish Man deserves some sympathy,' we have been told. What a hard time men are having of late, the poor, confused things. No longer assured as breadwinners, weekend fathers, unsure as to what demands women are making on them, these bachelor boys are now reduced to having to look after themselves. Can you believe it – grown men having to work microwaves?

As you can tell, my sympathy is limited. If you look at the statistics, we are all having a hard time, but it is still women who are doing the double shift of working both inside and outside the home. The issue does not seem to me to be one of men's inability to shake off social conditioning, but men's refusal to give up a good deal. This is about power. And those who have someone to shop and cook and clean for them will always have more power than those who don't.

Female disgruntlement at this situation reflects their powerlessness as, more often than not, it is only manifested through individual 'nagging'. There is no pressure group powered by exhausted women with dusters, no lobbying of MPs on the issue; indeed, it is hard to imagine a less 'sexy' topic in media terms. And this is because, as was pointed out a long, long time ago, housework is largely perceived as a private issue. Something that takes place between mutually consenting or, as it turns out, not so consenting adults. Campaigns such as Wages For Housework were formed to make the point that domestic labour is a form of unpaid work. There were long and tedious debates among feminists in the seventies about how domestic labour oiled the wheels of capitalist exploitation. But we still carried on doing the dishes.

During the eighties, while you could get thousands of women to sit in the mud at Greenham Common or march on the streets in protest at the sale of pornography in newsagents, housework remained something to be swept under the carpet. Yet I would bet that if you gave most women a choice about what on a daily basis would most affect the quality of their lives – the banning of porn or the men in their lives taking more responsibility for the domestic routine – they would plump for the latter.

Apart from the inestimable time 'nagging' must take up, the average woman has fifteen hours a week fewer than her partner because she is busy with 'essential activities'. Hardly fair. However, the survey also shows what odd ideas we have about men in that we think it's strange if they have to live alone and look after themselves.

Some of this, of course, is not men's fault at all. In the past, women have had an enormous amount invested in maintaining the mystique of housework: after all, if they were being kept to do it, they had to make out it involved some mysterious skill. Indeed, it wasn't until I left home that I realized there was nothing particularly intellectually taxing about washing up, going to the launderette or even cooking. The dull truth dawned: it wasn't hard to do but it was very hard to keep doing it over and over again.

But just as women gained a scrap of self-respect from knowing how to be very good at doing these boring jobs, so men have gained an enormous amount of freedom from either never learning how to do them, not noticing that they need to be done in the first place or, the old favourite, doing them so badly that they are never asked again.

I remember once, when interviewing Paula Yates, she told me that after ten years of living with Saint Bob, he asked her if they had a washing machine. This charming anecdote may relegate him to the sub-sloth category but even Bob must have realized, the times they are a'changing. His kind must eventually go the way of Nanette Newman who is to be replaced in the Fairy Liquid ads by what we can only presume will be a specimen of Newish Man.

For Newish Man apparently believes in women's 'right to work' (gee, thanks); some are even 'happy cookers', preferring to entertain rather than do the everyday cooking. Some can even iron their own shirts. All this in a week in which this very paper asked 'Are Men the Real Victims?' Victims, maybe, but still victims on to a pretty good thing, if you ask me.

Somehow I suspect the results of this latest survey will be quickly forgotten. Instead we will have to put up with more guff about how difficult it is for men to change and more speculation as to What Women Really Want, as though we haven't been telling everyone for years. The answer to the question 'What Do Women Want?' strikes me as neither abstract nor mystical. It is, as my friend Deborah says 'Six hours of cunnilingus a week and someone who wipes down the worktops after washing up. I want someone who can do both jobs properly.' Now surely even Newish Man can get his head round this one.

FREEDOM OF A CLOSED ROAD

It is hard to use the word freedom today without lapsing into banality. Freedom is what we are promised if we purchase the right car or use the right kind of sanitary towel. Freedom is what we shall have if we punish criminals more heavily and let our hospitals, schools and prisons be run by an interchangeable set of bureaucrats. Freedom is efficiency. Freedom is value for money. Freedom is the right to choose one John over another. Freedom is the right to buy.

Beyond this, the idea of freedom gets embarrassing – personal even. One man's freedom is another woman's slow death. When John Major evokes imagery of warm beer and amateur cricket matches to stir the heart of the freeborn Englishman, mine sinks. Is that all there is? But never mind, if people want to gather together in pubs or in fields to drink warm beer then I have no interest in stopping them. They must surely be guaranteed the freedom to indulge this particular lifestyle, if that is what they so desire. Their vehicles should not be seized on the way to the cricket match, nor should police computers be used to monitor their movements.

Imagine, though, that the clan of warm beer drinkers were twenty years younger and that their preferred leisure activity was also to gather in fields and deserted spaces. Not to watch men in white jumpers playing with bats and balls, but to dance or just simply to listen to music or to be together. Imagine another lifestyle.

For that is what freedom might mean, isn't it? Quite simply, the lifestyle of one's choice. Yet the news that the police are aiming to 'log about 8,000 travellers on computers with details of their vehicles, nicknames and associates' is a sure indication that certain lifestyles are not to be tolerated. Liberty, the organization for civil liberties, is concerned that the police are seeking to implement many of the public order provisions of the Criminal Justice Bill before they have been properly debated in Parliament. The rest of us might wonder more pragmatically if this is the correct use of police resources. Do we really want the police to spend an enormous amount of time and money stopping raves, gatherings and free festivals?

The wider issue, however, is what Liberty refers to as 'the criminalization of diversity', in that the bill's proposals will make that way of life of gypsies, New Age travellers and even those attending raves at weekends not only difficult but actually illegal. Clause 45 of the bill, for instance, would give the police power to break up a gathering where there are more than six vehicles. They would also be able to end outdoor festivals, seize vehicles and sound equipment, to stop people they 'reasonably believe' may be going to the event and direct them not to do so. Other proposals would make squatting virtually impossible.

We have seen this coming for some time, of course. The demonization of New Age travellers over the last few years has produced some ugly confrontations between police and travellers. But, while the number of hardcore travellers remains quite small, the number of people attending raves is much larger and the rave scene itself is under attack. The policy of the Surrey constabulary that 'raves will not happen, illegal or otherwise' is extraordinary. Substitute the word 'party' for 'rave' and you can see what I mean.

What is it about these raves and gatherings that is so threatening? Is it that they are organized by young people, is it that they might be enjoying themselves or is it, as increasingly seems to be the case, that any large gathering of people is in itself suspect? Nowadays a crowd itself is regarded as dangerous, as something that has to be broken up by the police. What matters is the sheer number of people involved. The fear is that of the mob out of control. Remember Heysel?

Or is it the lifestyle itself that must be stamped out? While the police and some sections of the press lump together New Age travellers, ravers, inner-city squatters and gypsies, this is not a movement in any recognizable sense. If anything, it is characterized by its rejection of politics as it is commonly understood, though by criminalizing these various lifestyles such subcultures are automatically politicized. Yet everyone knows that there is a world of difference between someone who has taken to the road and someone who works all week and enjoys going to raves at weekends.

Quite what this continual harassment is supposed to achieve is debatable. By continually stopping and searching travellers, do we really expect they will see the light, give up their dogs on string and return to the fold of 'sensible' society. If their alienation forced them out of society, their further alienation is hardly going to force them back in. Yet, whenever given the chance to be heard, what many of these people articulate, albeit in a rather vague manner, is not so different from what many of us feel anyway. The strange alliances we have seen lately over proposed motorway developments at Twyford Down and Wanstonia have seen resolutely middle-class protesters fighting alongside dreadlocked eco-warriors. While one group might have been concerned only with saving their 'Darling Bud' countryside and the other with saving the entire planet, there is at least some crossover.

Throughout the eighties the commodification of rave culture into clubs was heralded as a thoroughly Thatcherite enterprise, fuelled by feisty young entrepreneurs. That this itself should now be outlawed suggests establishment paranoia, to say the least. For the issue goes beyond that of personal whim. You may have no desire to take to the road, you may be appalled at the idea of a rave, although your children probably won't be, but do you honestly think therefore that no one else has a right to these activities? In a free country is it legitimate that the police can turn you back if they suspect you might be on the way to one of these events? There was an outcry during the miners' strike when the police used their powers to stop people on the way to pickets and demonstrations, when they made whole counties no-go areas. And so there should be, because the implications of this bill mean that any largish gathering of people for whatever purpose is now suspect.

As Martin Kettle pointed out in his recent essay on democracy in *Guardian* Weekend ('The Big Lie'): 'Polls show that the British place freedom easily at the top of the list of institutions and characteristics that they most value – far above the royal family, for example.' Kettle also talked about the reinvention of democracy – no small measure, but an interesting one at a time when such discussion is focused more and more on the rights of individuals to pursue the lifestyle of their choice whether they are gay, New Age travellers or just trying to have a good time. For the notion of a good time is at risk if leisure pursuits are now the subject of proposed legislation.

It is not possible to invest so much in the idea of freedom if we are not prepared to live with what freedom means in practice. It means, as it always has in this country, that there are groups of people who reject the dominant lifestyle and strive, however messily, to find some alternatives. Shouldn't we be proud of this tradition instead of trying to police it out of existence?

DEATH AND THE MAIDENS

'We are in the House of Horror.' We used to chant this as kids when we played a game we called levitation. One of us would lie on the floor like a corpse as we repeated after one another: 'She looks pale. She is pale. She looks dead. She is dead' before trying to raise the body. A childish fascination with death – well, it's normal, isn't it? Something you grow out of when you come to realize that death is serious, very serious indeed.

Reading about our very own 'house of horror' this week, though, I wondered how grown-up we really are about death. The bodies found at 25 Cromwell Street and the arrest of Fred West have given us another mass murderer to salivate over. As bodies have been found almost daily, the 'gore-score' has grown. Maybe there is even a record involved. If the body count should rise to twenty, 'that would surpass the worst multiple murder cases – those of Dennis Nilsen, who confessed to fifteen victims in 1983, and Hungerford gunman Michael Ryan, who shot dead sixteen in 1987' wrote the *Daily Mail* excitedly.

We – that is, you and I – would not spend our days hanging around outside number 25 in the hope of glimpsing . . . what? An actual decaying corpse? A murder weapon? No, we are not like the ghouls who bring their toddlers in pushchairs to show them 'what wickedness is', as one tired mother explained on the news. No, we are not like that at all. Instead we study with appalled fascination the details of the house itself.

So what does wickedness look like? It looks very much like the grim-faced policemen carrying out boxes of human remains draped in black. The truth is that there is not much to see really. Death remains invisible, as ever. So we focus on the plans of the house itself, as if a building can yield up its secrets if we stare at it hard enough. Can we locate the heart of darkness somewhere between the fitted kitchen and the four-poster bed? As with Dennis Nilsen and John Christie, who also kept the bodies in their houses and gardens, we wonder how it would be to live in a house with dead bodies everywhere.

We wonder, too, how this could happen in Middle England, how the neighbours didn't know, how he simply got away with it for so long. Emerging day by day in this case is not the England of neighbourliness and family ties but a place of dislocated people and fractured families, of lives lived and lost and never missed at all, of wives, sisters, daughters who have somehow just disappeared, of the disposability of a whole section of society. We have come to expect this in the wastelands of America, where serial killers are born and bred to achieve their life's ambition and become the subject of a TV special, but here? No.

Yet we are catching up. According to John Stalker, alongside America 'we are cornering the market in this crime. Serial killing – from John Christie forty years ago to gays' murderer Colin Ireland last year – is the new British crime speciality. We are in danger of leading the world.'

Not every sick individual captures the public imagination in the way Fred West has done, however. As Stalker asks: 'Who now remembers Kenneth Erskine, who murdered seven elderly women in London less than eight years ago?'

Instead, it is the lads who get away with it for so long – Nilsen and Peter Sutcliffe and now West – who assume an almost heroic status and who now come presented to us as existential loners, supreme individualists, what Joyce Carol Oates has described as the 'eerily glorified Noble Savage'. They have acted out the alienation that late twentieth century life produces through taking the lives of others.

These men, whose names are etched on to our consciousness, have been to the edge and never come back; they have transcended the scumminess of their sad little lives by the one act that will mark them out for ever. They have felt the power of choosing who shall live and who shall die, 'playing God in their lives', as Edmund Kemper the American 'co-ed killer' put it. Sutcliffe claimed he was 'just cleaning the place up a bit'; Henry Lee Lucas was 'death on women. I didn't feel they needed to exist.'

And while we know what these men said, we don't even remember the names of their victims. There are simply the rows of old photographs of fresh-faced girls and middle-aged women who are now dead. Or worse, perhaps, photos of women who are missing and have never been found.

As American poet and novelist Ntozake Shange has observed, such women 'died for their country'. Yet this is no monument to them, for already the most disturbing aspect of this case – that West appears to be just another man who thought women were disposable – is being underplayed in the knockabout reporting of the story, the black humour we must use to diffuse what disturbs us. There is a sneaking admiration for the man who got away with it for so long, who gave the phrase DIY sinister undertones.

Although we know from history that even mass murderers are 'somebody's husband, somebody's son', we are still surprised to find that this is actually the case. And already on the scene is a different kind of ghoul from the one that loiters outside the house of horror. Here comes Colin Wilson with another look 'inside the brain of a serial killer' and doubtless Brian Masters will be wheeled in to tell us, probably, that West had low self-esteem and came from an impoverished background. An expert with a huge database will give us yet another psychological profile, with details about his inability to form meaningful relationships and the probable death of a grandparent. We will focus on the minds of these warped individuals as though these men themselves can explain away their crimes to us.

Sometimes they almost can. Nilsen, for instance, is incredibly articulate. What he did made some sort of sense. He wanted his lovers to stay with him. So he made sure they did. He was an 'incurable romantic'. Does that explain it to you? Does that make it all right?

Many of the notorious American serial killers are so skilled in explaining their crimes that they will regurgitate tales about their domineering mothers at the drop of a hat. Women figure as tormentors or as unavailable objects who must later pay the price for making them feel impotent. It remains primarily women against whom these holy wars are launched. Or homosexual men. It is heterosexual men who have the least to fear.

In this latest case, it appears that some of the women murdered may have been the most disposable of all. Prostitutes. Sir Michael Havers, when prosecuting Peter Sutcliffe, remarked that the real tragedy of the case was that some of his victims were *not* prostitutes. This is but one of the reasons why we need an explanation that goes beyond individual psychology and looks at what messages the culture is sending out.

When the body count is finally settled and the beastly builder comes to trial, we will be flooded with scientific, psychological and religious perspectives on this case. The vicarious identification with which some sections of the population have lapped up each grisly detail will go unquestioned. It will be easier to turn West into another monster, different from other men, than to ask how he might be the same as them. As philosopher Sylvère Lotringer says: 'Our society desperately needs monsters to reclaim its own moral virginity.' The tragedy is that we continue to create the most ordinary monsters of all.

LIES, DAMNED LIES AND MEMORIES

I don't know whether it's false memory syndrome but I'm having a job sorting out the good guys from the bad. A headline in the *Sunday Times* about the death of Richard Nixon said: 'America unites in grief for statesman now seen as great'. But somewhere in my consciousness is a memory of a bad man doing bad things. I was fifteen or so at the time, not much interested in history, but I watched a lot of television and there he was, all hamster-faced and lying through his teeth. Or, as John Updike tells it in his novel *Memories of the Ford Administration*: 'This was, of course, August. Nixon, with his bulgy face and menacing slipped-cog manner, seemed about to cry. The children and I had never seen a President resign before: nobody in the history of the United States had ever seen that.'

He had tarnished the presidency, he had tarnished the political process. This man who once said 'Let us begin by committing ourselves to the truth' did not even see that truth mattered any more. In those days, such things were left to journalists. Nixon, who hadn't gone down so well on TV at the beginning because he couldn't stop sweating in front of the cameras, was one of the first politicians to bring in the image-makers, the back-room boys who make a fortune out of making the unacceptable slightly more palatable. And he has won after all: in death, his image has finally been remade once and for all.

The Queen and John Major rushed to send messages. Yeltsin declared him 'one of the great politicians'. Clinton announced a day of national mourning. Watergate, his involvement in the 1973 coup to overthrow Allende in Chile, not to mention small matters like his responsibility for the devastation of Cambodia, now become simply blips in this elder statesman's career. His presidency has been repeatedly described as 'flawed' rather than corrupt, which begs the question of how flawed someone actually has to be before they are denounced.

We keep on hearing the phrase 'the rewriting of history' and, as Martin Walker reminded us this week, no one was more interested in this than Nixon himself, who spent the last twenty years beavering away towards 'this final vindication'. It takes more than one man to rewrite history, though: it takes the rest of us too. It involves the suppression of all kinds of memories, a *laissez-faire* approach to fact and a decision just to go with the flow.

As history speeds by this week in South Africa, another man is also vindicated. Nelson Mandela also emerges as a good guy. Well, we knew that all along, didn't we? OK, there were some other blips in this story: twenty-seven years in jail, the massive investment in South Africa by this country, our dogged refusal to exercise sanctions, Margaret Thatcher's view of Mandela as a typical terrorist. But what the heck, we were all united in the struggle against apartheid, weren't we?

By the self-congratulatory tone of some of the recent media coverage, it is easy enough to believe this is the case. After all, that Jerry Dammers song 'Free Nelson Mandela', now that was a good record, wasn't it? You could dance to that one. It was a shame that when Mandela finally appeared on stage at Wembley, smiling that floodlight smile of his, some of the audience thought he was there as the lead singer in some groovy African band of world musicians.

We were all vaguely anti-apartheid. Some of us even bothered to go on demonstrations and avoid Cape oranges. Some of us, anyway. The others, the ones who voted for a government that deliberately slowed down the coming of democracy to South Africa, the ones who carried on selling arms, the ones who propped up the evil of apartheid while talking publicly about the inevitability of change – where are they this week?

Now, perhaps, they, too, are in the same historical laboratory, retouching and reshaping the past to show that they were on the right side all along. For what they said could never happen in their lifetimes is happening before their eyes as old, sick Africans are carried to the ballot box to make their small but indelible marks on history. Of course we should be celebrating but to pretend that all of us were in this thing together is an insult to those who gave their lives or years of their lives for this long, slow struggle.

Even those who endorsed Francis Fukuyama's complacent thesis that we have now reached 'the end of history' must feel some kind of jolt. The same kind of jolt that I got in the midst of reading all the respectful obituaries of Tricky Dickie when I came across Tariq Ali's remark that he still regarded Nixon as 'a war criminal'.

For history now comes in several versions. There is no longer official history versus popular memory but the whole new layer manufactured and inserted by the media. The nearest most of us will ever get to a gut feeling about democracy comes from watching the elections in South Africa on our TV screens. The actuality of trooping down to the local school to vote for one councillor or another pales in comparison. Which feels more real?

Perhaps, then, it is churlish to worry about the revision of history that we are currently witnessing. Instead, we should merely be grateful that things are happening at all. Jean Baudrillard in *The Transparency of Evil* jauntily proposes not just the end of history but 'its systematic reversal and elimination. We are in the process of wiping out the whole of the twentieth century. We are wiping out the signs of the Cold War one by one, perhaps even the signs of world war two and those of all the century's political and ideological revolutions.'

This smoothing out of the past, he argues, will give us a clean slate with which to start the new millennium. We are truly beyond good and evil. So to ask whether Nixon was good or bad appears embarrassing. To wonder, as apartheid dies, how it was sustained for so long seems inappropriate. To erase the past we must accept that we are suffering from collective false memory syndrome. But however hard I try, I can neither forgive nor forget because I can still remember. Please, someone tell me that I haven't made it all up.

I-WAY? I'D RATHER DO IT MY WAY

Emma Goldman once said: 'If I can't dance then I don't want to be part of your revolution.' I guess I feel much the same about the revolution that is before me . . . You know, all this computer business, life on the Net, shmoozing and cruising on the information super-highway. But I know who Emma Goldman was and my swanky new computer doesn't. It doesn't recognize the words Emma Goldman and suggests that I replace them with the words Me Goddamn. Now I don't know what Me Goddamn would have made of 'the I-way' but I know that I'm having a few problems with it.

My own personal software, that squidgy, raddled part that I laughingly refer to as my brain, may be severely lacking in the megabyte department but, hey, I'm trying to process all this exciting information just like the rest of us.

I wish I was as cool as Kevin Kelly of *Wired* magazine, which talks in hallucinogenic detail about the culture of the I-way. He doesn't just describe the future. He has taken up permanent residence there. I wish that I could say as casually as he does: 'I live on the Internet, and I hang out with Silicon Valley Visionaries'.

But unfortunately I live in a house and hang out with people whose idea of mastering technology is being able to programme the video. The nearest we get to cyberspace is moaning about how a cash machine has chewed up our credit card. For one way of under-standing the concept of cyberspace is apparently that this is the place where your money exists. Or, as is so often the case, doesn't exist at all. We live in hope of virtual sex or, on bad days, Luddites that we are, would even make do with the real thing.

I must admit therefore to being something of an old-fashioned girl at heart because, however hard I try, I just can't kick the reality habit. There is still a huge gap between the reality of information technology and the glorious visions that are being conjured up.

This is the gap we actually inhabit. As wonderful as the free flow of ideas that are exchanged on the Net every minute of the day might be, we still don't have the centralized networks necessary for an efficient screening for breast cancer. The police may be able to use their technology to monitor the movements of a few New Age travellers but never to catch serial murderers. And yet it seems that any Tom, Dick or Hacker can find out my credit rating just like that.

Obviously the technology is still in its infancy but, in the white heat that it is generating, surely it's worth remembering that much of what has promised to revolutionize our lives ends up changing them only ever so slightly and then only in fairly mundane ways. Do you remember the video revolution? Power was to be removed from the centralized media. Everyone would be able to create their own films. The whole process of television would be totally de-mystified. This has happened but only to a small extent. We wanted the revolution. We ended up with Jeremy Beadle. We've been framed alright.

The Utopian promise of the I-way is equally strong. On the Net no one knows who you are. No one can hear you scream. You can be whoever it is that you want to be. The old differences of class, race, gender can be digitally remastered. That doesn't mean that they cease to exist. If so, how come that so many of the female users of the Net are actually men who prefer for their own reasons to borrow a feminine identity for their onscreen communication?

And while the democratic potential of the Net is thrilling stuff – no one controls the Internet, no one is actually in charge – the old problems of access still have to be addressed. I may be able to talk to a farmer in Buenos Aires about crop yield but I still can't talk to my mother if she doesn't have a PC or know how to use one.

Maybe I should just chill out and go with the flow and accept, as Kelly says, that while thought shapes technology, technology also shapes thought. But, strangely enough, I want to know what those thoughts are rather than just reading another blurb for these new industries. Knowledge may well be power. But knowledge is not the same as information and we should not confuse the two things. What we are seeing is an information explosion, but you can have all the information in the world and be totally powerless unless you have the ability to analyse and interpret this mass of data.

Likewise we should not confuse the word communication with community. The imagined community of the Net is as real as the imagined community of print readers.

The enormous amount of help, of practical problem-solving as well as improvised theoretical winging that takes place, is inspiring. On one level, we must recognize that the notion of community is less and less dependent on locality. On another, however, while we may be thinking global, we still have to act – to participate, if you like – in the local.

I-way thought at its best may be cooperative and non-linear. At its worst, though, it is hard to avoid thinking of it as anything but a souped community of trainspotters, of tinier and tinier interest groups who speak to each other but no one else. Fragmentation may be a condition of living at the end of the twentieth century but fragmentation works both ways.

The workings of the Net may inevitably question the authority of the text, and indeed the individuality of the author, and make it possible for some fantastic interdisciplinary discoveries that no one person can lay claim to. But this kind of fragmentation does not, in itself, do away with the authority of multinational capital.

It isn't that no one owns anything anymore, it is rather, as we have seen with the case of George Michael, that the person who creates something no longer automatically owns it themselves. George Michael may not own his own songs but it doesn't mean that the rest of us do. Sony owns them. Ownership has not stopped, it has simply become more complicated.

However much we want to celebrate our fragmentation, which still feels remarkably close to psychosis half the time, what we are actually witnessing in the communication and media industries is a greater centralization of power than ever before. We have the illusion of choice – there are more and more things to know, more and more people to exchange ideas with, more and more things to buy – and yet we exert choice over smaller and smaller areas of our lives.

We can communicate twenty-four hours a day on our mobile phones, fax each other senseless if we so desire, but let's not mistake the speed with which we can communicate with communication itself.

Of course it matters how we say something, but more and more it also matters what we end up saying. Often that urgent fax or that crackly call from a mobile says nothing more than: 'I've got one of the machines so I want you to know I've got one.' The medium may be the message but the message is increasingly the mediocre: I fax therefore I am.

I want to believe, I really do. The anarchy of the Net is too good to refuse but my own limited understanding of this new technology tells me that sometimes it's not all that it's cracked up to be. If, for example, I took any notice of the tools that my PC is equipped to write with, you wouldn't be reading this column.

It is not particularly interested in fragmentation. It could rival John Patten for trying to instil a bit of grammar into the proceedings. Nor, for a thoroughly modern device, does it have much of a sense of irony. It suggests that the quote from Kevin Kelly should be rewritten as it is not a complete sentence. It refuses to recognize the word 'Internet', replacing it, rather sinisterly I feel, with the word 'Internment'.

I asked it why but it wouldn't tell me. Maybe it knows something that I don't. Maybe it really is connected to something that I don't know about.

Or maybe too much time onscreen is making me paranoid. Either way it's time to switch the bloody thing off and get interactive. And I don't mean with a machine.

A FEW JEWELS SHORT OF A CROWN

You might think he has suffered too much indignity already. Isn't it enough to know that the man who would be king would actually rather be a tampon? But no, we must all suffer alongside him. Two and a half hours of televised tedium and we are still no nearer knowing what Prince Charles is for. What was this programme for? A party political broadcast on behalf of the republican cause is fine by me, I just wish it were a little more exciting.

As Charles rambles around doing the job we are continually told no one else could do because they haven't been prepared for it, I come over all Yosser Hughes, 'Gissa job. I could do that. I could.' I could meet the public if it consists of nothing more than conversations like: 'How old are you now?' 'Twenty-five.' 'Are you really, jolly good.' I could sip exotic aphrodisiacs in a tent in Dubai. I could, honest. At a push, I could produce the odd watercolour and stalk a deer. I could have more of a sense of belonging to this beautiful land, especially if most of it belonged to me personally.

But life isn't fair. I will never be the monarch and Charles will never be on the dole and anyway, or so people say, you have to feel sorry for him. This is the worst argument for retaining a monarchy I have ever heard. The idea that we retain hereditary privilege as a job creation scheme for these sad individuals is preposterous. In a country in which it is now debatable whether we fund hospitals, we are expected to fund a monarchy out of nothing more than sympathy.

This, surely, rather than when exactly he canoodled with Camilla, is what we should be worrying about. Instead, we are expected to concern ourselves with this man's confused musings on the meaning of life. He admits it is difficult to know how to play the media. Yet surely, if he is born to inherit anything at all, it might be an inkling of media savvy. While we read that Diana is negotiating an interview with Princess Oprah herself, Charles gets plodding old Jonathan Dimbleby. Still, like I said, life just isn't fair.

His royal highness has clearly not been the beneficiary of even the most rudimentary advice on TV. Look at the camera or even the person you are speaking to. Try not to fidget all the time. Try to answer the question in short, sharp sentences. This is what you or I would be told if we ventured in front of a camera for even thirty seconds. Instead we have a hand-wringing, ear-tugging, thoroughly bewildered man who, however hard he tries, just doesn't seem to get it.

The impression is one of a man whose sum is less than the total of the parts he seeks to play. One minute he is an old hippie into the great chain of being, the next he is some kind of international arms dealer. There is the prince concerned about releasing the latent talents of dispossessed youth, then he suggests, in all seriousness, that Britain should use its armed forces as mercenaries. But then anyone who thinks he can help unemployed youth by inflicting Phil Collins on them is a few jewels short of a crown.

He is interested, he says, in floating ideas for discussion, but how do all these strange notions that float in and out of his head fit together? For someone who professes an interest in a more holistic approach, the unhappy truth is that his philosophical meanderings are simply incoherent. They do not make sense any more than his role in contemporary Britain makes sense.

As this documentary showed us, much of what he has to do is boring. But no more or less boring than many of the jobs at which his subjects work. He keeps going by maintaining a belief in sacred duty and by apparently entering 'another dimension' when painting pictures of castles. I don't begrudge him that. Yet if you unpick all these musings about spirit and duty, what sustains him and indeed the whole institution is the belief that he is better than the rest of us. How do we know he is better? Because he has the divine right to be? Because that's his job? If this is the case, how come, the whole way through this embarrassing programme, I kept thinking of people who could do it better?

If his job is to be a roving ambassador, to amuse the natives, to conquer the world with reticent English charm, then why isn't Michael Palin king? He is not king because he was born at the wrong time in the wrong place. Charles will be king, even though he appears to have been born at the wrong time if not the wrong place. He is not in favour of a bicycling royal family on Scandinavian lines on the grounds of tastelessness. What, pray, is more tasteless than setting up photo opportunities with your own children as part of a PR campaign?

The function of the monarchy looks increasingly tasteless from all sides. The repeated pleas for privacy, while understandable, are implicitly protests against the kind of accountability that more and more people are demanding. What most of us do behind closed doors is of no interest to anyone; what Charles does is of interest primarily because we pay for it. While he professes deep concern for what is wrong with this country, as part of the monarchy he remains a symbol of it.

The political arguments about the constitution are overshadowed by his personal failings. The question is not whether an adulterer can be head of the Church of England or whether a divorced man should be king, but whether anyone at all should be king. After the long haul of *Charles: The Private Man, The Public Role*, one senses that the time has come to put him out of his misery. And if he can't do it himself, then it's up to the rest of us to do it for him.

ANGST AND ANGER IN MIDDLE ENGLAND

Your children watch too much television. You cannot breathe in this heat. You think they should do something about pollution. You think they are building too many roads. You worry that you will not be able to find a parking space. You have negative equity. You are working on a short-term contract that you hope will be renewed. Your house has been burgled and your car radio stolen three times. Someone was mugged on the street where you live. You have ants in the kitchen and rats in the basement, you had to wait three hours just to see your GP. And then she was half your age. She asked you if you felt reassured by Tony Blair.

When you answered 'Yes', she diagnosed you as suffering from nothing more than middle-class *angst* and sent you on your way. No wonder the health service is in decline.

Don't despair, though, for someone still wants you. They really want to help, to soothe those troublesome feelings, to massage away those everyday aches and pains, to offer you a Radox bath of policies that might relieve the stress. For Tony Blair and Kenneth Clarke are anxious to address the anxieties of the middle class. In return they ask for nothing more than your vote. The battle of ideas to capture Middle England is a strange sight to behold, for Middle England now refers to a state of mind rather than any geographical location. But it is here that the next election will be fought and already the middle class is being cast as the new downtrodden, the most likely contenders for the prized crown of victimhood. Their class struggle is not about trying to change the system, just feeling peeved that the system hasn't delivered quite as much as it should.

In the eighties they thought the future would belong to them. In the nineties they feel more insecure, less trusting of institutions and politicians and the glories of the free market. There are sound structural reasons for this. The much-vaunted flexibility and streamlining of the work-place has meant that, as Blair says, there are no longer jobs for life, simply skills for life. The recession eventually hit the middle class, which is still reeling from the shock. What they are experiencing, as John Gray has pointed out, are just 'the insecurities and risks that have always plagued working-class life'. No wonder then they are unhappy. No one voted for this.

The classlessness which we were promised – we are all middle class now – has backfired. It's not that we are all working class now, but instead of the trickle-down effect of wealth there has been a gradual downgrading of middle-class lifestyles. So class, which of course has never gone away, is once more on the agenda – but in a decidedly topsy-turvy way. The language is no longer one of class warfare, of proletarian uprising, but instead something far vaguer: a kind of collective disappointment by those who do not even consider themselves part of a class. In an insecure world the old guarantors of privilege no longer hold good. *Angst* turns to anger.

Class once more means something apart from money. Material wealth, we were told, was the key to everything. The Labour Party could never capture the hearts of those who just wanted to move on up. Yet the Tories made the mistake of thinking that the aspirations of working people were limited to a bigger fridge-freezer and another package holiday. Those other more blurred aspirations about the quality of life were trampled on in the quest to privatize the very souls of the electorate. Hence the scramble now for the ownership of concepts such as community, civic duty and a tolerable public as well as private sector. Kenneth Clarke describes Blair as a 'political cross-dresser' – an interesting choice of phrase, implying, as it does, a kind of perversion and effeminacy. Yet, if Blair is trying on clothes that he hopes will appeal to the middle classes, at least they suit him. Clarke himself makes an awkward transvestite. He may dress himself up in softer tones but he still has to accept that his

Government's policies on education, health and the benefit system have not been at all popular.

However, in appealing to the middle class, Blair is doing something quite different. The cliché that those who vote Tory do so out of self-interest, while those who vote Labour do so out of an altruistic concern for social justice no longer appears viable. This is the difference between wanting homeless people off the streets because in this day and age it is an outrage that they have nowhere else to go, and wanting them off the streets because they literally get in your way, they make your life slightly more difficult than you would like. Now you can have two for the price of one.

Self-interest is thus being redefined. What is the point of bettering oneself, of saving and investing for the future, if you live in fear of the multitudes who have far less than you do? The fear of rising crime cannot be answered simply by more expensive burglar alarms, any more than it can by characterizing the underclass as 'the new rabble', incapable of the most basic kinds of morality. Society – in other words the connections between us all – may have been a dirty word under Thatcherism but it has come back with a vengeance. While New Age travellers are ridiculed because of their attempts to opt out of society, this in fact was a delusion shared by many in the eighties, that it was feasible somehow to opt out. Now that has become reality – schools, hospitals and prisons can choose to opt out – many people are desperate about trying to opt in. Meanwhile, though the middle classes are disgruntled, the sufferings of those who live in actual poverty are still difficult to talk about. Though it is no longer fashionable or indeed politically advisable to talk about the working class, they have not disappeared just because Middle England feels sorry for itself. Inequality, Blair tells us, is expensive. Expensive for the tax payer. Again, the appeal is to get rid of inequality, not just because it is a bad thing in itself but because it is bad for your pocket.

It's a little weird to be having a conversation about class at all at this late stage of the game. Both the modernizers of the left and the stalwarts of the right have been 'in denial' about its existence for so long. We talk about the problems of the inner city, for instance, without mentioning the word at all. The language of class has felt both too archaic and too abstract to describe what is going on – until now, that is, when suddenly it's OK for there to be a panic about the middle classes because they are being squeezed.

Those who have been severely squeezed for such a long time now that they can hardly mumble, are still not heard. But what I hear in all these middle-class complaints is not new. The sense of powerlessness, of the precariousness of their ways of life, of a basic lack of control, is what characterizes life for many people in this country. Ideally this should generate empathy but so often it invokes apathy.

For me, the difference between having money and not, security and not, of moving from one class to another, is symbolized by one thing. I do not have to wait as much as I used to. The long waits at the bus stop, in the DHSS, at the phone box, at the launderette, have stopped.

The endless waiting for things to get better is awful. So now that the middle class find themselves waiting for interviews, waiting for hospital places, waiting for what they feel is their due, I am not without sympathy. The question is whether they have waited long enough to try a different way of doing things. I hope so.

AN ID THAT IS FOOD FOR THOUGHT

Tired and emotional and trawling through the long walkways in the arrivals lounge at Heathrow this week, I began as I always do, to get vaguely paranoid. Customs, passport controls, baggage checks always make me nervous. I don't know why; I am not a small-time illegal immigrant or a big-time drug smuggler. I haven't got a gun in my pocket and I am never pleased to see anyone in this situation. All I know is I don't like immigration control one little bit.

This feeling was not helped by the 'art' in this anonymous environment. Along the walls are huge black and white photographs of stunning-looking people of all genders and races. They all have the same shaved heads and on the side of their scalps are printed bar-codes and letters indicating their nationalities.

If this is supposed to welcome us to Britain, to reassure us that we are part of one nation under a groove – I'm afraid it had the opposite effect on me. I haven't got a bar-code tattooed on my scalp, unless of course, 'they' did it while I was asleep on the plane. Waiting in the lottery that is baggage claim, I felt the ghost of Patrick McGoohan in *The Prisoner*: 'I am not a number'. I had to stop myself repeating it to the man at passport control. When he asked the purpose of my trip, I heard myself saying 'business'. It never seems appropriate to say 'pleasure' on these occasions. This is England, after all.

The bar-code idea is nothing new. Sci-fi novelist William Gibson did it long ago. Various artists and film-makers have used it with great panache. And it is a lot more effective than the all-purpose identity cards that are being proposed at the moment. A quick tattoo at birth and we will all know where we are or at least who we are supposed to be.

Along with bar-codes go the proper dietary requirements. A trip to the supermarket in search of egg-shaped spuds and three-quarters of a Kit-Kat, or whatever it is we are supposed to limit ourselves to, is a scary prospect. Perhaps some number on our ID cards could flash up on the shop till if we have strayed from the true and rightful path on our quest for a healthier way of life.

Oh no, it's not at all like that, the proponents of ID cards tell us. It's simply to make life easier. Easier for whom exactly? Well, the police for one. One advantage of the all-purpose identity card would be to end the possible discrimination against the auto-challenged – poor souls like me without cars. I mean, we may not have much of an identity because we haven't got a car, but hey, we are still people, aren't we?

The argument about identity cards, like so much current political discussion, is not one that can easily be divided along old left/right lines. Roy Hattersley is in favour of them even though he says he is an 'avowed civil libertarian', whereas *Sun* columnist Richard Littlejohn is against them. No, this is an argument between those who want more state regulation and those who, like me, want less.

It is an issue about which areas of one's life one is prepared to accept are other people's business and not just a matter of personal choice. If I want to live on a diet of saturated fat and more units of booze than is good for me, I do feel that this is my prerogative. If that makes me a burden on the NHS, so be it. But I would extend this freedom to everyone else too. Most of us are destined to be burdens of one kind or another. Most of us will get sick and grow old and frail at some point. That is life.

As Dennis Potter once said on *Question Time*, when asked if those suffering from smoking-related illnesses should go to the bottom of NHS waiting lists: 'All I know is that if I don't have a fag within the next half an hour, I am going to DIE.'

Not only do I refuse to believe that you are what you eat, I also refuse to swallow the notion that I am what someone else tells me to eat. But that, of course, is an infantile reaction, one that should surely be indicated on whatever kind of identity card I am made to carry.

As usual this government is hoist with its own ever-more ragged petard. If you leave things entirely to the free market then advertisers and food manufacturers will spend a fortune encouraging us that Pop-tarts are a great way to start the day. In the interests of public health, nutritionists are brought in to tell us otherwise, and to remind us that we have not yet reached the situation in the US where, if school meals are provided at all, ketchup is counted as a vegetable.

But what is repressed in all these debates is what nutritionists know and what George Orwell knew long ago – that people's diets are mostly dictated by income. Poor people eat things that are bad for them because they want things that are bad for them, because they are cheap and convenient and because, when all else fails, sugar and fat make you feel better.

Soaking pulses may be a much healthier and possibly cheaper proposition than a bag of chips but they never quite hit the mark. Brown bread is better than white bread but children don't like it as much.

At the end of a hard day, it's easier to give them what they want than whatever they might actually need. To deny these things is to deny how we really live. It is still largely women who shop and prepare food, and women, who in their exhaustion, are grateful for whatever instant gratification is available to them. Guilt over such things is a prerogative of privilege, of having the time and energy to really worry about monosodium glutamate instead of wondering how you are going to pay the gas bill.

Nothing is harder to stomach than when some well-meaning MP or public servant takes it upon themselves to show that you can live on benefit and still eat healthily. The image of someone living on forty quid a week and searching for fresh fruit and fibre bears no relation to the reality of the stresses of never having enough money.

While the effectiveness of dietary guidelines is debatable, no one is talking about the effectiveness of identity cards. Should they be introduced it is assumed that they will work. But how do we know that? Fraud is not a thing of the past in countries where they have ID cards; fraud is simply more professional. They become part of a system of ever greater checks and controls. In the US, a credit card is not enough to guarantee a cheque; instead, you stand in queues while they make even more checks on your credit-rating. A passport is not enough proof of identity and fake driving licences are two-a-penny.

One strange side-effect is that one's standing in the world has little to do with how much money you have and everything to do with your mysterious credit-rating. I remember trying to hire a car in New York for someone else. He had the driving licence but I had the ID and the cash. Having discussed in great detail what kind of car we would get, I offered to pay on credit card, by cheque or quaintly, even with cash. After several phone calls, the woman – who by now even knew my star-sign – said to me: 'I am sorry, ma'am, you are not cash-qualified.' Having the cash did not actually qualify me because I didn't have enough of an identity.

Perhaps then, my paranoia is not totally unjustified. But I can't help feeling there should be less of these controls not more. It's a free country, isn't it? If you want to ration your intake of cheese sandwiches I'm happy for you but I say, 'let them eat cake'. Why? Because we want to, and because our diets, like our identities, are our own precious affair. Bar-codes are fine for chocolate biscuits, for populations they are something else altogether.

A LESSON IN MISH-MASH MORALITY

Even the headmaster of John Major's old school can't hack it. He is refusing to comply with the law on religious assemblies in schools. According to government guidelines published earlier this year, assemblies should be 'in the main, Christian'. They must also accord 'a special status' to Jesus Christ. For believers, it must be a pretty sad day when the Son of God only gets special status because of a government guideline. For the rest of us, it just reflects the muddle that religious education has become. Ninety-five per cent of schools inspected last year were not holding Christian assemblies. So what has replaced them? It is not that 'Onward Christian Soldiers' has been replaced by the Black Mass – that would be far too definite – but most kids are now subject to the vague moral mish-mash propagated in the name of multiculturalism.

In practice, faith has become a pick'n'mix affair and all religions are presented as equally valid. Songs which offend no one are sung. My daughter used to sing 'We All Live in a Yellow Submarine' and Rod Stewart's 'Sailing' in her assemblies. My three-year-old is convinced we are Muslims because she has 'done' Ramadan at nursery and thinks we should be doing it at home. Her friend thinks that all the Hasidic Jews who live in the area are policemen. They argue over whether Jesus is a girl or not. 'Anyway,' says the eldest, 'Jesus is just a story, like Batman' and finds it hysterically funny that some people like her grandad actually get down on their knees and pray.

The nativity play at her old school where many of the kids were Muslims, was a spectacle to behold. We were celebrating the birth of a very special baby. No names, no pack drill. No mention of why this baby was special. A prophet was in there, somewhere. Obviously. And for no other good reason than the school was full of Australian supply teachers, the finale included an Aussie version of 'A Partridge in a Pear Tree' – 'An Emu up a Gum Tree'. No one was offended but most were as bewildered as the children as to what it all meant.

Attacks on multiculturalism usually come from the right. Yet the left can no longer keep quiet about this and hope just to muddle through. The result is that with nothing better on offer, parents will welcome a return to moral and religious teaching that they can at least understand. Many of us are uncomfortable with what passes in the name of multiculturalism. Parents talk about it at the school gates. Kids know that however many Bob Marley songs you sing in assembly, racism is endemic. The Tories want schools to be what black sociologist and author Paul Gilroy calls 'repositories of authentic national culture'. School is where this culture must be transmitted from generation to generation. It is hardly surprising that the Government wants to impose a monoculture of Christianity on to children even though we live in an increasingly secular society. If we don't want this to happen, and I don't, then we have to be honest about the failures of so many approaches to multiculturalism. I also think we have to be more honest with our children.

In private few of us let Jehovah's Witnesses into our homes because we think they are nutters. Not all religions are the same, not all of them are tolerant. People kill each other over these beliefs. Let's not pretend that Islam is a cosy little belief system in the multiple choice approach to world religion. Let's talk about Islam as it is lived if you are a twelve-year-old-girl or a gay man, for instance. The blanding out of cultural difference into a range of equal opportunity festivals doesn't fool anyone any of the time. Those children brought up in religious homes will feel secure in their beliefs anyway, those who are not will cobble something together like the rest of us. For while multiculturalism recognizes culture only as some kind of ethnic property, it cannot recognize the culture that produced it.

The one faith that doesn't get much of a mention, that no one studies, is secular liberalism. We are too embarrassed, too self-conscious of our own lack of belief, that we simply bow down to organized religion however much we find it distasteful. Floating voters of the spiritual realm, who may be any colour and of any cultural background, end up simply as the negatives in this approach. Just because we are non-believers, however, does not mean that we believe nothing. Yet there is no room at the inn for us. The culture of doubt fits neither the sugar and spice approach to faith nor the insipid right-wing attempts to rebuild Jerusalem in the middle of a school assembly.

It is up to us, then, to be less apologetic because we don't have brightly coloured gods the kids can do collages of. It is up to us to say, look around, culture is not inherently tied to race. It is a fluid thing that moves between all of us. But sometimes there are limits to its fluidity.

Those limits are set partly by where we come from. Not many of us are converts, so it is also up to us to insist that children of what-ever faith understand how they got to be living in the society they are in.

I do not want Christianity shoved down my children's throats but more and more I want them to know about Christianity, which is a different thing altogether. Without it, I fail to see how you can explain the relationship between nation and state, between politics and religion. It is a paradox, of course, that multiculturalism actually de-politicizes culture, that in its rush to respect difference it so often denies it. For children who have been taught that Christianity is just another soft option it must be a shock to find out that the reason Prince Charles can't get divorced is because he will be head of the Church of England. Religion suddenly moves out of the soft-focus vision of 'Some people believe this while others believe that' into the bloodier world of power and politics. You try explaining Ireland or what was wrong with Wallis Simpson or what Henry VIII was doing to a child, as I have recently, without talking about the Church. 'What church?' they will ask. 'The Church' is something they have no concept of. Churches yes, mosques and temples sure, but not The Church – religion as a powerful, highly organized political force has not figured in their education. Why should it? Well, I guess that would be to include the nastier stuff. It would ruffle the 'I'd like to teach the world to sing' notion of religious education. It would show that most organized religion is not enamoured of a multicultural approach and would actually prefer separate schools. It would show that multiculturalism is not the same thing as anti-racism, though it's often carried out in its name.

Perhaps most of all it would make us secular liberals question what it is that we get, or want, or mean, when we preach tolerance and respect of other cultures. What does it mean, for instance, to respect a faith that you never want to be part of? The comedian Dave Allen signs off his act with the phrase 'May your god go with you'. As heartening as this may be, it should hardly be the basis for our children's education. May your god go with you. Sure. But don't expect me not to ask you where you are going.

MAKE WAY FOR THE THIRD SEX

Some days I just feel like a woman trapped in a woman's body. I wonder if there is some sort of help I could get. It's not an operation I'm after, more a quick fix. Actually a quick fix of testosterone might be just what I need. It would be wonderful to have more energy and to see the world in brighter colours, which, according to a recent interview with a woman taking testosterone regularly, is one of the side effects of this wonder drug.

Other side effects are more of a hassle, such as having to shave regularly, but what the hell? What other drug makes you want to drop to the ground and do fifty push-ups as this one is reported to do? The goal of the increasing number of women taking male hormones in the US is not necessarily to change sex but to create a new one altogether.

It's a risky business and not just in terms of the physical risks to their health, which no one is sure about yet. Regarding gender as nothing more than virtual reality, something that can be keyed into and exited at will, is a transformation that most of us have not yet made.

It is a brave new world that has such people in it. Sex-change operations, the removal of bits and bobs after years of therapy, are still only judged to be successful when the individual involved can pass fully as a member of the chosen sex. This is deception on a grand scale and documentaries on British television that have traced the history of George who became Julia and was still miser-able, serve as a warning that one should not tinker with one's equipment. It hasn't really worked, we say, holding on to the belief that it could never really work. Instead, let us dwell on voices that are too deep and hands that are too big or reduce it all to the level of fashion.

Elle magazine's new 'trend for November – The New Unisex – the end of gender', is about gorgeous boys and girls who trade on sexual ambivalence. At the heart of all this wonderfully aesthetic blurring even the writer admits 'the new unisex is still pretty heterosexual'. And heterosexuals, however pretty, do not disturb us too much. Sexual equality must amount to something more than whether you can borrow items from your boyfriend's wardrobe.

No, what is unsettling is the idea of being neither one sex nor the other. The creation of a third sex – though why stop at three? – is a very old idea but one that is, once more, gaining currency. Up until now, even the script of transsexuality was written solely in terms of a dialogue between two entirely discrete genders. You may be born one thing but with surgery could be the other, if you wanted it enough and could prove to a psychiatrist that the core of your being did not resemble the sexual apparatus that you were born with. Hence all this talk of being trapped in the wrong body, which is still how we understand transsexuality.

This desperate search for the politically correct body, the body that means what it says, the body that looks on the outside as it feels on the inside (though is any body really like that?) is limited to a few sad individuals. They have to try so hard, so that we don't have to. But is this actually the case?

What about the amount of effort and time we spend trying to be natural men and women. The huge performance in order to display femininity – the waxing and work-outs, the dieting, the skincare, the make-up, the accessorizing and the clothes – that goes into producing an acceptable face of womanhood over a lifetime costs more than a sex-change operation. Just ask a natural woman like Princess Diana.

I am not saying that woman are all honorary transsexuals, but I wonder at what point a certain type of body modification begins to question gender. We don't regard piercing, breast implants, hysterectomies or cosmetic surgery (with the exception of Michael

Jackson) as a part of gender-bending. Yet the injection of male or female hormones is considered profoundly problematic. What does it actually take to change sex? Or, more precisely, to change gender?

The transsexual inevitably presents a challenge to the neat binary of male and female but also to the opposition between sex – what you're born with – and gender – everything you learn. Yet recently, the Sunday supplements have been full of exotic people who defy the either/or of gender law. The new freak-show includes self-proclaimed gender-transients, she-males, cross-dressers, 'reverse drag-queens' (lesbians dressing up as gay men) pre- and post-operative transsexuals. The list goes on. Whatever these people are up to, the old script of being trapped in the wrong body is woefully inadequate.

The medicalization of transsexuality, as a disease for which there is a cure, involves therapy which is quite unlike any other in that it demands its patients invent a past they never had. A male to female transsexual will discard his boyhood in favour of an imaginary girl-hood. Whose benefit is this for, I wonder – this kind of forced assimilation? Why can't we just accept that some people are really neither one sex or the other, nor will they ever be?

One of the difficulties is that many of the campaigns for homo-sexual equality have been premised on insisting that we are all the same really. Transsexuals are not necessarily homosexuals or vice versa but the link is often made in the public imagination. However, both in practice and theory, new moves are being made towards a politics that can include anyone who chooses to play with gender. Kate Bornstein's *Gender Outlaw: On Men, Women and the Rest of Us* (Routledge) is one such book. A male to female transsexual, Bornstein doesn't regard herself as either male or female. Like the women shooting up male hormones, she makes all of us question what it is to be a man or a woman. She says that she spent thirty-seven years trying to be male and eight trying to be female. 'I've come to the conclusion that neither is really worth all the trouble. A lot of people think that it is worth all the trouble, and that made me think why?' Why indeed? After all, this is someone who clearly thought it worth the trouble to get himself castrated, who then became a lesbian, whose girlfriend is now becoming a man. So are they ending up as a perfectly heterosexual couple? For however fluid gender may be in theory, in practice it seems that on the cutting edge – literally – people are still having to resort to biology to feel good about themselves. I'm all for transcending gender, myself. I thought the person who stood up at a conference I was at and proclaimed themselves 'omni-sexual' was pretty cool. None the less, after years of feminists and gay activists and anyone else who came along for the ride, arguing that biology wasn't destiny, we now have to face up to people who believe biology *is* destiny, if only it can be tampered with slightly. After years of women complaining about how men are socially conditioned to be aggressive and never cry, we now have women telling us that after an injection of testosterone they feel much the same way. Sexual radicals end up endorsing the most conservative force in the book – good old mother nature. It's just them good ol' hormones that makes us the way we are. Confused? You should be so lucky.

INTELLIGENT NEW LIFE FORMS

We ask, mirror, mirror on the wall, who is the cleverest of them all? Blacks or whites, men or women? Is the future for females so bright that we are going to have to wear shades?

This week's *Panorama* presented us yet again with highly competent girls drawing graphs, excelling at languages, diligently recording the result of experiments, while their gormless brothers read comics, played Sonic and congratulated each other on getting chucked out of the classroom for 'messing about'. Meanwhile, Charles Murray has regaled us recently with his not-so-new theories about IQ and race.

It seems that the best of all possible worlds would be to be an East Asian babe. East Asians score, on average, higher than European Americans who, in turn, score higher than African-Americans in Murray's IQ tests. Or, in the words of Paul Johnson, 'the twenty-first century will be the age of Madame Butterfly – still beautiful, I hope, but no longer the hapless victim, more the perpetrator.'

Let's face it, girls, what matters when you look in the mirror is your ability to score, and I'm not talking IQ tests here. What is obvious is that the mirrors we hold up to measure intelligence don't look so clever after all. People see what they want to see, though they may disguise it with jargon like 'cognitive ability' and 'information assimilation'.

Finding reassurance that your soaring IQ puts you in the same club as Gary Bushell may not strike the rest of us as a mark of intelligence. Indeed, it is an indication of the limitations of such markers of intelligence in the first place.

Intelligence is yet another arena in which the culture-versus-nature debate is played in increasingly bizarre ways. So, on one hand we have the Murray gang believing they can measure innate intelligence, and just happening to find blacks fare less well than whites with – as Murray stresses – no policy implications whatsoever. (If you believe that you really are stupid.) On the other hand, we are told that in terms of learned intelligence – exam results and continuous assessment – girls are out-performing boys at all levels. These findings throw a spanner in the works of those who deem intelligence to be God-given – because no one wants to say that girls just *are* cleverer than boys, so we rush around looking for cultural explanations. Girls are doing better because they are parented differently, their expectations are different and the culture of laddishness does not value swots.

Panorama featured a series of experts trying to explain this phenomenon. Those who look to nature for an answer end up sticking electrodes on tiny babies' heads in order to prove that girls' facility for language is better than that of boys, even at a week old. Teachers, meanwhile, prefer to talk in terms of girls' linguistic skills and their ability to present information well. Increasingly, the old myths about boys being slow starters, but catching up later, are being shot to pieces. Slow starters remain slow, yet, shockingly, the education system has been in the business of fixing results in favour of boys from the 11-plus onwards, in order to achieve the 'natural' male/female balance.

Many of those who argue vehemently against quotas and positive discrimination in favour of women have actually been part of a system that has positively discriminated in favour of boys for decades. Yet, in looking for cultural explanations for girls' achievements, no one mentioned the word feminism which – whether you like it or not – has been part of the culture for around twenty years or so and coincides almost exactly with the period in which women started to move up the educational ladder.

I am not suggesting that feminism has made girls brighter, but feminist attitudes have certainly raised women's expectations and freed them from the notion that the pinnacle of achievement is baking the perfect soufflé.

However, while the current debates focus on who is the more clever, no one seems to be asking the vital question: what kinds of intelligence do we need for the twenty-first century? If the new jobs favour women because they require linguistic ability, multi-skilling and co-operation, how is the education system to be changed? If the information superhighway means that we no longer need people who have learnt amazing numbers of facts and figures – because we can call them up onscreen – then why should we still require our kids to learn parrot-fashion? The future must lie in the hands of those who can comprehend, assimilate and manage information, all skills that the girls appear to be 'naturally' better at.

The name of the game is now 'information management', which is a very different concept from the old model of an all-round education. What still dominates public debate are those tedious point-scoring exchanges which those processed by Oxbridge excel at, exchanges which assume that debating-society codes operate through the rest of society. This approach to information comes from the top down, and with it comes the assumption that there are things that we are better-off not knowing. But it is increasingly at odds with the ways in which we work and live.

Showing off one's own software (the size of one's brain) is increasingly irrelevant when everyone's software is on display, via computer technology. We do not need to pick an individual's brain when we can, if we want to, pick brains all over the globe. The new codes will be based on access as well as ability, on analysis rather than argument.

What matters is understanding, rather than the facility for simply accruing more and more information. We used to ask of any new fact or insight: Is it right? Is it true? Is it good? We now ask: What is it good for? What can we do with it? Those in the business of inventing the electronic codes we use, for example, the computer technocrat Bill Gates – 'the new Henry Ford' – give us some indication of what will be required. In the beginning, there was the word, and the word was Microsoft, which is currently installed on fifty million computers around the world. Microsoft has made Gates a millionaire guru.

It's OK to feel uneasy about all this, as Bryan Appleyard obviously did when he interviewed Gates for the *Sunday Times*. Gates is certainly a genius, but the worry that 'from this computer-freaked gang of self-confessed partial personalities the future is emerging' is a worry that many of us share.

Gates may be an all-American visionary. The computer language of roads and highways could only have come from the United States. But Gates doesn't seem to appreciate art, or even aesthetics. This man who imagines the future does not have sufficient imagination, and does not fit into the humanist model of a well-rounded individual; he knows that computers can make up for the deficiencies of his brain. Why clog up your mind by memorizing information when a computer is so much better at it than you? The optimistic way in which people speak about information technology is premised on this single idea – that our minds will be liberated to do other much more important stuff. But the related anxiety is that none of us will know anything properly any more, and so all the information in the world will be useless. Knowledge only gives power when you know what to do with it.

In such an environment, discussions about IQ belong to the last century, not the next one: yet the revaluing of skills that have traditionally been deemed 'feminine' do not. Phrases like 'the future is female' – the title of *Panorama*'s report – are almost meaningless, if in the virtual world anyone can be 'female'.

If, instead of asking 'why can't a woman be more like a man', we now have to ask 'why can't a man be more like a woman', we also have to ask 'where is the female Bill Gates?' Or, more mundanely, what happens to all these sharp young girls once they hit the workplace? The problem, as it stands, is that we already have access to such information. The real changes will come when we can assimilate it.

TAKE IT SLOWLY, FROM THE END

Please stop me if you've heard this one before but this is the end, my friend. A week does not go by without the end of some, rather large, idea being declared, as the millennium vultures hover over it to pick its bones. If the end of history, Francis Fukuyama's unlikely death wish, wasn't enough, we have also recently been treated to the end of politics and the end of liberalism, the end of the establishment, the end of institutions, the end of Western dominance, the end of the left, the end of the monarchy, and the end of any cultural authority whatsoever.

Amazingly, life goes on much as it ever did. Ideas get recycled, of course, although it's all rather exhausting. We limp forward in a kind of collective ME, the passing of time becoming just another post-viral syndrome that drains us of our energy. As melodramatic as this may be, the truth is rather less imposing.

It seems to me that we are so preoccupied by these big ends that we tend to ignore the smaller ones. Perhaps, finally, we have seen the end of the eighties, although, as John Gray wrote, they have been a long time dying. Or at least the part of the eighties that was synonymous with Thatcherism. As Michael Heseltine's plans for the Post Office were aborted, the man himself looked tired, as well he might. Ronald Reagan, Thatcher's brother-in-arms, announced officially that his brain was disintegrating.

As these eighties ideologues entered the twilight zone once and for all, people have started asking the question of the Tories that has long beleaguered the Labour Party. What are they for? What do they represent? If they continue to dither over Europe and are unable to privatize everything that moves – then just what do they stand for?

While Thatcherism was a clearly identifiable programme, if there is such a thing as Majorism, it is rather a muddle. But it is not yet impotent. Remember, somewhere between the drift of the Cabinet and the parroting of underclass dogma by the Portillos of this world, is a Government that has managed to pull off one of the greatest assaults on individual liberty we have seen for a very long time – the Criminal Justice Act. None the less, the excitement around Tony Blair at the moment is simply that instead of reacting to an agenda set by the right, the rest of us left, leftish or just not right can have a go at fixing one ourselves.

Yet, just as the derided symbols of the Thatcherite enterprise – the Filofax and the mobile phone – have now become detached from their moorings and become commonplace, so too the fall-out from this period has entered parts of our culture that other politics have yet to reach.

The sleaze factor, and the subsequent lack of faith in politicians, is a direct result of one of the central contradictions of that era in that it reflects the tension between, on the one hand, centralizing power whilst, on the other, spouting rhetoric about the freedom of the individual. If people in public office are allowed to act according to their whims, you end up with the pantomime of David Mellor, which, while providing good knockabout farce, is actually small fry compared to the corruption of Westminster's Shirley Porter.

For, as Stuart Hall writes in *The War of the Words*, Thatcherism 'redefined contours of public thinking'. It grasped that the way to people's hearts was not just through Westminster but through the other spaces in people's lives that they did not even consider to be 'political', areas formerly deemed miraculously free of boring old politics – morality and culture.

So far, Blair has been better on morality than on culture. Having your photo taken next to Bono, even if he dressed as a pimp, is not the way to do it. You cannot embrace the superficial in pursuit of depth; instead, a stranger thing happens. The rock star, whose life's work it is to play with superficiality, ends up with more *gravitas* than the politician. Blair, looking like a suit with teeth, managed the improbable feat of making Bono look cool. The lesson is that it is not enough merely to borrow the dreams of pop culture if you don't actually inhabit them.

It was the politicizing of the private arena that made Thatcherism radical. So it is not surprising that it should also prove so difficult to renegotiate, either by her own party or any other. What is going on at the moment strikes me as far subtler than the end of politics, or life, as we know it. What we are edging towards is a redefinition of exactly what is public and private. And what's in between.

The old categories have been broken down primarily by the media, and we are not sure how to redraw them. Almost every major news story resonates with this unease. The sleaze factor is about what public figures do in private, as is the 'crisis' of the monarchy. The rows over single parenting and the CSA are to do with how much the state can interfere in the personal relations of its members. No one is clear about this, nor do the arguments conform to a left/right divide. There is no longer any internal logic, even within political parties. So, for instance, while the Tories are responsible for the Criminal Justice Act, they are also responsible for lowering the age of consent for homosexuals and are considering the decriminalization of cannabis.

The message is becoming even more mixed. Consenting adults can do some of what they like in private, but not too much of it. If, however, they enter any public space, be it a street or a field, and do what they like, the full powers of the state can be ranged against them. While public space is ever more policed, the Blairite vision involves the conjuring up of public space that is benign rather than merely threatening. This is called 'a community' and it feels like a new deal because the valorization of private property that took place in the eighties produced an almost tangible disdain for anything that was not privately owned. As a psychic state this was tolerable, but when people saw it enacted in their cities, schools and hospitals, the decay of public space, bad enough in itself, became symbolic of something even more rotten at the heart of government. To talk of civic society, never mind civic duty, is difficult among broken-down playgrounds littered with old condoms and screwed-up tin foil, lifts that don't work, streets you wouldn't want your children to roam.

Yet the answer to all this is not to simply reclaim the public space on behalf of the state, as though the eighties never happened. If you listen to what people are saying, they want less government not more, but they want the few things that it can do, done properly. If we are going to have quangos, or the CSA, or trusts running hospitals, then why do they have to be so bloody incapable of doing what they are supposed to do? It is not ideology that irks people so much as inefficiency.

In going 'back to basics' with the discussions about Clause Four, a window could have opened up to ask what we really mean now by public and private ownership, and the role of a government – any government – in people's lives. Instead, it has been suggested that we replace an archaic clause with a meaningless one that babbles: 'Everyone has the right to be fully and meaningfully employed or occupied.' How is a government ever to guarantee such a right, and if it can't, what is the point of having it and who is to say what 'meaningful employment' is anyway?

If any kind of new agenda is to be set, it must be done with a recognition that there is no going back lazily to the old assumptions about public and private, left and right, as currently all the definitions are sliding into each other. Nor can any talk of community or, equally vaguely, 'social justice', be entered into as though these were policy issues alone.

It is civil society, not party politics or the old leftist version of the state, that may, or may not, produce communities of whatever description. It is in, and through, culture that the lines between public interest and private affairs will be drawn up. This is what Blair and his allies must understand. Winning an election may prove easier than conquering this terrain, as Clinton has just found out. But, if Thatcherism is to be truly ended, then just such a beginning will have to be made.

HARD MEN WITH SOFT HEADS

I wanted a quiet night in. I didn't particularly want to be by myself but I didn't want company either. I turned on the TV and watched an Everyman film about Jeffrey Dahmer – the American serial killer who killed and dismembered seventeen young men. They showed some movies of the young Jeff goofing around. A shy boy but ordinary enough. His father tried to piece together what had gone wrong; or, as he says in the book he wrote about his son, *A Father's Story*: 'I dwell on the small, pink hands and in my mind I watch them grow larger and darker as I think about all that they will later do, of how stained they will become with the blood of others.'

This wasn't *Pulp Fiction*. Or *Natural Born Killers*. Or even Des Lynam's *How Do They Do That?* Dahmer killed, ventured the police officer who interviewed him, out of the need for human contact, to stop people leaving, to keep his victims with him. This is also what was said of Dennis Nilsen. There was, then, a logic to it. It meant something. The court ruled that Dahmer was sane, even though he had murdered and cannibalized his victims, which makes you wonder what insanity might be like. It was a subdued programme, no special effects, no gory details – unless you count the pain that seared through every second of it.

This was screen violence in the real sense. You couldn't look away even if you wanted to. It made me want some company, too. But as a sign of life, not death, because I am also sane. If this was screen violence it was also the opposite of *Pulp Fiction*, which is bursting with energy, which makes you feel really good to be alive.

Yet the debate about violence in popular culture does not have much time for the dullness of reality. Those who want to censor images never understand that what scares us most, even in fictional terms, can never be censored. Will you stop children seeing the witch in *The Wizard of Oz* because it scares them senseless? Will you cut out the scene of violence in *The Piano* which made me feel sick to my stomach? Will you stop young men reading Andy Mcnab's best seller *Bravo Two Zero* because it gives lonely young men the idea that killing is a rite of passage to manhood?

Clearly, censorship may not be the answer, yet on the other side nor is the critical and moral evacuation that passes for holier-than-thou hipness. That adolescent boys particularly want to see on video dismembered entrails is, one hopes, a phase they are going through. Let's not elevate it to the status of art or, even more daftly, commentary about society. Yet there seems to be an awful lot of macho posturing about all this – a kind of silly dare about who can stomach the most grossness. If we are going to be macho about it, I can stomach an awful lot of blood and guts on screen. I was a film critic for two years. I got hard, if you like. Haven't we all?

Still, it seems to me that some of the hardest men around are soft in the head when it comes to this stuff. Tarantino, who learnt how to film violence from watching violent films, is a brilliant, brilliant film-maker. That does not mean, however, that he is not responsible for some of his dumb followers who hang on to his quote about violence being just another colour, who forsake moral judgement for hand-me-down aesthetics.

It's good to talk. No one, not even BT, knows this more than Tarantino, who fills his movies with some of the best talk around. His characters talk as if they were in a movie and the thing is, they are. The rest of us unfortunately aren't, however hard we pretend. No amount of Nietzsche or Camus poking out of pockets or ultra-fashionable nihilism can change that. But we might ask each other where all this nihilism is coming from? Why all these boys want to be quite so bad?

Was Kurt Cobain bad enough for you? His was not, as so many people lazily commented, another rock 'n' roll suicide. That is when you take a lot of drugs and one day just happen to take too many.

His was an extremely violent death. And it touched even those who felt there was no point in anything anymore. It made them feel, even though it wasn't part of a movie or a song.

At least, I suppose, the current anxiety about screen violence has foregrounded our concerns in a far more sensible way than the silly worrying about showing people having sex. We have cut to the heart of the chase, and whether bodies are naked is neither here nor there when they are being sliced up on screen. The most frightening thing that Tarantino ever shows us is not severed ears or splattered heads but fear itself. What does fear look like? How do people react when they know they are about to be tortured? After the complaints that Arnie/Rambo-style action movies turned violence into a cartoon, Tarantino gives us some kind of context for the violence. Instead of making it better, though, it makes it worse. Just as with the Everyman programme on Dahmer, there is no context that can make this behaviour palatable. We still keep on searching for one. If Dahmer was sexually abused as a child, for instance, would that make what he did more comprehensible?

If the fictions that concern us, the films of Tarantino or Oliver Stone's new one, or the writings of Bret Easton Ellis, try to turn real-life horror into something that we can identify with, that we want to pay to see or read, then of course they have somehow to heighten the violence, to make it worth our while. So, to say that this is at odds with the peculiarly flat testimony of those who have killed for real is to miss the point about what it is that we require from fiction.

Yet it is this very flatness that is so disturbing. The lack of connection with other human beings, the inability to understand the consequences of their actions for their murder of a taxi driver. What they wanted was a fictional buzz but in reality it didn't last for long – if they got it at all.

The problem comes, however, when fiction or fantasy tries merely to represent this flatness. Bret Easton Ellis got into trouble over it with *American Psycho*, although in the new climate the book is being reclaimed as a classic. An anonymous member of the British Board of Film Classification recently said of Oliver Stone's new film, *Natural Born Killers*: 'I would happily cut bits of it, but it is like a stick of rock – the violence is all the way through.' Even when fiction tries to empty itself out it must still be full of something. Of Ellis's stylistic detail, of Tarantino's bravado, of Stone's demons. It cannot actually be devoid of content. It cannot give up the ghost altogether. That we leave to the real victims of violence, to the families of those who kill and are killed. Dahmer's father has tried but failed, as he must, to understand his son's actions. He has be-friended the sister of one of his son's victims, a remarkable woman, who spoke of hope and forgiveness in the midst of all this grief.

Words like hope and forgiveness and bravery don't figure much in the work of the new nihilists. They don't push you back in your seat or make you gasp. They don't tell you much about how awful society is. They are words devoid of cheap thrills and even cheaper ennui. They may not take us, as we increasingly demand of fiction, to the edge. In real life, though, they just might bring us back again.

WATCH THIS SPACE: IT'S THE COMMUNITY

Love may be all you need, but no one can promise that. It is difficult to know how we might get people to care about each other more than they already do, so instead politicians talk continually of the magic word 'community'. We must have more of one. We must be in one. We must strengthen a sense of community to cure all the assorted ills of society. Community, like peace or freedom, is something we can agree that we should have, but it remains a vague ideal.

We take for granted the idea that our communities have been weakened primarily by economic decline. The task, then, is to rebuild them and produce active citizens. Dick Atkinson, in a Demos pamphlet entitled 'The Common Sense of Community', starts from the common sense position that 'our sense of responsibility for each other has atrophied'. He goes on to suggest ways in which this sense might be resuscitated, from encouraging self-governing institutions of all kinds, like trusts to manage local parks, to making schools more central as support systems for the whole family.

Much of what he argues makes sense; like many others, he is looking for ways to decentralize power away from local authorities and promote self-sufficient institutions in their place. This strikes a chord, especially because of the current disillusionment with politicians and with government itself.

Copying the world of commerce, the sub-text of much 'radical' thought is to do with the downsizing of government itself. We want a slimmer, trimmer political system. Government can get on with the lean cuisine of administration – as for the rest of it, we can manage by ourselves, thank you very much.

It is worth noting that this is taking place at a time when communities which want to think for themselves or just muddle along – squatters, travellers, good old-fashioned hedonists – are being penalized more heavily than ever before. But then that is the trouble. One person's idea of a blissful community is the next person's nightmare. I must confess that the idea of community as some all-encompassing Neighbourhood Watch scheme, in which everyone knows your business and is always concerned about it, is not one that I can get excited about.

It's not that I don't care or won't do the shopping for my next-door neighbour when he can't make it up the road. But let us not deny the claustrophobia of much small-town life, nor the fact that we need different things at different times in our lives. When you are old or ill or have small children, your world shrinks and you become more involved in the place you live in than at other times.

However, it is the fundamental rupturing of the automatic link between place and culture that Atkinson's pamphlet does not begin to address. What constitutes our sense of place is less and less dependent on the place itself. Likewise, 'community' cannot simply be thought of in terms of geographical location. Although Demos brings together political theorists of all persuasions, it would do well also to draw in some cultural analysis if the argument is to move on.

Bea Campbell has rightly criticized Atkinson for failing to place gender at the centre of his discussion. If we see the family as the building block of community, then the changes in the family have to be acknowledged.

It is women, usually mothers, who forge the links, who lubricate the wheels of community action, who care about decent parks, schools, safer streets, childcare networks, and all the things we think would make the world a better place. This work is voluntary and undervalued and a long way removed from Atkinson's suggestions of qualified neighbourhood officers acting as 'social entrepreneurs'. Such people couldn't be more 'involved' than they already are. What they need is greater power. As David Morley has written: 'Small (or local) is not necessarily beautiful; it can sometimes mean powerless.' Apart from bringing gender into the equation – though it seems ludicrous that in discussions of urban policy it can still be ignored or slipped in by the back door under the guise of 'family centres' – we also have to look to other huge changes that are taking place.

Community surely rests on a sense of belonging and that sense has shifted dramatically. The gay community – and that term itself is debatable – doesn't live in one place. Many people in the gay community don't feel themselves to be part of a community or don't like what this community has become. Community in this sense is something both that you escape into and escape from – something that forms part, not the whole, of one's identity.

Indeed, closed, self-sufficient communities – such as the Hasidic community in the area where I live – arouse a mixture of bewilderment and hostility, precisely because their sense of community is so strong. But they would live like that wherever they were in the world. For others, a sense of community is bounded by a sense of place which can be equally reactionary, resulting in the worst kind of nationalism. More mundanely, modern cities are increasingly full of enclosures for the professional classes, such as Docklands, which are designed to keep others out.

This obviously is not the kind of community that Atkinson is proposing, but if community is about keeping others out then we have to acknowledge that our sense of belonging is coming from elsewhere. In other words, the spaces that we choose to occupy are much more than the physical spaces in which we live. What we call 'home' is increasingly defined by what is outside, not by what is in. Whether this is due to the globalization of capital, the massive influx of media, of electronic communication, the place we feel at home still matters. It is the place we ingest all this information, all this 'foreign-ness'. As Morley points out, one of the reasons that much of America is more provincial and 'localized' than any other country is because it does not import most of its media.

The feeling of disorientation produced by the global flow of information and culture has led to the phrase 'time-space compression'. What this means is that distance is not quite what it was. You don't have to be 'there' to experience what 'there' is like – you can see images or buy products from all over the world without actually going anywhere. Yet there is a confusion still when we talk about mobility. On one hand we live in a fantastically mobile culture, but on the other when people do move they tend to stay in quite a small area; recent research suggests they remain within a three-mile radius of where they started from. Having brilliantly described 'a reeling vision of hyperspace' full of new formations of global hierarchies, the geographer Doreen Massey reminds us that 'most people actually still live in places like Harlesden or West Brom. Much of life for many people, even in the heart of the first world, still consists of waiting with your shopping for a bus that never comes. Hardly a graphic illustration of time-space compression.'

So we must locate our sense of community somewhere between a bus stop in Harlesden and simultaneous electronic communication. It is no wonder that people want to go back to how it was, whether it's the toy town that Prince Charles is constructing or the requests for bobbies on the beat. Again though, there is no going back — or even forward — unless the modernizers of the Labour Party or Demos (they are not quite the same thing, yet) take on board some of the basic ideas. If community (which is the way we now talk about idealized social relations) is the answer, then we must understand how those relations are changing. When we say 'local', what do we mean when what is local is more and more made up of that which comes from beyond its borders.

One response is to try to reorder public space — so that we can get our bearings, so that we know exactly where we are. Atkinson suggests clear signs, like postal district indicators, to mark boundaries, 'clear entry and exit points' to signal where our communities start and end. I guess this would provide a kind of mapping for us lost urban souls. But we need much more. You cannot legislate a community into existence where there is none, nor can we become so mired in nostalgia that we cannot celebrate much of what is liberating about some of these changes. The struggle in Docklands was soon polarized between a notion of the old unchanging community as essentially good and the new more mobile one as essentially bad. It was a struggle over a place once called the Isle of Dogs, a fight between the authentic residents and horrible yuppies. This is not the answer. Who is to say who were the most 'active citizens'?

There may be no place like home but maybe that is because home is not in the place it once was. The job of those who care for the community, then, is to find the new places. They might even find it's where the rest of us already live.

THE HONEYMOON HAS ENDED

On 26 May, Hugo Alvarez Perez, a civil judge in the Dominican Republic, asked Michael Jackson: 'Do you take Lisa Marie to be your wife?' Jackson replied in English 'Why not?' or, as it was translated into Spanish, 'Si?'

Why not indeed? As the judge himself remarked after the wedding, 'It was all very strange, but it is not my job to ask why people are getting married.'

The rest of us have been less sanguine. The marriage of Elvis's baby, Lisa Marie Presley, to Michael Jackson has not, on the whole, been well received. It has been regarded variously as a hoax, a public relations exercise, or a straightforward business merger. The word 'love' has been notably absent.

The announcement last month that the couple are 'to live apart' has fuelled speculation that this was never in any sense a real marriage in the first place. But it was always going to be difficult for either Lisa or Michael to have a real marriage, not least because they are not real people. We speak of them mostly as inhabitants of the spirit world of celebrity. Each of them embodies a bundle of contradictions that tells us what we want to hear. About America, or fame, or fortune, or ultra-stardom. About too much too soon. About money not buying happiness. So what has love got to do with it?

Nothing, unless you count our love for a good metaphor. And now we're talking. For here is a couple who between them carry the genes of pop culture, the DNA of rock 'n' roll and the blood rites of sweet soul music. She, with her father's face eerily superimposed on to her own; he, desperate to remove the face that he inherited from his own abusive father. What would such genetic inheritance produce? What would such a pop baby look like?

We don't know because we don't know what Michael Jackson looks like any more. He freed himself from nature a long while ago. And this is the darker side in this luminous melting pot, for this is mixed marriage after all. She is the daughter of a white boy who could move like a black man; he is a black man who is widely considered to be deracinated after all he has done to himself. Yet all that Jackson has ever done is that which we demand of our greatest performers – expressed outwardly what normally stays on the inside. He has gone too far, but stars are stars because of their ability to do just that. Nothing succeeds like excess. By showing us his innards, by remaking his face into that of another – a Caucasian, a female even, or some life form that we don't yet understand, Jackson has taken literally the alchemical power of popular culture to transform that which it touches.

Conversely, if Elvis stole, or 'appropriated' black culture, he remained to his dying day pure white trash – though he always denied it. Sure enough he was poor, he said, but his folks were never prejudiced. Why was it then, that after Priscilla – the fourteen-year-old he pursued in Germany, taught to wear two rows of false eyelashes, and re-created as 'his living doll' – gave birth to Lisa Marie, he never had sex with her again? And why, when she ran off with her part-Hawaiian karate instructor in 1972, did the Presley circle refer to her lover as 'the half-nigger'?

What Sam Philips was seeking before he found Elvis was 'genuine, intuitive Negro music' not 'nigger music' as Albert Goldman rewrote it. But while the critic Lester Bangs universalized Elvis's appeal – 'I can guarantee one thing, we will never again agree on anything as we agreed on Elvis' – race is once more on the agenda. As a member of Public Enemy said: 'Elvis was a hero to most but he never meant shit to me.'

And we cannot even begin to agree on Michael Jackson. We don't even know what colour to call him. We simply know that he is beyond weird and that he did what all good Americans are supposed to do – he created himself. He is a self-made man. The surface of his skin is as deep as we care to go, so we are inclined to read his marriage and separation as little more than a play of signifiers. To bring reality into the equation is more than it can bear. To attach depth to his actions would be truly scary. Peter Guralnick, who has often written about Elvis, always quotes William Carlos Williams: 'The pure products of America go crazy.' Greil Marcus rewrites this line as: 'But you might say that the crazy products of America are pure.'

Burdened with such a heavy metaphorical load, the marriage itself is seen to be meaningless. It means too much for it to mean anything at all. And, alas, our cynical hearts tell us that this absence of meaning can only mean one thing. Money.

So what can I tell you about this marriage that's real? That Elvis speaks to us from beyond the grave, watching his only child move from Graceland to Neverland and out again, and says he doesn't like it one little bit? That he speaks to us through the Elvis Presley Burning Love fan club, whose members are not pleased at all? Or that he communes through his stepmother, Dee Presley: 'I know Elvis would never accept it'?

He would, she says, have been deeply troubled and concerned about Lisa Marie's children, given the child molestation charges that have until very recently been hanging over Michael Jackson's head. 'It leads you to wonder,' she said darkly. But there is something here that's more offensive to the Presley dynasty than Jackson's tarnished reputation, and that is the idea of young Michael as a pretender to Elvis's throne. 'I would like to say to Michael Jackson that there was one King and that was Elvis Presley.'

The King himself is worth more dead than he ever was alive. Elvis Presley Enterprises, run by Priscilla, rakes in millions of dollars from the shrine at Graceland. Michael Jackson had tried to obtain the Presley catalogue and already owns the copyright to 'Long Tall Sally' and 'Lawdy Miss Clawdy'. He has had a crush on Elvis for years. In 1984 he even considered hiring Colonel Parker as his manager.

He's not the only one obsessed with Elvis, as Greil Marcus's book

Dead Elvis creepily reminds us. Elvis inhabits the body of popular culture, not as a bloated corpse, but as a voodoo spirit able to take over the souls of others. Among the apparitions that have figured, Marcus lists: 'Elvis Christ, Elvis Nixon, Elvis Hitler, Elvis Mishima, Elvis as godhead, Elvis inhabiting the bodies of serial killers, saints, fiends.' After Madonna's oft-quoted remark about k d lang, 'I've just seen Elvis and she's beautiful', we can also add Elvis Dyke to his reincarnations.

To bring him alive again, all we need to do is remember Lester Bangs's reaction when he saw him in the flesh for the first time in the seventies. By then the King may have become the Burger King but he could still move Bangs to say that seeing Elvis gave him 'an erection of the heart'.

In such a context, then, how do we talk of his real-life flesh and blood, of Lisa Marie, who at six said of her father, 'I looked up at him and said "Daddy, Daddy, I don't want you to die". And he said, "OK, I won't".' She had been staying with him three years later when his eighteen-stone body was found. At fifteen she would be living with her mother Priscilla and her mother's lover Mike Edwards, who was later to reveal that he fantasized about having Elvis Presley's little girl while making passionate love to her mother.

Soon she was taking sedatives, then other drugs, and dating un-suitable men. She even went to live with Jerry Lee Lewis at one point, though he was old enough to be her grandfather. All this until she found Scientology, and dyed her hair black, Elvis black. She ended up in a Scientology detox clinic going through what they call a Purification Rundown. She once commented flatly, 'If I didn't have Scientology, I'd be dead now. It's a way out, it works.' Her two children, Danielle and Ben, were born in accordance with strict Scientology guidelines: 'No noise, no drugs, no help.'

Now, at last, Lisa apparently needs her space. She is to move out of Neverland, the ranch that her husband built, to live with the children in a £2 million mansion in North East Los Angeles. The children, apparently, have not been happy in Neverland, the place that Jackson created in order to make children happy. Danielle misses her dad, the little-known bass player Danny Keough, whom

Lisa divorced to marry Jackson. The little girl preferred living with her grandmother Priscilla.

Unsurprisingly Keough is reported to be none too enamoured of the idea of his children living with Jackson, although one of the two witnesses at the ceremony in the Dominican Republic was Tommy Keough, his brother and also a Scientologist. What Priscilla really thinks of the marriage changes according to whichever tabloid you read. She is either furious or standing by whatever her daughter does. From the Jackson camp only LaToya, Jackson's marvellously eccentric sister, is prepared to do the dirty, which is after all her only real claim to fame: 'It is an obvious PR exercise aimed at portraying Michael in a more manly, heterosexual light, but girls are not really part of Michael's life.'

Michael, as we know, has had a hard time of it lately. The charges of child molestation against him have finally been dropped, following an out-of-court settlement to Jordy Chandler. After Jordy received his $2 million trust fund, no other boys have been prepared to come forward to testify against Jackson, though David Schwartz, Jordy's stepfather, is suing him for breaking up his family. There are also impending lawsuits from five of Jackson's former bodyguards who claim that they were fired for 'knowing too much'. Pepsi had by this point cancelled his contract, and Jackson fled to Europe to be cured of his addiction to pain-killers just after the LA police obtained a warrant to strip-search him in order, supposedly, to verify remarks that Jordy had made about his genitals. Suspicious minds at that time suggested that Jackson was having yet more plastic surgery, this time on his penis. And while Lisa was weaned off drugs via Scientology, Jackson's route was somewhat different and slightly easier, according to the tabloid headlines which proclaimed 'Jacko weaned off drugs on to Hob-Nobs'.

Still, maybe theirs was an old-fashioned love story after all, involving, as it would have to, their shared love of other creatures. According to Jackson: 'One of the things that most attracted me to Lisa is that she gets along well with the many animals in my zoo.' There are many animals in Jackson's zoo and let's not forget that this is the man who once tried to woo Whitney Houston by sending her a llama. It was an unsuccessful move, Houston replying: 'That's just what I need around the house – a llama!'

However, if proof were needed of Lisa and Michael's affection for each other, we have about as much proof as we are ever going to get. Though Jackson's new calendar features him kissing babies, and even more unwisely, dressed as a scoutmaster surrounded by young boys, at the MTV awards ceremony Jackson engaged in his first public kiss with a woman by planting – in tabloid speak – a 'sizzling smacker' on the lips of his bride. Madonna, in her new-found role as marriage guidance counsellor, was convinced. 'It was a great moment. I realized they're real happy.' They also took part in that other guarantor of marital bliss, featuring on the cover of *Hello!* magazine; Michael laying his hands on Lisa's body rather gingerly, caused a 'body language expert' to comment that he was resting his hands on her as if she were 'a hot plate'. Still, if Madonna believes that they were real happy, then isn't that enough?

They were real happy on honeymoon too. In Budapest. Just the two of them. Oh and forty-seven friends, a male dance troupe, five bodyguards, a PR team, a film crew, 2,655 cuddly toys and, according to the *Mail On Sunday*, a dwarf named Misha that 'Jackson had delivered to his room'. For, apart from honeymooning, Jackson was also making a video in which he plays a freedom fighter who delivers a tormented East European people from communist tyranny. The actual people of Hungary weren't so impressed, as their role was to dress up as Soviet troops for the video or watch while Jackson delivered toys to a children's hospital which needs resources and wages for the doctors rather than Barbie dolls for the patients.

All of this could be true. Or a version of the truth. Or I could have made it up, or the tabloids could have made it up, or Lisa and Michael could have made it up. But I swear to God that I want to believe, I really do. I want to know deep in my heart that stars are not like us. Their lives are made of something altogether different. They can never be normal. They cannot even have sex with each other, for Chrissake. Or is that just another line – that what brought this odd couple together was their shared dislike of sex?

At least they didn't want each other for the money. Or unit sales, as it's daintily referred to. Besides, if you grew up as Michael did, watching yourself as a cartoon character on TV, then the only girl for you would be the girl who grew up in a boulevard named after her father, who saw a £2 million airliner with her name emblazoned on its side. The child who had toddler mink coats and diamond bracelets and Harley-Davidson golf-carts to play with was once flown to Utah for twenty minutes to play in the snow just because she had never seen snow before. This was Elvis's idea of quality time. And yet she never really knew if she would be dislodged in his affections because of the fans that always surrounded him.

So it makes sense that such celebrity royalty has to intermarry, just like our own royal family, because no one else can survive it, no one else understands the pressures. No one else wants to.

You might say that as long as we turn our stars into empty vessels into which we layer meaning upon meaning we cannot feign dismay at their hollowness. We need them to be hollow in order that we can fill them up with our heart's desires. Why trouble ourselves over the emptiness of their real lives? Why worry about the absence of a centre when the tabloids can produce a life from the edges, from the detritus of fame?

Yet whatever metaphors we produce out of this melding of icons, this merger of the gods and goddesses of fame, they tell more about ourselves than is sometimes good for us. Lisa Marie Presley and Michael Jackson have everything money can buy, yet in the stratosphere that they inhabit all we can see is a sexless, dysfunctional, horribly disfigured union. That which made them what they are must be denied to them. The ability of great pop music to mean everything and nothing, to move us beyond belief, is lost somewhere in the great distance between Graceland and Neverland. And you know, I wish them all the luck in the world. For the one thing that they could do to make the house come tumbling down again, to change our lives as we want them to be changed, would be for them simply to love each other. And be loved in return.

BALANCING THE BOOKS

If I made the statement that I would never consider educating my children privately, would that make me (a) an unreconstructed socialist; (b) politically correct; or (c) a liar?

Actually, I'm not any of these things – but it's true that I've never thought of private education as an option for my children. It has never been part of my experience. Yet, according to this paper and just about every other one, this is a huge moral dilemma for the Left. Or the middle-class left anyway.

Presumably the rest of the country doesn't have to trouble itself with its children's schooling. It just bungs them off to the nearest school and hopes for the best.

In many ways this strikes me as a healthier attitude than this endless agonising over which school, but often I feel increasingly alienated from many of these discussions. Like being at a dinner party and finding yourself next to someone who wants to tell you how they did their own conveyancing, my attention soon wanders, but that's probably because I went to a state school and never grasped what the important things in life really were.

It's not that I am not concerned about my children's education. It's just that it seems we are not really talking about education at all. Not in the true sense. Instead, a kind of code is in operation that masks our real anxieties. If we send our kids to an inner-city school – inner-city now has purely negative connotations – how are we to guarantee that our children remain resolutely middle class. How will Sophie manage with crack and guns and black people even if we spend a fortune on violin, extra French and tennis coaching?

The fear is not just about exam results but about contamination.

This is a real fear – the squeezing of the middle classes and all those potential Labour voters has produced this dreadful defensiveness, the desire to stick to what we know, rather than imagine a future that is in any way different. How better then to guarantee this future than through our children? It is no longer a case of giving our kids what we never had, but of trying to ensure they have *exactly* what we had, even though we didn't like it at the time.

Tony and Cherie Blair's decision to send Euan trekking across London to the Oratory strikes me as mad, but for personal as well as political reasons. Politically, I can see how this could operate as a signal to former Tory voters who can see that Blair is just like them. Personally, however, anything that makes you have to get up even earlier than you already do is insane. This ten-year-old will have to be ferried across London by car during the rush hour. Whatever happened to the idea that we should rely less on cars? Or is that just another piece of politically correct whimsy no one really has to take any notice of now?

It is interesting that the charge of hypocrisy should now rest on the choice of school. Over the years it has become far more acceptable to buy private health care, though of course we all support the NHS. I have never done it, but I'm not sure I wouldn't – you know, if it was a matter of life or death. School, however, doesn't strike me as a matter of life or death, although it is increasingly presented that way. To say it isn't, that one school is much the same as the next, in the current climate, means that somehow you are an uncaring parent. I don't think this is the case at all.

Perhaps this is because, as the Californians would say, I am so in touch with my 'inner child' that I have not completely forgotten what it was like to be at school. And I hated it. I did not have a 'child-centred' education, but the kind that people are prepared to move house to ensure that their children get: that is a desk-centred one full of pettiness and uniforms and arbitrary rules and regulations. I did not go much and left as soon as I could, at sixteen, feeling that the subjects I wanted to learn about could not be contained in such a ridiculous institution. I guess I was lucky in that I could already read and write, but that came from primary, not secondary, schooling.

Many years later, when I wanted to be part of a structure in which to learn, I found a course for mature students, most of whom had had experiences similar to mine.

I do not underestimate the importance of education, but what matters for me is those first few years and the opportunity later in life to retrain, or do a course just for the hell of it. Those intervening years of adolescence have never struck me as the right time to focus on education. Proper adolescents have always got better things to do.

In these days, when we have to get down on our knees before league tables and examination results, such talk is unfashionable. Anyway, my friends say it's different now. There *are* no jobs. Young people cannot leave home like they once did and are dependent for far longer on their parents. Basically, if you want them to leave home, you have to make sure they can; therefore schooling has even greater psychological investment in it than it once did.

So we now talk of consuming education, while sneering at the working classes for their mindless consumption of other pursuits. Education has become a kind of banking system. In the guise of individual choice, we regard children less and less as individuals and worry more and more that they should be the same as everyone else in our socio-economic patch. We no longer ask each other whether our children are happy, but whether they got into the right school. Even those who were miserable at their private schools are prepared to inflict this on their own kids to ensure these enclaves of properly educated individuals. Those who don't want their offspring to mix with 'deprived' children are perfectly willing to deprive them of computer games, TV, social interaction with all kinds of people. In the name of what, exactly? Choice? Opportunity? Who's kidding who?

Since I have been doing this job I have met a lot more people who have been privately educated. I can definitely see the benefits of this kind of education. They are confident that they are educated, even when they are being stupid. They have a greater grasp of macro-theory than the average person, alongside pockets of quite useless information. For every erudite and charming public-school boy I have met, there exists his counterpart – the Dim-but-Nice type that Harry Enfield plays so well. But I guess this is what you are shelling out for, if all else fails. Niceness.

State schools are just much more nasty, full of horrible working-class children who are being encouraged to express themselves. We don't want any of that, thank you. The idea of education as libera-tion, or even the idea that it can go on outside a school building, now seems terribly idealistic. Those who sent their kids to free schools are disillusioned – like a friend of mine who found that the only thing her daughter could construct was a dope table.

Summerhill – and similar schools – only seemed to work as long as its charismatic founder, A. S. Neill, was still alive. We have all grown up now and education is about jobs, even if there are none to be had. The slacker generation is, on the whole, educated and has not dropped out, but has never found anything worth dropping in to.

This is a problem that stretches far beyond schooling. Surely, though, if education is to be relevant for the next century it has also to be about self-sufficiency. There will be more and more out of work for longer periods. Skills, rather than jobs for life, means a more flexible approach, yet we are bogged down with ever-more rigid requirements about what our children should learn. You cannot teach self-sufficiency, but it is crazy that what dominates debate at the moment is this banking concept of education in which what we feel is right is deposited into our students. In an-other context, the great educator Paulo Freire wrote of how this turned students into 'containers' to be filled by teachers. The teach-er 'makes deposits' which the students must memorize and repeat. Feeling that schools and teachers are somehow failing us, certain parents now rush around to try to make the right deposit, to buy the right insurance policy for the future, as if their children, too, were empty vessels waiting to be filled up. We will have vouchers instead of gift tokens in order to pretend that there are equal opportunities where there are none. When school becomes the only way we try to control our children's future, we are giving up the notion that there might be other ways. In the absence of a collective solution, some parents will always opt for an individual solution. I cannot blame them, but I think in the guise of seeking a broad education they are instead narrowing it.

And as poor Euan Blair is roused from his sleep for the long drive to school, I wonder what exactly is being deposited in this child. I hope it pays off. But who knows? The returns on such an individual investment can never be absolutely guaranteed as long as Euan grows alongside those in whom no such investment is being made.

That may be uncomfortably close to a socialist argument, but as long as parents are expected to act as educational entrepreneurs on behalf of their children, let's not kid ourselves this is about choice. It's about hopelessness. And in this case, the personal is as desperate as the political.

CALF LOVE WE WON'T GROW OUT OF

Those who oppose fascism without opposing capitalism, wrote Bertolt Brecht, 'are like people who wish to eat their veal without slaughtering the calf'. What he would have made of the ranks of animal protesters, many of whom don't mind capitalism much at all but do not want to see calves slaughtered, I do not know.

Those who want to have their veal and eat it will no doubt be delighted at the publication of William Waldegrave's wife's recipes of delightful things that you can do with this melt-in-the-mouth flesh. Perhaps, too, they will be pleased to know that food writers have recently told us that the next trend in exotic meat is kangaroo.

You do not have to be some balaclava-clad fanatic to feel that actually no one needs to eat either veal or kangaroo to have a full and varied diet or to satisfy some dubious meat-lust. I have never eaten veal but my reasons for this are as valid or as muddled or as purely emotional as the next person's. Yet the recent protests – which now extend to sheep, though not as yet to chickens, which I'm told have an even worse life – have prompted several conversations which have made me think.

Many of the discussions I have had with perfectly decent souls over the last couple of weeks go something like this. Yes, farming methods may be barbaric and (surprise, surprise) profit-fuelled but aren't there far worse things in the world? What about people? Where are the protests against Rwanda, poverty, homelessness, etc? Animal protesters are dubbed single-issue loonies or middle-class do-gooders who will get all sentimental over a watery-eyed calf but do not object to many other evils in the world. This position was summed up most eloquently by John Naughton writing in his television column in the *Observer*, after viewing *Shoah* and Richard Dimbleby in Belsen. Linking the cattle trucks that men, women and children were herded in for transportation to the death camps to the trucks in which the hapless veal calves are exported to Holland, he wrote: 'And eventually the thought comes to me that only half a century ago the Germans carted human beings about in less humane ways, and subjected them to an infinitely worse fate, and nobody in authority here apparently gave a damn.'

This is a powerful argument and is usually followed by some pleas to redirect the energy of the animal protesters into some more worthy cause. I have made it myself but increasingly I feel it is missing the point or at least exposing an ever-widening gap between politics as we have traditionally understood them and the kind of personal politics that has bloomed over the last few years. To dismiss these protests as not properly political or as simply mis-guided is to dismiss vast sections of the population who feel strongly that things are not as they should be. Proper politics are rational, we say, but these protests are governed merely by emotion – as though political action and emotion are mutually exclusive activities.

The biggest demonstrations of the last year over roads or the Criminal Justice Bill have been similarly described. These, after all, are not life or death issues but they are all infused with the vaguer notions of social justice, of basic fairness, and the right of people to have a say in how their lives are lived. The fuzzy logic of many of the demonstrators may be caricatured as Utopian, juvenile or hope-lessly optimistic, but to deny their energy is not the answer. It is simply to further disenfranchise people from a political system they already feel alienated from.

There is in the direct action of so many of these demonstrations an instant gratification, a feeling that is missing from much more established political organizations. You can go home feeling that, yes, *you* have saved a crate-load of calves, released a few chickens, made the Government think twice about building another motor-way link. There is a purity in such activities that is missing from the average party political meeting, which is so consumed with its own internal affairs that very little ever seems to be achieved and leaves most of us feeling even more powerless.

If only these protesters would connect their issue to other more fundamental issues, I hear you say, the world would be a better place. Surely, though, the point is that these protesters are making connections that conventional politics still feels largely oblivious to. To say that how we treat other species reflects on our own humanity, that we do not have the right merely to take from the environment without giving back, conjures up a different moral universe than the one which John Redwood described in this paper this week which sees the unfettered market as the highest expression of our humanity.

If leaders such as Tony Blair are trying to redraw policy on a moral basis, it is because morality and politics as it is lived feel like such separate worlds. The issue of how we treat animals, then, is debated in terms of rights or of considerations of supply and demand, both of which are inadequate. The notion that we can grant beings rights that they are themselves unable to exercise is misguided, as is the idea that we should so blindly follow the market. Some people may be happy to buy slaves but we do not on the whole think this is a good idea. Some people may want to kill endangered species for the skins but we now look down on this too. There are few fur coats on the streets of our cities these days. This victory for the animal rights lobby may be a peculiarly British affair but it is a victory none the less. It indicates the possibility of change.

The 'if only' brigade may wish that our consciousness had been similarly raised over more crucial issues concerning human beings, and point laughingly to the fact that Hitler was a vegetarian, but let's not dismiss small victories in the name of larger more elusive ones. I neither think Meat Is Murder nor that You Are What You Eat but my own position has shifted over the years, largely, I think, because of watching my own children's and their friends' response to these issues.

Never having been a great animal lover, I have also felt that environmentalism has been rife with all sorts of ideologies that I have no time for, literally. A green household inevitably means more domestic labour and we know who does that. So in the past I could have put my kids' concern over dolphins and ducks down to the endless green brainwashing that they get at school or to the fact that we read them stories about Henrietta Hen before serving up the chicken nuggets. Or I could put it down to the fact that on this score Seeing Is Believing, and we are so far removed from the process of meat production that it was a real shock for my kids to see a carcass hanging in a market on the Continent. They thought meat only came in plastic packets from the supermarket.

'What is it, Mummy?' they kept asking. And when I told them, they could not believe it. 'But what is it really?' They refuse to gloss over the contradictions that most of us do – 'Be kind to animals but, here, eat this one or you won't get any pudding' – and have drifted in and out of vegetarianism ever since. They do not contort themselves with arguments about whether it's OK to eat something that has had a good life (we do not know what a good life is for a person, let alone a turkey) and instead have a childish but fundamental sense of fairness. To call this mere sentimentality is wrong. Nor does it mean that they care about animals at the expense of people.

At five most kids – not even mine, you'll be glad to know – do not intone the slogan 'the personal is political' but instead wonder if fish really do have fingers and whether it's OK to eat them once they are covered with ketchup. Like most vegetarians they would kill for a bacon sandwich. They may, as they get older, direct their passions into a concern about world farming, they may have more grasp of the arguments about resources and so on. This may, of course, as many of my friends have suggested, just be a phase they are going through.

To patronize them in this way – 'It's just a phase, it's infantile, unrealistic, one day they will grow up and see how the world really is' – is to use exactly the arguments being made against those crying over veal exports. This is not the world of grown-up politics. It is not adult enough, rational enough, to be taken seriously. All this youthful energy must be channelled into something far more deserving. Yet if it is just a phase it is one that more and more of us are going through. And if you want people to grow out of it then you must offer them something to grow into.

To say this is not to put the rights of animals above those of people. On the contrary, I say it out of concern for the quality of human life, another phase that I have not yet matured out of.

SHOPPING AND THE DEMEANING OF LIFE

When the going gets tough, the tough go shopping. Or we used to. There was a time when the feel-good factor could be bought as easily as a new washing machine. No down-payment necessary. Instant credit. Buy now. Pay later. A quarter of households now have three or more TV sets. Dishwashers and microwaves are no longer sold as labour-saving devices so that a busy housewife can put her feet up but as the necessary tools of every working woman. Perhaps, once upon a time, fan-assisted ovens, chest freezers and CD-players made us happier than we had ever thought possible. But no more.

The feel-good factor cannot be reduced to consumer durables. It cannot be reduced even to the odd trip through Harvey Nicks. Feeling good apparently depends on that most elusive of products – confidence in the future. People need to feel not just that they can buy more but that they can hold on to what they have already got. They don't, and that is why they are not spending, even though they are continually told that the economy is on the up-turn.

It's difficult to say exactly when shopping ceased to be the meaning of life. In the heady days of the eighties people like Wally Olins said things like 'marketing is to the 1980s what sociology was to the 1960s', and we believed him, expecting marketing men to understand our hearts' desires far more than a politician of any hue.

We no longer wanted to be classified by what we produced but by what we consumed. This was what a classless society meant. If you blanked out the poverty you saw all around you could aspire to the purity of untrammelled market forces. It even seemed kind of noble – giving the people the right to buy whatever they wanted. The talk was of freedom and infinite choice, grand abstract concepts. The reality was a Sock Shop in every railway station, a Next shop on every high street and the homogenization of retailing which made every town centre interchangeable.

Now, as Rumbelows closes down, giving way to the out-of-town superstores, the high street looks increasingly barren. Even city shopping centres are full of empty 'units'. My local Rumbelows in Hackney will doubtless be replaced by yet another shop that sells everything for the price of 99p. Should I need to buy another TV or even just a hairdryer I guess I'll have to drive miles to some godforsaken warehouse somewhere on the North Circular. The thing is, I haven't got a car, and when I tell this to people they invariably say 'You really should learn to drive and buy a car.' And when I say 'What for?', the answer is always that 'it would make shopping so much easier'.

Not having a car puts me, in marketing terms, alongside pensioners and the unemployed. In ABC terms, I'm an E and sadly locked out of the vast 'retailing experience' currently on offer. So I do rely on shopping locally, not out of some quaint notion of community but because it is the easiest thing to do. Once tele-shopping becomes the norm I will apparently be able to shop by just using my computer, and shopping will have become a completely private experience, not a social one. As I also work from home, there will be little reason for me ever to leave it. And this is marketed as something to look forward to?

It's not that I have anything against shopping centres, it's just that the dramatic celebratory spaces that they were supposed to provide never really materialized even at the height of Thatcherism. Stuffed full of bored security guards, surveillance cameras, slow fast-food these strange, weatherless environments have become so many end zones. Kids who would hang around these places as kids do are ushered out not so gently. Old people sit staring at the inevitable fountain. The buzz and hum of a market-place is often absent in such a sanitized space. At night the lights are turned off and these temples of consumption cease to exist. Where are we to go? What does it mean to hit the town when there is nothing left in town and the town centre is on the outskirts of town?

Urban planners talk about the importance of the evening economy, the twenty-four-hour city and yet, despite the huge changes in work patterns, British life still seems to revolve around the notion that we all work nine-to-five and go home. Public service broadcasting stops at midnight as if to tell us to go to bed so that we can be up for work in the morning. Cities, too, operate in this way. The city is something to get away from after work. It is dark, dangerous, unpredictable. You wouldn't want to be there after the shops close, let alone after the pubs shut.

Fewer of us live in our city centres and fewer of us will visit them if the shops are closed down. The myth of the bright lights, of Fridays on your mind, of waiting for the weekend so that you can hit the streets, is somewhat different to taking the family to B&Q on a Sunday afternoon. I spent my youth, as countless others have, going 'up town'. And it was never about consuming anything other than a coffee that you made last two hours in the local Wimpy.

There is a great deal to be said for hanging around. It is what young people with no money do. And while my mother could never understand why I spent so many freezing evenings sitting on a wall outside a chip shop, all I can say is that it was a formative experience. It sounds melodramatic to call the endless lurking that I and my friends did on street corners 'streetlife', and I'm aware that the phrase has different connotations for girls than it does for boys, but in our own small-town way that's what it was.

It is reassuring to find that when I go back there the various subcultural views – I'm afraid there's only one per subculture so that the punk, the rasta, the goth and the skinhead all know each other – still sit on the steps of the old post office just like we did twenty years ago. But the thing is that they go 'up town' to do it, to what is recognizably the town centre. The closure of a few electrical shops does not mean the death of the high street but it should remind us that our streets should be places for people to sit in and watch the world go by as well as places to buy things in. We already know what happens if we leave the creation of civic space to market forces alone, and it is nothing more or less than these out-of-town superstores that pile it high and sell it cheap and that are certainly not in the business of caring about social interaction.

These vast stores, with their crèches and restaurants and the promise of everything under one roof, will carry on in their quest to give us, in their jargon, 'the perfect retail/leisure mix'. The postmodernists among us will write gloriously of these excessive, hyperreal spaces, in which we are what we buy and have become simply desiring machines with credit cards. Meanwhile, the places which could give us the perfect leisure/retail mix, the high streets, are struggling. If the going gets so tough that there is nothing to do but window-shopping, where will we go when all the shops close?

GENETIC SCIENTISTS LOST IN INNER SPACE

Picture this: you are delighted to find yourself pregnant and anxious to do everything to make sure you have a healthy baby. The doctor recommends a few tests. 'It's just routine, nothing to worry about.' You are called in to get the results. Everything seems fine. No Down's syndrome. No spina bifida. 'But there is just one thing. We have made an antenatal diagnosis and feel that we should give you this information. What you do with it is your decision.' The doctor then goes on to tell you that the foetus, while perfectly normal in every other way, may be carrying genes which predispose it to aggression, antisocial and possibly criminal behaviour.

Do you demand a termination of pregnancy? Do you say, can you be more specific – will this foetus have a predisposition towards serial killing or are we talking tax evasion here? Or do you say loftily that criminals are not born, that there is such a thing as free will and that you will have none of this 'neurogenetic determinism'?

A scientist at a private conference in Britain at the Ciba Foundation last week suggested that the technology may already be available for such antenatal diagnosis. Dr David Goldman, from the Laboratory of Neurogenetics at the US National Institute of Health, said that such information should be given to families, though any decision to abort should be made privately. The conference has been criticized by many other scientists and criminologists who are wary of attributing crime to genetic factors.

There was also talk at the meeting of whether genetic evidence could be used as a mitigating factor in court. This will soon be tested, when the Georgia Supreme Court will have to rule on an appeal by lawyers to introduce genetic evidence for their defence of Stephen Mobley. Mobley is on death row for shooting a pizza parlour manager twice in the back of the neck after robbing the till. He has no underclass credentials to explain such behaviour. He is from a white, middle-class family which did not abuse him as a child. His lawyers, however, have unearthed violent and criminal behaviour over the past four generations of his family. Mobley's father sent his son to many institutions when he was growing up to try to curb his violent behaviour and now the antisocial behaviour of his aunts, uncles and cousins is being used as a mitigating factor for this murder. The boy couldn't help it. It was in his genes.

Even if genetic evidence is ruled inadmissible, many lawyers and scientists believe it will be used in the future in the way that evidence of pre-menstrual syndrome and hyperactivity is now being used in some cases. It is worth noting that the debate surfaced in the same week as the Rowntree Foundation's claims of growing inequality between the richest and poorest in Britain, and as a report from the Employment Policy Institute that, whatever the Government may say, rising crime and rising unemployment are connected.

It's tough being tough on the causes of crime if we can't agree what they are, and if such arguments become so ridiculously polarized. We are actually a complex combination of nature and nurture, a product of the way that our 'raw' genetic material has been 'cooked' by the environment. To identify a 'criminal gene' seems as primitive as Lombroso's nineteenth-century notion of dividing up swindlers from murderers on the basis of facial characteristics. Yet why does this kind of genetic reductionism hold such sway? Possibly because so few of us really understand much about neurotransmitters, the amygdala and the controversial claim that there is a link between 'a point mutation in the structural gene monomine oxidase inhibitor' and abnormal behaviour.

Certainly I never did brilliantly in the course I once took in 'Biological bases of behaviour' which involved a lot of sticking electrodes into rats' brains in order to establish that they had 'pleasure centres' somewhere in there. In retrospect, though, it was worth taking for the curt comment that my tutor wrote at the bottom of one of my essays: 'Not bad until the end when you lapse into hysteria.' Anyway, my ignorance is shared by most of the population and, as a result, we swallow whole chunks of popularized, over-simplified and often suspect sociobiology and neurogenetics.

Any geneticist worth his or her salt might care to locate precisely the gene which causes a predisposition to abandoning all our critical faculties so that we do indeed become blinded by science. Social scientists on the other hand could undertake a study which would show us who is funding this sort of research and why.

Many scientists, such as the admirable Steven Rose of the Open University, are always careful to explain, as he does in the journal *Nature*, that 'the phenomena of human existence and experience are always simultaneously biological *and* social and an adequate explanation must involve both'. But in recent years a number of 'scientific' theories about behaviour have filtered down that are worrying, to say the least.

Charles Murray's and Richard Herstein's book, *The Bell Curve*, has resuscitated the argument that there is a link between intelligence and race in order to explain the huge black underclass of America. Simon Le Vay claims to have found 'a gay gene' and even 'a gay brain'. Genes have been found which, it has been claimed, cause violence and alcoholism. Cause is a key word here. If primacy is given to genes as causal mechanisms then we can forget environmental or experiential factors. In other words, we begin to believe that some people are just born bad and nothing much can be done about it. If this is the disease, then the cure veers between vague social engineering in which we find it sensible to eradicate, if possible, the chances of babies being born with congenital abnormalities, and a far more frightening scenario that I conjured up at the beginning of this article in which babies are aborted because they are perceived to be carrying antisocial genes.

In such a scenario we are relieved of our duty to alleviate the stresses that poverty and unemployment and homelessness cause, whereas the one fact that most geneticists agree on is that if there is any predisposition towards destructive behaviour it will be activated by such conditions. Why look for the roots of violence in the serotonin-re-uptake of incarcerated criminals, Steven Rose asks, when you could achieve as significant an impact by taking measures to reduce the 280 million handguns on the streets of the United States?

The study of the inner space of genetics has altered our lives as profoundly as the study of outer space, and it is producing the big moral dilemmas. Yet the popular understanding of much of this research is coloured by an older kind of magical thinking which resonates with much of this biological determinism. We all know families where everyone has turned out all wrong, we still speak of bad blood, we still use the notion of essential evil to explain certain crimes. Indeed, such determinism slots in all too easily with much New Age guff about unchanging essences and energies, which also emphasizes the individual at the expense of any social context.

A predisposition to a particular kind of behaviour is misread instead as predestination. These things are written in the stars. Or, if not in the stars, in the long strings of DNA that make us what we are. Our fate is decided in the womb. Will I be happy, will I be gay? Will I be locked up? *Que sera, sera.* If it is your personal biological make-up that makes you do the things you do, then don't blame it on the conditions that you grew up in. Giving you a job, an income, a decent place to live won't change your life. You can forget all that dreary social work stuff. No dear, we have a little something to help you get your neurotransmitters sorted once and for all. Remember it's not your fault. And it's certainly not ours. You were just born that way, and though I fear I'm lapsing into hysteria again, perhaps you should consider yourself lucky to be born at all.

ROCKERS ON THE RUN FROM MOTHER

The cover of this week's NME says it all. There is a picture of the scowling Stone Roses bearing the legend 'we're still arrogant sods. The Stone Roses take on the world.' Arrogant sods; don't you just love them? And where would rock and roll be without them? If you are not actually in a band you can take on the world from the privacy of your own home. You could listen to the music that makes you feel you could. This is the buzz. You could call it empowering, though what it empowers you to do is not really the point. It is empowering enough to feel, to react, to be messed around and messed up by it. This is the energy, the life force. This is how we grew up.

There is a burgeoning genre of writing in which writers, mostly male, chart their own development by their musical tastes. They own up to liking what may now be considered naff. It is an effort to undo the selective memory of so much music criticism which pretends that we came out of the womb liking John Coltrane rather than Mud. Certain of what is fine and proper, they can now laugh ironically at their own bad taste because, after all, if you can't judge a man by his record collection, how can you judge him at all?

Maybe it is different for girls. For a start we have always been allowed to like a fluffier kind of music. It is taken as given that we have a purchase on commercial, disposable pop music, that we like what is meaningless, from the Bay City Rollers to Take That because, well, we just don't know any better. When I was growing up, meaningful was what boys did, mostly because they couldn't dance. Various boyfriends of mine spent the seventies boring me to death in a thankless effort trying to get me to appreciate the likes of Cream. They went to an awful lot of trouble organizing the right drugs at the right moment for the right track. I really tried because I wanted to be sophisticated and that meant not liking the music that other girls liked. But I remained immune, preferring Sly Stone's voice to any guitar solo, a sign which of course I now realize was indicative of my superior musical tastes.

Punk happened at around the same time I first heard the word misogyny. There was a lot going on. Young women could garb themselves in the skewed trappings of male fantasy – leather, rubber, stockings and suspenders – and look untouchable. Softness was a sin. We purged our shelves of any trace of Joni Mitchell, wandered off to Clash gigs and wondered why Joe Strummer took to dressing up as a soldier. Once we understood the look of Sandinista rather than squaddie we were reassured. But not that much. How come we like music that, if not bad for us, was not actually about us at all? Was punk just rejigged cock-rock? Hell, let's get off on the excitement of rebellion, we'll worry about the revolution later.

Anyway, everything and everyone was horrible back then. It seemed tetchy to quibble about the lack of representation of women in such circumstances. Why be articulate when you could just be angry? In retrospect, the men had monopolized that too. No one in the world could be as angry as Johnny Rotten when he screamed out the options for the phallic principle: 'be a man, kill someone, kill yourself'.

All that was long, long ago. Nowadays *some* men are more sensitive at least; they boast of their impotence, like Morrissey, or sing lines like Beck: 'I'm a loser baby, so why don't you kill me?' To be honest, I guess, it's been a while since I worried about the ideological content of the music I got off on. The question most women ask of the Rolling Stones's 'Under My Thumb' is still not whether it is obnoxious but whether they can dance to it. I was reminded of all this by a fascinating new book, *The Sex Revolts; Gender, Rebellion and Rock and Roll*, by Simon Reynolds and Joy Press (Serpent's Tail). This is not a book about 'women in rock'; rather, it is about men in rock viewed through the almost mutually exclusive lenses of feminism and fandom. I say this because, right from the start, the authors admit that what they like best emotionally is almost always at odds with what they should like politically, ethically and intellectually: 'Some of the worst offenders – the Stones, the Stooges, Nick Cave, etc – are among our all-time favourites.' What is liberating about their music is 'inseparable from their entrenchment in "unsound" gender politics'. What feels like freedom is rooted in their 'seeds of domination'. And you just liked the tune?

Identifying the powerful and violent dynamic of cutting loose, of breaking away, as the essence of rock and roll, they wonder whether it is possible to imagine rock and roll that isn't fuelled by the drive to free oneself from the feminine domain. Women feature as good for sex or shelter, but eventually they try and tie you down when all that matters is to keep moving. Their analysis goes beyond actual lyrics and also finds another strand in music – from the avant-garde, cosmic sounds of the likes of Eno and Van Morrison to various kinds of rave music – in which femininity figures largely in the abstract, as a desire to come home, to return to the womb, to Nature itself. Again, real women do not appear much in this idealized evocation of femininity. The questions that Reynolds and Press ask could indeed be asked of most popular culture, although it is still not *de rigueur* now that we are all post-politically correct. Now that we all like Scorsese, Tarantino, Oasis, William Burroughs and John Updike, the charge of misogyny has become the retreat of the politically retarded. To even raise the issue is to be seen as not understanding what is going on, or even worse, it is to commit the ultimate crime, to not know how to enjoy oneself. Seeing as we are all so desperate to communicate to everyone else what a good time we were having, we shrug our shoulders and say: 'I'm a ballsy kind of chick. I worship Nick Cave, the man who says "I've always enjoyed writing songs about dead women". I can give as good as I get. I can rap back, I can applaud Courtney Love. I think there should be more women in rock.'

More than this, however, anyone who asks what all this stuff might mean is working from the deeply unfashionable premise that pop culture might be about more than itself, that it might be about other things that go on in the world. This is an increasingly tenuous position when we know that Tarantino makes films about other films, that what influences most musicians are other musicians, that the literature we like is not misogynistic but about misogyny, that you can learn from your enemies; you can learn so much you learn to fall in love with them.

Much of what I love the best is not in any straightforward way anti-women. It just has nothing much to say about them. Or it can only say what we've heard a thousand times before. Women's lives have changed, are changing. So have men's, but the archetypal rocker/rapper who regards women as 'the architects of conventional life' is still in revolt, still on the run from mother. Meanwhile, in the real world, mothers are blamed for the delinquencies of a generation of young men. Music is still the ritualistic way in which we mark out our individuality, our separation from all that is grown up and suffocating, however grown up we really are. Men might need to do this more than ever. But so do women. Isn't it time to put another record on? Hey Joe – by the way are you still wandering around with that gun in your hand?

BARKING UP THE FAMILY TREE

Love, it seems, may sometimes be free but it is never cheap. According to a new book, *The Rising Price of Love* by Dr Patrick Dixon, the cost of the sexual revolution is an awfully high one: £124 billion, to be exact.

Please don't ask me how this 'self-styled emotional actuary' arrived at this figure: we must, in these times of value for money, ask whether it's worth it. Most of us bought it for a lot less than the price of dinner for two and a packet of condoms, though that, of course, is a selfish, morally reprehensible view that has no place when we consider, as he does, the cost of divorce, or the bill for children in care or for looking after people with AIDS.

Once it was only cynical feminists who were ridiculed for reducing marriage to little more than an economic contract, a cost-cutting exercise that sustained the efficient reproduction of capitalism. Now our moral guardians talk in the same language. The Archbishop of York's proposal for tax breaks as an incentive for married couples has been taken seriously. If floundering 'family values' cannot be buoyed up by moral pressure alone then they have to be supported economically. Yet, this yoking of economic forces to personal relationships is coming at the very same time that economic forces are pulling us in the opposite direction.

As John Gray wrote in this paper earlier this week: 'There is, on the contrary, a close – and unsurprising – correlation between economic individualism and family instability.' Globalization demands job mobility and families demand double incomes simply to survive, let alone flourish.

Rather than face these changes head on and ask how we can support all kinds of families, we are once more subject to moral crowing that insists that yes, we can go back to the good old days of the idyllic nuclear family.

We are told we can do so as a matter of choice. We will have to accept that we have responsibilities as well as rights and that, out of the fragments, we can rebuild something wholesome. The family is the place where we can refute our damaging individualism. To those who say there is no going back, the Chief Rabbi, Jonathan Sacks, says: 'The family can be recovered because it is, first and foremost, a moral institution. It is made or unmade by our choices. It is built on the bonds of commitment, fidelity and self-restraint.'

Melanie Phillips, writing in the *Observer*, has harsher words. She sees a conspiracy of 'self-serving intellectuals' who, when they aren't busy wrecking other people's marriages, are busy suppressing the evidence that it is better for children to grow up with two parents rather than one. Those presenting this view, she claims, are treated as 'intellectual and political pariahs', which is funny when you consider that most politicians, religious leaders and, indeed, newspaper columnists regularly regale us with such opinions.

There is a paradox in all this. I agree that the free-market doctrine of sexual entrepreneurship, combined with the compulsory quest for personal gratification, has altered the traditional family set-up and it has flourished precisely because the illusion was sustained that individual choice was all that mattered.

Since that particular bubble has burst, it seems insane to suggest that we can recover the family again via individual choice. The whole point is that, nowadays, having a child is presented as a private matter of individual choice rather than, as a communitarian like Etzioni argues, 'an act that has significant consequences for the community'.

Certain choices are encouraged by social pressure and most of us aspire to bring up our children in the most stable and secure circumstances possible, just as most of us aspire to finding a partner with whom we can share our lives. Choosing these options, however, is not enough to secure them.

Flaunting one's idyllic marriage and achieving children does little to help those who have tried and failed, not because we are immoral, irresponsible people but because we are full of human failings and may have made wrong choices or felt that there was no choice to make.

I am sick and tired of the moral high ground being divided up between the haves and the have-nots. If this is the high ground give me the low ground any day. I am at home in the low ground – this is where I grew up and where I see women on their own struggling to bring up their children as best they can with little money and support. It is in the moral foothills that I see people look after their dying relatives day in and day out. Amongst this misery I also see more ingenuity than in a thousand sermons. Here it's hard to recognize the idealized family that such sermons are full of.

It is easier to be reminded, perhaps, that the family is the place not only of enormous support but the place where people abuse their children and each other. It is the place where women still do most of the work. When they are good; families may be very, very good; when they are bad, they are horrid.

The current PR for the family reads like a glossy commercial. The family warts and all, the family disturbed by changing work patterns, gender expectations, gross dysfunction does not figure much. Yet surely one of the reasons that families produce so much unhappiness is because our expectations of them remain, against all odds, so high. The traditional family has become part of the heritage industry, a kind of emotional theme park which we visit from time to time to remind ourselves of how things used to be. It's nice for a day but would you really want to live in one?

It is a strange thing to be writing this on International Women's Day which, of course, is also National No Smoking Day. Talk of liberating women is as exciting as talking about giving up smoking. We know both things would improve our health and we really are going to get round to it one of these days . . . yet in all these discussions of the family, morality and community there is a striking absence of gender, or indeed reality. The basis of the family is the woman and child, as the number of marriageable men who can support a family, in either economic or emotional terms, is in decline. The moral carrot cannot compete with the stick of the de-regulated labour market. The result is global too – the international feminization of poverty. Children are suffering through material, not maternal or paternal, deprivation. This, for me, is the real moral issue.

Adversarial gender politics are not only unappealing to today's young women, as the new Demos report predictably told us, but were always difficult to bring to bear on the complex allegiances of family life. I am glad to see that young women and men now want to work alongside each other.

I trust that we will see more young men campaigning for women to earn the extra 40 per cent that they do, that they will happily support the children they have fathered, that they will be filled with joy at the idea of working for female managers, that they, rather than their partners, will fill the gap in 'the parenting deficit' so that feminism actually becomes as irrelevant as their partners already think it is.

The family is, of course, the place that such changes are felt the hardest. I am not in the business of denying, as Melanie Phillips accuses the 'media libertarians' of doing, the huge damage caused to children by divorce and family breakdown – nor do I believe that all the problems associated with new family structures can be overcome.

This may be because I would never argue that all the problems associated with traditional family structures could be overcome either. Surely, though, there must be a way of having this discussion without such ridiculous polarization. Those who want to reinstate the mythical nuclear family present themselves as 'for' the family and imply that everyone else – including myself, who sees that there can be no turning back – is somehow 'against' the family.

This is nonsense. Where do they think we live? The argument has become like those of divorcing spouses battling over what is best for the children. What unites us, surely, is that we all claim to want what is best for the children. Pronouncements about the social good of the marital institution do little apart from propagating the idea that, when it comes to families, some are more equal than others.

The choice we have left to make – socially, economically and politically, rather than individually – is whether we treat all families equally whether they are 'proper families' or not. There is much moral huffing and puffing done 'for the sake of the children'. Until we are prepared to act on it, it is so much hot air – as the children huddling on the stairs listening to the grown-ups argue know so well.

STRAIGHT TALKING

So Peter Tatchell has finally been 'outed' as a martyr. What a surprise that is. The man has been crucified this week following his organization's (OutRage!) 'victory' that they got the Bishop of London, the Rt. Revd David Hope, to admit his sexuality was 'ambiguous'. Although the news is his 'confession', Tatchell's letter was actually written a while ago.

Tatchell has since been denounced as a hypocrite, a blackmailer, one of the least 'attractive characters in British public life', a fascist, a terrorist and, in the words of the *Sun*, 'an Australian-born Vietnam draft-dodger'. Australian-born, hey, how low can you go? This is a Murdoch paper after all.

The spectacle of the press denouncing outing is a sight to behold, since the business of journalism has become more and more about outing over the past couple of years. Outing adulterous MPs, public figures who cream off private perks, or indeed fumbling footballers and mumbling monarchs. This is not called outing, this is called 'scoops' and newspapers such as the *News of the World* win awards for such endeavours.

Dishing the dirt – it is in the public interest that hypocrisy is revealed, you understand – is part of the growing climate that is pushing towards greater accountability. We all think it is a good thing. Tatchell stands accused of blackmail.

When a journalist says to a public figure we have certain information about you that we will publish if you don't tell us first, no one cries blackmail. When the *Sun* discovered the MP Michael Brown in the company of a young man it ran the story. Later on, he decided to be open about the fact that he was gay. This was not called outing but investigative journalism.

Actually, I have never supported outing but I understand where it comes from. In the condemnation of Tatchell no one has mentioned the word AIDS, not one person has attempted to explain the history of this kind of activism.

In America it was groups like ACT-UP campaigning around health issues for gay men, for funding and education, which began to use outing strategically. It was always controversial. While many gay people were involved in the long, slow struggle for equality, there were others who felt there wasn't enough time for dainty debate, for polite political discussions. Maybe if you had seen your friends dying, you might feel the same way too.

'Don't die of ignorance' remember? That was the slogan that was used to try and educate us into safer sex. The opposite of ignorance is knowledge, but it still seems many of us would rather not know the truth. It is fine, in fact almost mandatory, for heterosexuals to flaunt their sexuality, but if a man stands up and imparts the knowledge that he is gay he is somehow flaunting something that is best kept behind closed doors. No one could have watched the *Newsnight* interview with Bishop Derek Rawcliffe and not felt unbearably sad that this deeply sympathetic man had spent so much of his life in turmoil. The church talks of love and yet this man had been made to feel bad about those he loved, and this is the tragedy.

Most of us believe that some level of acceptance about what we are is healthier than denying it. How we achieve this, as long as homosexuality is regarded as an entirely private affair, is what needs to be debated. Unlike Tatchell, I do believe in grey areas. I think that the odd ambivalent feeling or act is not proof of innate homosexuality.

I don't think it's all so black and white, probably because I do not think homophobia is so black and white either. As we leave the twentieth century behind, the clergy is struggling to enter it. Their congregations have long shown that kind of Middle English, middle-class tolerance for what the clergy choose to regard as a human failing. Regarding homosexuality as a human failing may in theory constitute homophobia. In practice I'm not so sure.

I always think of my mum in these matters. When one of my 'uncles' phoned to tell her that he had AIDS, her immaculately politically incorrect response was: 'Well, dear, you always were a hypochondriac.' Her actions on the other hand told a different story. She immediately went to visit him when others would not and offered to nurse him when the time came.

This is the grey area and this is what most of us inhabit. I dislike outing because it presupposes two options: one is gay or one is straight. The whole point of the queer politics which Tatchell claims to champion is that it liberates us from the strait-jacket of such categories.

A bit of blurring is no bad thing. Besides which, any historical or anthropological study of sexuality demonstrates that the idea of a distinct homosexual identity is a relatively new one. It depends entirely on heterosexuality being an equally watertight category. In terms of legislation this is a nightmare which, when unpicked, becomes a nonsense. This is why both Clinton in his muddle over gays in the US military and Cardinal Hume in his recent 'acceptance' of gay Catholics make the distinction between a homosexual identity, which is somehow OK, and a homosexual act, which isn't. In other words, you can be it as long as you don't do it.

Not only is this entirely unworkable, it misses the point completely. No one actually needs permission to drink cappuccino all day and listen to the Pet Shop Boys. What they need is a world in which their private sexual practices have as much or as little relevance to the other parts of their lives as the rest of us. This is the heterosexual privilege that we take for granted.

The vilification of Tatchell has shown just how far gays are from attaining it. He has been delving into that fragile area – the gap between what is private and what is public. His detractors claim that he has no right to poke his nose into the private lives of priests. Gayness is seen as an essentially private issue in the way that heterosexuality is not. No one says to the adulterous politician: 'How dare you flaunt your private sexual practices in front of us in the form of your wife, your mistress and your two lovely children.' They say: 'Don't say one thing and then do another.' Or they say: 'There should be some correlation between how you live and how you tell others to live.'

The case against Tatchell is that he uses homophobia as a weapon to lob at those in the closet and this can and does backfire. The cause is elevated over the individual, and the public has far more time for suffering and confused individuals than it does for militant activists. In Tatchell's black and white world 'the gay community' is a necessary myth that will entice these people out of the closet. In practice, even he must know this is not the case. Many members of this community thoroughly oppose his activities. An agenda upon which gay men and lesbians can agree is far off. The priorities are different. The issue of lesbians becoming mothers is a different one to arguing for more research towards helping people with HIV and so on.

Outing is premised on the idea that the personal is political. The reaction, in recent days, has reduced a political argument to personal terms once more, with confused clergy as victims and Tatchell and his gang as persecutors. However ambiguous David Hope may be, he knows a good PR opportunity when it hits him. To be pictured clutching a cross sets him up as some kind of human sacrifice. What is really being sacrificed here is much more than one man's 'right to privacy' – it is the chance to have an open discussion about what we expect from those who set themselves up as our moral guardians. I am not gay, nor militant, nor a supporter of Tatchell, but the refusal of the press to countenance such a discussion strikes me as extremely narrow-minded.

Tatchell may be wrong in his methods but no one that his group has targeted has actually denied the allegations made against them. The pressure that has been used against them is clearly distasteful, although this pressure is daily applied when it comes to matters other than homosexuality. What is distasteful is that while on the one hand the press has encouraged us to think that it is their moral duty to pressurize public figures into revealing their private doings, it will destroy anyone else who does so on a freelance basis. You cannot have it both ways, it would appear, unless, that is, you are straight.

ANGELS WITH DIRTY BOSSES

I have no problem with people being paid what they are worth. Top salaries for top people and all that. As Ed Wallis, chief executive of PowerGen, wrote in the *Financial Times*: 'We must win public confidence that pay is independently set and reflects the market rate; that bonus incentives are directly related to short, medium and long-term performance and that there is full public disclosure.' He should know. Already paid £300,000 a year, he earns an extra £36,000 from three other 'little jobs' that require four days' work a year. He has share options worth £332,000 and stands to receive a bonus payment of up to £100,000 for last year.

The market rate for chief executives is obviously higher than the market rate for nurses or midwives. Under the 1 per cent pay award offered from central funds, staff nurses would get an increase of just £115 a year, taking their salaries up to a whopping £11,435.

The option of a further 2 per cent, to be negotiated locally, is also on the table but has angered the nurses' unions, who want a 3 per cent pay increase 'full stop'. Midwives, traditionally the most conservative of health workers, voted by 82 per cent to rescind its policy of no industrial action.

It is unfair, we have been told, to compare pay in the private sector to pay in the public sector because it's different; it is unfair to compare what a guy like Ed Wallis does to what the average midwife does because it's not the same thing at all. It's unfair to make comparisons because life is unfair.

Anyway, nurses are wonderful. Sentimentality may not pay the mortgage but you don't become a nurse for the money just like you don't become a PowerGen exec to show what a caring person you are. I've yet to meet someone who doesn't support the nurses, who says it's fine that they should be treated so shabbily. Phone-ins are filled with callers telling stories about particularly noble nurses. I could regale you with some myself.

Having spent a lot of time last year in hospitals and hospices with my dying mother, I know what nurses do. Sometimes they didn't go home when their shift ended; they would stay and have a drink with my mother when that was the only pleasure she had left. I don't know how percentages fit in here really. I don't suppose they were being paid overtime when they came to her funeral either but there you are.

No wonder so many of them talked of giving it all up. Because they couldn't get the jobs they wanted, because they had done their backs in lifting patients, because almost any other job would have been more lucrative, because they were tired, because they knew and I knew that no matter what Mrs Bottomley says, the Health Service is falling apart.

Anyone who denies this has not been in a hospital recently. Even terminally ill patients cannot have a bath unless they are able to clean the bathrooms themselves, which of course they can't, because there are no cleaners to do it. Patients who need special food do not get it for days on end because the hospitals simply don't have it.

When my mother, who had not eaten for three months, said the only thing she fancied was a piece of fresh fruit, there was none to be had. When she was sent home on two drips – they like to empty the wards at the weekend – one of them went wrong in the night and I had no idea what to do. When I called the doctor, she said that not only should my mother not be at home but that she should be in intensive care.

Nurses work in these conditions yet are publicly told things are getting better. There is something about medical training that makes everybody unbearably breezy, even when things have gone very wrong. I guess that is how they survive.

A few hours after my mother was told she was dying, I asked one of the nurses how she was doing. 'A little under the weather,' she replied. If you were told you had three months to live I think you would be more than under the weather. So is the Health Service in decline as it rearranges itself into a two-tier system? No it's just feeling a little poorly.

While over the years we have quietly acquiesced in the market as the only model worth following, the Health Service – even more than education – has become the place where somehow we let our hearts rule as well as our heads. Even though it is riddled with trusts and quangos, we feel patriotic about the NHS. We feel, quaintly perhaps, that life is more important than money, which is why all the fuss was made about the ten-year-old girl with leukaemia being refused treatment. We may no longer have the right to a job for life, to walk the streets without fear of crime, to educate our children for free, but when push comes to shove we feel we have the right to health care that is 'free at the point of access'. It has become the last marker of a civilized society and we are losing it.

Such feelings may be soppy, they may even be socialist, although one hears them from people of all political persuasions. The boundless energy of the market stops here. Indeed, it rebounds into obscenity when the talk turns to saving money, rather than lives.

We value those who work in the Health Service for their expertise and dedication, but we don't value them enough to pay them what they are worth. That nurses and midwives have had to threaten strike action is but one sign of how out of touch this Government is. The flaunting of vast salaries by executives indicates that the ever-widening gap between private and public sector pay is something over which we have no control. If huge salaries are a sign of a competitive organization, then low salaries are inevitable in loss-making enterprises. And here in the profitless zone of health care, we give birth, die, stub our toes and go to casualty.

As long as the idea of paying people what they are worth only applies to the private sector, nurses will remain in the glorious position of being highly valued by everyone at the price of being expected to look after all of us for little more than £25 a day. The

Government's proposed pay award will now give staff nurses six pence an hour more.

Performance-related pay? In your dreams.

ALL NUTS AND HALF-WITS

All men are retards, sexual inadequates whose idea of a good time is setting fire to their own farts. They sit miserably on sofas boasting of imaginary relationships with imaginary women. They watch TV non-stop and live in piles of beer cans and dog-ends. They like football, baseball, anything with balls in it. And air guitars.

They fancy the girl upstairs, the girl next door, the girl on screen, but in their hearts they know it will never happen. Instead they share their lives with a similar sort of bloke and spend long nights irritating the hell out of each other.

Hey guys, I'm only kidding. I know you are not really all no-brainers, no-hopers. It's just that I've seen rather a lot of you recently who choose to represent yourselves as such. The wonderful world of Wayne and Garth, the sluggish Fantasy Footballers, the adventurous Bill and Ted, the *Men Behaving Badly*, the brilliant Jerky Boys, Ricky and Eddy in *Bottom*, the muthas of obnoxious ignorance, Beavis and Butthead, and now Harry and Lloyd of *Dumb and Dumber* is full of odd couples who are getting odder. The game is on to be the most stoopid. The sequel to *Dumb and Dumber* is already being discussed. It will be called 'Dumb and Dumbest'. The stakes are high when it comes to idiotic behaviour.

Following the success of *Forrest Gump*, snobby English critics have diagnosed the 'Dumbing of America'. Over the water they love idiots. Hell, they turn them into icons, make them presidents even. This is a bit rich when you consider that one of our national exports is Mr Bean, a man so backward that he has not even graduated to the all-important friendship with another similarly retarded guy. Rather, it's easier to slot this new breed of comics into the noble tradition of funny men from Laurel and Hardy to Morecambe and Wise, men who live together, sleep in the same bed (no questions asked) and are, to use the jargon, co-dependent.

Forrest Gump belongs to a different genre altogether – that of great actors playing characters whose limitations give them an opportunity to show their range: Dustin Hoffman playing autistic in *Rain Man*, Robert De Niro playing cerebrally challenged in *Awakenings*, Daniel Day Lewis multiply-handicapped in *My Left Foot*.

The new brand of idiots weren't born this way. It makes them hot property. Jim Carrey can now command $7 million a movie. Who needs sex appeal? While a few years ago movies such as *Big* and *Vice Versa* – in which little boys were trapped in the bodies of adult men – were in vogue, we no longer need such complicated fantasies to play 'Young, Dumb and Full of Fun'. Regression, somehow, is no longer a process but a product. Lad culture flaunts its immaturity, defying age by simply denying it. It is men rather than women who have taken to lying about how old they really are and we roll about in the aisles because, yes, it is very funny.

Dumb and Dumber is a hoot. Seriously. Carrey with his cartoon face and Jeff Daniels looking like the scarecrow in *The Wizard of Oz* do those weirdo things they do and try to get off with women with whom they have no prospects. When Carrey asks the love-interest in the movie what his chances with her are, she levels with him: 'One in a million.' 'So you are telling me there is a chance?' comes the reply. In real life Carrey is involved with her, so maybe he's on to something.

The ad before the movie started was for No. 17 make-up. Hard-bodied models instruct the boys 'out there' with military precision about what it is girls want. They want pecs, washboard stomachs and well-groomed men. The slogan for the campaign, 'It's not make-up. It's ammunition', points to another kind of battle that is going on, though you wouldn't know it from those endless surveys in women's magazines in which women consistently rate the most important thing about a guy as being his 'sense of humour'.

You've got to hand it to the no-brainers. They have humour

coming out of their backsides. By the bucketful. The *pièce de résist-ance* in *Dumb and Dumber* involves a joke about Turbo Lax and violent diarrhoea. 'Could you want anything more in a man?' I ask myself. When not at the movies, we worry about our young men, about their poor performance at school, at college, as partners, as fathers, as people even. They are not worthy, we say. Thank God, then, we can become hysterical when they reflect back to us that they are not. Underneath they are all lovable, as the bra ads used to say in the days before a bit of uplifted cleavage torpedoed them into submission.

For these new idiot savants, whether they are actually Cambridge graduates or well-brought-up Canadians, may be fuelled by the anxieties that always make the best comedy but the best of them are genuinely disturbing. Beavis and Butthead still reign supreme, probably because they are genuinely disturbed and because they are milking the benefit of being animations, and the writers can take the logic of their characters to its sick conclusion, deconstructing MTV culture more profoundly than any semiotician. When they lose the image on their omnipresent TV screen, they panic because they can hear a woman panting and gasping and think they might be missing out on a sex scene. When the picture comes back, what they have been so excited by is a woman giving birth and they are 'grossed out'. Men masturbating to Cindy Crawford exercise tapes is small fry in comparison.

It is not that these new breed of dumbos are misogynistic – they all love women, as they keep explaining – it's just that there are no laughs to be had in relating to women except as out-of-reach fantasy figures. When Harry explains to Lloyd in *Dumb and Dumber* that he is in love, he says: 'She actually talked to me.' The response is incredulity: 'Get outta here.' They do not relate to women because these odd couples only ever really relate to each other, to their own kind.

While female friendship currently features in popular culture as a hot-bed of jealous, sometimes murderous intensity, from *Heavenly Creatures* to *Ab Fab* to *Muriel's Wedding*, male bonding is delightfully low-maintenance, requiring only the ability to get tanked up and act half-witted. As escapism it makes a lot of sense because, although we know they aren't really like that, we all know that some guys are fools to some of the people some of the time. Anyway, what humour is to be had amongst consenting adults? It's just far too bloody difficult, this business of negotiating with the opposite sex. Why go to all the trouble of exchanging bodily fluids when you can piss in a bottle, with your best friend watching, while cracking jokes about 'homos'?

Brainlessness is in. As in getting 'brained' and being bored with issue movies such as *Schindler's List* and *Philadelphia* which, according to film executives, left audiences feeling 'brained out'.

So how low can you go? As low as a 12-certificate will let you, I guess. Well, you have to giggle, don't you, and believe me, I do. And I'll laugh even louder when two girls can sit on a couch, talking out of their arses, like Ace Ventura does, watching Jeff Stryker videos all day, vomiting their Babychams all over each other while trying to get off with Keanu Reeves and Brad Pitt. Laugh? I think I'll phone my agent.

MOURNING SICKNESS

Some day you will ache like I ache. So sings Courtney Love in her single 'Doll Parts'. To ache like Courtney aches – is that a threat or a promise? Surely no one can ache like she aches and that is why we love her: she has been to hell and back. She has lived through her husband's suicide and carried on touring, being a mother, being a star. She has mourned and ranted and raved in public.

She has shown us how it is to be on the edge. Our fascination with her is entirely morbid, like watching a road accident, as some have said, yet somehow she's coming through, coming into her own. She will be bigger than Madonna, bigger than Nirvana, so they tell us.

She is the anti-Madonna. A rock chick to Ms Ciccone's pop tart. Madonna is hard-bodied and always in control. Courtney is fleshy and continually threatening to lose it, big time. Madonna, saint of health and efficiency, with her pip squeak of a voice, inhabits a different world from Courtney's rocked-out Scotch and smack rasp. Madonna's sexuality is entirely inner-directed, her object of desire is fundamentally herself.

Courtney's sluttish, Blanche du Bois persona draws in whoever will watch her. She behaves, not as a widow and a mother should behave, and for all Madonna's calculated taboo busting, Love effortlessly blurs the lines between the prescribed behaviour of a mother, a whore, a grieving widow, a young woman.

Which part of Courtney is real? Which parts are skilful image manipulation is not a question that can be answered. We assume her pain is for public consumption even though the burden of representing other people's fantasies contributed to Kurt Cobain's misery. And here she is on the cover of *Vanity Fair*, photographed by Herb Ritts to show us how far she has come.

Last time she featured in this magazine, she was pregnant and said to be taking heroin, resolutely a bad girl providing a little *frisson* of freakiness, of celebrity low life among the usual *Vanity Fair* gloss.

The bigger she gets the less we can have of her and the resentment starts to build. Already it's there. In this week's *NME* she is accused of signing 'Faustian pacts with the voyeuristic tabloid sordids so as to keep the celebrity machine whirring, while knowingly exorcising their torment.' She is lost to the underworld of those who study their *NME* as if it were the Bible, and has become a creature of the mainstream media. She no longer belongs to that cult because we all know about her. She's not the same any more, she's not so real. Maybe it's true but why isn't it said of the boys, too? Are the Gallagher boys of Oasis lost now? Is Damon Albarn as real as he used to be? Why can Courtney not make her own myth? What do you want her to do – open her veins on stage?

Sylvia Plath is mentioned. Of course, Courtney has become a Sylvia Plath replacement. Elizabeth Wurtzel, the author of *Prozac Nation*, a book about depression, is also being marketed as the Sylvia Plath of the MTV generation. Instability is in. Madness is kind of sexy. Depression drips authenticity and depth when nothing else does these days. To be depressed is at least to feel something and something is better than nothing. But Sylvia Plath didn't take Prozac, she put her head in an oven. Courtney has not committed suicide, though the public seems to have judged her guilty of this act by association. Ever astute, Love has said 'One of the largest duties I have is to report on that madness and to try not to become a victim of it in the same way as Anne Sexton or Sylvia Plath or Zelda Fitzgerald.'

The recent anniversary of Cobain's death has sparked a recognition of a culture of suffering that has afflicted the young, who pour their tormented little hearts out in the pages of the music press. Anorexia, bulimia, self-cutting, all the *angst* turned inwards eventually spills out. Love used to cut herself, she says. Elizabeth Wurtzel describes in her book the patterns she used to make on her legs with razor blades. Now her story of self-laceration is to be made into a movie. Wurtzel is to be found this month posing topless in *GQ*. Having exposed her tortured psyche, she tiredly exposes her breasts. Is this to make us believe she is a better writer, or more depressed than ever, or so zonked out on anti-depressants she couldn't care less, or fully recovered? God only knows, although the copy that reads 'Feeling down? A little depressed? Sounds like a job for Prozac girl' simply trivializes whatever it is she is trying to achieve. Prozac girl, it seems, is so depressed she might even sleep with a *GQ* reader.

Some might say that our authors are now rock stars and we like our rock stars to live their lives for us. We want them to be extreme, to have bigger lives than we do. To pose in the nude for us. As Courtney's mother puts it, 'Her fame is not about being beautiful and brilliant, which she is: it's about speaking in the voice of the anguish of the world.' Wurtzel's writing is so thoroughly self-involved that she can barely acknowledge the anguish of any world but her own. Courtney's job is bigger – to absorb all the pain that is projected on to her and throw it out again. If anger turned in on itself causes depression, we are among a lost generation who see no future in getting angry. Depression is on the increase, especially among young people. Women are three times more likely to suffer than men and, as BBC2's excellent *States of Mind* series on mental illness reminded us, there is not much glamour about being mentally ill.

There was a woman where I used to live who roamed the streets in mid-winter, wearing nothing but a nightie and begging for money for Lucozade. 'Lucozade aids recovery' she used to intone whenever I gave her some change. With her matted hair and calloused feet, she was a far cry from today's psycho-babes whose mental disarray adds to their allure. A far cry from the artists who, on the programme *Prozac Diary*, took the drug as if it were Lucozade in order simply to unblock them creatively. The media obsession with Prozac points to a generation gap not just between doomed youth and mystified elders, but between those who seem surprised that a drug can make you feel better and those who grow up taking drugs precisely because they do make you feel better. We are unhappy about offering Prozac as a cure-all because we feel that chemicals cannot truly be the answer to existential crisis.

It is no coincidence that the young find no meaning in their lives when so many of our bigger belief systems have imploded over the last twenty years. It is almost twenty years since punk first proclaimed that there was no future. A generation raised in its shadow finds it could only claim its alienation second-hand and so couldn't be bothered.

Thus the new heroes and heroines, from Courtney to P.J. Harvey to Kurt, sing of deep, dark things and show that all this suffering may be worth something, even if that something is only a pop song. They show that madness is not ordinary, even though we know differently. They emote for us because we are too numb to feel anymore. Is Courtney Love and her media circus for real? 'Is this what you want? Really?' an anguished *NME* writer asks. Yes, it's what we want. Really. Or, as the woman herself, drawls it: 'I fake it so real I am beyond fake.'

LOOK WHAT'S UNDER THE PATIO

For one reason or another I have been thinking a lot about female solidarity this week and in order to switch off, switched on the box. I thought I had stumbled into one of those BBC2 theme nights, the theme being 'All men are bastards' but in fact I was watching Channel 4. First there was The Verdict on the Mandy and Beth Jordache trial in *Brookside*, then a programme on Ike Turner and how he used to bash up Tina. To top it all came the first episode of *The Politician's Wife*, written by Paula Milne and focusing on a Tory sex scandal and the effect that it has on the wronged wife.

There may be those who feel that to engage with popular culture is a waste of time and we should be concentrating on more important matters. Clearly I do not belong to this precious gang. Nor does the wife of the next Prime Minister – Cherie Blair – who chose to have her photograph taken with Sandra Maitland, the actress who plays Mandy Jordache in the soap opera. The photograph, which appeared on the front of a national newspaper, was taken to help launch a campaign of cinema advertisements by the charity Refuge intended to increase awareness of domestic violence.

The plight of Mandy Jordache, the fictional character, who has been sentenced to life imprisonment for the murder of her abusive husband, has touched a nerve in a way that the plight of Sara Thornton hasn't. *Brookside* has demonstrated just how the law continues to fail women and generated sympathetic publicity that will doubtless help those who are trying to change it. The issue of what constitutes provocation is precisely the one that *Brookside* has highlighted and that various groups have been campaigning around for some time.

What *Brookside* has so cleverly shown us is the background to the case, the brutality of Trevor Jordache, the desperation of his wife and daughters, the powerlessness that women feel in such dreadful situations. The magnificent acting of Sandra Maitland and Anna Friel, the melodrama of the last-minute wedding, the voyeurism as well as the kindness of neighbours, has pulled us into a plot which at first felt like a gimmick – a body under the patio – and has ended up reducing us to tears.

No one believes that it is legitimate for women to go around stabbing men, but without understanding the appalling circumstances in which these things happen, we cannot easily make a judgement.

A popular soap has contributed to that understanding in a way that has reached all kinds of people. *The Politician's Wife*, on the other hand, is, in its own glossy fashion, as topical and gripping a deconstruction of patriarchy as you could wish for. Flora Matlock, played by Juliet Stevenson, is married to a Tory MP who wants his wife to stand by him after his affair has hit the tabloids. She is surrounded by men (including her husband, his aides and her own father) who put the requirements of 'the Party' and political power over any consideration of her feelings.

To discuss feminism in the abstract in such a context, as though it belonged simply to a few strange women, misses the point entirely. There is little mileage to be had in arguing over which particular feminists are allowed to speak and which aren't, an old and trivial dispute which, at the end of the day, is of little concern to anyone except those who make a living flogging dead horses and even deader books.

What is much more interesting is the way that feminism has entered the culture to such a point that popular drama, from *Prime Suspect* to *EastEnders*, is increasingly full of feminist attitudes, although no one actually mentions the horrible F-word itself. The place we are now most likely to hear debate about sexual politics is in the pub after a night out at the movies. This is obviously unsettling to those who want to own certain ideas, those very souls who, while asking for wider debate, actually feel threatened when 'ordinary people' manage to do it all by themselves.

It's not the case that there has been a concerted attempt to make feminism popular; it is rather that those who make the products that become popular culture are young women and men who have grown up with feminism. It matters not how they choose to describe themselves; it matters enormously that what they see as hooking in viewers, as intelligent drama, as relevant, doesn't come in a box marked 'women's issues' but is literally the stuff of everyday life.

I am happy to say it is becoming increasingly difficult to demarcate what is said to concern over half the population in this manner. One reaction is simply to ignore what is in front of our eyes and to revert to older certainties. The rise of the boorish lad at a time when traditional masculine identities are crumbling is but one example. Another is to focus on what we believe to be the truly important issues for women today – cellulite and make-up. What all this misses, however, is that at a time when fewer women want to actually define themselves as feminists, they are already defined by implicitly feminist attitudes.

It's too late to try to contain what's happened. The image of feminism has never been so far removed from the reality. I understand perfectly why so many young women refuse this sort of labelling. Countless female stars, musicians and actresses give interviews in which they say that they want to be judged on what they do and not merely as a representative of some outdated cause. When women are equally represented in all walks of life that burden of representation will be lifted. We will have what men take for granted – a set of political opinions that weave in and out of lives but do not act as a strait-jacket preventing all room to manoeuvre. Feminism is not about the power of faith but about understanding how power currently operates.

Here, popular culture comes to our rescue. Mandy Jordache and Flora Matlock are not feminists, but it would be fair to say they have had a few problems with men. Their narratives are driven by their experiences rather than a few batty theories about the position of women in society. Just like real life, eh? Even David Crosby, the token fogey of the Close and hardly any sort of liberal, has had his view of British justice 'severely dented' and is helping organize the 'Free the Brookside Two' campaign.

Jimmy Corkhill is 'gutted'. Well, so am I and it's a rum do when prime time is where we find such progressive entertainment. Or maybe we shouldn't be shocked that while we are constantly told feminism no longer has a home to go to, something that bears a remarkable resemblance to it has found a way into all our homes. I wouldn't miss it for the world. And now that both Mandy and Flora have stopped shaking, the real stories will begin.

Revenge is always sweet: it's even sweeter when you don't have to leave the house to get it.

STRESSED OUT ON LIFE

Children today grow up far too quickly. One minute you're changing their nappies, the next they have turned into that hulking teenager out of the Harry Enfield show. They no longer communicate but sit with their Walkmans on in front of the TV, lost in the alien world of youth culture.

You cannot reach them. They cannot even hear you. All over the country parents who can no longer talk to their own children are obliged to ask each other, what on earth has happened to our babies? How come it all went by so fast? And they worry about what their babies get up to because there are now more and more opportunities to get into trouble than there ever were. The choice is endless. You can abuse yourself from an early age in various ways with drink and drugs. You can abuse others by involving yourself in countless criminal activities. You can sink into depression. You can starve or binge and vomit your way to misery. If this isn't enough you can, of course, always commit suicide. Increasing numbers of our young people are doing all these things.

As the physical health of our nation has improved over the past fifty years, the mental health of our youth has deteriorated. A study published this week by Professor Michael Rutter, head of the Department of Child and Adolescent Psychiatry at the London Institute of Psychiatry, and David Smith, Professor of Criminology at the University of Edinburgh, details the rise of these 'psycho-social disorders' in young people since the Second World War.

Though the study shows that these increases 'are not related to deprivation or to increasing affluence in any simple way', it has already been used as evidence by the right to demonstrate that the link between economic deprivation and criminal behaviour is entirely false. What matters above all else is 'the stability of family life'.

An editorial in the *Daily Telegraph* mocks the conclusion often drawn by those 'on the left, that crime is a mute protest at social injustice'. Certainly the study illustrates that the rising levels of crime, suicide, depression, alcohol and drug abuse were most marked during the period of two to three decades in which living conditions improved dramatically. 'Between 1950 and 1973 there was a "golden era" of economic growth, low unemployment and improving living conditions throughout the developed world. This coincided with the post-war rise in psychological disorders.'

The wide scope of the report, which groups together anorexia nervosa with criminal behaviour, means that to slot its findings into any preconceived political framework is actually rather difficult. You can see what you want to see and the familiar rants against 'progressive teachers' and that other bogeyman of the right – 'modern child-rearing methods' – are pouring into the letters pages, though the report does not even touch on these issues.

What is overwhelming about this study is not its usefulness as party political dogma but the great gulf it delineates between, for want of a better phrase, 'youth culture' and the rest of society. We see our young people as having greater freedom than ever before, yet their unhappiness appears often to be directly connected to the stresses that these freedoms bring with them.

Stress is notoriously difficult to quantify but the authors of the study point to the likely stresses involved in parental marriage break-ups, the prolongation of education with its possible risk of failures and rejections, the stressful decision-making about whether to engage in drug-taking as well as the familiar struggles around adolescent sexuality and sexual relationships.

These stresses, one could counter, have always been around in some shape or form, but what has changed since the war is the meaning of adolescence itself. The birth of the teenager, in the late fifties, documented by the likes of Colin MacInnes, marked the transition between the austerity of the war years and the rise of what would be called 'the sixties'.

The teenager, the young blade with money to burn, became an iconic part of what Stuart Hall described as 'the libidinization of consumption'. Spending was not only modern and sexy but integral to the process which we have now all become part of – the construction of social identity through consumption.

The exploitation of this newish market in the fifties and the sixties put the adolescent experience at the very heart of Britain's popular culture. Now, however, this process has reached its sulky apotheosis in that youth culture appears an impenetrable bubble, a virtually autonomous state that grown-ups rarely visit and many have washed their hands of.

When I wrote recently about Courtney Love in the context of an article about young people and depression, several other commentators congratulated themselves on the fact that they hadn't even heard of her. As with those judges who have to be told who Gazza is, being 'out of touch' with everyday concerns is still ridiculously worn as a badge of cultural superiority. Why bother to ask why young people feel so alienated when we openly scoff at what they hold dear? The other side of the coin are those who struggle to keep abreast of youth culture, like the character of Eddy in *Absolutely Fabulous*, fetishizing every passing youth trend while despising actual young people themselves.

Yet, it is not just the meaning of adolescence that has changed over time, but its actual length. While the onset of the start of puberty is falling for both sexes, the length of time that children are dependent on their parents is increasing. Unemployment may not lead automatically to psychosocial disorder, but it has undoubtedly forced many young people to carry on living with their parents well into their twenties as they have no other financial option.

Government policy, too, has pushed fiscal responsibility back on to parents. So, while the authors of the report identify 'a possible increasing isolation of adolescents from adults' they recognize 'a greater financial dependence on parents'. The tension arises because this 'coincides with greater autonomy in other respects'.

No wonder that these kids are stressed out. Being young, they are continually informed, is about doing what the hell you like, yet at the same time their mums tell them to stop treating their home like a hotel. They are not able to make the natural break from the nest as young adults but are forced into the childlike position of living at home.

The reality is that they are dependent, but the recurring fantasy of youth culture is always one of impossible independence, of individualism so rugged that you need nothing and no one.

The dislocation that the report highlights must in some way be a result of the gap between the rising expectations of our young people as compared with their experience. The *Daily Telegraph* laughably finds it easy to blame the 'rising tide of crime' on that essential triumvirate of sex, drugs and rock 'n' roll. Yet the consumption of sex, drugs and rock 'n' roll is in many ways part of a freemarket philosophy which emphasizes individual gratification above all else.

The right are in the contradictory position of endorsing the freedoms of the market while seeking to limit those freedoms when they are enacted socially. While the market promises flexibility, this flexibility puts unbearable pressure on the rigid moral system that they are currently proposing. The report comes back again and again to the somewhat vague notion of 'increased individualism' as a root cause of disorder.

For boys this individualism may find its outlet in crime, but for girls it turns inwards into depression and eating disorders. Even existential crises, it appears, are gendered. Alienation for young girls means not only alienation from other people but from their own bodies.

Instead of trying to prop up beleaguered moral frameworks on behalf of our young people, we would perhaps be better off to recognize, as John Gray pointed out this week, 'that we have the makings of a strong and deep moral culture in Britain today but its content is rejected by cultural conservatives'. Its content is the very context in which today's teenagers have grown up. This culture, as Gray pointed out, has not much time for traditional Christian values, is on the whole liberal about sexuality, and is concerned about the environment.

The new social-political forces in our culture tend to demand greater accountability: the campaigns against roads and on behalf of animal rights, those groups seeking to preserve the environment, are peopled by the very same young people who, we are told, have received no moral guidance from their dysfunctional families. Indeed, the report points undeniably to the role of family break-down in the unhappiness of teenagers. Predictably this has been seized upon by those who want to attribute every problem in society to the collapse of the traditional family rather than look at the larger social forces at work.

What the study shows unsparingly is that the reality is much more complicated. It is not a question of economic deprivation versus emotional deprivation, however much one skews these findings. Rutter and Smith have found that 'The poor, the unemployed and people living on sink estates are more likely to be criminal, depressed, suicidal and addicted to drugs than those in more comfortable circumstances.' The more general question then is why, when overall living conditions have improved, has adolescence become more difficult than ever. It is not family break-up *per se* which causes so much unhappiness, it is discord and the 'lack of parental support and involvement' that is so damaging.

As Elizabeth Wurtzel, in her self-absorbed memoir *Prozac Nation*, writes: 'It is no surprise that a generation of children of divorced parents have grown into a world of extended adolescence in which so many of them have slept with one another and remained friends, have put aside the conflicts of sundered relationships for the sake of maintaining a coherent life. Divorce has taught us how to sleep with friends, sleep with enemies and then act like it's all perfectly normal in the morning.' The 'show of civility', the accompanying pyscho-babble renders heartbreak 'a minor inconvenience'. The children are endlessly reassured, as if this is enough to numb the pain.

We may care enormously about our children but is that the same as respecting their feelings? We may worship the concept of youth but we jump to categorize youth's predicament through inane classi-

fications. Thus they are slackers, ravers, hooligans, the blank generation. We give them their head, let them do their own thing and
then feign shock that they feel adrift from adult culture. We do not
understand their language, nor want to, and insist that conflict between one generation and the next is inevitable, even desirable. In
order to grow up one has to reject one's elders, we tell each other,
not seeing that so many of the problems arise because they do not
want to reject us but simply have us accept them.

It is true sometimes that rebellion fuels enormous creativity but
sometimes it fuels only destruction. When it leads more mundanely, however, to an insularity which can only be penetrated
through consumerism, then we are all implicated. The producers of
youth culture give the kids just what they want when they want it,
but should they want anything more than another CD we wash our
hands of them. They want too much, these kids, they want it all
handed to them on a plate.

But who has fuelled these unrealistic expectations – a home of
one's own, a way of making a living, the dream of mobility? Who
has failed to meet them? To say that we, the supposed adults, are
responsible, too, is a lot harder than saying it is the fault of the
Government or of the increasing divorce rates or of a decline in
moral standards. If the transition to adult status has always been
fraught, pushing it to a later and later age has not been beneficial.
We may celebrate youth in the abstract but in practice we often
behave as if it is a foreign country rather than the place we all come
from.

We just don't get it. So we complain constantly that the kids
grow up too soon when it looks like the opposite is the case. We do
not allow them to grow up fast enough. To allow them to do so
would require that we treat our adolescents less as children and
more as adults – that we take them seriously. Maybe this is just a
phase we are going through but such a grown-up approach still feels
like a long way off.

SEA CHANGES IN POLITICAL TALK

If truth be told, not many of us know what goes on 6,000 feet below the surface of the ocean. There are, it seems, plenty more fish in the sea than we could ever have imagined. In the depths strange species lurk and, though we may never ever see them, we feel in our hearts that they should be left alone. Why must they share the great dark deep with bits and bobs from a dismembered oil platform?

Here is nature, raw and pure and unknowable, forced to cohabit with the detritus of a culture that pretends to itself that everything is ultimately disposable. Even that rundown shopping centre of a name, Brent Spar, adds to the unacceptability of using the sea as a rubbish dump. As Shell has backed down in the face of consumer boycotts and protests by Greenpeace, it looks as though the emotional argument has won the day.

It is a triumph over Shell, the Government and, some would say, reason itself; a battle that, according to the *Daily Telegraph*, the environmentalists 'did not deserve to win'. Traditional politics has once more found itself disempowered by a groundswell of what it chooses to dismiss as mere emotion. This is true of all the parties. Even though Labour grudgingly supported the consumer boycott, it would have preferred direct Government action to direct action. 'We shouldn't have to resort to boycotting Shell,' said Frank Dobson.

Greenpeace exists and is so widely supported because when there is so little faith in governmental action, such an organization offers a last resort. More than this, it speaks a different language — a language that is muddled, insufficiently scientific maybe, intensely romantic and heroic. This language is misunderstood as somehow anti-political or as a form of lesser politics because it speaks in terms of emotion and symbolism; as with the animal rights movement, it appears to have come out of nowhere rather than having a long and honourable tradition.

Others may still want to argue about whether dumping on land or sea is the best option for a decommissioned oil platform. Questions may be raised about Greenpeace's aggressive campaigns which have been criticized for being economic with the scientific *actualité*. Greenpeace tends to link the word 'chemical' with the word 'cancer' at every available opportunity; it overstates its case again and again. Many environmentalists actually think it would be safer to sink the Brent Spar, though Greenpeace's declared aim is to make sure that the Brent Spar does not serve as a precedent, to ensure that the rest of the North Sea oil industry is not allowed to litter the sea.

Yet the larger debate that should be occurring between these two forms of politics can scarcely start to happen because each side will not learn the other's language. On one side, Greenpeace is the hero, David against Goliath, fuelled by consumer power, which has shown us what true democracy could be about. On the other side are those who see the members of Greenpeace as irresponsible, publicity-seeking, over-excited, interfering know-nothings who feel 'little obligation to stay within the bounds of normal political behaviour'.

It feels rather late in the day to point out to the leader writers of the *Daily Telegraph* that Greenpeace's *raison d'être* is not to mimic normal political behaviour because normal political behaviour has got us into this fine mess in the first place.

Greenpeace, which itself seems rather taken aback that it has won, should not be so surprised. There is, one senses, a coming together of many issues around this particular campaign. What should never be underestimated is what a beautifully televisual campaign this was. A battered and ugly man-made structure in the North Sea, being buzzed by a Greenpeace boat and helicopter, caught the imagination because we could, for once, literally see what was going on. We may know that Shell is a huge multinational, exercising enormous global power, but it is difficult to conceive what this might actually look like. Now we have an image to go with the concept.

One of the reasons that Greenham Common was so successful was because it functioned as an easily understood visual aid to what those particular protests were about: in the middle of the base were the missiles, then there were soldiers guarding them, then there was a fence, and on the other side of the fence were women. This kind of over-simplification is an inherent part of symbolic politics. To trash it as mere sentiment neglects the fact that the sentimental and ritualistic traditions of Westminster are meaningless to most of us.

The highly effective consumer boycotts that were part of Greenpeace's strategy also seem to have taken everyone by surprise. There have recently been other successful boycotts. Two big UK paper companies pulled out of contracts in British Columbia last year because of protests against 'clear-cut' logging. Environmental groups in India have repeatedly used boycotting in the fight against multinationals. What was impressive about the boycott of Shell was that it was co-ordinated across Europe. Greenpeace's strategy – flexible, responsive, media-savvy – made the Government's seem even more rigid and isolated.

This kind of boycott has not come out of the blue. Nor should it be confused with the milder green consumerism of the eighties, when changing one's washing-up liquid to something less toxic and generally less effective produced a feel-good glow. There has been for some time a strong anti-consumerist, even anti-materialist tendency that tries to speak its name in poll after poll. Not only does the environment figure higher than the economy in many people's hierarchy of concern, but there is a growing feeling that enough is enough. No one can get a grip on this because it is not tied to anything to do with the left. It is not puritanical and self-sacrificing. Neither is it anti-technology. Even New Age travellers want their sound systems and PCs and mobile phones. In all the long-winded discussions about political correctness, no one seemed to notice that this kind of innate environmentalism, this talk of respect for the land, this concern for animal rights, was actually producing a generation that was not worried about what you called things because it spoke an entirely different language anyway. While we were tracking the fussy details of political correctness, suddenly something bigger was in the air that is being referred to as 'a new ethical climate'.

A change of climate is a much better way of expressing what is happening at the moment, rather than trying to search for new political 'formations' that resemble the old ones and that must be still evaluated in their terms, even though these criteria are as obsolete as the Brent Spar itself. This merely reproduces the line that the new politics is too vague, unfocused and naïve to be truly meaningful. This is to miss the point completely. Look at the 'McDonald's Two' – two North London anarchists accused of libelling McDonald's in their little pamphlets, who for months have been in court. They are embarrassingly well organized. Rather than refuse to make connections between a single issue and its context, they make them everywhere. This isn't about boycotting hamburgers but it is about the abuses of power of this huge multilocal company.

Ethical consumerism and investment are about self-imposed limits, about individual choice inspired by a collective consciousness. Such thinking bypasses the state and only asks of it that it imposes limits on itself too, that it must deal with the consequences of its actions, whether these are in pollution or the arms trade. We are becoming less forgiving to those who trespass against us, even if they have the power of ownership behind them. Our sense of what is actually ours and theirs is changing. As we have become used to the fact that, in George Monbiot's words, 'we are shut out of the land which was once ours', we now feel that nature itself resides in the seas and the skies. It is a romantic notion – the sea may be hacked up into fishing territories, and when one is sitting in a plane one hopes that air space is well regulated – but it is a powerful one. If Shell wants to trespass on a bit of the North Sea, 250 miles northeast of Aberdeen, we feel outraged, although most of us will never go there. No one owns the ocean. How can Shell be so arrogant as to think it does? Greenpeace has good reason to put the kettle on. It has saved the sea. Who from, and for whom, is not exactly clear.

Technically the protesters may have got it wrong even if demo-
cratically they have got it right. That is why this is not a victory for
the environment but for the politics of refusal – and that, as we are
coming to realize, is a different kettle of fish.

HAVING YOUR CAKE . . .

How much does a cheap blow-job cost? A lot more than a hundred dollars if you are Hugh Grant. For the sake of a 'lewd act' in a public place, Grant may have lost the chance to become the next Cary Grant and the love of the lovely Liz, who, if we are to believe reports, has taken to the smelling salts like some Victorian damsel in distress. Gorgeous Grant has been turned into 'Grubby Grant' overnight by the gentlemen of the press, none of whom would ever in a million years visit a prostitute. No one knows what goes on inside Mr Grant's head, or for that matter any other part of his anatomy, but this charming man with his floppy hair and oh-so-English reticence has metamorphosed into a demented sex beast overnight.

We have been offered startling insights into his behaviour from such experts in male psychology as Cynthia Payne: 'What makes a successful, attractive man act like this? They just can't help them-selves, that's my theory.' This hardly constitutes a theory, more a resigned shrug of the shoulders. This is what it always comes down to – what women are saying to each other. Men can't help it, even men who have to fend off Madonna in the middle of the night. Sometimes they want meaningless sex, devoid of emotions, some-times they want to take risks, sometimes they do stupid, pathetic things, sometimes they get a little crazy . . . and so what?

One of the perks of being famous is that you get more opportun-ity to do this than the average guy, and part of the reason that the average guy wants to be famous is just so he could get to behave in this way. Let's not kid ourselves.

But kidding ourselves is, of course, our speciality. Without it, whores of all persuasions would be out of business and so would many of our fragrant tabloids. Family newspapers such as the *Sun*, which have been encouraging us to speculate on whether Pamela Anderson is going to breastfeed, but would no doubt condemn that sub-genre of pornography which features lactating women, are experts in such contortions. What pleasure to be had in this story, especially when we have had to content ourselves with the deeply unsexy spectacle of the Tory party destroying itself, is in hearing of a young man possibly destroying his career for the sake of a moment's 'relief' in the back of a car. If Michael Portillo could be found to be having a torrid affair with Liz Hurley, the circle could be squared.

Already it matters very little what the truth is. I cannot honestly see that the evidence that a sex symbol actually has sex is so very damaging. Still, the charade must continue. Hurley is the wronged woman, Grant has gone 'insane'. The pragmatic notion that in a long-distance relationship maybe both of them occasionally 'lapse' has not been entertained because it doesn't fit the script. Instead, there have been numerous outpourings of the 'why oh why do high-flying men go to prostitutes?' variety. Because they *can* might be the simple answer, but surely we can do better than that? They are addicted to risk, to forbidden fruit, to something dirty and low-down. They do it because stars are given unconditional love, because fame entitles one to a prolonged adolescence. God forbid we might conclude that they do it because they choose to do it, that this is what they want to do. The idea of men being responsible for their own desires is still not one that our culture has much time for. Grant says he has done something 'completely insane'. Silly yes, insane no. I don't think so.

Michael Douglas, whose wife Diandra is divorcing him after nearly two decades, also subscribes to this testosterone-driven view of insanity. 'Sex is a wave that sweeps over me – the impulse, that is. And when the urge comes, I'm helpless every time. I run the most impossible, incredible risks. The consequences are the loss of my marriage and possible disease.' Poor little Michael, the boy can't help it and as long as he believes he can't help it he will presumably carry on doing it. He really isn't a boy at all, the man is fifty years old. If a woman the same age were to talk like this she would be depicted as a sad and suspect creature. Grant cannot say that whatever he did on Sunset Boulevard was just what he fancied doing at the time, because that would mean he was in control of his behaviour and the sorry little incident has to be cast in terms of momentary madness brought on by the pressures of stardom.

Quite a few men in Hollywood and elsewhere pay for moments of madness on a regular basis. Those men, whose names are in Hollywood madam Heidi Fleiss's little black book, are mostly men who could have and do have successful relationships with beautiful women. If it were only men who could never have sex unless they paid for it that visited prostitutes, then prostitutes would not make the kind of money they do. Likewise, if the buying and selling of sex was restricted to a few red-light areas, Hollywood would not be raking in the bucks.

Hugh Grant and Elizabeth Hurley are in the business of selling sex. Their relationship, however it started, has now become a professional one. The feigned moral outrage is because someone who sells sex isn't supposed to buy it. In the sexual market-place this golden couple cannot be seen to be punters. If their mutual image is based on a version of classiness, then for Grant to indulge in such behaviour as paying a black hooker immediately casts a shadow on his class credentials. An Englishman abroad should not settle for any old broad, let alone one you have to pay for.

Unfortunately, Hugh and Liz have a duty to perform. We are strangely bereft of golden couples. Diana and Charles no longer fit the bill. John McCarthy and Jill Morrell have proved themselves to be human. Damon of Blur and Justine of Elastica will soon be the only model of a successful heterosexual relationship that we have left. That is why Grant's small failing is such a big deal; but in the great scheme of things I cannot see that he has actually done anything so terrible.

One might think that the Hollywood police had more urgent cases to pursue than this one. There were no children involved, no homicide, no coercion of innocent people. Compared to current

Hollywood scandals this is remarkably small fry. The fact, as Dominick Dunne reported in one of his letters from Los Angeles in *Vanity Fair*, that cynics are now suggesting that it is likely that Heidi Fleiss will do more time than either O. J. Simpson or the Menendez brothers *is* something worth getting worked up about. That Michael Jackson can buy off those who would testify against him, that justice now depends on how much you can afford, is surely far more worthy of moral indignation than an actor shelling out for a lewd act.

But hell, it's hot – and mugshots of Grant are a damn sight more appealing than mugshots of John Redwood any day of the week. In the fantasy factory of Hollywood, prostitutes look like Julia Roberts not like Divine Brown, the literal bit-player of this escapade. I trust that she will now make more than a paltry hundred bucks for putting her mouth where the money is, by sucking up to a better class of individual altogether. A partnership with John Wayne Bobbit surely beckons. Film stars may be paid to put out and talk at the same time; whores, on the other hand, know that sex may sometimes be cheap but it is never free. What Grant actually paid for was a woman who would put up *and* shut up. Even in such a man's world, the moral of this tale, if there has to be one, is that you don't always get that for nothing.

POPE ON A ROPE

I greet you all most cordially, women throughout the world! No, this wasn't Hugh Grant grovelling on American television, but the way that the Pope's 'letter to women' starts. Saying sorry is *de rigueur* these days. Love has little to do with it. Grantie will have to apologize for the 'bad thing' he did forever now. The Queen has apologized to the Maoris for stealing their lands, as you do. 'Most dreadfully sorry for colonizing you and all that.'

And now old John Paul is in on the act, trying to plead his way out of thousands of years of discriminatory behaviour by his own church with a quick sorry and a nod to the twentieth century, just in time for the UN conference for women in Beijing. Has the man no shame? Does he truly expect us to forgive and forget and carry on being content to bear children we do not want because celibates in frocks tell us that it is our true destiny as women?

So this may be a little harsh. There may be other ways to view the Roman Catholic Church than as an all-male hierarchy that rules over the minds and bodies of women, but there are enough intelligent women out there who explain that Catholicism is in many ways a 'feminine religion', the 'Marian' principle having been drummed out of Protestantism a long time ago. Indeed, for a definition of uptight, paranoid masculinity, complete with rolled-up umbrellas and quasi-military insignia, it would be hard to beat the spectacle of the Orangemen prepared to squabble to the death over which road they could walk down. There was not an Orangewoman to be seen. The pomp and circumstance of patriarchy is certainly not the prerogative of Roman Catholicism any more than it is of any other organized religion.

Cynics suggest that the Pope's letter is prompted by the need to distance himself somewhat from the Muslim fundamentalists with whom he found himself aligned at the Cairo conference on population. We also point to the fact that the Pope's sudden conversion to feminism has not made him alter his position on birth control, abortion or the ordination of women. Mary Kenny in the *Daily Telegraph* writes that the response to the letter 'will be hollow laughter at *Spare Rib*', which would be interesting if the defunct magazine were still in existence. It closed down some time ago, so hollow laughter will have to be found elsewhere, perhaps even among the many pragmatic Catholic women who do use contraception.

Kenny is right, though, to point out that as befuddled as this letter may be, 'Thank you, *every woman*, for the simple fact of being a *woman*!' (eat your heart out, Lionel Ritchie), it is a tribute to the success of feminism that the man has at least addressed it. As always, though, it is not simply feminism that is pushing through changing attitudes but the conjunction of feminism with larger social and economic transformations. Just as locally we are feeling the ramifications of what happens when women enter the work-place in vast numbers – in all sorts of ways, from the shifts in family life to the so-called crisis of male identity – then globally we are seeing that the key to population control lies in improving the condition of women through education and economic independence.

The next century will see increased urbanization, as all over the world people migrate into the new super-cities. In the next twenty years the world urban population will grow by half. Access to family planning is still unavailable to 350 million couples; of the world's illiterates, two-thirds are women. For women such as these there is little chance of making any kind of choice in their lives. The Pope's talk of the 'genius of women' will be meaningless to them. Nor will his words do much to alter their chances of dying in childbirth.

Even the Pope must have realized that issues of reproductive rights alongside population control are no longer feminist issues –

women's issues – but political, ethical and environmental debates that all governments must participate in. It is disingenuous in the extreme for the Pope to express his admiration 'for those women of good will who have devoted their lives to defending the dignity of womanhood by fighting for their basic social, economic and political rights, demonstrating courageous initiative at a time when this was considered extremely inappropriate, the sign of a lack of femininity, a manifestation of exhibitionism, and even a sin!' – yet not to acknowledge that for most women basic social justice involves, at some level, some degree of control over reproduction.

While at first it may be difficult to work out exactly what kind of feminism John Paul is espousing, it soon becomes quite clear that it is the rather familiar defence of men the world over: 'Oh, but I love women really.' Pornographers love women really, politicians love women really, and now the Pope presents himself as yet another Man Who Loves Too Much. The great thing about loving women so much is the enormous respect you can have for a mystical conception of womanhood – in this case, the blessed Virgin in whom the Church finds the highest expression of 'the feminine genius' – whilst ignoring anything that flesh and blood women actually say.

The theoretical prop for such monstrous arrogance always comes down to the universal principle of complementarity. Men and women are just . . . you know, different. Difference shouldn't, but inevitably does, translate as old-fashioned inequality. The Pope himself falls back on this old staple time and time again to explain why things are different for girls. What he describes as the 'iconic' complementarity of male and female roles, leads (surprise, surprise), to a 'certain diversity of roles' which means that there can be no female priests because Christ himself chose only men to be his 'icons'. This, the Pope argues, is not prejudicial to women. To think it is confuses the signs with reality. For you see, the codes of Roman Catholicism operate a kind of semiological system which bears little relationship to the outside world. Thus the icons and representatives of God belong to 'the economy of signs' which He 'freely chooses in order to become present in the midst of humanity'.

These signs, then, must not be tampered with, least of all by women who are deemed, indeed doomed, in such a signifying system to represent nothing more or less than virginity and motherhood simultaneously.

If the Roman Catholic Church, through the icon of the Pope, needs to apologize for anything, it is for the immense damage it has caused women throughout the ages by loading them with immense symbolism while emptying of significance their daily experience. The Pope's letter is yet another attempt to rejig the signs somewhat, to bring feminism into an heroic, self-sacrificing and dignified tradition that the Church finds manageable. Feminism becomes but one idealized offshoot of the 'cultural and spiritual motherhood' that Catholicism idolizes, but the point is surely that feminism, even in its most simplistic manifestation, ruptures the signifying system through which Catholicism operates.

Women no longer regard themselves as empty vessels into which meaning is poured, nor, if they ever have, as a homogenous mass. Can you imagine the Pope saying that he greeted men most cordially throughout the world? Of course not. His patronizing birthday card greeting might as well have said 'Hello, Earthlings'. Maybe it should have. We are forever alien beings as far as the hierarchy of the Roman Catholic Church is concerned and all the saying sorry in the world won't change this. Perhaps we are glad he values our minds, but unless he can deal with the reality of our bodily needs as well as our spiritual ones, then I'm sorry to say playing with the signs of the 'sacramental economy' amounts to little more than playing with himself.

He may take to wooing his female followers with the information that they are 'Once, twice, three times a Lady' but as long as he remains a fundamentalist then the answer to the familiar question 'Is the Pope Catholic?' will remain, unfortunately for women, 'Yes'.

DEALING WITH THE DRUG DEMON

There is, we are told, a generation that sees drugs as 'no big deal'; as just a routine part of the 'leisure-pleasure landscape'. Are they talking 'bout my generation? No, this new report refers to the fact that many children will try drugs of one sort or another before they are sixteen.

This is a normal, rather than a deviant part of teenage behaviour, but the tut-tutting has begun already. So too has the dividing up of the world – the upstanding, just-say-you're-uptight non-drug users versus the seedy underbelly of evil chemical abuse. There are two cultures, we are warned – an insular adult culture and a secret garden where children whisper to each other about doves and penguins while listening to tracks called 'Feel the Rush', where they come in all bleary-eyed and giggly and their parents *don't know that there is anything going on at all.*

I have to say I find all this quite incomprehensible. No, not the habits of the young but the feigned ignorance of the parents. I am not surprised that today's kids grow up with drugs all around them. I am thirtysomething and I also grew up with drugs all around me. Those who would be in government surely did too, although they all make loud exhaling noises when it comes to discussing the subject.

I had tried most drugs before I ever got properly drunk. I did it because it was exciting, because drugs appeared to offer a kind of knowledge that I considered worth possessing. I did it because lots of famous people did it. I did it because my boyfriend did it and he said it would make everything better.

It wasn't all so cool. One guy I knew went mad doing so much speed that he saw the devil coming out of a cut in his thumb. Another boy broke into a vet's and died injecting himself with the stuff they used to put horses down. Teenage kicks.

Other friends had elaborate systems where they could use heroin and not get hooked. Some of those who became junkies got off it, but only by going to prison. The weirdest thing that happened was when one of the biggest dealers in my small town gave it all up to become a chiropodist, a sign, if you ever needed one, that drugs can really mess you up.

Still, I guess, for all the feeling of danger and rebellion, it was pretty average. Most drug-taking is. We are not all William Burroughses. And, anyway, for all the scaremongering about drug use and young people, let's not get carried away: the drug we are really talking about is cannabis, not heroin.

If there is a generation gap here, it is this continual muddling up of all kinds of drugs. Finding your kid smoking dope does not mean that he or she is an 'addict' who will never have the chance of a normal life. The biggest generation gap emerges from the use of ecstasy and LSD. Acid has moved out of the realms of revolution and re-established itself as just another recreational drug. Rave culture has pushed its way into the living room via its own brand of graphics, music and imagery. Everything from soft drinks to banking ads now depends on rave-type imagery and language. You don't need to be on drugs to know what it's all about, but it helps. Each generation has its own attitude to a particular drug and this changes. Once, acid was treated with deep reverence as a tool for self-knowledge. We are shocked to find the same drug can now be taken just to dance in a field all night.

For serious drug use, one only has to browse the Internet, where lists of chemicals are passed among the brethren, alongside information on how to make various drugs. Most of this is boring beyond belief, although the odd human cry for help is there: 'Anyone have a recipe for making quick and dirty psychedelics from natural precursors?' to which the answer comes, 'Try this and you will see God in short order.'

Seeing God, of course, is a more grown-up concern than simply wanting to get off your head or wanting to have a good time. And wanting to have a good time is probably something you don't feel like debating with your parents.

The authors of the report, which is called 'Drug Futures', point out that there is no discussion about drugs between parents or children or between head-teachers and pupils and that kids are quite simply terrified of adults finding out.

All of this must be a great boon to the dealers because part of the thrill of drug-taking is that it is illicit. You wouldn't really want to do it with your mum's blessing, as if it was something you could buy in Boots. The kind of parents who buy their own kids hash to stop them mixing with nasty dealers are positively nauseating.

While we can blame kids for wanting to maintain a separate culture, to use drugs precisely to make them feel as if they are in their own world, how can we justify adult behaviour which wilfully misunderstands all drug use as bad? Anyone who has been around drugs knows that certain drugs, both legal and illegal, are extremely bad for certain people in certain situations. They also know that some drugs make some people feel wonderful. To suggest that all drug use will lead to sordid addiction is simply not true.

Yet politicians and public figures, especially those who bow down to the market economy, feel duty-bound to come over all doom and gloom when it comes to any mention of drug use.

Blair Inc. may wear his background of playing in bands and having long hair as a badge of pop culture credibility, but where is the MP who will stand up and say, 'I not only inhaled but used to drop acid like it was going out of style'. Or are we to understand that all politicians have inhabited entirely parallel universes to our own?

Edwina Currie once told me that one of the biggest shocks when she first entered the House was just how much alcohol was drunk slowly through the course of the day. She found herself, she said, like many MPs, never really drunk but never really sober either, until she decided to stop drinking. This we must regard as an entirely different issue, because alcohol is legal, yet many teenagers point to their parents' patterns of consumption of legal drugs when asked about their own use of illegal ones.

Another generational difference is pointed up in the fact that drug-taking amongst the young has become more democratic. It is no longer the province of young men or of particular social classes. Drugs no longer belong purely to seamy subcultural groupings in the margins of society, but are part of the mainstream.

This has clearly been happening for some time, although there are those who pretend it hasn't. There are those who feel sentimental and secretive about their own drug use because they can then kid themselves that it's somehow subversive. There are those who are just going through a phase.

But one thing's for sure, the gap is not so much between one generation and the next as between those who admit that drugs are a part of their lives – rather than part of some grubby underworld – and those who, when asked if they have ever taken drugs, always just say no.

TIME FOR ALL GOOD WOMEN TO BE
PARTY POOPERS

As we all know, women are the grooviest people on the planet and it's about time we celebrated this fact. We may also be the poorest people on the planet but let's not get bogged down in all that, let's rise above such crass materialism. Instead it's time for a bit of feel-good feminism. Women getting together, being together, giving each other massages, aromatherapy and guides to starting up small businesses – that's what women want, isn't it? Well, it is 'What Women Want – A Global Celebration' that will take place at the South Bank this weekend.

As you may have already guessed, I won't be there. Lynne Franks, who is organizing the whole shebang, will be. 'What Women Want' was conceived partly in order to publicize the Fourth United Nations Global Conference on Women. Though on a somewhat smaller scale, the idea is that it replicates the exchange of information about what grassroots women's organizations are up to.

Franks's ambition is, she says, 'that, as women, we feel good about ourselves'. As a feminist I have to say that I don't feel good about either of these events, but then, party pooper that I am, I always thought there was more to the struggle for women's equality than feeling good anyway. Who knows, maybe my energy needs un-blocking with a good karmic going over.

Actually, many other people have expressed reservations about the Beijing conference, the chief one being that it is being held in Beijing. China is hardly known for its commitment to free speech or to women's rights. It is, as someone said to me the other day, like holding a conference on anti-racism in South Africa in the days of apartheid. Women's organizations from Taiwan, Tibet and Hong Kong have already been banned. Yesterday the Chinese government said it would turn away any women 'whose activities are deemed by China . . . as running counter to the principles and politics of the UN Charter, the relevant General Assembly resolutions and the purpose of the conference'.

It is probably just as well that I am not planning to apply for a visa. When I recently wrote an article complaining about China's treatment of girl children and mentioned the documentary shown in Channel 4's *Secret Asia* series, *The Dying Rooms*, in which girl babies were neglected and even left to die in state orphanages, the Chinese Embassy promptly sent me a letter explaining how the documentary was 'nothing but sheer fabrication'.

Aside from the constraints placed on the conference by the Chinese, several other problems are also emerging, an important one being the difference between the official governmental conference and the non-governmental one held some fifty kilometres down the road which, surprise, surprise, has a somewhat more controversial agenda.

There are those who will ask what such conferences can achieve anyway. Aren't they just a form of diplomacy to make us think that something is happening when actually it isn't? Is the UN any more capable of acting in the area of women's rights when it has proved so impotent elsewhere?

Yet the real difficulty is that much of what affects women's lives, and what would improve them – availability of contraception, freedom from domestic violence, access to education – is controlled not just by governments or states but by cultural, traditional and social arrangements that many governments are loath to interfere in. It is the linking of the private to the public sphere that is feminism's greatest insight and is proving the most difficult obstacle to overcome. If basic human rights are to include reproductive rights which means, simply, that women have a degree of control over their own bodies, then we still have a long way to go, as we saw at the UN conference on population in Cairo when fundamentalists of all persuasions lined up together in order to block such a debate.

These thorny issues, however, will not be dwelt on by those attending the Lynne Franks extravaganza at the weekend. Instead, one can gaily trip from a workshop on female genital mutilation to a session on tantric sex and take in some counselling on freedom of choice called 'Issues for Me Personally'. If you are wondering about the changing role of women in the twentieth century you can listen to none other than well-known writer on women's issues, Shelley Von Strunckel, perhaps better known as a *Sunday Times* astrologer. If you want to think about what's happening in China before tripping off to the Goddess Party, the nearest you'll get is a session on Chinese herbs. Bel Littlejohn couldn't make this stuff up if she tried.

If I sound grumpy with all this absolutely fabulous New-Age feminism, it's because I am. The closest you'll get to a debate on politics will be a discussion on women's rights as – you've guessed it – consumers, which is only to be expected at an event in which feminism is measured by how many Body Shop products one can rub into oneself.

There is no sense of feminism as a historical enterprise, with a past, with rifts between different kinds of approaches, with strategies for achieving power. The organizers did try to bring in some other voices: I know because they phoned me, but they were so unfocused that most people who had something to say apart from 'Aren't women wonderful' refused to take part. The result is feminism with the politics taken out because, as Franks says, she is not interested in politics and therefore expects other women not to be too.

I understand completely that there is huge disillusionment with traditional forms of politics, but if you want the world to change then I would say you need to be interested in some sort of politics, and that this may occasionally lead to some sort of confrontation rather than the cosmic unity Franks is seeking.

Her brand of high-energy, low-calorie feminism means we can celebrate being women as long as we can afford to buy the necessary accoutrements – the acupuncture, the therapies, the exotic oils – that we need to get in touch with ourselves. This is not the personal as political but the personal as entirely privatized, as the only potential space in which women can kid themselves they are powerful. Consciousness-raising may be outmoded but instead it has been replaced with this kind of global psychobabble.

In many ways the two conferences are mirror images of each other. One cannot discuss the private for fear of rupturing diplomatic relations; the other cannot talk about what women have to achieve in the public sphere because it has retreated so far into the private that to talk about power, real power in the world, is impossible. To do so might make some of us feel powerless when the goal is to feel relentlessly good.

I am, of course, no expert on What Women Want but neither is Lynne Franks, because they clearly don't want Viva radio. But I imagine the last thing we want is to be patronized by being told that possession of a womb alone is cause for celebration.

This Feminism Lite may be the flavour of the month – you can consume vast quantities of the stuff without anyone even noticing the difference – but surely I am not the only one who knows that however much of the ghastly stuff you manage to swallow, there is no getting rid of the bitter aftertaste.

WHY SEX IS HARD TO SWALLOW

There is too much sex in popular culture. It is everywhere you look and unnecessarily explicit. It bursts out of women's magazines, it writhes around in front of you on TV, it teases from every billboard you clap eyes on. It pimps everything from fridge-freezers to instant coffee. It slithers down from satellites. It bonks out of the tabloids and MTV. It has no shame, it doesn't care who sees it – men, women or children, it flashes at us all. It has no limits. It is cheap and degrading and we pay more and more to see it. We need to do something about it.

Or: there is not enough sex in our culture because we can't talk about it openly. Teenage girls get pregnant because they don't know about contraception or no one will talk about it with them. People die sad, lonely deaths because they are consumed with guilt about their sexual desires. We don't tell our children the truth about sex because we don't know what the truth about sex is. Paternalistic cultural authorities in turn treat us like children, banning films and videos that they think we should not see. Moralists always link images of sex with images of violence as though they were the same thing when they are not. We are too uptight, too repressed, too frightened to be honest about sex. We need to do something about it.

Whichever way you swing on this one, the unease over what we see and hear signals a loss of control by those who are used to defining what 'common decency' consists of. You can feel it in the air. The Calvin Klein ads featuring prepubescent-looking models showing their knickers have been so 'misunderstood' as child pornography that they have been withdrawn. Fifty per cent of the women recently surveyed complained that there was too much sex in women's magazines; the editors, however, are determined that sex is part of the mix. Discussion at the Edinburgh TV Festival reveals all kinds of anxieties about how to keep viewers when channels are proliferating. Does that mean inevitably that the boundaries of taste are to be consistently pushed back? Does accessibility mean more sex, more lottery and more sports? Is that what the people want? More significantly, should cultural producers merely give the people what they crave or what they deem to be good for them?

Part of the worry about the increasing sexual content of most forms of pop culture is that it represents a kind of downgrading, a tabloidization, of all forms of media that centres inevitably around the lowest and most horribly common denominator.

Television executives are having to face up to changing demographics as much as politicians; the mass audience has fragmented into many smaller groups who do not have such predictable allegiance or interests. This may have displaced a lot of TV people who believe that TV is, or could be about more than ratings and entertainment. Simon Jenkins, who has the grace to see that television is no longer aimed at him, writes: 'The days of cultural evangelism through TV are over.' Yet, is the choice always between a paternalistic approach that is trying to better its lumpen audience, and a shift ever more downmarket? Actually, if we look outside the world of TV – something that Street Porter was sensibly arguing for – we see galleries fuller than ever before. Art is no longer the prerogative of a cultural élite. People are interested in other things than tits and bums.

The assumption that the market is unassailable in every single area is patently wrong. Culturally speaking, people are very weary of everything being used as marketing devices. Otherwise why would we mind the Calvin Klein ads? Why would *Campaign*, the advertising industry's own journal, argue for the banning of these ads? Why would the readers of all those sextastic women's mags admit they were getting a little bored with all the articles on how to give a blow-job. Let's face it, there are only so many variations on a theme and only so many ways to swallow this particular set of instructions.

Klein's defence of his ad campaign is risible: that it was supposed to convey 'the idea that glamour is an inner quality that can be found in regular people in the most ordinary setting'. If we are to buy the notion that glamour comes from within, then we certainly don't need to buy all the outer trappings of glamour in the form of Calvin Klein underwear, jeans and fragrance. While we may feel that we live in a culture that is sexually saturated, there are clear limits as to what we may and may not see. The problem, though, is surely not how many of these images abound but how similar they all are to each other. How samey all these pictures of women turn out to be. No wonder photographers run the gamut of perverse sexual practices to try to liven up their images. We've done rubber, leather, bondage, how about some underage sex? Our relationship to this endless sexual imagery, always intrinsically voyeuristic, becomes even more so. It is now commonplace to have seen images of practices that we ourselves would never indulge in but that vaguely titillate us. It is not surprising that the Calvin Klein ads took this just one step further; he has already been pushing the boundaries of acceptability with his Kate Moss shots, looking (as *Campaign* pointed out) all of thirteen years old.

Such voyeurism which encourages us to see everything and feel little about it except the urge to buy something or other – 'to bridge that gap' – is worth worrying about. There are, though, differences between the various forms of media. One cannot avoid billboards in the way that one can turn over the page or switch channels. When Stuart Cosgrove, commissioning editor at Channel 4, said at the Edinburgh Festival 'people are interested in sex on TV', he was simply being honest. We are all human, all curious. What unsettles us is to see sex out of context, popping up all over the place, so to speak. This is what we feel is bad for our kids. It is not sex on a late-night programme about sex that should be the concern, but sex on every street corner that bothers us. As the old cultural authorities and institutions break down, there is a fear that the masses, malleable as ever, will be happily downgraded and degraded. Yet what do all these supposedly passive couch potatoes do? They do something else besides watching TV. What will set the limits on what we can see is a cultural force that nobody talks about much. Boredom. On planet tabloid you cannot talk about 'doing it' enough, no one ever manages to shut up about it; in the real world something else happens.

You just do it and get on with the rest of your life.

ON THE REAL MEAN STREETS

It is fashionable these days to reclaim the streets. We claim them from cars for the people. We must reclaim them from the people who live in them for the people who don't. We must reclaim them from the graffiti merchants, squeegee men, beggars, skagheads and alkies who roam them, for the ordinary citizen who just wants to feel safe.

How all this divides up on traditional left–right lines, I don't know. I do know that people are fed up, that I have lived in areas where you can't take your kids to the local parks because of the tramps congregating there. I know people aren't happy when they read that a toddler has been hospitalized because it has picked up a used syringe and sucked it. I know that while there are those who see graffiti as urban art, there are others for whom these squiggles signify another no-go area in which youth has run riot. I know people don't want to be approached for money every time they use public transport. I know women who roll up their car windows tightly the minute they see a squeegee guy. I know people feel unsafe. I know that sometimes I do.

To say these things, which is all that Jack Straw did, is deemed somehow right-wing. It is even, according to the letters page of this newspaper, bordering on Nazism. This is a ludicrous situation. To not say them, to ignore the experience of many of our citizens, is to sweep street people under the carpet, to use them as pawns in some spuriously ideological argument. It is OK, apparently, to blather on about parks and public spaces and community in some idealized form. It is not acceptable to point out why it is that public space is not the benign, harmonious arena of the communitarian dream.

Overnight, mild old Jack Straw has transmuted into Travis Bickle of *Taxi Driver*, cruising mean streets and ranting on about flushing the scum 'down the fucking toilet'. He'll be sporting a Mohican hair-do next. All he did was tell it like it is. It's fine and dandy to do this so long as you blame everything on Government policy, if you stick to the mantra 'tough on crime, tough on the causes of crime', like it was tattooed on your forehead. Straw's crime was not to mention the dismantling of the welfare state; his punishment is to be compared to Michael Howard.

Sooner or later New Labour is going to have to talk about how it plans to dismantle the welfare state, although it will be done in the guise of reform. It is being done, it will be done by whichever party wins the next election. But there must be a safety net to stop the numbers of young people drifting on to the streets; that the withdrawal of benefits and forced financial dependence of teenagers on parents is producing massive social problems is undeniable. Yet to merely state that many of us are uncomfortable with the numbers of people sleeping rough, that occasionally we are intimidated by the odd aggressive beggar is not to 'criminalize' all homeless people.

To see the homeless as simply failures of Government policy is often not to see them at all. There are those kids, and I have worked with some of them, who do not want to sleep in hostels, who are not all innocent victims. There are alcoholics and junkies for whom no amount of time in therapeutic communities or detox centres will ever do the trick. There are, of course, many who need greater help and more facilities than are currently provided. There are those trapped by poverty, those who can be helped to help themselves, those who are so ill you wonder how they survive at all without any care in any community.

The presence of such people in our midst may serve as a reminder of the failure of Government policy, of the inequalities of the way we live, but I doubt it. Those who can afford to, avoid face-to-face confrontation if they can. They don't use public transport. They don't live in areas in which adolescent crusties huddle with decrepit winos and their pieces of cardboard that say 'Hungry homeless diabetic'. They don't take their kids to playgrounds covered in dog shit and broken bottles, screwed-up tinfoil and used condoms. They don't see it the same way. Those of us who do can't help but feel uneasy in our streets. We feel that no one cares, that there is no one or nothing to stop bad things happening, that it's all out of control.

There is a line of thought about how to run communities which says that as soon as a window is broken, it must be repaired. If one window in a building is broken, it is tempting for someone to come along and smash another one. Once a couple are smashed, it becomes obvious that no one is going to do anything about it and all the windows get smashed. Soon the building, indeed the surrounding area, becomes rundown and neglected. If, on the other hand, that first broken window is replaced straight away, it is a sign that someone cares, if only about the appearance of things.

Graffiti signals to people a lack of care. The piling of rubbish in the streets says the same thing. So did grids and shutters in every doorway. In an ideal world congregations of homeless beggars wouldn't frighten us but in such a context they do. One solution to all this is to deny the experience of ordinary people and talk about macroeconomic policy instead but, however much the next government achieves in redistributing benefits, some of these problems are just not going to go away.

Some of our cities already have areas that look like parts of the huge American cities. We are told that they only look like that because of the lack of a proper welfare system. In linking 'the brutalization of the street' to increased crime, Straw put himself in the firing line. In talking about mugging, Paul Condon did the same thing. We cannot say in public what we experience the case to be in private, that in some areas a disproportionate number of muggings are carried out by young black men. To say this in some quarters is to criminalize all black people at the same time as denying the greater number of other crimes committed by white people. So everyone has to shut up about it.

If to talk about feeling afraid, feeling unsafe in the street and the sources of those fears, real or imagined, instead of talking about racism, unemployment and the failure of Conservative policy, is to be tainted a right-winger, then I am obviously tainted. Still, if Straw is playing the hard man, then there is something equally macho about those who rush to oppose him by automatically turning the argument into one of public policy rather than personal safety, as if to prove they are indeed tough enough. This denial of fear plays into the hands of the right more than anything else.

To be properly concerned, it appears, we must take squeegee merchants to our hearts even as they harass us. We must fumble for spare change (we don't like to carry around too much cash, you know) to give to the guy who was ranting at passers-by on the corner and we must continue to step over the damage we see all around us. The last thing we must ever admit is that sometimes, just sometimes, like Jack Straw, like Travis Bickle, 'we just can't take it any more', because if the streets no longer belong to us, why should anyone care what happens on them?

BEWARE OF DANCES WITH UNDERWOLVES

There is a line in the film *Gregory's Girl* where she says, 'Why is it that boys are so obsessed with numbers?' and he says, 'Actually, that's not true, only 98 per cent of them are.' Another woman reminded me of this on Monday at the Demos conference to publicize the final report of its Seven Million project, a year-long study of the lives and values of the young. Demos, in case you weren't sure, is an 'independent think-tank committed to radical thinking on the long-term problems facing the UK and other advanced industrial societies'.

This new report, 'Freedom's Children', concentrates on work, relationships and politics for eighteen- to thirty-four-year-olds in Britain. In other words, Demos wants to find out just what is wrong with young people today.

What is wrong with the young people who work for Demos is another matter. Their chief problem appears to be an unnatural attachment to numbers, statistics, and graphs of any description in order to explain the meaning of life. I have never seen so many charts and diagrams and 'findings' presented to an audience in such a short space of time – but then I am not a pollster nor do I frequent marketing 'presentations' in which clients are dulled into submission by endless flip charts.

There is, of course, nothing wrong with asking people what they think – which is what Demos do a lot of – but that is not the same as asking them what they feel, or even a clear indication of how they will behave. 'Freedom's Children' is the culmination of a year's work on the 'nature and depth of generational shifts in values –

through in-depth qualitative and quantitative research' on the fourteen million people in the target age range eighteen to thirty-four.

Much of what the report tells us could have been easily anticipated. It confirms what we already knew about the rising power of women, the fragmentation of values, the changing landscape of family life and the disconnection that many young people feel from traditional politics. Asking people what their attachments are to certain values may provide a snapshot of 'where we are at' but it certainly does not give us the whole picture. It is rather like cutting open someone's brain to see if they love you. Such dissection leads to a fetishization of facts and figures at the expense of something far vaguer but equally significant; what Raymond Williams described as a 'a structure of feeling'.

It is fine to take the temperature of society via opinion polls, but this should not be confused with a complete diagnosis. As we saw with the recent *Guardian* poll on infidelity, what people think they should do and what they actually do are two different things. As we saw at the last election, sometimes opinion polls just get it wrong.

What such polls cannot explain (but is the most intriguing) is why we are able to hold contradictory values at the same time. So, for instance, while the Demos report shows us that young women have little time for feminism, they have internalized many feminist values, and while the young are tough on law and order issues, they are liberal on issues of personal morality.

The degree of tolerance and understanding demonstrated towards Michael Barrymore when he 'came out' could not have been simply forecast by a poll on attitudes to homosexuality. For the tabloids hounding Barrymore, the only question was 'Is he gay?' For the great British public the more important question properly remained, 'Is he funny?'

The structure of feeling – the political subconscious, if you like – cannot be polled no matter how sophisticated the new methods for market research have become. One of the media-sexy issues that the Demos report highlighted was what it calls the 'masculization of female values'. It found a greater attachment to violence in young women than it did in young men and therefore predicts a growing problem of female violence in the years ahead. (A less provocative issue is the violence that so many young women do to themselves through the rise in eating disorders, but such things still remain secret.)

How do we know that young women may be more violent in the future? Because 13 per cent of eighteen- to twenty-four-year-old females agreed with the statement, 'It is acceptable to use physical force to get something you really want'. Agreeing with this proposition seems to me a long way from the prospect of having more girls than boys going round mugging, breaking into houses and beating each other up on a Saturday night.

More evidence of this trend is scooped up from popular culture where we see females identifying with bad women — the anti-heroines of *The Last Seduction, Tank Girl, Basic Instinct* and *Thelma and Louise*. To use pop culture to prop up a statistical argument fails precisely because there is no room for the very thing that popular culture sells us — fantasy. Cultural analysis occurs in a different world to the one that Demos currently occupies, yet its thinking will be limited if it continues to ignore it.

While Demos finds a rejection of national identity, there is something more complicated happening — we see all around us a reworking of what Britishness means from the likes of Blur and Pulp, in the writing of Kelman and Rushdie, in the work of artists from Mark Wallinger to Gilbert and George, in the romantic attachment to the land of the environmentalists, in the call to return to Albion, to Avalon itself.

The point, I guess, for Demos is to use all their information to try to suggest solutions for this unsteady world. It worries itself a lot about the old generation gap, seeing the possibility of intergenerational conflict when today's twenty-year-olds will have to pay high taxes to finance an ageing population. Generation rather than class will be a determining factor in tomorrow's world, yet it will still be predicated on differences of economic power.

It worries even more about what it calls underwolves — the third of eighteen- to twenty-four-year-olds who take pride in being outside the system. It fears they might bite back. I hope they do. There is really little point in being classified as subhuman if you don't do anything about it, is there? And it worries that politics has become a dirty word for alienated folk who don't bother to vote, let alone join a political party.

The shift away from traditional forms of politics to single-issue groups – whether they be environmental, anti-consumerist, animal rights, the Criminal Justice Bill protests, or AIDS activism has been well documented. Many young people are fundamentally interested in ethics and see no room for this in parliamentary politics. This is hardly surprising for a generation that has grown up with the reality of seeing that government has less power to change things while decisions are made elsewhere in the global economy – but has at the same time organized a state that has had disastrous effects in their lives.

While the state has washed its hands of financial responsibility for the young, trapping them into economic dependence on their parents for longer and longer, it has intervened enough to tell them that many of their leisure activities are illegal. The idea of voting once every four years is no compensation for the lack of say in the rest of their lives.

Many of the new pressure groups feel that what matters is not when you vote but where you vote. What opportunities are there in your life for voting about decisions that affect you? There are many lessons to be learnt from this new politics of refusal but Demos, I fear, refuses to learn them. Instead it is trying to filter this energy through the tired mechanisms of party politics.

It proposes, as Peter Hain also does in his new book, *Ayes to the Left*, that we bring in required voting. Required is a much nicer word than compulsory but it means the same thing. Required voting has been a success in Australia, argues Helen Wilkinson, one of the authors of the report, providing a kind of political education. It would still be possible to abstain and there would be small fines for those who didn't vote. There would also be room on the ballot paper for stating why you had chosen none of the above. This information would be processed and passed back up to the politicians who would then have to learn to be more accountable. Ha bloody ha!

I find it incredible, but not so surprising, that an organization that is so concerned with asking people what they think should then ignore their thinking and try and tell them what to do. Tinkering with the rusty machinery of a floundering political system doesn't count as very radical in my book. Indeed, as one member of the audience pointed out (and was promptly ignored), Demos has a touching faith, indeed a huge investment in the ability of politicians to manage a situation which is largely beyond their control. As Andrew Marr writes in the new magazine *Prospect*, the state 'has lost huge amounts of macro-power, not simply to Europe, but to a host of multinational bodies, to the bond market, to international corporations, even to cyberspace'. Its ability to control money, tax, unemployment is largely illusory.

The new forms of politics recognize this instinctively. Many young people recognize this emotionally, the rest of us flounder around trying to connect old and new. To think that the state can make itself more popular by coercing those alienated from it into voting is another illusion. We all agree that we have to do things differently but Demos is just too straight to be different enough.

It could do with a few underwolves lurking in its midst. The only thing is they just might 'bite back' and swallow a few flip charts and social contracts. To be honest, who could blame them?

OUTSIDE, LOOKING IN

'Non-stop shagging. Women with dangly earrings,' says my friend Andy authoritatively when I tell him I am going to the Labour Party conference. 'Men in suits with beer guts – you'll love it,' says Stella. Have either of these experts actually been to the conference before? No. But then nor have I.

It may be naïve, but I am going for the politics. Or at least some version of politics. I want to see how it is, which these days means seeing how it looks. I want to see Dennis Skinner's trainers and Scargill's hairdo and Tony's teeth in the flesh because I never have. In some small way, like many delegates at the conference, I am looking for something authentic.

Ingénue that I am, I spend some time on the phone trying to find out from the Labour Party press office who is speaking and when. It seems a simple enough request. You know – a programme, a time-table, that sort of thing. There is not one available. These things are not known in advance. It is because of these things called composites. 'The conference is a living thing. It's democracy,' I am told. 'Relax.' So I try, but can't quite get a grip on the looseness of the conference arrangements. There is a code in operation here. On one hand, people keep telling me these things have not yet been decided because of the wonderfully democratic process of the party, on the other hand they clearly have. Not only is there some sort of timetable, but people will tell you what's in the speeches if you ask them nicely.

I realize on the first day that if you want to know what's happening you have to watch television. The first person that gives me a running order that I can comprehend is a reporter being filmed in a hotel room very close to my room. I watch him on the TV in my room. This could be post-modern, it could be ludicrous; it certainly helps.

Eventually I tear myself away from the telly and wander down to the actual event. There is an awful lot of wandering around involved. You wander from one hotel to the next in search of fringe meetings. You wander up and down the seafront, in and out of the conference centre, into more hotels and bars, and Brighton itself ceases to exist as a place and becomes a 'venue'. The infrastructure of the whole affair is serviced by numerous waiters and receptionists and maids and Group Four security staff, and occasionally the odd reporter takes a break from talking to other media folk and notices that some of these people earn way below any proposed minimum wage and interviews one of them.

I go to see Gordon Brown talking but can't help thinking that the pink of the stage set is the colour of cheap toilet paper. It looks nicer on the box. As Brown talks, I wonder what it would be like if he was the leader, but he isn't, and I wander out again and meet a lady I saw in the café earlier on. She is already disappointed. 'You may see the overweight body of a fifty-five-year-old woman,' she says, 'but inside there is an eighteen-year-old with true socialist views.' And presumably thinner too.

She then reminisces about the good old days. Conference just isn't the same any more. This is a view I will hear over and over again. Everyone seems nostalgic, even for what they despised at the time. Apparently, to get into the conference hall, you used to have to run the gauntlet of the hard left, of Militant newspaper sellers.

The only demonstrators outside the hall this year are a weird coalition of animal rights people, pissed-off pensioners and the Free Kashmir lobby. I am fascinated by them. With their 'Ban Live Exports' banners they chant 'Live Export Tony Blair'. Tony Benn appears and they shout 'Scum, Scum, Scum', and either because he is incredibly benign or incredibly deaf, he smiles and waves at them. The bloke next to me is more mild-mannered. 'Glenda Jackson can't act,' he yells. Later on I see him up the road. He has donned a balaclava and looks slightly more dangerous. He is part of a gaggle of non-specific demonstrators that the police seem particularly worried about. His friend holds a sign saying 'Freedom not Boredom', which doesn't seem too unreasonable.

I bump into Barbara Follett who is very sensibly wearing a hat because walking up and down the seafront plays havoc with your hair and you never know when you are going to have to be on television. She invites me for dinner with her and Ken but then has to cancel because she has to be on television. At lunchtime the *Guardian* debate gets going. New Labour means that the man in the street is replaced by the man in the BMW.

I look in at Peter Mandelson's meeting on how to win marginal seats: Operation Victory. The evil genius promptly chucks out the media. I had met Mandelson the week before and liked his campy, almost Carry On, northernness. 'You're very controversial, aren't you?' he said to me, and I found myself waiting for, 'Ooh, er, missus'. He has a stillness about him that makes people lean into him. It's a good trick. There is also more than one of him, which helps. He is everywhere you look.

So is Derek Draper, one of his assistants, who also works for Rory Bremner, whom he keeps claiming is Britain's top light entertainer. Draper is worried about his suit. 'Is it OK? It cost £89.' His friend tells him it reminds him of the inside of a cheap hotel room. The night before I had caught him musing about writing a novel about political betrayal: 'A sort of cross between early Bret Easton Ellis and Jeffrey Archer.'

Out of the corner of my eye I keep seeing Liz Davies followed about by various camera crews. She has now assumed the quality of a veal calf about to be exported. But it is not till I go to a 'wacky' fringe event on 'The Political Psyche', chaired by Jungian psycho-therapist Andrew Samuels, that anyone articulates the bizarreness of the whole affair. 'Conventional politics takes place within a fantasy of seriousness,' he says. Well, some of it does, though a woman from the *Sunday Times* is more concerned about the outfit that Cherie Blair wore to the races. She has checked with the fashion desk to see where she got that waist-clinching belt. 'We can't find anyone who stocks them except Anne Summers, you know.'

The battle for the soul of the party may reside in such details, but of course you can't say that to sulky old Scargill, who makes yet another speech about being an unashamed socialist. The politicians' capacity for repetition is amazing. How do they do it? Over and over again. Because they believe it? Maybe some do. I am starting to believe some of it myself but it's an exhausting business. This may be less to do with the politics than the amount of alcohol one feels obliged to consume. The Labour Party drinks while the Tories dine, someone tells me. The Tory conference is an entirely different affair because 'they bring the wives'. Labour people do dine though. They cannot live on bread alone, or even on the tempting 'Roast meat in a bap' offered in the conference centre. The restaurants are chock-a-block with conspiratorial kalamari eaters. The receptions are brimming with champagne socialists.

In fact, I soon grasp there are really only two kinds of fringe meetings: the ones with sandwiches and the ones without. Some even have vol-au-vents too. The comrades, on the whole, may be hungry for ideas but they are ravenous at buffets, shoving you out of the way for the sake of a few peanuts. One fantastically grumpy old woman realizes I am 'press' and tells me of her outrage, not about the National Health Service but at 'dried-up little sandwiches' at the BMA meeting. 'Disgusting,' she says. 'Anyway, I don't like the *Guardian*. Nothing in it. I get *The Times*.'

The hall is buzzing by Tuesday afternoon. Everyone is waiting for Tony Blair to speak. There is a warm-up act in the shape of the merit awards and then he gives us his vision of free laptops for all. Unlike most politicians, Blair is bigger in real life than he is on screen. He is tall, whereas Kinnock is shorter than you think he is going to be. I feel this must be significant. He goes on for an hour and you don't notice, which must mean that it is a good speech, but it's strange to be sitting with the press. While the delegates clap and cheer, many of the journalists sit quietly. This does not mean they don't like it, because they do, but they are waiting to react not only to this but to the O. J. Simpson verdict. By six o'clock the news is

O. J. and not Blair, and the hacks are complaining that what with this and the Rosemary West trial, there is just too much news for one day.

There are film crews filming the reaction of the media to the Simpson verdict. We are all huddled around a TV set in the media centre, as if what is real and what is important can only ever be seen on screen and through the eye of a TV camera. We are watching and being watched. This makes my head spin, it is so profoundly weird and so taken for granted.

Yet, at the Tribune meeting later that evening, where Roy Hattersley, Peter Hain and Robin Cook are speaking, the audience is up in arms. They can't see the speakers because of the TV cameras in the way; they can't see the wood for the trees. A chant goes up. 'Move the cameras.' This direct action works. The media people bow to the pressure of the audience and get out of the way. Tribune meetings didn't used to be like this, I am told; you couldn't buy a ticket. Now there are empty seats and Hattersley is speaking, honorary left because of his views on education. He is relaxed, freed up maybe by knowing that he is leaving office; what he says is passionate and funny and sensible. It reminds me of when Ted Heath started spouting sense about the Gulf war, and right and left became meaningless terms simply because someone was telling the truth. This is still somehow different to providing a vision, to making a myth, to remoralizing a demoralized electorate that Blair is up to, though of course we all agree these days with the necessary fiction.

Clare Short tells me that it is normal to feel weird at conference. 'Is it your first time?' she says and invites me for a drink. She is great and her clan are with her: her sister, her brother, her brother-in-law, Angela Eagle, Angela's twin sister and Dad. It is a family affair and Clare claims she can drink like this and get up in the morning because she is of peasant stock. Everyone is drunk and happy enough to rule the world – or this little world anyway. But I have to leave the bubble and go back to real life. The minute I do, I put the TV on.

WHAT'S LOVE GOT TO DO WITH IT?

Inspired by Andrew Sullivan, I'm thinking of writing a book myself called 'Virtually Impossible, An Argument About Heterosexuality'. I'll leave the definitive work, 'Frighteningly Normal', to those better qualified than myself. It's not that I want to muscle in on Sullivan's act, more that I feel it is impossible to talk about homosexuality without talking about heterosexuality or indeed homophobia. Sullivan's book may not be – despite the hype – *the* most important book ever written about homosexuality, but it is important for a number of reasons, not least of which is that it is being shot into the mainstream in a way that most books about gay politics are not.

Certain gay activists may mutter to themselves that this is because Sullivan is known for being right-wing and his views are unashamedly 'assimilationist', but this is somewhat unfair. *Virtually Normal* is a powerfully and passionately written work that will appeal to a wider audience because it is written for a wider audience and this in itself is no bad thing. Too much of the discussion about gay politics takes place in an insular world which those uninitiated into the vagaries of academia and queer studies find difficult to comprehend. The world of sexual politics is a place in which 'the narcissism of small differences' abounds, yet at the same time, AIDS has created a sense of urgency. Death, as James Baldwin said, 'clarifies our responsibilities'.

On the ground, so to speak, homosexuality is everywhere. Only this morning, my family watched a man pretending to be a woman interviewing a woman whose husband had left her for another man.

Lily Savage was talking to Carrie Fisher on the bed in *The Big Breakfast*. How such a phenomenon feeds into a discussion of what legislation is needed to stop discrimination against gays, I am not sure. All I know is that this may be the argument of Sullivan's life, but the rest of life cannot be reduced to the legal system alone. The 'politics of homosexuality' that Sullivan advocates, though, are remarkably reductionist in this aspect. He asks simply that public, as opposed to private, discrimination against homosexuals be ended 'and that every right and responsibility that heterosexuals enjoy as public citizens be extended to those who grow up and find them-selves emotionally different. *And that is all.*' The two reforms he argues for – ending the ban against gays in the military and allowing gay people to get married – require 'no change in heterosexual behaviour and no sacrifice from heterosexuals'. They can be slotted into the current system without our noticing much change and that is all there is to it. Or is it? Far from being a new argument, this is, in fact, a very old one. As this week sees the 25th anniversary of the Gay Liberation Front, it's also a pre-Stonewall one. Thirty-five years ago, the Wolfenden Committee pointed out: 'Unless a deliberate attempt is to be made by society, acting through the agency of the law, to equate the sphere of crime with that of sin, there must remain a realm of private morality and immorality which is, in brief and crude terms, not the law's business.' The law's business, then, is to tell us what's socially acceptable, not what is morally pure. And that is all. The law itself, as we have seen, cannot stop prejudice once defined as 'a vagrant opinion without visible means of support'. It cannot address a culture of homophobia.

In some ways, it appears Sullivan is drawing a line around what a politics of homosexuality might be about. By relying on legislation, and an absolute split between private and public life to maintain it, he is de-politicizing gay politics. This is not so much a politics of transformation but of negotiated withdrawal. Gay people can be integrated into society without disturbing that society, yet the Utopian promise of sexual politics, whether gay or feminist, is its capacity to touch upon all aspects of life – to make it different. We know that, in the absence of God, the state can give and the state can take away, but we also know that, when we are talking about love, which is a word that – rightly – Sullivan is not afraid to use, then we have to work out a way in which we can love who we want and not be hated for it. There must surely be a politics that runs parallel to Sullivan's which goes beyond the traditional language of liberal rights claims, the claims of excluded minorities. For while arguing that the right to what heterosexuals already have is important, what is being claimed is essentially negative. As Jeffrey Weeks writes in his new and equally important book, *Invented Moralities: Sexual Values in an Age of Uncertainty* (Polity Press), to claim 'freedom from interference from and discrimination by the law on the grounds of equal status' is separate from 'any attempt to claim a right to be different'. It also fits easily into our existing notion of citizenship.

Weeks talks of two moments in sexual politics – the moment of transgression and the moment of citizenship. The politics of transgression which deliberately represent a challenge to the law have appeared recently in the form of confrontational queer politics and as a direct response to the epidemic. Sullivan discusses this in his chapter on the liberationists. However messy such politics are they are precisely about claiming the right to be different. Advocates of such politics usually believe that gender is socially constructed and constantly in flux. This makes most of us, gay or straight, uneasy because we tend to feel along with Sullivan that our sexuality is not a choice but something that just is.

At the extreme, theorists such as Judith Butler see gender as simply a kind of performance. Heterosexual men and women perform their masculinity and femininity as well as homosexuals and in this mix of high theory and low culture we can identify many actual performers – from Madonna to Schwarzenegger to Barry Humphries – who consistently play with themselves and with us in this way. This may be exciting stuff but the reality is that even if we are to accept that most people are merely 'performing' their gender, we have got our act down to such a degree that it is now our reality. What compels us to keep on performing in much the same way is not a question that is ever really answered because the stress is always the amazing fluidity of the whole process. However, as Weeks writes, 'Homosexuality has become a way of life that for many begs acceptance rather than continuing transgression.' This is where Sullivan and the politics of citizenship comes in.

For Sullivan, the logical conclusion of the liberationists and of Foucault is the spectacle of outing. I disagree and would use Foucault, whose value was his very slipperiness, to argue against, rather than for, outing, but the point is that the right to be different is something we should take seriously rather than try to sweep under the legislative carpet. The buzz word may be diversity – even Blair used the phrase 'sexual diversity' in his speech last week – but in order to live with diversity then we have to ask ourselves just what is it about homosexuality that is so threatening to the rest of us? Why has a vast edifice of homophobic ideology, in the form of all the various myths about homosexuals, been created throughout history that speaks of gayness as representing an end to life as we know it?

What are we protecting ourselves from by a discriminatory legal system and culture? More importantly, can the same mechanisms that we use to protect ourselves now be used to give homosexuals the freedoms they desire? Marriage may still be the pinnacle of achievement for heterosexual normality but it is crumbling from the inside out. What is to be achieved by offering this right to gay people? The muddle over gays in the military, where they are allowed homosexual acts but not a homosexual identity, shows how far we are from accepting what gayness, as it is currently practised, is actually about. Sullivan has every right to present homosexuality as a blip on the way to being virtually normal; for others, though, it will always mean that normality itself must be challenged. To want to enter the most patriarchal institutions around – marriage and the military – can never and will never be their aspiration.

Sullivan's most radical proposal, which he underplays somewhat, is in asserting the right of gay people to adopt children. This is because this is not merely a matter of law but strikes at the heart of what homophobia is about: the contamination of children by gays, the fragility of heterosexuality that it can feel itself so easily tainted.

If the integration of gays into society can be achieved without any effect on me whatsoever, you might wonder why I care about all this in the first place, beyond the usual 'some of my best friends . . .' apology. Well, it is because I hope this book is part of a wider argument than just the one about homosexuality. It is because I can see Sullivan, like so many contemporary thinkers, trying to work out a system of values that secular society can live with. His recourse is the supreme rationality of the law. Blair's is Christian socialism. Hillary Clinton's – and now, it would appear, Naomi Wolf's – is the quasi-spiritual language of soul. Other languages exist, too. What Jeff Weeks is trying to do is talk about 'the ethics of love' and he does not see the family, and therefore marriage, as the only repository of values. Instead he looks to other networks of community and friendship as providing a good place to start. In an age of uncertainty he looks elsewhere, whereas Sullivan simply resurrects the old certainties as though nothing has changed. Even in his conservative heart he must know it already has, which is why a homosexual version of 'Back to Basics', however popular, must have its self-imposed limitations.

I hear the term 'Get real' all the time. It has replaced 'Come off it' or 'You've got to be kidding', but is somewhat more edgy. To tell someone to get real implies that they are not facing up to the world as it is. 'Get real,' says Tiffany in *EastEnders* when Robbie tries to give her a puppy. Get real is what most of us think when our politicians cannot even debate the issue of cannabis legislation. Get real is what we feel when they argue that what they earn from all their little extra jobs is somehow irrelevant.

Get real is my reaction to the Chief Rabbi, Jonathan Sacks's claim on the programme *Who Killed the Family?* that soap operas rarely portray any conventional morality whatsoever. Has the man never watched *Neighbours* which, when it isn't lecturing us about skin cancer, is telling teenage kids to wait before they have sex?

Yet Sacks's claim, repeated in the programme by others, is that popular culture does not lead by example. Instead of propping up nuclear families and stable relationships, it continually shows adultery and family breakdown. At its worst it even celebrates divorce – as with the Volkswagen ad. A sense of humour is obviously not a prerequisite for the post of moral guardian. All of this apparently gives children the wrong idea about the right way to live. Popular culture rumbles on, venerated by some and experienced by most of us for what it is – and yet it is still subjected to these periodic attacks for its general looseness, whether it's the tabloids homing in on Pulp singing about raves and drugs, or the worry about too much illicit sex in *EastEnders*.

Just when you think having to defend pop culture is a thing of the past and it's safe to turn on the TV and wallow in the complexities it offers, you are forced back into justifying its very existence. It is something of a joke that the new editor of the *Daily Telegraph* can come on like those 'Who is Gazza?' judges and admit his ignorance of the television of the past ten years. These people don't need to be in touch because they are in power. Or so it would seem.

However, it is beyond a joke when things that can be argued about in front of a family audience (drugs, domestic violence, divorce) – as they have in all the soaps recently – cannot be aired properly in the Commons. It is not that our popular fictions can answer the questions that they raise, but at least they acknowledge what some of those questions might be. They are certainly providing a much-needed public service.

Some programmes that I have refused to miss over the past few weeks include *Pride and Prejudice*, *Cracker* and *EastEnders*. Judging by the viewing figures, many others found them as compelling as I did. Has the nation become debased by watching them? Well? No, not unless you count Darcy fever and endless discussions about the appeal of breeches and riding boots. If anything will undermine the nuclear family it is dreams of Darcy, rather than our rush to follow in the path of 'Chelle as she heads off to America carrying the spawn of yet another psychotic publican.

For this version of *Pride and Prejudice* rammed home the triumph of romantic love over the workings of property and inheritance. It was as if Andrew Davies had taken one look at Jane Austen and said 'lighten up'. So in the end marriage for Jane and Elizabeth looked like a free choice, even though we were reminded that too often it wasn't. To marry for love and money, what modern girls they were, after all; and what Darcy came to represent was a version of strong, silent but decent masculinity. No wonder we were weak at the knees. Now he is no longer on television, pray where else shall we look for it?

Certainly not in *Cracker*, a dark and dangerous piece of work cranked up by Technicolor Catholic ravings and an implicit understanding that all is not right in the world between the sexes. I am unsure what Jonathan Sacks would make of *Cracker* and what it says about conventional morality. It says ultimately that it's bloody difficult. *Cracker* exists in a cesspool of prostitution, rape and murder. The victims are women but the men suffer too. At the end of each episode the address of a helpline for those who have been raped or assaulted appears. This may be over-egging the pudding somewhat. *Cracker* wants to appear socially concerned rather than just socially voyeuristic as it shows us graphically all sorts of horrible injuries inflicted on women. To be frank, I can't imagine a woman who had been raped sitting through till the end of an episode. It would have been like having the number of Childline at the end of *Twin Peaks*.

While there was an enormous fuss over whether *News At Ten* should be moved to make way for Fitz's bulk, no one seems to mind that a storyline involving the murder of several women is being shown at the same time as the Rosemary West trial is going on.

Just as it would appear that, despite ourselves, we want to know the worst that one human being can do to another, and we find ourselves reading details of these murders (which we afterwards wish we hadn't), so *Cracker* appeals in its attempt to take us to the depths. And Fitz is deep. Too deep. As he says himself: 'I am too much.'

Cracker is too much. In the guise of naturalism there is nothing natural here. You can feel the struggle in the writing to wrench it up, wrench it out. Every character has a guilty secret, every exchange is heightened, every emotion just under the skin. Gripping stuff. The police station is crackling with sexual fear and loathing. The streets are full of tarts and the churches full of hypocrites. Men rape and murder women because they hate 'that thing between their legs' and then they protect each other. All women except prostitutes are so sexually jealous of each other that they wish rape and murder upon each other.

In this jungle one feels Jimmy McGovern try to tell us something about power and the lack of it. Beck, the rapist, acknowledges to Fitz (who knows that there is more than one way to take someone apart) that what makes men weak is not actual impotence but their desire, over which they have no control. Men are 'impotent when they have an erection' and women 'abuse that power'. When Fitz is trying to get a confession out of a murderer he says he understands and talks the shorthand of psychosexual neurosis: 'innocence; virginity; catholicism'. For McGovern's shorthand is sex and death, preferably at the same time, and his world is one in which women don't stand much of a chance. I wouldn't want him to write it any other way. You can't make brutality politically correct. You can, however, ask what makes it so appealing. You could also ask why some of our best writers, like McGovern and Bleasdale (*Jake's Progress*), are moving their drama from the political to the personal, to the private space of families and the relationships between men and women rather than dealing with overtly political structures and institutions. What can they explore here that they couldn't before? Where are the logical conclusions of living in a climate of moral relativism more finely expressed than in these series?

You could also, if you are in the business of deriding popular entertainment, watch some of the damn stuff. If you do, then you could never make such simplistic claims about soaps and dramas doing anything as simple as undermining the way we live. Fiction represents, reflects, challenges and – thank whatever god you like – it is not in the hands of those who would give us join-the-dots morality plays. If viewers are sophisticated enough to switch from *Cracker* to *Pride and Prejudice*, how come our moral guardians aren't?

Or do they still fear that *Pride and Prejudice*, with its elegant deconstruction of the workings of patriarchy and capitalism, might bring about the decline of marriage? Will *Cracker*, watched by the same eclectic social mix of viewers, empty the churches and fill the brothels? Will the claustrophobic adultery of Albert Square inspire a wave of copy-cat behaviour in previously monogamous couples up and down the country? Get real.

HELLO! AND GOODBYE RADICALS

Paula Yates poses on the cover of *Hello!* in a faux-princess outfit, and we are promised a glimpse of the house she has bought in London and shares with Michael Hutchence and her daughters. Just below is a much smaller picture of a distraught Leah Rabin. Rabin's widow Leah reflects the world's grief as the man of peace is laid to rest. Such shameless juxtapositions are *Hello!*'s speciality. B-list celebs mingle with the parents of murdered children. We share their pain and their ruched curtains and we say isn't it terrible and what a horrible sofa.

I doubt that *Hello!* will be discussed at tonight's Radical Journalism Forum in London. But perhaps it should be. *Hello!* is a kind of 'mental chocolate': you know it's not good for but you can't help these cravings. Cravings that remain totally unsatisfied by the *New Statesman, Red Pepper, Tribune, Prospect* or any other supposedly 'radical' publication.

These journals rely on a notion of commitment in a world of instant gratification. Circulation remains low because of our cultural failure to commit. That's one excuse, anyway. Another is that the Blairite Labour Party stifles discussion and is only interested in the kinds of ideas that fit into a tabloid agenda. Public disillusionment with the Government should, one imagines have bolstered the sales of these left-wing magazines but it hasn't. It is more comfortable to blame potential readers for their lack of interest than editors and writers for their lack of popularity.

I hope the speakers at tonight's forum – Alexander Cockburn, Christopher Hitchens, Darcus Howe, Steve Platt and token woman

Hilary Wainwright – will explain what radical journalism means now rather than what it meant fifteen years ago, because I would like to know.

Radical can mean merely being in opposition to the Government or increasingly being in opposition to the Opposition. It can refer to terrific investigative journalism, a luxury in a downsized profession, or it can mean intrepid undercover reporting. It can mean feminist, gay or green writing. It can mean insisting on an international perspective when newspapers are being forced to buy in their foreign coverage from agencies. It can mean the socially concerned reporting of a Nick Davies or the bravery of a war correspondent like Martin Bell.

Radical journalism depends on the myth of the journalist as hero, very rarely heroine, I'm afraid. There is nothing wrong with all this except that it is an expensive business and the context in which it appears has changed. Magazines of the left – and there aren't that many left – have not done well in adapting to these changes and they have only themselves to blame. They are complacent, narrow-minded and, while perceiving themselves to be on some cutting-edge that appeals to their mates in the housing association, seem to have little respect for their readers.

They start from the ideological position that people should read their magazine rather than ever asking the most basic questions. Why should they read it? What can it provide that other media cannot? Is it pleasurable in any way at all? Why should someone buy a publication when they get increasing comment from newspapers, TV and radio? Why should anyone read dull but worthy writing laid out in visually uninspired fashion when for the same price they can buy something that looks like a million dollars?

The response is that style costs a million dollars and they can't compete. I don't accept this – look at the fanzines, the student mags, the football rags, the art journals that are produced on shoestring budgets but which at least look like fun. Look at the exciting work of young graphic designers who need a break and never get it.

As long as the left considers a concern with the visual somewhat superficial it misses the point entirely. But these publications not only ignore our increasing visual sophistication but all things cultural. I was pleased that *Soundings*, which launches next week, is a journal of politics and culture and includes pieces about mountain-biking, music and gay consumerism. My heart sank when I saw that the first issue of *Prospect*, with its 6,000 word essays, couldn't manage a single piece on books, film, TV or the arts. Does one have to be so serious to be taken seriously? Does seriousness inevitably mean that one always has to prioritize an incredibly narrow definition of politics? And surprise, surprise – these publications find it hard to get women writers and consequently women readers.

If I sound bitter, that's because I am. I spent a long time working for these sorts of magazines. All those debates that took place in the eighties about the importance of culture, of widening the space of politics, might as well not have happened. The true and rightful path is still one that requires the utmost dedication and, believe me, you have to be dedicated to make it through so many of these journals. The hegemony – and there's an appropriate word for you – of the fortysomething lefty male continues. His world view prevails and he knows what's important. Content not form. Statistics not style. As Eduardo Galeano once wrote: 'Hermetic language isn't the invariable and inevitable price of profundity. In some cases it can simply conceal incapacity for communication raised to the category of intellectual virtues.' Thus the *New Statesman* relegates its best writers, its arts and books reviewers to the back section. Never once do they get to play up front with the big boys because, hey, why discuss something as frivolous as cinema when you can have another three-page spread on taxation alongside some lovely graphs.

It is only fair to point out that my objections to the *New Statesman* are personal as well as political as, when I worked for it, it only gave me four weeks' maternity leave and then asked me to take a pay cut. I guess that is the joy of working for a left-wing employer. You do it for love not money and if your idea of love is being touched up by some menopausal male after he has downed ten pints of real ale then everything in the garden is rosy.

I don't want to appear ageist and so I'll just be plain rude and say that one of the problems with 'radical journalists', or those who define themselves this way, is that they are getting on a bit. They assume a constituency of readers where there is none. They talk of 'modernity' but they do not actually like what it produces very much – and that is young people who do not experience life as full of political certainties on which they must take the correct position. Where are the young writers on the left, people ask, forgetting that the left as they understand it never really existed as a viable option for someone of twenty. Instead, if you look at youthful magazines from the *Big Issue* to the *Idler*, you will see signs of life that cannot be co-opted easily into any one political programme. Preaching to the converted is one thing but what we are talking about is a generation of the deliberately unconverted.

The bottom line for radical journalism must surely be that it somehow challenges power, and power is both institutional and political, cultural and personal. Traditionally much of the left has had vested interests in tackling the first two at the expense of the last two. That is why the definition of what is radical needs to be widened considerably.

Doubtless this is a tall order but a programme like Molly Dineen's *In the Company of Men* did it in a delightfully unmacho way. No one watching could have thought that what the Army was doing in Ireland was anything less than ridiculous, yet at the same time one had a sympathy for the individuals involved. This is radical documentary-making. Next week's *Panorama* interview with Diana may also be radical if it shows the impossibility of her situation.

While radical journalists may be huffing and puffing about republicanism in their next issues, I suggest they might also enlist Diana's support for some other more unlikely radical causes. In Liverpool last week, a 'cheeky' Scouser waved a hand-rolled cigarette at her and asked: 'Have you gotta light, girl?' Diana giggled: 'Is it weed?' To which he replied: 'Do you want some?' The source of this intoxicating piece of gossip? *Casablanca*? *Prospect*? *Private Eye*? No. Stone me if it wasn't that radical journal *Hello!*

BEWARE OF GEEKS BEARING GIFTS

I have been part of the digital community for some time now and I'm still waiting for it to change my life. I may be wired but I'm still not convinced. I feel I must try harder but it's all a bit of an effort. My main technological problem of the day is that my oven won't work – but what the hell, I can get my Tarot cards read on-line. They were bad. I hate my computer. I hate my oven. I checked my e-mail and found as usual I'd got two exciting messages from friends who now also have e-mail. They say things like 'I've got e-mail. E-mail me.' Often they say 'I'll phone you later.' When I first had a fax machine we all faxed each other senseless, just because we could. We didn't actually say anything that we couldn't say via much more old-fashioned technology but that's not the point, is it? The point is to be modern and show off about it, to pretend you're at the cutting edge, at the centre of thrilling conversation, that you have the world at your finger-tips.

Geekhood beckons with its promise of revolution and yet I still can't make the grade. Perhaps it is because I don't believe. Or I don't believe enough. In Douglas Coupland's new novel, *Microserfs*, people say to each other 'Who's your Bill?' They are referring to Bill Gates, head of Microsoft and the god of geeks the world over . . . The man, everyone tells you, is a genius. He is clearly a genius at selling, at doing business, but reading the extracts from his new opus *The Road Ahead*, I remain sceptical. You can, if you are extremely lucky, even get a glimpse of God, or Bill, at a special multimedia workshop at the Science Museum. Just answer a couple of easy-peasy questions like 'What does MS-DOS, Gates for operation system stand for?' The thing is I don't know and I care less, because while I accept information is power this kind of information bores me stupid. I guess this is a further sign of just how boring and stupid I am, but there you go.

When Bill talks about his first experience of computers, playing games on a slow prehistoric machine that actually took longer to do things than if you were using pen and paper, I find it somewhat eerie. 'There was something neat about this expensive, grown-up machine that we could control; we were too young to drive or do any other fun adult activities, but we could give this big machine orders and it would always obey.' Now Bill has a much bigger machine to give orders to and not only does it also obey, its employees are prepared to work fourteen hours a day to keep Bill happy. The division between work and leisure scarcely exists for many of Bill's workers; indeed, such division belongs to the old world not this one.

He describes a world in which everything is made smoother, easier, by having computers do it all. Access to information will mean that the concept of distance will vanish. Everything will be here, now, if you want it. Or rather, if you want to buy it, for the information highway turns the whole world into a more efficient market-place than ever. If you are worried about too much information, too much overload, fear not – other machines will sift through all that is on offer, tailoring it to your individual needs. These machines, intelligent agents, are what everyone is getting excited about. These agents will know your preferences and tastes about everything and scan what is going on before they relay what you need. So, for instance, if you hate this column you can have your *Guardian* delivered without it. Now, as even Bill admits, all this could sound creepy. We wouldn't want these agents to be too smart, to anticipate our needs too much and to perform unwanted tasks, but rest assured, we will come to like it. Back to Bill: 'Researchers in this area have found that people give mechanical agents with personalities a surprising degree of deference.'

The promise of digital democracy is reduced to consumption and deference; no wonder some nerds see Bill as Satan and are waiting for the anti-Bill to rise up and save our souls. Coupland's book, while masterfully sketching the world of some youngish Microsoft employees, actually takes us back to some very old questions about soul and identity and the meaning of life. The geeks he portrays mark themselves out as individuals primarily through the products, both material and cultural, that they consume. The nearest they get to a spiritual discussion is when they talk of their shared obsession for *Star Trek*. They may be living in the future but they are obsessed with a seventies version of what that future will be – apolitical, colonial, hierarchical. Dan, the main character, admits 'I think nerds secretly dream of speaking to machines – of asking them "What do you think and feel – do you feel like me?"' The primary relationship is geek and machine. People are a problem. While all the characters say they would like to have a relationship, they can't deal with real live women. It's not their fault. It's a user interface difficulty. They'll just wait for the next version to come out – something more 'user friendly'. What Coupland does so brilliantly is show the various ways in which they try to reconnect and they do it through that imperfect, slightly embarrassing and uncontrollable soft machine – the body. They do shiatsu, body-building. The female characters are anorexic or bulimic or have taken so many steroids that they are not quite sure of their gender. Michael (the recognized genius among them) meets a potential partner on the Net but is not sure whether it's male or female. In cyberspace, you see, the word becomes flesh and the body melts away and you can be anything you want to be.

It is, I know, too easy to counterpoise a world of flesh and blood with a hard-techie world, but Coupland's old-fashioned concern with the loss of the body in cyberspace must be taken seriously. For some, freedom from the body can mean a liberating freedom from gender, from age and race, but it is not enough to say that it is simply that. The same confusion about where the body starts and ends is to be found in Dale Spender's new book *Nattering on the Net: Women, Power and Cyberspace*. In it she talks about the concept of data-rape. She is referring to abusive and pornographic e-mail, the on-line sexual harassment that many women are subject to on the Net. I understand this is a violation but I don't understand this as part of the same category as physical violation, with its suggestion that mind abuse should have the same status as abuse of the body. She concludes that virtual rape or harassment are on the same conceptual continuum as rape as we usually understand it.

I cannot accept this because, as Coupland hints, there are very real boundaries to our bodies and while it is exciting to imagine a bodiless existence, we are a long way off from any such thing.

Women need not worry so much about potential violation which, though annoying and upsetting, is not the main problem with this technology. We have to concern ourselves much more with the question of access. Many older women are scared of cash machines, never mind intelligent agents and if the world is not to be divided into the information-rich and the information-poor along old class and gender lines, then clearly we must demand access. I remain optimistic because I see that my daughters, like most young girls, have no fear of this technology. It is part of their lives.

Increased access would also, I hope, stop the worrying reverence that we are supposed to have for Bill Gates. I am happy that he has a vision of the future but there must be others, ones which see human needs as being more than merely the need to consume. What is appealing about the Gates vision is that I wouldn't have to bother to get my oven repaired because my own intelligent agent would have sorted it out for me. I can't help but wonder whether cooking and eating and all those other pleasures of the flesh would get much of a look in, in Bill's future.

SHE WHO MUST NOT BE OBEYED

I have always detested the ads for *She* magazine – '*She* is for the woman who juggles her life' – which depict some model as the perfect mother, career woman and lover. If women are so adept at juggling so many balls, why don't they lob a few where it matters? An advert is, of course, a fantasy, an aspiration that most of us never achieve. Yet, somehow, the image of the woman who wants to 'have it all' is discussed in the media as if it were a reality. In journalistic shorthand, Ms Have It All's caring, sharing partner is the equally fictitious New Man. Together this wonderful couple would smooth over the cracks in the problematic relationships between men, women, children and work and take us hand-in-hand into the future.

Now that Linda Kelsey, the editor of *She* magazine, has resigned due to stress, the cracks are being brought into focus once more. I take it for granted that it's possible that occasionally some men resign from high-powered jobs too, but that this does not usually precipitate a discussion of whether it is feasible for men to combine a career with being a father and a husband. Poor Kelsey now has to cope with the added stress of being representative of a whole generation of women, rather than just being someone who has recognized that they need a break.

If she can't hack it, the gloating implication is that neither can the rest of us. It serves women right for wanting it all in the first place. Having it all might mean, in essence, simply wanting what men have; but we have known for a long time that if we want what men have, we need what men have got – and that is a wife. Without such support we have, as Erica Jong once said, simply fought for the right to be terminally exhausted.

Yet the discussion about Kelsey and her ilk also takes place in some media stratosphere where all jobs are careers, where all work consists of a series of meetings and lunches, where people do have more than enough money to live on, but still want something else. Most women with children do actually work. They work part-time, which hampers much chance of a career, and they do underpaid, unstimulating jobs – not to have it all, but simply to have enough. Likewise, the stress they suffer is not to do with the circulation of a magazine they edit, but to do with wondering how they can afford to get the washing machine fixed and buy all the presents their children are demanding at Christmas. They might worry about whether they are spending enough quality time with their partners and children, but there is the shopping to do, the meal to cook, the floor to vacuum. It may come as a surprise to some journalists but teachers, nurses and shop assistants have children too. And they manage. Just about.

Why I am so grumpy about *She* magazine is that in the guise of supporting women, it implicitly supplies a whole new set of pressures. Women are already too hard on themselves and each other; we spend our lives keeping up appearances. A nineties magazine for women would forget the spinach flan and understated camel suit. It would tell its readers to live in a tip, only have sex if there was nothing on the telly, throw up at parties, to dress in a bin-liner if they so desired, phone in sick and yell at the children. It would say that mess is fine, it is healthy, it is life, that feeling out of control and veering from one crisis to the next is perfectly normal. It would say 'Let it go', and it would of course have to let all its lucrative glossy advertising go, too.

However, women's magazines are still imbued with what feels like an increasingly eighties ethos, in which the answer to every problem is either work or consumption. If anything marks out the difference between the decades, it is this changing attitude to work. It has been forced upon us. And it has been forced upon men, too, who can no longer assume a smooth progression through one career. Many men are now having to find an identity outside work, in the way that women have always had to. All of this is being done in a vacuum. The old infrastructures of extended family have gone and nothing has yet replaced them. The Government is perfectly happy to drive down wages for part-time work and to deny paternity leave for fathers. Child-care is expensive. Job-sharing is still looked on as a rather peculiar practice. Work and family are still constructed as separate spheres and never the twain shall meet. No wonder the stress of holding it all together is high.

Add to this a generation of women who are having their babies later and it all becomes too much. The impact of women becoming mothers in their thirties rather than their twenties is not much taken into account, but it should be. These are women who have more to give up and are therefore more resentful. They know that having a child changes your life but they never realized quite what the extent of that change would be. Does anyone? Unless they are the privileged few, they find that children cannot be slotted easily into a busy schedule.

This has caused us to question what exactly those words that are thrown around all the time, words like 'equality' or 'equal opportunity' actually mean. Equality means working fourteen hours a day. Equality, it turns out, means the double-shift in which some are clearly more equal than others. We talk of children as a choice, as an option, but once they are here there is less choice and fewer options for women. *Options* is, by the way, another women's magazine in which your options involve one kind of make-up or another. I don't think any legislation can change the fundamental fact that women have babies and men don't and nor do most feminists, contrary to popular belief, but it could certainly be made easier. Working practices, as we have seen, can change overnight if the desire for change is there.

But as long as women excel at juggling and doing it all, change is unlikely. We are victims of own ability, if you like, and arguing for equality in the work-place has resulted in us having to pretend that we can function on men's terms, that we are not in fact the primary care-givers in our families, and that work is the be-all and end-all of our existence.

It is no shock that the talk now is less of equality – why should we even want to be equal to miserable men who have no other life? – but of quality itself. Women want quality time, not just with their husbands or with their children, but selfishly enough occasionally for themselves. Just like men. The eighties obsession with quantity has been replaced by a concern with the quality of life and this is a debate in which both sexes have a stake. What is the point of having it all if you still feel something is missing? Perhaps it is better to have part of it at different times in your life and enjoy what you have. But as long as men can function in the current system then it will carry on; let's not fool ourselves that they have much investment in arguing for female equality. Yet if they see that they, too, are malfunctioning and can promote a better balance between work and family and the quality of life, some version of equality may slip in through the back door. This is a difficult thing to suggest to an already cowed workforce, but without it none of us, I'm afraid, can truly claim to have it all. Rather, we will continue to feel we've all been had.

Anyone who hankers after a traditional Christmas may find him or herself sorely disgruntled as so many of our cherished traditions are falling by the wayside. In order to avoid such seasonal disappointment, here is my guide to what has changed, so that you may celebrate in true contemporary spirit. Here's wishing you a thoroughly modern and cool Yule.

Father Christmas

The growing distrust of all authority figures has spread to Santa himself. It is no longer fashionable to regard him as a benign patriarch who puts us in touch with our inner child. Rather, his role is considered more problematic by those who see him as just another absent father who needs reminding that a child is for life not just for Christmas. Anti-Santa feeling is certainly running high in Tyne and Wear where a Santa has had to seek police protection to stop him being attacked by 'stone throwing youths'. Children as young as ten apparently were shouting 'fat bastard' and throwing beer cans as they tried to overturn his sleigh (a heavily decorated Land Rover). In future he will be accompanied by a police officer and two special constables. This is not simply a British phenomenon. An Australian Santa was also attacked by children in the outback. He and his assistant elf 'fled to the local police station for help and had to continue their mission from a police wagon'.

Christmas trees

While Santa may be a male fertility symbol, the decorated Christ-

mas tree is female one. Originally a weapon used by German Prot-
estants in their fight against Catholicism's tendency to depict everything in human form, the Christmas tree could signify the festival in
an abstract manner. Decorating it with baubles was a magical process which the whole family could be involved in. Not any more,
folks. Christmas trees, like everything else in the house, have
become design statements about your very soul. They have to be as
morbidly style-conscious as the rest of us. This year the thing is
evidently to hang chilli peppers on your tree. The fashionable colours for decoration this year are less garish. No more red and gold –
rather russet and bits and bobs made of straw. Tinsel is out. Twigs are
in. Fairy lights yes, but obviously not on the tree itself, sweetie. If
you are not prepared to pay five pounds for a pine cone in Habitat
then people will talk about you behind your back. 'Did you see that
tree?' 'I know, tragic.'

Carol singers

Carol singers apparently used to do it in the road and do it for free.
Now they come only in sullen pairs managing to render 'Silent
Night' a threat. They don't like singing, don't know the words and
they don't like you either. As soon as you give the money, they run.
They make squeegee merchants seem the most charming people on
the planet.

Mistletoe

This charming reminder of our pagan past used to be for kissing
under. Now it is for boycotting as it mostly comes from France, the
home of a certain Mr Chirac. We can't help feeling that nuclear
testing in the Pacific is not the ideal way of spreading goodwill to all
men.

Parties

People used to have fun at parties. Now parties are a problem.
Officially. Experts confirm this. Julia Cole of Relate, the counselling agency, says that the Christmas party season is a minefield of
temptation and indiscretion. Well, would you go if it wasn't? Office

parties, unfortunately, she explains, 'encourage intimacy and the indulgence of long suppressed desires'. This, of course, is a bad thing and the number of complaints about sexual harassment soars at this time of year. Cases that have gone to court include harassment by 'chocolate willies' as well as, even more bizarrely, men claiming to have been harassed by their secretaries. The advice from those who give advice about this sort of thing is to take your spouse and stay sober to avoid this sort of nastiness occurring. My advice is to ignore theirs.

Christmas dinner

'Christmas is carnage,' flapped the duck in the new film, *Babe*. And so those who wish to avoid carnage in their homes this year will opt for a meat-free Christmas. No dead ducks, no sausages made from little Babes, no deceased mad cows and no yukky turkey. Anyone who hasn't jumped on the animal rights bandwagon didn't see the documentary *The Turkey Business* and *Babe* in the same evening as I did. My children have long been vegetarian ever since my eldest claimed to have seen a 'Chicken Drummer' bleeding on her plate. Anything fleshy revolts them, and like many children they won't eat anything resembling an animal unless it is a pizza shaped as a dinosaur. Those who go on about Christmas puddings being made in July and steamed for hours should stop boring us with such details. The tradition is now that we buy them in December and do them in the microwave.

Turkeys

It is hard to feel about turkeys as we once did. They are no longer regarded as a treat and nor are they selling so well this year. Gobblers are not gobbled up with such relish any more. The more we know about turkeys the more we realize what stupid animals they are. They may not deserve the gruesome deaths that Channel 4 so vividly showed us but they are so intensely foolish that they can become enraged by unusual rocks. The eyeballs of these primitive fowl fit so tightly in their sockets that they have to turn their whole head to see movement. Cocks will display to a wooden carving of the head of a hen if it is held at the properly seductive right angle but unfortunately, because geneticists have so enlarged their breasts, many of them can barely stand and are incapable of copulating.

Stuffing

This was what we used to do to turkeys. Now any mention of stuffing is laden with *doubles entendres*. For example, 'a saucy *Sun* Reader' faxes Pamela Anderson inviting her to come around and sample 'some of my traditional English stuffing'. Similar references are made to crackers and the pulling of. The *Sun*, though, should be congratulated for bringing Pamela over here in order to make us all feel more festive. Dressed as 'a snowflake', sick of spending Christmas on a beach, and revealing a fondness for Dickens, no one could ever suggest that Pamela with her enhanced breasts has the same problems as a poor old turkey.

Nativity plays

These used to be events where the story of Baby Jesus's birth was acted out by cute kids whose wings would fall off or who would say, 'But I don't want to call it Jesus, I think Julie is a much nicer name'. Nowadays, the Baby Jesus barely gets a look in. He may be referred to as 'a special baby', but there is no mention of God being his father. Christmas is but one festival among many that the children learn about. Thus this year my children performed a Ghanaian legend about Ananse the Sky God and a reworked version of *Sleeping Beauty* with Eric Cantona as the bad fairy.

White Christmas

We used to dream of a White Christmas but after *Miss Smilla's Feeling for Snow* and the politically correct realization that the Inuit have a huge number of words for snow, perhaps we should be more specific. What kind of snow do we want exactly? Soft snow – *maujaq*? Snow with a hard crust – *katakartanaq*? Compressed snow – *aniugaviniq*? Sparkling snow – *pataqun*? Crystalline snow – *pukak*? I could go on, but I won't.

Soft shoe shuffle

I had actually been out buying some shoes, turquoise, strappy, satiny numbers, when my editor at the *Guardian* phoned in a dreadful state because he thought Germaine Greer had gone mad. Her comments about my hair, shoes, cleavage and manner of speech, in a column unpublished by the *Guardian*, were soon to be leaked everywhere. Germaine resigned and this dispute was then picked up by all the other newspapers, which like nothing better than seeing two women fall out, all the better if these women are supposedly feminists. I didn't respond publicly to Germaine's outbursts. I didn't want to join in this stupid row or dignify her criticisms of me by answering them. Anyway, I had no interest in giving the boys what they wanted. It all reminded me of being told off by my mother, who, like countless other mothers, used to say: 'You're not going out of the house dressed like that.' I was and I did and doubtless I shall soon be saying this to my own daughters.

Far be it for me to guess what Germaine's motivation for all this really was. All I know is that at the time I was asked a lot of questions about it by other journalists. Had she simply gone doolally? Was it about self-publicity, age, being Australian? Or was it about something deeper, some real generational difference within feminism? That the writer of *The Female Eunuch*, a brilliant book, should choose to grow old disgracefully and refuse to celebrate an entirely spurious notion of sisterhood never struck me as a bad thing. That a woman who has posed with her ankles behind her head should choose to make an issue of 'fuck-me' shoes, though, did strike me as a strange state of affairs. But then icons are not expected to be consistent – they are simply expected to be.

The media at the time were looking for another story, one beyond the obvious plot-line of female envy and one that could be used to diminish the project of feminism itself. When men fall out publicly, their gender is not an issue; when women do, gender becomes the issue that overshadows all others. What was so daft about the whole affair was that, because of the tone of Dr Greer's remarks, very little sensible discussion was had about the differences within feminism. Such a discussion may be far less media-sexy than that of an older woman bitching about a younger one, but it was the only one worth having. We have over the last few years merely imported American feminists to do it for us. Naomi Wolf, Susan Faludi, Camille Paglia, Rene Denfield *et al.* may have important things to say about what is going on in their own country, but their views cannot simply be superimposed on to British culture.

We are living at a time when feminist attitudes have filtered down through every level of the culture, yet at the same time there is no movement, no leader, no centre for this form of politics. Even before the Greer attack on me, there was a tangible sense that an older generation of feminists were disappointed by a younger generation. At times we were not even speaking the same language. The vocabulary of socialist feminism was meaningless to many of those who had only known a woman prime minister. Likewise, it was incomprehensible for me to be attacked by another feminist primarily on the basis of my appearance. As someone who grew up with punk and Madonna, I take it for granted that women dress to please themselves and not men; that pleasure, irony and sexuality are part of the fashion system of which we are all part; that arguments over the politics of appearance were a thing of the past; that feminism should be inclusive, not exclusive; and that if it makes that mythical object – the ordinary woman – feel that she has got everything from her ideology to her lipstick wrong, then it is doomed.

Some of this, and let's be clear here, is about class. I sense that some women may feel that people like me are not respectful enough to our elders and betters. It's true, I'm not. I do not tug my forelock sufficiently to those career feminists whose main contact with working-class women is to employ them as servants. Yet class plays itself out in far more complicated ways. Some commentators complained that while Germaine writes about Shakespeare, I had written about Courtney Love. They wore their ignorance of Courtney Love proudly, assuming naturally that an interest in popular culture is of itself an indication of irrelevance, evidence of a low-class act. Such a position is ludicrous to many of my generation. It is not that Courtney Love is somehow equivalent to Shakespeare, or will ever be as significant (though to some of the people some of the time she may well be), just that an interest in one does not preclude an interest in the other. If one is concerned by the representation of women, then one looks at the culture one lives in as well as its history. Why be embarrassed about such populism? Surely feminism as a political project is nothing if it cannot understand how it might make itself more popular. Much valuable work has been done by feminist scholars on popular culture, on the forms of it that appeal to women and the ways it is constantly negotiating the changes within women's lives. If you want to hear a discussion of sexual politics, listen to the conversations of cinema-goers after they have seen *Thelma and Louise* or *Disclosure*. No one uses the word feminism, yet such movies would not be possible without it.

Similarly, the pioneering work done by those like Greer around issues of women's health is now to be found in women's magazines and the pages of certain newspapers. It may not be in a pure and rarefied form, it may be surrounded by cosmetics ads, but it is there none the less. However imperfect in reality, most women of all classes now expect to have some sort of control over the way they give birth.

Yet the success of feminism has also been its downfall. Many young women see it as profoundly old-fashioned and unnecessary. It is hard for them to imagine their mothers' lives, let alone their grandmothers', and they optimistically expect to be treated as entirely equal to men. They have grown up with freely available contraception and easily obtainable abortions; they have outstripped the boys educationally; they assume that a working woman is the rule, not the exception. It is not until they have children or fail to climb past middle management that it occurs to many of them that all is not well in the world. Statistics about the rise of eating disorders or the feminization of poverty may niggle, but feminism as a form of collective politics still figures in their imagination largely as some sort of whingeing.

A crisis of faith in feminism is hardly surprising when all forms of collective politics are undergoing similar transitions. The grand narrative of socialism is difficult to maintain after the revolutions in Eastern Europe; the idea of women's rights sometimes feels like an anachronistic cause to be arguing for when every day we read of the fate of the unemployed male, the educational problems of boys, the lack of opportunity for young men.

The question, then, is about the primacy of gender. Are all social relations to be understood in terms of gender? Clearly, they cannot be. Such a narrow focus has produced what Wolf and, before her, Paglia identified as a 'victim feminism'. The task for the contemporary feminist then is to point out where gender is a factor rather than to reduce everything to its presence. There are limits to the discourse of much old-style feminism, limits which if not recognized as such are so much ammunition to our opponents. Feminism may have buoyed itself up with a fantasy about the moral superiority of women, but such fantasies are no longer tolerable or workable.

As someone who often writes about the representation of women, I found it more than interesting to see how the conflict between myself and Greer was represented in the media. If this was to be a dispute between younger and older schools of feminism, how were such schools to be defined? Had younger women betrayed their elders? Had we lost the plot completely? Was the wearing of red lipstick indication enough of political differences? I suspect not. Indeed, much of the support I received was from women of Greer's generation who seemed to have no problem at all with my choice of shoes or anything else. Had a man attacked me in these terms, it would have been dismissed as sexism of the grossest kind, they wrote.

The lesson that I learnt was that age has little to do with how we identify ourselves politically. Just as I may find a nineteen-year-old who professes a radical politics that seems to come straight out of the sixties, it is possible to find a sixty-year-old who has moved on from then and rejoices in the bolshiness of young women today. What I admired about Greer's work is that she herself has sought redefinition on issues such as rape or contraception. The differences between us seem to me to rest on our different interests, backgrounds and institutional bases. Greer is working within academia. She belongs to a literary tradition. Her focus is predominantly high culture. I, on the other hand, work as a journalist and refuse to apologize for my preoccupation with television, advertising, pop music and cinema. This culture may be low, but its vibrancy helps shape the meaning of my life. It has never occurred to me that one might have to make a choice between high and low culture. Such demarcations were, I thought, shattered long before the word 'post-modernism' was bandied about by every style journal in town. Yet the central question for anyone interested in feminist politics is how it may survive or even flourish in these post-modern times. The promise of much that has been described as the post-modern condition was that, in some ways, the loss of meaning would be a democratizing process. A plurality of voices could be heard, the master narratives would give way to a diverse series of subjective voices. This simply has not happened. What is emerging are those who hold on to the old certainties more than ever. The rise of fundamentalisms, of nationalisms, are desperate indications of this. To talk of women as a class, of patriarchy as a monolithic entity, to speak of an international feminist agenda in such circumstances, is well nigh impossible. A feminism that cannot deal with local and cultural differences becomes little more than spirituality. In a global economy we still act locally. Generalization may be comforting, but it underestimates the complexities facing the average woman.

One tack is to follow the path of so many of the US feminists and set up a single problem with a single answer. So we have seen a series of works that tell us the answer to women's oppression is to get rid of pornography, the beauty myth or housework. There has also been a concerted effort by many younger writers to do away with dogma about the sexual relations between men and women that casts feminists as moral puritans unable to see that women must take responsibility for their own sexuality. The backlash perceived in America has been seen as applicable to British culture, despite the fact that we do not share a large and organized religious right-wing to fuel that backlash.

Meanwhile, recent debates here have focused on a far more straightforward agenda – the number of female MPs, the use of positive discrimination in order to get more women into public office, equal pay and the ongoing problem of funding decent nursery education. It seems to me that this is a sign that some people are thinking far more strategically about what feminism might achieve. In order to further this process the time has come for us to look back, not in anger, but to evaluate the successes and failures of the feminist project. A tactical feminism has to deal with the world as it is, not as it was twenty years ago and not as a Utopian future. It has to be alert to the nuances of the way that women are represented; it has to be part of the mainstream rather than marginalized as a special interest or eccentric obsession. It has at times to be pragmatic, to translate itself into everyday language in order to leave the ghetto of so much feminist scholarship. It cannot assume an audience without creating one. It cannot create an audience without paying attention to the way it represents itself. We are no longer innocent of image, and the great irony of Greer's attack on me was that it reduced us to stereotypes – once again giving the image of feminism itself a bad name.

The Female Eunuch was part of the populist tendency that I am arguing for and I would assume that any feminism worth its name had room for the likes of myself as well as its illustrious author. It was a shock to find that there are those who do not think that this is the case. If it isn't, then we have learnt nothing, and feminism has become too old and tired to encompass personal differences and has become merely quarrelsome. This is not my vision at all. But if I am forced to take sides, then I must renounce the old in favour of the new so that we might begin all over again.

Index

Index

Index

Index

Oasis 195, 215
Oates, Joyce Carol 122
O'Brien, Richard 1
Obscene Publications
    Squad 32
Olins, Wally 185
'On the real mean streets'
    (7 September 1995), 253
'Once upon a time in the
    nuclear family' (5 March
    1993), 10
Operation Rescue 55
Orangemen 237
Orwell, George 141
'Out of action' (17 July
    1993), 40
outing 52, 202–5
OutRage! 202
'Outside, looking in' (5
    October 1995), 262

Paglia, Camille 70, 88, 96,
    294, 296
Palin, Michael 134
Parker, Colonel 170
Parker, Dorothy 17
Parker-Bowles, Camilla 86,
    132
Patten, John 66, 75, 76, 82,
    83, 84, 99, 131
Payne, Cynthia 233
Pet Shop Boys 204
Pfeiffer, Michelle 60
Philip, Prince, Duke of
    Edinburgh 89
Philips, Sam 169
Phillips, Melanie 198, 200
Pitt, Brad 213
Pizzey, Erin 69
Plath, Sylvia 215
Platt, Steve 276
political correctness 99–
    102
'Pope on a rope' (13 July
    1995), 237
Porter, Shirley 156
Portillo, Michael 234
Potter, Dennis 140
PowerGen 206, 207
Presley, Dee 170
Presley, Elvis 168, 169, 170,
    174

Presley, Lisa Marie 168–74
Presley, Priscilla 169–72
Press, Joy 194, 195
Pride and Prejudice
    (television programme)
    273, 275
private education 175–9
Proops, Marje 85, 94
Public Enemy 169
Pulp 259, 272

Quindlen, Anna 25

Rabin, Leah 276
radical journalism 276–9
Radical Journalism Forum
    276
rape 11, 71–4, 282–3, 297
Rawcliffe, Bishop Derek
    203
Reagan, Ronald 155
Red or Dead 3, 4
Redford, Robert 60
Redwood, John 36–7, 182,
    236
Reeves, Keanu 213
Refuge 218
Reich, Wilhelm 16
Relate 289
religious education in
    schools 143–6
Reynolds, Simon 194, 195
Riches, Valerie 75
'RIP the "real" Roseanne'
    (28 May 1993), 29
Ritts, Herb 215
Riviere, Joan 22
Roberts, Julia 60
rock music 193–6
'Rockers on the run from
    mother' (2 March 1995),
    193
Roe v. Wade decision 27
Rolling Stones 194, 195
Roman Catholicism 237–
    40
romance 61–4
Ronay, Edina 1
Rose, Steven 191, 192
Rotten, Johnny 194
Rowntree Foundation 190
Rumbelows 186

Rushdie, Salman xiv, 259
Rutter, Professor Michael
    222, 226
Ryan, Meg 63
Ryan, Michael 121

Sacks, Chief Rabbi
    Jonathan 198, 272, 273
Salt 'n' Pepa 13
Samuels, Andrew 264
Savage, Lily 267–8
Scargill, Arthur 262, 265
Schwartz, David 172
Schwarzenegger, Arnold
    40–50, 161, 269
Scorsese, Martin 195
screen violence 159–62
'Sea changes in political
    talk' (22 June 1995), 228
serial killers 121–4, 159,
    161
serial monogamy 12, 17
Seven Million project 257
Sewell, Brian 105
sex 13–17, 233–6, 249–52
sex education 75–7, 82–4
sexism 33, 34, 296
Sexton, Anne 215
Sexton, Sean 80
Shakespeare, William 102,
    295
Shange, Ntozake 123
'She who must not be
    obeyed' (7 December
    1995), 284
Shell 228, 229–30, 231
shopping 185–8
'Shopping and the
    demeaning of life' (9
    February 1995), 185
Short, Clare 266
Shriver, Maria 44
Simpson, Mark 111
Simpson, O. J. 236, 265–6
single parents xii, 12, 36–9,
    157
Skinner, Dennis 262
Sleep, Wayne 86
'Sloth about the house' (25
    February 1994), 113
Smith, Professor David
    222, 226

303

Index